HOOKED

Tiffinie Helmer

This is a work of fiction. Names, characters, places, brands, media, and incidents are either the product of the author's imagination or are used fictitiously, and any resemblance to actual persons, living or dead, business establishments, events, or locales is entirely coincidental.

HOOKED
All rights reserved.
Copyright © 2013 by Tiffinie Helmer

ISBN-13: 978-0615791050
ISBN-10: 0615791050

The Story Vault
c/o Marketing Department
P.O. Box 11826
Charleston, WV 25339-1826
http://www.thestoryvault.com

Cover Designs by Kelli Ann Morgan
Website: www.inspirecreativeservices.com

Publishing History: First Edition
Published by The Story Vault

ACKNOWLEDGEMENTS

First to my mother, Barb Blanc, who dove into commercial fishing back in the 1970s. I used to hate that you dragged me to Bristol Bay as a kid, away from my friends and civilization. Funny, now that I'm grown, I look forward to unplugging and going fishing. Thank you for the unique experiences, the unforgettable summers, and the killer skills.

To my brother, Indy Walton, who fights the line every summer as he pilots the *Double Dippin'*, determined to catch as much salmon as he can, and for keeping his crew safe in some extremely dangerous situations. Now, if you can just stay under the radar of the fish cops.

To Tayt, Montgomery, Tess, Bristol, and Dagen for being the best fishing crew in South Naknek, Alaska. You started fishing as kids and still upstaged every other fisherman out there on the water with your work ethic, attitudes, and your ability to find the fun in everything. I can't wait to see what the fab five will do now that you are all adults.

Fish on!

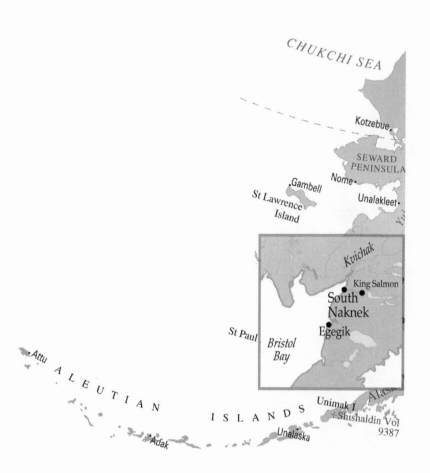

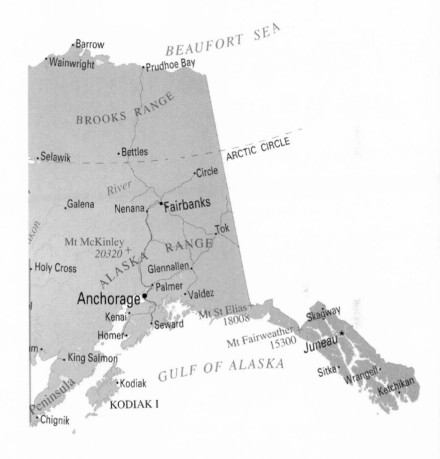

To my oldest son and diehard fisherman, Tayt Helmer. Always remember how very proud of you I am, and that good things come to those who bait. Love you, babe.

PROLOGUE

She'd always known she'd die this way.

The strong tidal current dragged her farther into the unforgiving depths of the Bering Sea. She kicked and lashed until her limbs grew heavy, cold. Useless. Everything inside her screamed. She was too young. She had too much to live for.

She had to kill that fucking bastard.

Salt water burned and blinded. Filled her mouth and nose. Smothered and squeezed the life out of her.

She'd cheated this bitch of an ocean fifteen years earlier, but she knew she wouldn't be able to again. She'd never been destined to live through the sinking of the *Mystic*.

Pain exploded in her chest, and her lungs flamed with the need for air.

Blackness swallowed her.

CHAPTER ONE

Sonya Savonski screeched her ATV to a stop alongside the dirt runway as the puddle jumper touched down. The prop airplane had just made the fifteen-minute hop from King Salmon to the small fishing village of Bristol Bay, Alaska.

"That was *not* a fair race," Peter hollered, parking his 4-wheeler next to hers.

"Only because you lost."

"I'm towing a trailer," he pointed out, tossing his head to the side, and clearing his eyes of dark hair. At seventeen, Peter hated to lose at anything.

"An *empty* trailer," Sonya said. "It comes down to the better driver, little brother."

The plane taxied toward them, the noise deafening. The engines thundered down and welcomed silence followed. A door opened and passengers began to climb out. Most gazed around, not surprised by the wind-whipped banks, low-lying tundra, and the gray-green waters of the Bering Sea promising adventure, money, and possibly death. This wasn't the tourist-friendly part of Alaska.

Fuel and exhaust mixed with salty sea air and the smell of fish. Call her crazy, but it was a scent Sonya loved. The scent of fish meant money. Hopefully this fishing season they'd get stinking rich.

"There they are." Peter pointed to their grandparents as they stepped down from the plane.

Gramps chatted animatedly while Grams seemed to listen with rapt attention. Sonya knew that look. Margaret Savonski was woolgathering.

Peter rushed up to them, and Gramps' face spilt into a grin as he grabbed him in a man hug. It had been weeks since they'd all seen each other. Sonya and Peter had headed out to open camp for this summer's commercial sockeye season, knowing it would be one for the books—they were drifting *and* set netting this year.

Their nonconformist plan was bound to upset some fishermen.

Gramps greeted her with a bear hug. "How's my favorite granddaughter?"

She responded with the expected, "I'm your only granddaughter."

Nikolai Savonski's dark brown eyes twinkled, and dimples cut deep grooves in his salt-and-pepper whiskered cheeks. A navy seaman's cap hung lopsided over his thick wave of silver hair. He was a breed apart.

"Nikky," Grams said, "you and Peter get the bags, while I say hello to Sonya." Margaret, with her regal bearing, immediately had the men jumping to do her bidding. The sweet-as-sugar smile, which accompanied the request, had paved a long road of men bending over backward to fetch anything she needed. The woman had skills.

"Sonya, my girl, I've missed you." They embraced, and Sonya breathed in the scent of English roses. "I've been too long in the company of men," Margaret said, indicating Nikolai. He and Peter were pow-wowing with a group of fishermen waiting for the plane to be unloaded. "We must make time for some girlie stuff before the season starts."

Girlie stuff on the Bering Sea of Alaska? They'd have a better chance locating an ice cream shop.

"We'll make a point of it," Sonya said, her attention snagged by Gramps who'd thrown his head back and let loose with a booming laugh. He was conversing with a sandy-haired man. The man had broad shoulders powerful enough to haul in a boatload of fish without breaking a sweat. Gramps motioned for Sonya to hurry over.

"Looks as though Nikky has another suitor to introduce you to." Grams chuckled while smoothing her platinum—never gray—curls back from her face as the Bristol Bay wind puffed teasing gusts around them.

Sonya moaned and moseyed over to Gramps and Peter. For some reason, her grandpa had decided she needed to get married. She was only twenty-nine for heaven's sake. There was plenty of time for that nonsense, but Gramps was bull-headed, so she went to be paraded in front of another "potential."

"Sonya, I'd like you to meet Garrett…uh…what's your last name?"

Great. He was so desperate to get her hitched that he wasn't bothering to screen the men anymore. For all they knew, this man could have murdered a string of women.

Peter turned his head to the side and snickered.

"Hunt," the stranger supplied. "Name's Garrett Hunt." He reached out a hand for her to shake. "It's nice to meet you, Sonya."

Yeah, yeah, blah, blah, she wanted to say, but then her attention caught on his ice-blue eyes. Eyes that color shouldn't project heat. Somehow she found her hand happily engaged in his. It wasn't just his eyes that gave off heat. A slight smile crooked his lips.

"Same," she said, "to meet you, that is." She gave Garrett Hunt a second look. The man wasn't handsome…

more interesting. Tough, muscled, and weathered. He looked like he could hold his own in any situation. Anywhere. Anytime. Chiseled jaw, sharp cheekbones, spiky military haircut, with a scar by his left temple. The only thing soft about him was his lips.

Dang, she did not need this kind of distraction this summer.

"Well, how do you like that?" Gramps commented with a hum, breaking Sonya out of her trance and reminding her of where she was. Gramps slapped Garrett on the back. "How about you join us for dinner tomorrow night? Red Fox Camp is about five miles down the beach. Can't miss it. We should be ready for company by then, don't ya think, Sonya?"

"Uh…sure." Even though she wanted to tell her grandpa to keep his busybody nose out of her business, she couldn't.

Garrett gave her that crooked smile again. It was quite sexy on him. "I'd like that."

"Hunt!" the pilot of the plane hollered, walking toward them carrying a surfboard. "You have any idea how hard this was to stuff into my plane?"

"Thanks, Harry," Garrett said, taking ownership of the board. "I appreciate you making the room."

Surfboard?

"You owe me a drink for it," Harry said. "I plan on collecting as soon as I get that swarm of fishermen flown over here."

"You got it," Garrett said.

Harry waved them goodbye and boarded the plane for the return hop to King Salmon. The fishermen were all coming in now that the fishing season would be opening in a few days. In that amount of time, the population went from around a hundred to thousands.

"What are you going to do with that?" Peter asked, eyeing the surfboard.

"Catch a wave," Garret said.

The man was a nut. Gramps had to stop introducing her to just anyone. She looked at her grandfather and was glad to see that even *his* brows had risen in question.

"Why?" Peter asked.

Yeah, *why*, Sonya thought.

"For the thrill of it," Garrett said with a grin.

"Nobody gets in that ocean for fun." Sonya shivered. "You only get in it when you're forced to." The memory of the last time she'd been in that deadly ocean sliced through her like a cutting edge of an arctic wind. *The freezing water, the screaming, and then the terrifying silence followed by death.*

"Well…hmm…hope to see you at dinner," Gramps said, dragging Sonya back to the present. "Wait a minute, Garrett." Gramps took another look at the man, as though sizing him up. "You military?"

Garrett nodded. "Former SEAL. You?"

Gramps' smile stretched from ear to ear. Garrett had seen through the meddling grandparent to the seasoned warrior beneath. "Merchant Marine."

"Combat?" Garrett asked.

"Vietnam. You?"

"Iraq."

Nikolai nodded to the surfboard. "Well, being a SEAL explains the water toy." He then offered his hand for Garrett to shake. "Very much looking forward to seeing you at dinner."

Garrett shook his hand. "It was nice meeting you, sir." He looked at Sonya. "And your family."

Garrett pursed his lips and whistled under his breath as Sonya Savonski swaggered away from him, easily toting a duffel bag over her very capable shoulders. She wore a ball cap with a ponytail of dark hair hanging out the back. It seemed to tease him as it bounced in time to her step. She was garbed in faded jeans, and a t-shirt with a picture of a king salmon. The words, "Size Does Matter" blazed in red lettering across her ample breasts.

Now there was a woman. Full mouth, full breasts, full hips. The trifecta. He'd never been able to resist that sexy combination.

She must have sensed his scrutiny for she glanced back over her shoulder. He smiled. She frowned. He smiled wider. This summer was showing some promise.

Sonya straddled the 4-wheeler, and Peter jumped on behind her. Nikolai had commandeered the other ATV for him and his wife. In a cloud of dust, they took off rumbling down the dirt road.

Garrett was definitely showing up for dinner.

Waiting for his own ride to manifest, he took a moment to look around. South Naknek didn't have the postcard beauty of the Kenai Peninsula that he'd flown out of that morning, but it had a rough and ready appeal. An appeal that fit his mood as of late. He could use some getting back to nature and there wasn't anything but nature at present. He'd spent too much time indoors, riding a desk, and needed some space around him. Nothing *but* space here. The only building next to the dirt-packed runway was a six-by-eight shack with a broken window and a doorway with no door. Someone with a sense of humor had painted a sign on the shed that read, "South Naknek International Airport."

There wasn't a tree to block the wind or the view. Bright green tundra with the bloom of summer ended in silt cliffs that broke the ocean as she tumbled her destructive way to shore. Industry dotted the coastline in the form of canneries to help process the catch of the "Red Salmon Capital of the World."

As an Alaska Wildlife Officer, he'd come to this place under the guise of policing the craziness that the combination of money and cutthroat fishing brought out in people.

"Yo, Hunt!"

Garrett turned from surveying the area to see Judd Iverson stepping out of a brown, rusty Jeep. Garrett hadn't seen Judd in two years, but he looked as though he hadn't changed much, still had that playful swagger as though he hadn't a care in the world. Judd had grayed more at the temples, but it looked good on him. Straight dark brows slashed over eyes that noticed the slightest infraction, unless a woman was in the vicinity. It would be fun working with Judd again, as long as Garrett remembered not to be coerced into joining in any poker games.

"Iverson, you dog. How ya been?" he asked, slapping his hand out for a bone-crushing shake.

"Same as ever." Judd focused on the surfboard. "Couldn't have left the board at home, could you?"

Garrett's face split into a grin. "Not a chance. Gotta have something to do on my off time."

"Right," Judd scoffed. "Like we're going to get any time to breathe once fishing starts. Your memory's fading, old man."

"Last I heard, you had a few years on me. Like five."

"Damn, it's good to have you here." Judd slapped him on the back. "I was glad to hear you wanted a change of scene. We can use all the help we can get. I take it Homer's not treating you well?"

Homer had lost its appeal since his "friend with benefits" had revoked his bedding rights. Garrett shook off the melancholy. He'd had his chance with Mel Bennett and hadn't taken advantage of it, though she might have been the one woman who wouldn't have tethered him. He disregarded the thought and focused on Judd.

"Homer's fine," Garrett answered. "I just wanted a little more action."

Judd grabbed Garrett's bag and threw it into the back of the open Jeep. "There's no shortage of action around here."

Just what he was after.

CHAPTER TWO

Garrett boarded the *Calypso* and stowed his gear below deck. He then met Judd and the other trooper they'd be working with, Skip Ozhuwan, in the cabin above. Skip was an Alaskan Native and had grown up on the Kuskokwim Delta. No one knew the waters of the Bering Sea like the Aleut. He had dark almond-shaped eyes and a round happy face that belied a shrewd cop.

Garrett took a seat, and stretched his legs out in front of him, crossing his ankles. Judd threw a Coke to him and offered one to Skip, who declined. Judd popped the top of his own and leaned against the bulkhead.

Skip commandeered the captain's chair with a clipboard in front of him and began listing where other troopers would be stationed in the Naknek/Kvichak District. It was the job of the Alaska Wildlife Troopers, or AWT, in conjunction with the Alaska State Troopers, to police the fishing and make sure everyone adhered to the fishing and safety regulations.

"We have the usual hot heads present," Skip began. "The Harte brothers gave us some trouble last summer. Earl Harte is a little trigger happy and likes to shoot at the drifters. He's yet to hit anyone, but there's always a first time." Skip adjusted his seating. It seemed as though his uniform was getting tight in the trunk.

"Then there's the drifter, Chuck Kendrick, captain of the *Albatross*," Skip continued. "Last summer, Aidan Harte cut Kendrick's net when it wrapped around his buoy. Kendrick threatened to get even."

Judd added, "As we know, Kendrick always follows through."

Skip nodded. "Yeah, that was a bad situation with the sinking of the *Miss Julie*. Thankfully, we didn't lose anyone. That time."

"It sure stuck in my craw that we didn't have enough evidence to pin that on Kendrick." Judd addressed Garrett. "It's common knowledge Kendrick had a hand in her sinking."

"If it's common knowledge, why wasn't he arrested?" Garrett asked.

"Same reason he wasn't brought up on charges in the burning of the *Mystic* fifteen years ago," Judd said. "Not enough evidence. That time we lost three and one was a fifteen-year-old girl. Kendrick's got everyone scared shitless out here. I'd sure like to catch him at something and throw his ass in jail."

Skip brought them back to his list. "We need to keep an eye out for the *Mary Jane*. Word is she's doing more than fishing. We'll need to inform DEA if we catch any drug activity." Skip glanced at his clipboard. "Last on the list are the Savonskis."

Garrett uncrossed his legs and sat up. "Who'd you say?"

"Savonskis. You familiar with them?"

"The grandparents were on my flight." Garrett didn't feel inclined to mention he'd been invited for dinner tomorrow night.

"Sonya Savonski has thrown in with the drifters. According to the district registration cards she turned in, she's planning on set netting *and* drifting this summer. There's bound to be trouble."

"That's it." Skip laid his clipboard down and stretched out his own legs. "Unless you guys have something else to add."

"I've got something," Judd said. "What's that new wife of yours been feeding you?"

Skip actually blushed. "Wren's pregnant, and I guess I've been a little sympathetic to her situation." He rubbed his belly. "I've been cutting back on the carbs."

"Well, with this knucklehead's surfboard, and you eating for two, the fishermen will think we've gone soft and take advantage."

"Just let 'em try." Garrett smiled.

Sonya slowed the 4-wheeler down as camp came into view. Red Fox Camp was situated on the edge of Tory Creek, which cut a gully through the tundra—the only place for miles where the bluff lowered enough to allow for cabin sites.

Wes Finley, family friend and seasoned crewman, jogged toward them as she parked the 4-wheeler high on the beach out of reach of the incoming surf. Grams and Gramps followed right behind.

"I was getting worried you guys wouldn't make the tide," Wes said, with a ready smile. High tide would flood the available beach, making getting to camp impossible.

Wes was a man with steady brown eyes and trimmed brown hair. Even when he let his beard grow during the fishing season, he kept it neat. He was like a rock, solid and sure, and wise beyond his twenty-three years. Wes gave both Grams and Gramps a warm hug and then reached for the luggage.

Peter grabbed a duffel and hefted it over his shoulder, and Sonya seized the last bag.

Gramps started to sputter. "Give me that, young lady. I'm not so old I can't fetch and carry anymore." He held out his hand.

Sonya handed it over. The man was built like a moose and sometimes showed the stubbornness of one.

Grams settled her hand on his arm. "Nikky, let Sonya take the bag. I'd like to stretch my legs a bit after all that traveling. I was hoping you'd take a walk on the beach with me."

True to form, Gramps tossed the duffel at Sonya—who was braced to receive it—and took his wife's hand, kissing her fingers. "Sounds like a dandy idea, Maggie May. See you kids in a bit."

Grams's laughter caught on the wind as Gramps wrapped an arm around her and pulled her close. The man was still besotted with his wife after forty-five years.

Someday, Sonya thought, she'd find a man who would love her like that.

"You coming, Ducky?" Peter's voice broke into her thoughts.

"Call me that one more time and you're going to be on dish duty tonight," Sonya threatened. She hitched up the bag and began the twenty-foot climb up the bank to the cabin perched on the bluff.

"Quack, quack," Peter countered, already halfway up the trail. "My hands need a good soaking anyway."

"All right, you two," Wes said from near the top of the bluff. "Want to fill me in on the name calling?" He was always the level voice of reason between Sonya and Peter. It didn't hurt that he was getting his masters in psychology, planning to work with underprivileged children. At the age of sixteen, Wes had been caught by Gramps trying to hotwire their SUV one winter. Instead of calling the troopers, her grandfather had dragged him into the house, fed him dinner, and then put him to work shoveling the driveway. He'd been a part of the Savonskis' extended family ever since.

"I made the mistake of sharing family stories," Sonya said. Sonya filled Wes in on their mother naming her and Peter after characters in the Russian fable "Peter and the Wolf." Wes, who was always quick to laugh, didn't disappoint.

They reached the nest of cabins dotting the tundra. The main cabin housed their grandparents. Rustic and weathered, the cabin was completely shingled to help withstand the intense Bering Sea weather battering its walls all year long. It consisted of one room, a kitchen with a table and benches, and a built-in bed used for extra seating during the day and curtained off at night. A loft provided extra storage and sleeping quarters if necessary.

The bunkhouse stood behind the main cabin along with the gear room and an outhouse. Running water was a luxury that had yet to manifest itself this far from the village of South Naknek.

They dropped off the bags, and Wes and Peter returned to the beach to mend nets. Sonya decided it must be up to her to start dinner. She grabbed three mammoth cans of beef stew and opened them, dumping them into a pan, and lit the propane stove with a match. Then she set a box of saltines on the table. That was about as good as she could do without a microwave and a take out menu. Grams would take over cooking now, much to everyone's relief.

While the stew simmered, Sonya rang the come-and-get-it bell hanging from the eves on the small covered porch

Peter was the first to traipse in. "Stew again?" he whined, wrinkling his nose.

"You want something different, you volunteer to cook." Sonya brought the pot of stew to the table, plunking it down on a hot pad.

"Smells great," Wes said, following behind Peter. They took their seats as Grams and Gramps entered.

"That climb gets steeper every year." Grams pressed a hanky to her forehead. "It's good exercise for my legs."

"And mighty fine legs they are, Maggie May," Gramps said with a grin. He turned to Sonya. "After dinner, I want a tour of that new boat of yours. I figured that's her out there anchored off shore."

"Yeah, that's her." Sonya scooped a bite of stew and felt a shiver of uncertainty. Last summer, Gramps had turned the fishing operation over to her, stating it was about time for a younger generation to step up.

Boy, had she stepped up.

She just hoped that step didn't send them all tumbling. She'd sunk what money they had into buying the boat and drift permit, and mortgaged the rest. If her gamble didn't pay off, winter would be lean and the chance for Peter to go to college in the fall, iffy.

After dinner, she and Gramps outfitted themselves in chest waders and traipsed down to the beach. Across the creek, she noticed activity. The Hartes had arrived, which meant Aidan was there. She tried to put that thought out of her head. Aidan was the past. A mistake.

The differences between the neighboring fish camps were night and day. The Hartes embraced their helter-skelter attitude while Margaret Savonski wouldn't hear of anything out of order on her place. The serene quiet of the fish camps would end now with the Hartes in residence.

Sure enough, Earl hollered over the creek, "That's a funny-looking boat anchored out there, Nikolai."

His brother, Roland, added his two cents, "That's what happens when you let a woman start running the operation."

Gramps turned and acknowledged the two old men in rusty lawn chairs, lazing away the afternoon on their sagging porch. "Earl. Roland. Hope you had a good winter."

Earl couldn't see the shiny side of a gold coin and Roland's good fortune always ended up being someone else's misfortune.

"Hey, Sonya. Aidan's been looking forward to seeing ya," Earl called out with a cackle.

Sonya stiffened her shoulders and kept on walking. Last summer's unfortunate fling with Aidan Harte was over. While the match between the two of them had made sense in theory, it had quickly paled in reality.

Live and learn.

Together, she and Gramps pulled the running line with two of their set netting skiffs tied to it, bringing the boats into shore. Set net fishing had been a way of life for the Savonskis since the 1950s when the first Savonski, Great Grandpa Slava, began fishing these profitable waters. Since then, the family had purchased three more coveted set net sites. They now owned four of the most profitable sites on the beach, much to the envy of the Hartes and many others.

Now she was stirring the waters by throwing her net in with the drifters. She'd always wanted to fish with the big boys. That's where the real money was. Drifters literally drifted, they could drop their net wherever they wanted to fish—within the rules and regulations of the Fish and

Game—while set netters set a thousand feet of net anchored from the beach and had to wait for the fish to swim to them.

There was an unspoken code that drifters and set netters didn't fraternize, much like a feud between opposing families. They each resented the other for taking any part of catch they deemed as theirs, due in part to each party believing the Fish and Game tipped the scales in the others' favor. It was a cutthroat way of life. You picked your team, stood on one side of the line, and never crossed it.

At least, no one had until now.

Gramps waded out into the surf, boarded the skiff, and Sonya jumped into the bow after untying the line and giving the boat a hard push from shore. Gramps yanked the outboard engine's dinosaur pull cord. It coughed, sputtered, and died.

"Don't tell me this engine's giving us trouble again. I thought I fixed it last year." He gave the pull cord another yank. It spit and caught, black smoke bubbling out the back of the engine. "Now that's more like it." He smiled.

Sonya had told him they needed to buy another outboard engine two years ago, one with an electric start. Gramps had disagreed, figuring he could jerry-rig a little more life out of it. Someone was going to get stranded.

Gramps powered up the skiff and skimmed the short distance toward the anchored drift boat Sonya had purchased months ago and had shipped from Seattle to South Naknek on a barge.

"She's a mite different than any other drift boat I've seen," Gramps said, giving the whiskers on his chin a rub. "Sure sits high on the water."

"She's a flat bottom jet boat, which will give us better mobility, quicker turns, and more speed than the traditional gill netter. She's able to maneuver in shallow waters where the fish like to hang out." Sonya felt her nerves dart around like salmon fry as she waited for his reaction. More than anything, she wanted Gramps to be proud of her.

His bushy brows rose. "So we'll have an upper hand on the other drifters. I like that."

"With a jet engine, versus the propeller that most of the other drifters have, there isn't a prop for the net to get tangled on."

"She's wider than I expected."

Sonya tied the skiff to the painter's line attached to the stern of the drift boat. "She's thirty-two foot long, fourteen-feet-wide aluminum bow-picker." They took turns climbing up the ladder, leaving the skiff to drift behind.

Gramps didn't say anything as he made his way to the bow. He glanced around and Sonya started talking fast, explaining the benefits of the flat bottom bow-picker verses the other boats that seasoned fishermen had been using in the bay for decades.

"There are sixteen holds, each able to carry a thousand pounds of salmon with extra space on deck for more." She gestured to the rollers standing tall at the bow and stern. "The hydraulics will pull the nets over the front rollers rather than the stern like everyone else's."

"What's this pole doing hanging across the middle?"

"Well, I had this idea. Having a pole there would help hold up the net in the middle so it doesn't drag on the deck, making picking fish easier without bending over."

"Working smart, not hard. I won't need to see a chiropractor when the season's over." He moved to the starboard side and rested his arm on the rail. "The sides are tall. It'll take some effort to fall overboard." He turned and noticed the name of the boat painted on the reel under the pilot house. "You're calling her the *Double Dippin*?"

24

"That's what we're doing. Set netting *and* drifting."

"Yeah, but couldn't you have been a little more subtle?"

She met his gaze. "Have you ever known me to be subtle?"

"You realize the drifters aren't going to welcome you with open arms."

She barked out a laugh. "They're going to flat out hate me. Especially when I take most of the catch."

His eyes twinkled. "I like the way you think. Show me the pilot house."

Gramps followed her up the narrow steps. Windows framed all four sides, including the door.

"No blind spots," he said. "That's good. Sheltered so you can get out of the weather."

"We're as high up as any crow's nest on the other boats out there." Sonya pointed to the right where a ladder led down. "Bunks, the head, and the engine room are below us." She indicated the stove next to her. "Propane stove for cooking and heating. Mini refrigerator, small sink, some storage." She moved to the front of the pilot house where the wheel and control panels were. "Hydraulic levers for the reels. State of the art GPS system. VHF radio and fish finder."

Gramps turned a full circle, a dimpled grin splitting his face as he took in the captain's chair, and a small bunk crammed into the space to the left. "You did well, Sonya."

She let out a breath of relief. She'd known this was the boat to buy, but having his approval meant the world to her.

"We're going to make some enemies this season." Nikolai's eyes met hers. "You sure you're up for this?"

"Looking forward to it."

CHAPTER THREE

Aidan Harte narrowed his eyes as he focused through binoculars on Sonya aboard the *Double Dippin'*.

She'd gone and done it—bought herself a damn drift boat. Was nothing good enough for that woman?

Apparently, he hadn't been.

His boot crushed an empty soda can as he adjusted his feet. He lowered the binoculars and glared at the cabin in disrepair. So the Harte camp wasn't as well kept as the Savonskis'. Who cared? They were only here four weeks tops every summer. They didn't need comfort for that amount of time, especially when—God willing—they'd be fishing most of it.

Sonya needed to lower her standards right down to his level. Wait a minute, that didn't sound right. He turned as his father came up next to him and looked at the view through the cracked window pane.

"Checking out Sonya's new boat?"

"Nope. Looking for jumpers." Aidan set the binoculars down on a wooden crate doubling as a kitchen cabinet. This place really was sad. Why didn't they fix it up a bit?

"See any?"

"See any what?"

"Jumpers!" Earl slapped him on the back of the skull. "Where's your head, boy?"

Hell if he knew.

Earl took the half-chewed toothpick out of his mouth and gestured with it for emphasis. "Instead of playing like a Peeping Tom, you should be making tracks to get back into Sonya's good graces."

Aidan hated admitting his father was right about anything, but he had a point. Peering at Sonya through binoculars wasn't getting him anywhere. Time for a face-to-face.

He grabbed his jacket. "I'm going out."

"About damn time you got down to business." Earl picked up the binoculars, grumbling. "If I'd had a chance with a woman like that, she'd be shackled and pregnant by now."

Aidan let the squeaky door slam behind him, ignoring Earl's holler, "Don't slam the door!"

He'd slam the door if he wanted to. Hell, he hadn't been here more than a few hours and he wanted to leave. Putting up with his father became harder and harder every year. If it wasn't for the money he made fishing, he'd have told Earl to go to hell by now. He shoved his hands in his pockets.

No he wouldn't. He didn't have the backbone, which Earl was consistent in pointing out.

He kicked his way down to the beach just as Sonya and Nikolai jumped out of their skiff. As timing went, it couldn't have been better. As moods went, he was in a sorry one. Not the best shape to be meeting Sonya after their last conversation when she'd told him to get lost.

"Hey, Aidan, how you been?" Nikolai greeted him with a smile and a hearty handshake. No matter the trouble his father and uncle caused the Savonskis, Nikolai didn't blame him for his gene pool.

"Good. You?" He glanced at Sonya, her face flushed from the ocean breeze. She always looked so…fresh. Smooth skin, dark eyes, dark hair pulled away from her face, and full red lips. Classically beautiful and way out of his league.

"Great. Couldn't be better." Nikolai glanced between him and Sonya. "Well…I'm going to head to the cabin and see if there's anything for dessert. See you kids later."

Nikolai left them alone, and Aidan found himself lost for words. Sonya had always represented all that he'd ever wanted in life. Love, success, and a happy, well-adjusted family.

"Aidan." Sonya hooked her hands in the straps of her chest waders.

"Sonya," he copied her greeting, taking his cues from her, when what he wanted to know was if she'd missed him? Had she thought of him over the long winter? The memories of their sweet lovemaking was like a hunger he couldn't satisfy.

"How's Seattle been treating you?" she asked.

"Wet." He cleared his throat not liking where that one word mentally took him. "That is, we've had nothing but rain." He glanced up to the azure sky dotted by a few puffy clouds. "This is the most sun I've seen in a while."

She shifted on her feet. "Which could change at any moment."

Silence stretched between them until Aidan indicated the boat moored out in the bay. "I see you went and bought a drift boat."

She nodded. "I told you I was going to."

She had, and he'd argued with her, which was one of the reasons why they were no longer sleeping together. Something he was going to rectify this summer. "Who'd you get to captain her?"

"I'm her captain."

"You?"

"That's right. Got a problem with that?"

You bet he did. "Aren't you biting off more than you can chew?"

"I can chew it just fine." Her jaw tightened.

He shook his head, not wanting to rehash the old argument. "Who's your crew?"

"Gramps, Peter, and Wes."

"Who will be working the set net sites?"

"Not that it's any of your business, but the four of us will fish those as well."

"When are you going to sleep?"

"When the fish do."

"You're nuts, you know that?" Why did she have to be so damn pig-headed?

"I've been called worse. In fact, if memory serves, I've been called worse by you."

He took a deep breath and held it before letting it out in a rush. This was not where he wanted their first conversation in over nine months to go. It was like they'd picked up right where they'd left off, but they were wearing more clothes this time. "I don't want to go there."

"Then don't." She fidgeted like she wanted to leave.

"Aren't you worried about what the other set netters are going to think?" Couldn't she see the troubles she was about to bring down on herself?

"I don't waste time worrying about what anyone thinks of me."

"You should. Word's got around what you're planning this summer. A lot of people don't like it."

"I'm out here to fish, not to gain in popularity."

"I've heard things, Sonya. Not nice things. You need to be worried."

Her gaze hardened. "Do I need to worry about you?"

He sucked in a breath remembering what he'd done last summer. He never should have said those things. Did those things. "No. Not from me."

"What about Cranky and Crafty?"

He smiled at her nicknames for Earl and Roland. "I'll keep them in line." At least he'd try.

"I'd appreciate it." She made to leave, and he grabbed her arm.

"Listen, Sonya. About that night—"

She stiffened under his hand. "Forget it."

"I can't. If I hadn't—"

"I said forget it." Her voice hardened.

He let go of her arm and ran a hand through his hair. "I really messed up…and I wanted, needed, to tell you that I'm sorry." There he'd said it, finally apologized for being an ass. He should be getting pretty good at it by now.

She narrowed her eyes as though wondering if he was truly sorry or just trying another tactic. "Apology accepted."

He breathed a sigh of relief. "Want to take a walk?"

"Just because I accepted your apology doesn't mean I've forgotten." She turned away, and then looked back over her shoulder. "I won't be taking any walks with you, Aidan. I never repeat mistakes."

"You don't believe in second chances?"

"Not for you and me."

"I've changed, Sonya. I spent time working on my… issues. I won't ever do that again."

"Good. I hope you don't. But you won't get another chance at me. That boat's sailed."

"So how'd it go between you and Aidan?" Gramps didn't mince words when Sonya entered the cabin. He and Grams were sharing a cup of cocoa and a plate of shortbread cookies. Wes and Peter were nowhere in sight.

"Fine." Sonya had shed her chest waders and hung them in the gear room, taking a bit of time to compose herself after her run-in with Aidan. The man was still as handsome as ever. Black hair, always in need of a cut, dark stubble that sexed him up, haunted brown eyes. He seemed older and sadder, but she wouldn't let that sway her.

She grabbed a cup and mixed herself some cocoa, snagging a couple of cookies.

"What happened between you two? You were a mite cozy last year." Gramps bit into his cookie as he watched for her reaction. Sonya knew he hated being out of the loop.

"Don't pester the child, Nikky," Grams chided.

"I'm not pestering," he scoffed. "I'm concerned. Aidan's a good man. Good marriage material. Likes to fish. I want to know why she keeps turning men like him away." He narrowed his attention to Sonya. "You want to get married, don't you?"

She sighed and sat. "Yes, Gramps. I want to get married and have a family. I've got plenty of time for both."

"Well, I don't. I want me some great grandbabies and with your snail-like approach, I won't be getting any."

"So, you'd be happy with me shacking up with anyone as long as it gets you a great grandkid?"

"Don't get smart. Of course not. I want you happy too."

"I am happy." She softened her tone and gave him a crooked smile full of affection. "Gramps, I don't need a man to make me happy. I'm responsible for doing that all on my own."

He reached over and laid his hand over Grams'. "I want you to have what Maggie May and I have."

"Some aren't as lucky as the both of you."

"Hogwash. You make your own luck and right now you aren't even open to love. You need some romance in your life. You're way too serious."

"Why don't we take a break from this?" Grams picked up the plate of cookies and offered them to Gramps. "Have another cookie, Nikky."

"I've had enough cookies. I'm going to go help Peter and Wes with the nets."

Grams shook her head as she watched him leave. "He means well."

"I know. He's just stubborn and likes things his own way."

"He's not the only one." Grams gave Sonya a knowing look over the rim of her cup. "What's the real story between you and Aidan?" She took a sip.

Sonya set down her cup. "I'd rather not get into it."

"Did he hurt you?" Her eyes were steady, serious. There would be no flirting around the truth this time.

"Yes." Sonya gazed into her hot chocolate. If she told her grandmother the whole truth, there would be no coming back from it. The tentative peace between the Hartes' and Savonskis' fish camps would cease. "I thought I could care for him. It hurt knowing that I couldn't."

She wouldn't allow herself to love a man who'd hit her.

CHAPTER FOUR

Garrett had no problem finding the Savonskis' fish camp the following evening. A bonfire happily snapped in the slight breeze, and smoke peppered the salty ocean air. A group of people sat around the fire, laughter flickering along with the flames. They all turned as he pulled up on the ATV—the main mode of transportation for navigating the rough beaches of South Naknek.

"Well, if it isn't Garrett. Welcome, welcome." Nikolai met him as he dismounted the 4-wheeler and pocketed the key. "Have any problem finding us?"

"Not a one, sir."

"None of this 'sir' business. Call me Nikolai." He motioned for him to follow. "Come, meet everyone. You've already met my wife, Margaret, and Peter. This is Wes Finley, Aidan Harte, and his cousin, Lana. The Hartes have the camp across the creek. Ah, and here comes Sonya." Nikolai smiled. "Sonya, look who showed up."

Garrett thought her step faltered when she noticed him, but she moved so smoothly that he wasn't sure. She carried a cooler, and he hurried to take it from her. Obviously a little too eager, as her eyes widened and then quickly narrowed.

"I got it," she said not releasing her hold on the cooler.

"Let me." He thought, for a moment, he would have to fight her for it.

She wore jeans and a sweatshirt with "Fish Goddess" printed across the front. The air around them thickened as she held his gaze. She seemed to come to a decision and released her hold on the cooler.

This woman did something to him. With just a look he felt…singed.

"Bring the food on over," Peter hollered. "Some of us are starving here."

Yeah, it seemed he was hungry too.

"You've got the food." Sonya's lips tilted at the corners.

"What food?" Garrett asked, knowing he could drown in the depths of her eyes.

"The cooler." She pointed at what he held. "It's full of food."

"Right." He laughed. "I guess I'm holding up the festivities."

Her brows rose. "Oh, I don't know about that."

Heat infused his body. She turned and made her way to the fire and the group conversing around the open flames. Those very flames might as well have been licking down his spine. He followed and set the cooler where Nikolai indicated.

"Like the looks of my granddaughter, don't ya?" Nikolai said.

"What's not to like?" Then he remembered who he was talking to. "That is, Sonya seems like a very nice woman."

Nikolai chuckled and slapped him on the back. "Passion is a necessity of life, and Sonya has passion. She just needs the right man. You the right man, Garrett Hunt?"

Hell if he knew. It wouldn't be a stretch to be the right man for her, right now.

𝕁

Over the flames, Sonya observed Garrett talking to Gramps as he roasted a hotdog over the fire. The lowering sun highlighted the spiky ends of his short hair. She didn't know why, but she wanted to put her hands on him. A distraction this summer wouldn't benefit her situation. She was juggling too many balls in the air to add another.

Unless it was just sex.

Now there was a thought. Maybe that's what she needed to take the edge off. Lord knew it had been a while. Garrett definitely looked as though he could satisfy that need.

Aidan dropped onto the log next to her. "See something you like?"

She flicked a glance at him. "Got something to say?"

"Don't make me jealous, Sonya."

The warning sent a trickle of unease snaking around her insides. "I don't *make* you anything. It's up to you, what you feel." Just like it was up to her what she felt, and she refused to let Aidan make her feel intimidated.

"What do you want from me?" Aidan asked.

She tried not to be swayed by the hurt shining in his eyes. "I don't want anything from you, Aidan. I thought I made that clear."

"By the end of fishing, I *will* change your mind." He rose and moved toward his pretty cousin, Lana, who Peter was trying his best to impress.

As she watched him go, a pang of sadness intruded. No, he wouldn't change her mind. Garrett moved into her view, holding a plate loaded with food, and she gladly focused on him.

"Mind if I take this seat?" he asked.

Maybe a distraction was just what she needed. "Please."

"You going to eat?" He took a big bite out of his mustard-coated dog, leaving a smudge of yellow at the corner of his lips. She wanted to lick it off.

He wiped at the mustard with his napkin and paused, catching her gaze. "What?"

"Hmm?"

"You were staring."

"Was I?"

"Definitely."

Wow, it was getting hot. She'd have to move away from the campfire. "I guess I'm hungrier than I thought." His eyes widened over her words and she quickly excused herself to get some food before she helped herself to him.

Grams held out a roasting stick when Sonya walked over to her. "You seem to be hitting it off with Garrett." She pointed to Gramps who was retelling the story of when he'd bested a bear on this very beach to Wes, Peter, and Lana. They'd all heard it before, but never tired of it. "Nikky will be pleased."

Sonya skewered a hotdog with her stick. "Let's keep it between us. It'll just swell his head."

Grams laughed and handed her a plate with a serving of baked beans, potato salad, canned fruit cocktail, and a bun just how she liked it, smothered with relish and mustard. "You want onions with that?" she asked with a knowing smile.

"Not tonight."

"He does look like he knows how to make a woman's toes curl."

"Grams."

"I'm not so old that I don't appreciate a fine looking man."

Sonya took her plate and went back to Garrett. She set her plate between them. Better to be on the safe side. This attraction was coming on too hot. Needed to cool it down. A glance at Aidan glaring at the two of them reminded her of what happened when she didn't take time to think.

"So, where you from, Garrett?" she asked. Best way to start thinking was to begin finding out information. The man could be married for heaven sakes. Though she doubted it. He didn't have that "caught" look about him.

"Presently, Homer."

"Homer's nice. Scenic. Some great halibut fishing to be had."

"It's that all right." A shadow crossed over his features. He pointed to her hotdog sizzling in the fire. "Might want to pull that back."

"I like them blistered." She rotated her dog and then asked, "Married?"

"No." He coughed. "You?"

"Nope."

"Boyfriend?" He nodded his head toward Aidan.

"No boyfriend. You?"

"No boyfriend, either." He smiled and her insides fluttered.

So much for cooling things down.

Her hotdog caught fire.

Dinner with the Savonskis was proving to be a welcome-damusement. Garrett had been all work and definitely no play for far too long. It had been a long time since he'd felt this quickening of his pulse and heating of his blood. His relationship with Mel had been more friendly than frenzy. They'd used each other to scratch an itch when the need arose. Looking at Sonya, he felt more than an itch rising.

The fire had died down to a comfortable level. It was doing a good job of keeping the bugs at bay since the breeze had lulled. The sun hung steady on the horizon despite the late hour.

The sea hugged the shore as though content, but Garrett knew the calm surface belied the activity going on beneath as millions of salmon made the run up the rivers for spawning. The fishermen would be churning up the waters trying to catch them come tomorrow morning's high tide.

"Sonya," Nikolai said. "Maggie May wants to hear you play something."

"Gramps, I don't have my—"

Nikolai waved his hand. "Not to worry. I had Peter run and get it."

Peter smiled as he handed her an instrument case he'd stashed behind the log he'd been sitting on. "Here you go, Ducky."

Sonya narrowed her eyes, which seemed to promise retribution, and she took the case. Garrett wondered briefly over the nickname.

"If I have to play, so do you," Sonya said.

Peter shrugged. "I don't have my drums."

"I'm sure you can find something to beat on."

"The cooler's empty," Nikolai said. "It'll make a good sound." He thumped it for emphasis.

"Yes, Peter. Please, I've never heard you play," Lana said, her voice sweet and bright much like her blond cheerleader good looks.

Peter's cheeks pinked and he picked up the cooler, trying his hand at it. He sat, positioning the cooler between his legs. "Ready, whenever you are."

Sonya stood, opened the case, and picked up a violin, checking it for tune. She looked at Garrett. "Sorry about this. Gramps likes to show us off."

"Don't apologize. I'm enjoying myself."

Sonya nodded at Peter and positioned the violin under her chin. "Try and keep up." She strung the bow across the strings. It vibrated and sang with a voice of its own. The music she chose to play was a lively Celtic tune, and when Peter joined in with the beat of the cooler-drum, Garrett swore the flames of the fire flickered in time to the tune.

Here he was at a fish camp roast on the South Naknek side of Bristol Bay, much closer to Russia than the continental United States, with sand all around, gray cliffs towering over them, and the world's deadliest ocean at their backs. Not a theatre or opera house for three hundred miles, and he was being treated to a first class violin performance. He was captivated by Sonya's fingers as they danced over the chords, her hand commanding the bow as it stroked sound from the strings. Her hands would be picking fish out of a net come morning, yet tonight they brought forth music.

The woman had facets.

She finished with a flourish, her hair having come loose as she'd lost her ball cap with the fiery way she'd played. Her hair was dark and thick, longer than he'd first expected.

"Another," Nikolai requested. "Something sweet for my Maggie May."

Sonya gave the violin a slow caress of the bow, and Garrett felt the notes loosen something inside him. Nikolai rose and reached out a hand for Margaret, and she gracefully stepped into his arms. They swayed over the sand to the haunting music Sonya aroused from the strings. Peter sat this one out and let Sonya entrance the group. The music was potent, passionate, hypnotic.

And Garrett was snared.

ॐ

Sonya laid the violin lovingly back in its case. Her emotions were heightened whenever she played. The treasured violin had been her mother's. She always felt connected to her on a spiritual plane whenever she coaxed a tune from the instrument. It didn't matter if she played for a group, like tonight, or alone. Something about the music beckoned and bewitched.

"That was amazing," Garrett said. "Can you play another?"

"Better not," she replied, her voice too breathless for her liking. She cleared her throat. "Fishing tomorrow." They should be calling a halt to this evening anyway. They all needed their rest for their first day of drifting.

"Hey, Sonya. We forgot the makings for s'mores. Run up to the cabin and get them, will you?" Gramps asked, followed by, "Garrett, why don't you give her a hand?"

Sonya closed her eyes. What was Gramps trying to do?

"I'd be happy to." Garrett rose to his feet.

Sonya took the violin with her, and Garrett followed. They didn't talk on the climb to the cabin.

The cabin was shadowed when they entered. Sonya laid her violin on the table, and lit a candle to find the smore ingredients. The strong smell of sulfur dioxide from the match tainted the air and seemed to enclose the space, making it a touch too romantic with the burning candle.

"Nice place," Garrett commented, looking around. "You're pretty set up considering you're only here a couple of months every summer."

"Gramps likes to do for Grams." She opened the cupboard and took down the graham crackers, marshmallows, and chocolate bars.

"It's nice that he's still courting her after all the years they've been together."

She cocked her head to the side. "I've never thought of it that way, but you're right. He does court her." The man was perceptive to pick up on that. She wondered what else he was good at. Sonya started to bundle the ingredients into her arms.

"Here, let me help with that. After all—" he smiled and it reached all the way to his eyes "—wasn't that why Nikolai asked me to come along?"

Her matchmaking grandpa hoped something else would happen between them. Sonya handed the goods to Garrett and then thought, *what the hell.* "Why don't we get this out of the way?" With his hands occupied, she captured his face between hers, and kissed him.

Damn, his lips *were* as soft as they looked. It was the last coherent thought she had.

Garrett growled and yanked her flush against his chest. She heard the crunch of graham crackers beneath their feet and didn't care. All she cared about was getting closer to him, which was probably physically impossible unless they lost some clothes. But she was willing to give it a go.

They broke apart as suddenly as they'd come together as though simultaneously realizing where the kiss was headed. It wasn't the right time. Definitely not the right place.

"That was better than I thought it would be," she said, her voice huskier than she'd like, and for a moment she didn't recognize it as her own.

"That's an understatement." He leaned back against the counter, breathing deep. "Maybe it was a fluke." He seemed to be talking to himself more than to her, as if trying to convince himself that what had just happened hadn't really meant anything. She was all for agreeing with his argument. She didn't want that kiss to mean anything either.

"Want to try it again?" she found herself asking. "You know—" she shrugged "—rule out the fluke factor?"

His eyes burned into hers, and he pushed himself away from the counter. She swallowed. He was big and imposing as he stepped toward her. Their bodies came into contact as his hands framed her face, diving deep into her hair and forcing her head back. He lowered his mouth until their breaths mixed, mated.

He paused, just before taking her mouth. "If I kiss you again, we won't be leaving this cabin until after I get you naked."

Damn, her toes *were* curling. She wished she could deny it. Just having him this close, she was ready and willing to forget the people down on the beach and strip. The problem with acting on impulse was that when she returned to sanity, she always regretted her actions. She didn't know this man well enough to share herself with him. He didn't know her either, and once men really got to know her, they usually begged off.

She tended to intimidate.

"Well—" she swallowed "—best not, then." Her voice was breathless.

"It *would* be best," he said, his voice just as breathless. He still hadn't moved. Still held her as though he couldn't break away. She hoped he wasn't counting on her being the sensible one. She'd started this.

Slowly he let go of her and moved back. His step crunched, and he glanced down. "We might have a problem."

A bigger problem than their raging hormones? She glanced down at the floor and couldn't help but laugh. "This will be the last time Gramps sends me for dessert."

"If he does send you again, I hope I'll be along to help." He looked at her with enough yearning to cause her to envision pushing him down on the table hand-made from driftwood planks. It seemed sturdy enough to hold their weight.

She took a deep breath. "We'd better get out of here."

"Yep." He glanced at the table as though knowing what she'd been contemplating.

They made their way back to the beach, after salvaging the best of the broken graham crackers and chocolate bars—the marshmallows showed no signs of damage—and sweeping up the rest of the mess. Too bad she couldn't have swept Garrett's kiss from her lips as easily. The crowd was still going strong when they reached the sand. Peter was doing a cooler-drum solo while the rest be-bopped along.

That was, all but Aidan.

"All right, finally, here are the goodies," Wes announced. He had a wicked sweet tooth and was first to reach for the s'mores, opening the bag they'd stuffed everything into. He frowned. "What happened to the graham crackers?"

"Clumsy fingers," Sonya mumbled while trying not to look at Garrett, though she felt the heat of his stare.

"Hope you get them working for picking fish tomorrow," Wes said.

"By the way, Garrett," Aidan asked, "You working for the cannery or as crewman for someone?"

"Neither." Garrett paused. "I work for the State."

"State?" Sonya turned from unwrapping a chocolate bar. "Biologist? Fish and Game?"

He slowly shook his head, his eyes holding hers. "AWT."

"You're a *fish cop?*" *She'd kissed a freaking fish cop?*

He hardened his jaw. A jaw she'd wanted to nibble on a few minutes ago. "We prefer trooper."

"Trooper?" Gramps swiveled around, as though looking for the law, having just caught the tail end of the conversation. "Where?"

"Right in front of you, Gramps. Turns out Garrett's a trooper." She really needed to have that talk with him over screening his "potentials." Look at the position he'd put her in. Put *them* in.

"Well, who in the dang blazes invited the enemy?" Gramps grabbed an marshmallow and stuffed it in his mouth.

Who indeed. Sonya stared until Gramps pulled at his collar as though it was strangling him.

She caught Aidan's satisfied smile as he sat back, crossed his ankles, and watched.

Sonya faced Garrett, her hands anchored to her hips, when they wanted to be grabbing him by his shirt and giving him a good shaking. "Were you planning on telling us who you were?"

His brow furrowed. "Didn't think it would be that big of a deal."

"Liar," she said. "Why'd you really come to dinner?"

Peter pointed an accusing finger. "It's the fox in the hen house thing. He's sizing us up."

"Is this part of a new trooper undercover program?" Wes asked, his normally steady demeanor looking a bit ruffled.

"Find out anything useful?" Peter followed up with, not bothering to skewer a marshmallow on the end of his whittled willow branch. He held the stick like a rapier.

"Nothing criminal if that's what you mean." Garrett ran a hand through his short hair and Sonya could feel his frustration. Good. "Listen," he said, "your name came up on a list of potential problems. I thought it would be a good idea to see how much of a problem."

"Reeeally?" She dragged out the word until it sounded more like a challenge than a question. "You have no idea how much of a problem I can be."

"Now, Sonya." Gramps moved in between them. "The man's explained himself. He's just doing his job."

Was he doing his job when he'd returned her kiss and about burned her up from the inside?

"Cut the man some slack," Gramps added, trying to be the voice of reason. Someone needed to be. It sure as hell wasn't going to be her.

"But, Gramps," Peter said. "He came here and ate our food, schmoozed us into compliance, and watch, tomorrow he'll be fast to write us up for some stupid infraction."

"Am I going to need to?" Garrett asked, his voice having gone all trooperish.

Ooh, that shouldn't excite her. She was getting confused. That kiss had shifted something inside her. Time to get some distance and sort it all out.

"All right, that's enough. Garrett, it's time to say your goodbyes." Sonya pushed him back, trying not to let her hand linger on his brick house of a chest. "Peter, Wes, we'll be having an early start in the morning. Best clean up dinner and find your bunks."

"You're not my mother, Sonya. I don't need to be told when to go to bed," Peter was quick to point out. For the last year, he'd been bucking anything she'd asked of him that resembled parenting. It was past annoying.

"Right now, I'm your boss."

"Come on, let's listen to the Captain." Wes moved in front of Peter. "Garrett, it was nice meeting you…that was, before we knew you were a fish cop."

"Trooper," Garrett corrected with a clenched jaw.

Ah, sore spot, Sonya realized, filing the information away. She grabbed Garrett's arm and he willingly went with her. Good thing, because if it came to manhandling some-one, Sonya knew without a doubt that Garrett would be better at it than her.

Manhandle. Dang. She shook her head to get the image that one word brought into her mind. Yep, needed some space and fast.

Garrett mounted the 4-wheeler. He took the key out of his pocket and put it in the ignition, but didn't bother to start the engine. He captured her hand instead. "Sonya. About that kiss—"

"It's a conflict of interest for us to see each other." Damn, why did he have to be a fish cop? She pulled her hand out of his and backed up a step. "I don't play games."

"Neither do I…usually. But, when I do, I play for keeps." He started the ATV and engaged the gears. "I'll be *seeing* you, Sonya."

Not if she could help it.

CHAPTER FIVE

Sonya studied the skies from the pilot house of the *Double Dippin'*. An uneasy foreboding sank into her bones.

A red morning for the first day of drifting. The maritime warning echoed through Sonya's head. *Red morning, sailors take warning.*

Weather was predicted to blow in that afternoon. When didn't they get weather in Bristol Bay? She'd even seen it when the wind blew both directions just for the fun of it.

Right now the sea was gray, choppy, and dressed in whitecaps. The wind blew steady from the east at twenty knots. That would change. She stretched, trying to get the kinks out of her back. The bunk on the boat wasn't the most comfortable. Not to mention she was edgy over what today would bring. She had a lot to live up to. Her big mouth for one. She'd talked everyone into drifting. Her family had been happy set netting for over fifty years, and here she'd pushed for them to drift.

"Yo, Captain," Wes hollered from the starboard side. "Permission to come aboard."

Sonya opened the window and leaned out of the pilot house to see Wes bouncing like a rubber ball in the skiff. "Permission granted, matey." She rubbed her hands together as she noticed the individual cooler he had with him. Looked like she wouldn't have to settle for a protein bar for breakfast, after all. When he was safely aboard, and in the warm pilot house, she took the cooler from him. Her mouth salivated at the thought of what her grandmother had cooked for breakfast. Cinnamon rolls, blueberry muffins. "What did you bring?"

"Don't get too excited." Wes grimaced, unsnapping his rain jacket. "Margaret made salmon omelets. In my opinion, fish is never a good breakfast food."

They supplemented their food stores with salmon, living off the ocean as much as they could. Food was expensive to ship in and even more expensive to buy at the cannery. Then there was the problem of refrigeration. Salmon was caught fresh every day, healthy, and a great source of protein. Unfortunately, Sonya had to agree with Wes. It wasn't the most ideal breakfast food. Maybe she'd have her protein bar after all.

"I did grab you some nuts and the last of the apples, in case the omelet wasn't to your liking."

She grabbed the apple and took a bite. It was a bit mealy, but it was fruit. Probably the last she'd see until the season was over and she headed home. So she savored it. "Thanks, Wes. I appreciate it."

Wes settled himself on the small bunk while Sonya took the captain's chair and the bag of nuts Wes had stuffed into the cooler. She'd toss the omelet overboard later and let the seagulls fight over it.

"How are you doing today?" Wes asked.

She'd known Wes would show up before the rest of the crew this morning. He had a way of seeing things that no one else did. The talent would serve him well in his chosen career.

"Nervous. Excited." Sonya bit her lip and decided to speak her doubts and fears, knowing Wes would see them even if she didn't share. "Worried. Scared." Sharing with Wes had always served to calm and center her thoughts. "What if I've taken on more than I can handle?" What if she piloted her boat into the foray of the seasoned drifters and made a fool of herself? "What if this gamble doesn't pay off?" She'd literally laid everything she had on the line. "What if someone gets hurt?" There. Her biggest fear.

She couldn't lose another member of her family.

"Those are a lot of what ifs." Wes leaned forward and rested his elbows on his knees. "Let's start with the first one. Do you really believe you've taken on more than you can handle? Is that your thought or someone else's?"

"Oh, you're good." She hadn't realized she'd let Aidan get to her. How had she let herself doubt? She'd fished out here all her life. She *knew* fishing. It had driven her crazy when the Fish and Game opened the area for drifters and closed the set netters. The drifters cleaned up. They could go where the fish were, while the set netters were stuck fishing in the same place. She was in the commercial fishing business to make money, and there was a lot of money out there to be made. She just needed to maximize her take of the catch.

Drifting and set netting was good business.

"You're right, I can handle this," she said. "I've had to deal with tougher stuff." She discarded the apple, throwing it out the window into the sea, and then mimicked his elbows on knees posture. "Okay, on to the next what if."

Wes smiled. "That's the spirit. Gambling. You gamble every year out here. Other than the bigger stake, what's different?"

She thought about it. The game was still the same. The goal: to catch as much fish as she could. "I have better equipment to maximize my return." She tapped her lips with her fingertip. "I've spent all winter planning. I know what I'm doing, and I *do* have the best crew."

Wes smiled again and nodded. "Good. Now, onto the big one. What if someone gets hurt?"

Sweat broke out all over her body in a cold chill. She swallowed passed the lump in her throat. "I can't work through this one, Wes."

"Yes, you can. There are no guarantees, Sonya. Fishing is risky business. You know that more than most. You can't let the past paralyze your future choices."

He was right, but knowing that didn't silence the screams from the past that still haunted her. She was the captain. Captains were responsible for their crews. It was up to them to make sure everything was safe. She'd taken precautions. The *Double Dippin'* was hands down the safest boat in Bristol Bay. She'd seen to it. She'd put her crew through safety drills yesterday until they'd begged to stop, and then she'd put them through more.

She'd done everything physically possible to ensure the safety of her crew.

The only thing left to do was pray.

Garrett couldn't keep his head on the job. He was dressed in uniform. There was no doubt of who he was today. Regardless of the regulations to uphold, laws to enforce, safety to insure, he couldn't stop thinking of Sonya Savonski. The feel of her under his hands and the burn she'd started in his gut.

They'd just left a trooper meeting where it was apparent, as always, that the law was at a disadvantage. There were roughly four hundred drift boats to police out there, and not enough troopers.

"Hunt," Judd hollered. "You with me or not?"

"Yeah." He and Judd were doing a food run at the Cannery's General Store before heading out. Who knew when they'd have a chance at a warm meal? For now, quick and easy food for the man-on-the-go was the order of the day.

And it promised to be one hell of a day.

"Plain or peanut? Make a decision, would ya?" Judd elbowed him into the present, and he was struck by the colorful, amused woman waiting behind the counter for his decision.

"Peanut." The nuts in the M&M's would at least provide some protein.

"Why the hell was that so hard?" Judd tossed a dozen packages of peanut M&M's on the counter already littered with string cheese, pop, chips, beer nuts, and peperoni sticks.

"Lot on my mind." Not a thing on his mind but a woman. When was the last time that had happened? He'd always been able to compartmentalize. One of the talents that'd made him a good Navy SEAL.

Focus. He needed to focus.

Then he heard Sonya's name drift through the open window. He shook his head, figuring it had manifested itself because she was all he seemed to think about. When the voices lowered, and his second sense kicked in.

"I'll be right back," he told Judd, who could have cared less as he flirted with the clerk. Garrett doubled back around the building in the direction of the voices he'd heard. He smelled the bitter stench of cigarettes. By the shuffling of feet and flickering of a lighter, he estimated that there were two of them. He flattened himself against the wall, and waited. Sure enough, they started gabbing like a ladies Thursday night quilt circle.

"Seriously, the bitch never knew I was there. Sliced her hydraulic line while she slept. Easy as pie."

"You sure she's not going to notice?"

"Naw. Not until she tries to pull in her nets."

"Bitch thinks she can throw in with the big boys. It's bad luck, I tell ya. A woman drifting." The man gave a snort. *"We need to get her off the water and back on the shore where she belongs."* The voices started to waft on the wind, and he knew they were on the move.

Garrett peeked around the corner, hoping to catch a glimpse of the vandals. They'd meshed into another, louder group of fishermen dressed in hooded orange and green slickers. There was no way to tell who the perpetrators were.

He hustled back to Judd. "We need to get a move on."

Judd tore his love-puppy eyes away from the clerk. "Why?" He glanced at his watch. "There's time."

"Overheard a possible 10-59."

Judd turned back to the lady behind the counter. "Guess our fun's over, Davida."

"Only if you want it to be," Davida purred. "If you're free later, come by, and we'll see what kind of fun we can find." Her smile didn't leave much to the imagination.

"It's a date." Judd winked, and then signed his name to the receipt. Garrett grabbed the bag, hoping to get Casanova moving.

They left the General Store and made their way to the dock, where the *Calypso* was moored.

Skip greeted them with a grin as he spied the brown paper bag Garrett carried. "What did you get to eat?"

"Here." Garrett tossed the bag to him, which Skip immediately rifled through. "Judd, cast us off. Skip, take us out into the bay. We need to find the *Double Dippin'.*"

𝒥

With her crew aboard, Sonya weighed anchor and set a course for the mouth of the Naknek River. The Fish and Game had opened the river for fishing, hoping to limit the salmon escapement. As predicted, numbers of returning salmon were huge. Drifting in the river had the benefit of calmer waters, but with all the drifters jockeying for position, the fishing area would be tight, and that brought in another added danger.

It was called combat fishing for a reason.

Upon entering the wide mouth of the river, Sonya tamped down her nerves when she saw all the boats bumping and brawling for the best spot. Everyone was waiting for the clock to tick its way to nine-thirty, the time when fishing officially began. Tension and tempers were thick in the air in anticipation of the start of what was projected to be a record season.

Wes and Peter readied the net while Gramps kept her company in the pilot house. The windows were open, and she easily heard the normal insults and crass jokes—which came with men working together—traveling over the open water. It all mixed together and made a spicy soup.

Boats churned up the gray, silt waters, and engines rumbled. Diesel fumes permeated the air, while seagulls squawked like hecklers overhead. Sonya wasn't the only one needing to catch a lot of fish. For some fishermen, this was their only livelihood.

The juggling of constantly moving her boat, watching out for the other boats, and gauging the strong tide flooding the river took every bit of Sonya's attention. She barely had any left to keep an eye out for the troopers. They were everywhere, like gnats. Planes and helicopters flew above. The *Calypso*, and high performance RHIBs—rigid-hulled inflatable boats, or what Sonya referred to as sharks—patrolled the water. Planters were stationed on shore. All were outfitted with high powered cameras and binoculars, watching and waiting for the slightest mistake.

Garrett was out there somewhere.

Sonya locked the door on that thought and mentally tossed the key overboard. She had enough to concentrate on. She didn't need another distraction, and Garrett had already distracted her too much. It seemed in her experience that most fishermen were written up by the troopers for a loss of concentration. Something got away from them. There were the few cutthroats looking for any opportunity to bend the law to their advantage. After all, fishing was all about advantage. The best vantage point, the best fishing hole, the best boat, and the best crew.

"Heads up," Gramps said. "We have fish cops twenty feet off the stern."

Sonya glanced behind them. Sure enough there was the *Calypso*, a former drift boat the state used to "blend in" with the other fishermen. Any fisherman with any fish sense knew the *Calypso* for what she was.

A spy vessel.

"Looks like they want to board us," Gramps said.

Peter pointed at the *Calypso*. "Do you see that?"

"Yes." She nodded. They hadn't done anything. Hell, they didn't even have their net in the water. She glanced at the instrument panel and noticed the time. They didn't have time for this. "Wes, Peter, prepare to get the net in the water."

The *Calypso* angled alongside them. She heard Garrett's voice clearly as he yelled from the deck of the trooper's boat. "*Double Dippin'*, prepare to be boarded."

Damn it all to hell. If this had something to do with last night, Garrett was out of line. With no choice, Sonya did as the law ordered. A rope flew over the side of her boat and Wes caught it, securing the boats together. Garrett leaped over, looking lethal in his dark blue uniform, trooper hat, and sunglasses. He glanced around the deck, nodded toward Wes and Peter, then zeroed in on her up in the pilot house.

"I need to talk to you."

Oh no, he did not. "I'm busy here. You realize that we're about to drop our net."

He whipped off his sunglasses, his piercing eyes hard as ice. "Not before we speak. Don't make me give you a safety inspection."

Double hell! He could hold them up indefinitely if she didn't cooperate. "Gramps, hold her steady."

"Give him hell, Sonya. We need to get fishing."

"Plan to." Sonya slid down the rail of the stairs and stomped her way on deck toward Garrett. "What do you want?"

"You have a problem onboard."

"Yeah, I'm looking at it."

The *Albatross* puttered by, and Chuck Kendrick yelled across the open water, "Yo, Double D, better treat that trooper right. Show him your titties, and he might be kind enough to let you off with a warning."

She sent Chuck the finger, a message the dimwit would understand, and then caught Garrett's narrowed look.

"Not afraid of making enemies, are you?" he said, with a cocked brow.

"Just speaking to Chuck in the language he understands." She didn't need to explain herself to him and resented the feeling to do exactly that. She tried to hand him a copy of her permit and fishing licenses for everyone onboard.

"What's this for?" he asked.

"Trying to speed up the process." She flapped the papers at him again. "Come on, I've got fish to catch, and there has to be someone else you could be harassing."

"I'm not here to check that your paperwork's in order." His eyes snapped with temper. "You've pissed some people off, Sonya."

"That's nothing new. I piss people off all the time."

"I don't doubt it." He leaned into her, and she caught a whiff of that spicy mix of man and power. She didn't like it. It took a moment to clear her head.

"Are you listening to me?" he asked, advancing a step.

"Yeah." She waved her hands in front of her as though to scare off a pesky bug. "Say what you gotta say, and then get the hell off my boat."

"I don't know why I bothered trying to do you a favor. You'll probably ignore everything I have to say on principle."

"Probably." She nodded. "Just spit it out, so I can get my net in the water." His delaying her on the first day of fishing had better not be intentional.

"Check your hydraulic lines. I overheard someone say they'd sliced them."

"What?"

"Just do it." He turned and leaped over the side, back onto the *Calypso*. The man was in great shape to be able to do that so gracefully. Wonder what else he could do with such power and grace? Damn, she needed to get her mind off his body and back on the job at hand.

"What'd he want?" Peter asked, throwing the *Calypso's* rope back to her. Boats all around them were throwing their buoys in the water and laying out their nets in a roar of diesel engines. Garrett had kept them from getting a prime position, and she was already behind.

"Let's get the net in the water, and then we need to check the hydraulics."

"Hydraulics? Why?"

"Apparently, someone's tampered with our lines."

∫

"Damn ornery woman," Garrett muttered as he made his way to the cabin on the *Calypso*.

"You know her?" Judd asked. "Seemed to me that was more than just informing someone of a potential problem. After all, you could have informed them over the radio."

"Met her for the first time a few days ago."

"Well, she obviously made an impression on you," Skip added.

"That's one word for it." A few others readily came to mind. Hell, there she'd been spitting mad at him, actually wearing a t-shirt that said, "Have You Flogged Your Crew Today?" and he'd been doing her a favor. One that she'd probably ignore, because she didn't want anything from him. Anything that is, since she found out he was a trooper. Before that, she'd wanted plenty, and he'd wanted to give it to her.

He couldn't remember the last time a woman had gotten him so worked up, emotionally and physically. He didn't need this kind of aggravation.

"Hunt, you got your head in the game?" Judd hollered, pointing left of the bow where a drift boat had just rammed another boat.

His head was somewhere else entirely. He grabbed the binoculars and focused on the boat. A few weapons were already being aimed between captains.

Someone was going to get killed this season.

The *Double Dippin'* laid out her net.

Sonya tried to keep out of the way of the other drifters, packed into the mouth of the river, while her crew went over all the hydraulic lines. She wracked her brain, wondering when someone would have had the opportunity to tamper with her boat.

"Found it!" Wes hollered.

"Where?" she asked, hanging out of the pilot house.

"Someone's punctured one of the hoses on the rollers. We wouldn't have noticed it until we powered it up to pull in the net." Which would have caused them all sorts of problems.

"Can we fix it?" she asked.

"Already on it," Gramps said, holding up a roll of duct tape. "This will patch it up until we can replace the hose."

Sonya laughed with relief. There wasn't anything Gramps believed couldn't be fixed with a bit of duct tape. She sure hoped he was right in this case. If they lost the use of the hydraulic roller, the chance of catching a reasonable amount of fish, dwindled considerably. They'd have to round-haul the net in by hand. Having it full of fish, and fighting the pull of the tide, would make reeling it in tough, quickly exhausting the crew.

Garrett had saved them lots of time and back-breaking work, not to mention, money.

Now she'd have to find him and apologize for her snotty attitude. Worst of all, she'd have to thank him. Shit.

They pulled in their first net, yielding a respectable catch. Sonya turned over the wheel to Gramps under the pretense of wanting to be on deck when the net came over the rollers. When in fact, she didn't want Gramps overdoing it. The man wasn't as young as he used to be.

Everything seemed to be running smoothly after finding the sliced hydraulic line. Sonya promised herself she'd find the bastard responsible. Just because she was a woman didn't mean she was easy pickings. Then a member of her crew turned mutiny when she informed them that, as captain, she was upholding the long standing tradition of everyone kissing the first caught fish of the season for luck.

Peter screwed up his face. "That is gross on so many levels. Besides, I'm almost eighteen. It should be my choice what I kiss. It's a stupid ritual, anyway."

"No, it's not. As captain, I'm ordering you to do it." Fishermen tended to be a bit superstitious. She was no different. Every year she'd fished, Gramps had upheld this very ritual. It was Sonya's year, and they were fishing a new way, but a ritual was a ritual.

"Kiss the fish, Peter," Wes said with a dare in his eye. "You need all the practice you can get, especially if you want to try your luck with Lana."

"Lana? You want to kiss Lana Harte?" Sonya remembered the way Peter had acted at the campfire the other night. He'd paid more attention to Lana than he had his food. In the past, he'd picked on Lana. Pulled her hair, teased—kid stuff—but there had been a difference in the way he'd treated her last night. Taking food to her, offering her a seat, standing when she stood. A lot the way Garrett had treated *her.*

Scratch that.

She refused to think about Garrett.

Peter's blush rivaled the flesh of a spawning salmon. "So what if I wouldn't mind kissing her. She's hot."

Lana *had* grown into a beautiful young woman. "She's older than you, by what…two years?" Sonya pointed out. The Hartes could be trouble. Look at what had happened between her and Aidan. Sonya didn't think Lana handled problems with her fists, though being raised in that family, the girl could be seriously messed up.

"So what. Aidan's older than you. That didn't stop you from having a thing last year."

"You're only seventeen. That's a big difference and you know it." Sonya hammered home.

"All right, don't nag. I'll kiss the fish."

She *so* did not nag and was ready to tell Peter just that when she mentally took a step back. She had to remember that their relationship was changing. For so long, she'd spent all her time mothering him. Worrying about him. His friends, his choices, his future. It was time to back off and let him do some of his own choosing. The boy was becoming a man.

"Pucker up, lover boy." Wes held the fish by the tail and underbelly. Peter scrunched up his face and kissed the fish, spitting over the side of the boat afterward. Sonya laughed. Wes turned the sockeye around, making kissy noises, and planted one on its nose. "All right, Sonya, you're up."

Sonya rubbed her hands and sang, "Here, fishy fishy." She gave it a smooch. The fish was cold and slimy. Like Peter had said, it was a stupid ritual, but fun and who knew if it really worked or not. She wasn't going to be the one Savonski who threw caution to the wind and put a stop to it. Not when she needed every bit of luck she could get this summer.

The *Mary Jane* drifted next to them and her captain, Ringo hollered over from his crow's nest, "Sonya, you ever want a real man, look me up." He pursed his lips and blew her a kiss. "I'll promise you a party, sweetheart."

No doubt. "Thanks, *Mary Jane*, but this is all I want." She figured anyone seeing her crew kissing fish *would* do a double take.

One of the *Mary Jane's* crew shot off a question to Ringo, "Shouldn't we be kissing our fish? It's kinda like a blessing, right?"

"You want to kiss a fish, dude, knock yourself out," Ringo said. "Me, I'd rather kiss me a fine looking woman." He gave Sonya a "call me" signal that she wisely chose to ignore.

"Hey, I need a chance to kiss that beauty," Gramps yelled from the pilot house as he leaned out the window. "I'm ready to be relieved, captain."

"Be right up." She turned to Peter and Wes, who were already pulling the rest of the net into the boat. "Don't let him overdo."

"Got it, Captain," Wes said, picking fish out of the net as the duct-taped hydraulics pulled it in over the rollers.

"Don't worry, Sonya. We've got 'Operation Gramps' under control." Peter gave her a conspiring wink. She smiled at both of them, and then headed for the pilot house.

She'd talked with Wes and Peter yesterday about limiting the amount of work Gramps did. They'd all agreed that they'd have to be sneaky about it so he didn't catch on. The man was clever and had a lot of pride. The last thing they wanted to do was damage either.

The thought was quickly forgotten as they were rammed on the starboard side.

"Howdy, *Double D*," captain of the *Miss Julie II*, hollered. "Sorry for the nudge."

"Nudge me like that again, Treat, and I'm going to take it the wrong way."

"A sweet young thing like you wouldn't play hardball now, would ya?"

"There's nothing sweet about me. I have no qualms about busting your balls."

"Hear that boys? The *Double D's* a feisty one."

Chapter Six

Aidan reached the bluff that overlooked the mouth of the river. He hated that he felt like he *had* to get a look at what Sonya was up to. He lay down on his stomach in the tall grass and raised the binoculars. Deep down he knew what she was doing was wrong. It was a big waste of money, and time, and unnecessary risk. Or was it that he wished he had the guts to try and accomplish what she was doing?

In a sense, they'd grown up together, spending every summer fishing out here with their families. He focused the binoculars on the *Double Dippin'*. He was older and had a choice in where he spent the summer. Yet he still returned to put up with the same old shit. He was only biding his time. It couldn't be long now. The smoking, the drinking, and the cranky attitude had to be wearing on the old man. Earl would kick the bucket soon.

If someone didn't help him into a grave first.

Lana dropped onto the grass next to him. "Spying on her isn't going to help your cause." His cousin's breezy attitude, all smile and teeth, rubbed at his already nasty mood.

Aidan refocused the binoculars back to the deck of the *Double Dippin'*, catching Sonya throwing her head back with a laugh he wished he could hear. He felt a pang in his chest.

"Go away, brat," he said to Lana. He thought he'd lost her down at the docks. Guess she was more observant than he'd given her credit for. She'd been shadowing him all morning, and had just proved she was damn hard to lose.

"No wonder Sonya gave you the boot. Do you talk to all women that way?"

"You're not a woman."

"Last I looked I was."

"What are you doing here, Lana? I'm sure you could've found something better to do than bug me." He'd come here to be alone and chart his next course while he did a little reconnaissance work. At least, that sounded better than wasting his afternoon playing Peeping Tom.

"Nope. Been looking forward to bugging you all year." She picked a long blade of grass and twirled it between her thumb and forefinger.

He bit back a mean retort. He shouldn't take his anger and frustration out on Lana. She was a sweet kid. What had he learned in his anger management class? Think before you react. "How's your mom?"

Lana scrunched up her pretty face. "Same. Off to Brazil looking for her next affair."

"We sure got the bottom of the barrel when it came to parents, didn't we?"

When Lana's parents divorced, the courts had given Roland summer visitation, and Lana's mother had happily shipped her off to Alaska every summer after she'd turned thirteen. Aidan had lost his mother to the bottle, followed by the grave, when he was ten.

Lana nodded her head in the direction of the bay. "You see anything interesting out there?"

"Take a look for yourself." He handed her the binoculars and rolled onto his back, letting the stingy rays of the sun—playing chase with the gray clouds—warm his face.

She gazed though the binoculars in the direction of the *Double Dippin'*. "Peter sure looks different this summer."

Aidan chuckled. "Yeah, he got his man on over the winter." Aidan had a thought and turned his head to get a better look at Lana. "You aren't thinking of…"

"What? No. He's just sweet on me and it's—" she shrugged her thin shoulders "—you know…nice."

Aidan figured he wasn't the only one wanting to be a part of the Savonski clan. The Savonskis seemed to get along, as though they truly liked each other. Aidan hadn't heard Nikolai say anything derogatory to Margaret or anyone else at their camp. There was never any drinking, smoking, or yelling coming from across the creek. The Harte camp did enough of that for the whole beach. Instead, there was laughter, music, and fresh-baked cookies. He wanted to be a part of that. He'd almost been, last summer. To coin Lana's turn of phrase, Sonya and been sweet on him. Then he'd gone and ruined it. With one frustrated swing, he'd thrown it all away.

Now, he was after getting it all back.

What the hell was she doing?

Garrett refocused the dial on the binoculars. He'd seen the *Miss Julie II* intentionally ram Sonya. It was like bumper cars on water out here. The boats were too close and the fishing area too small for this many fishermen. Someone was going to get hurt, and he had a sinking feeling that "someone" captained the *Double Dippin'*.

"You want to run interference?" Judd asked, his binoculars pointing in the same direction, obviously catching what Garrett had.

"Let's head over there and see if our presence reminds people of their manners." Garrett tightened his fingers over the binoculars as Sonya gave another captain a hand gesture. At least this time she did it with a smile. She hadn't been kidding when she'd told him she didn't play well with others.

Judd hollered at Skip to power the boat toward the skirmish.

Garrett shook his head in disbelief as the *Double Dippin'* laid her net right in front of the *Albatross*, effectively corking them off.

"Did you see that?" Judd asked.

"Uh-huh."

"Kendrick isn't going to take that well," Judd said.

Sure enough, words were being slung, and then a pop can went flying toward Sonya. Sonya actually threw her head back and laughed as it missed, spraying soda against the pilot house. Garrett swiveled his binoculars back to Kendrick.

The face of the *Albatross'* captain was red as a heart attack. "Let's hurry this tug boat along, Skip." Before another weapon, more deadly, was produced. They'd already unarmed and cited another boat and the fishing period wasn't even half over for the day.

"The woman sure isn't out to make friends," Skip commented, clicking his tongue.

"Doesn't look that way." She was going to make his job a hell of a lot harder this summer.

"What's Kendrick doing?" Judd asked.

Garrett lowered his binoculars. "I think he just ordered his crewman to cut her line." The *Calypso* was too

66

far away to intervene. By the time they reached the feuding vessels, threats were being swapped and Sonya's net was about to be cut. Funny how the knife disappeared and the crewman dropped her cork line when he saw the troopers.

"What do you want to do, Garrett?" Judd asked, lowering his binoculars. "He hasn't broken any laws...yet."

"Let's board him anyway and see what we can find." It would dispel the situation between Sonya and Kendrick, and remind Kendrick that the law was watching.

Didn't Sonya know better than to cross men like him? Garrett caught her colorful threat of making Kendrick fish bait on the wind. Guess not.

Skip announced their intent over the loud speaker, and with the way Kendrick went off with his foul language, they weren't welcomed. Meanwhile, Sonya smiled ear to ear, and waved to the captain of the *Albatross* as her crew began pulling in their full net.

Before disembarking the *Albatross*, Garrett wrote Kendrick up for three safety violations. The fisherman was not happy, but he'd wisely taken the tickets, stone-faced and menacing. The man was imposing with his three-foot breadth of shoulders, lumberjack arms, and keg of a belly. He reminded Garrett of Brutus in the cartoon *Popeye*, though a lot smarter and more dangerous.

Sonya had better watch who she pissed off. Some tussles weren't worth the trouble.

Garrett reboarded the *Calypso*. "Where's the *Double Dippin*?"

"Are we policing her or protecting her?" Judd asked with a cocked brow.

"Both. She needs a friendly warning."

"Another?" Skip asked. "We babysitting the woman and no one told me?"

"Just do it."

"Would you look at the new guy, throwing his weight around?" Skip said to Judd.

"Just because he's a decorated SEAL, the man thinks he's hot stuff," Judd returned.

"Stow it, boys. And I *am* hot stuff." His comment was followed by snorts of laughter.

"Ahoy, Captain," Peter said in a sing-song voice. "The *Calypso's* back."

They'd finished hauling in their net and had moved closer to the beach to lay out the next one. Nice thing about the flat bottom boat was that they could position themselves in the shallows, as long as they were careful and didn't beach themselves when the tide turned.

Corking off the *Albatross* had been a smart, if somewhat risky move. The net they'd pulled in was stocked with fish. Looking at all the silver flashing on deck, made up for the gamble.

The *Calypso* drew as close as she dared in the shallow water. Garrett stood at the bow, his brows lowered, his face a chiseled mask of intent. "You got a death wish?" he hollered.

"No more than anyone else out here," Sonya yelled back.

Deep lines bracketed his mouth. "Chuck Kendrick isn't someone you want to be messing with, Sonya."

"You know what, Garrett. *I'm* not someone to mess with. Why don't you spread that around instead of telling me how to fish these waters?"

His eyes narrowed, and he anchored his hands on his hips. His stance reflected more than ever his position of power. He looked manly and macho, and frustrated as hell. It started private places of hers thawing, and she didn't want to thaw for him.

"I feel sparks in the air," Gramps commented, his voice easily reaching Sonya. Gramps turned to Wes and Peter. "You feel sparks?"

"Yep," Wes responded with an easy going grin.

Peter glanced around the deck. "Something on fire?"

"Your sister's about to go up in flames," Wes said, tongue in cheek.

"You ladies through gossiping?" Sonya knew her face was flushed. She just hoped Garrett couldn't hear the men's scuttlebutt.

"I'm not trying to tell you how to fish," Garrett said. "But if I have to intervene in another one of your squabbles, I'm going to write you up for harassment."

"Harassment! Squabbles! Listen, fish cop, I haven't been the one starting things out there."

"You started that last one."

She opened her mouth to argue, and then shut it. He was right. She *had* started it by laying her net out in front of Kendrick's, but he'd escalated it. Besides there wasn't anything illegal about what she'd done. Hell, she'd just been returning the favor as Kendrick had corked her off earlier. "There's nothing in your rule book that says I can't cork someone off."

"Don't make me find a reason to beach you."

"You threatening me?"

"You bet your sweet ass I am."

Sonya's mouth dropped wide open in shock. How dare he? Who did he think he was? *Sweet ass?* "I don't know where you've policed before, but it's cutthroat fishing out here. I'm only trying to fit in."

"Quit trying so hard. You're going to get yourself killed." With that, Garrett motioned for the captain of the *Calypso* to move about. She watched him until he was out of range.

"Damn stinking fish cop," she muttered, and then looked to her crew to see how they'd taken the trooper's warning. They regarded her with a mix of emotions— amusement from Peter, concern from Wes, and then the clincher, Gramps's solemn look.

"You're going to have to make nice, Sonya," Gramps said.

"I know it." She wanted to stamp her foot in aggravation, and would have done it, too, if it wouldn't have undermined her as captain in front of her crew. A captain needed a level head in order to make level decisions. Right now, she was so off balance with whatever she was feeling, she wondered what it would take to get her back on even keel again.

ↄ

The rest of the day proceeded fairly smooth. That was, everything except the promised rough waves and wind joining the party. They'd finished with a very respectable eight thousand pounds and had tendered, unloading their fish just as the weather started to bite. The storm had been threatening all day, but thankfully waited until the fish opening had closed to let loose her fury. Cold northwesterly wind cut like talons through the summer tease they'd been experiencing. The forecasted rain had yet to appear, but the waves had arrived. They were wicked enough that instead of returning to Red Fox Camp, where they'd have to traverse the open bay, they'd radioed to Grams, and she was meeting them at the cannery. Sonya would have to tie up to the docks for the night. It was too dangerous to be anchored out in the bay.

How dangerous would the docks be?

They tied up at the crowded dock. She wasn't the only one thinking safety tonight. Gramps studied the line of boats nestled together like the cork line of a net. "Sonya, I want Peter and Wes staying with you tonight." Before she could interrupt, Gramps continued, "Besides—" he punched Peter playfully on the shoulder "—the boy here needs a shower."

He wasn't the only one. So did she. It *did* made good sense to have someone stay with her, especially with the vandalism they'd already had.

Grams showed up with a cooler packed with salmon sandwiches, chips, canned green beans, and oatmeal raisin cookies. She was a welcome sight. Gramps returned with Grams on the 4-wheeler to camp.

Sonya, Peter and Wes chowed down, and then the men headed for the showers.

After they returned, Sonya informed them that she'd be late getting back since she had to find Garrett. Wes gave her a grin and wished her good luck with her apology. Peter was already engrossed with his hand-held video game and only grunted when she told him she was leaving.

Sonya grabbed her toiletries and headed for the cannery's showers. After washing the day of fishing off of her body, she took extra time to smooth on lotion and apply a bit of make-up, even though she normally didn't bother with cosmetics while at fish camp. She was going to see Garrett, and that girly part of her insisted she at least try to look her best. She wasn't out to attract. On the contrary, she was mad at Garrett. She hadn't liked the *Calypso*

71

shadowing her every move. She could take care of herself, thank you very much. She proved that today, even with Garrett's unwanted interference.

She was still a woman, and it made her feel good to take a few extra minutes over her appearance. That was all. Really.

Finished, she began the dreaded chore of tracking Garrett down. After giving him a thank you for the earlier heads-up, she planned on informing him that she didn't need him "protecting" her from all the other big, bad fishermen. She was a big, bad fisherman herself. Someone to be reckoned with. She was smarter, and had a faster boat. They'd all taken notice. Every move she'd made today had been cataloged and most likely used as gossip now that drifting was closed for the next twenty-four hours. Set netters got their chance tomorrow, which meant *she'd* still be catching fish. Just liked she'd planned.

She searched for Garrett around the docks where the *Calypso* was tied up. She also tried the mess hall, and the pay phone with its line of callers wrapped around the corner. This wasn't cell phone country, unless you could afford a satellite hook up. The two phones got a lot of business.

There was no sign of him. She was about to give up when she stopped in at the General Store. A place where you could buy a can of bacon and a marine battery all in the same shopping spree.

"Well, if it isn't the celebrity of the hour," Davida greeted from behind the counter. Davida with her multi-colored spiky hair of golds, reds, and deep browns, and her equally spiky attitude, ran the store much like an army general. She was the one person who knew everything worth knowing. "Let me pour you a cup of coffee and you can fill me in on what I've missed."

"Why don't you first tell me what you've heard? Could save time." Sonya took the cup of coffee, though she preferred tea. Tea was considered a sissy drink out here. She wasn't going to add to the stereotype.

Davida filled her in, taking her time since the store was empty. There wasn't much she'd missed. "You didn't actually cork off the *Albatross*, did you?" At Sonya's nod, she shook her head and chuckled. "Damn, wished I could have seen that. I like it when bad things happen to Chuck Kendrick. Lord, knows he should be plagued with bad karma, considering all the things he's done."

"Agreed." Sonya changed the subject before Davida decided to visit the many things suspected of Kendrick. Some of those things were against her own family and too raw for casual conversation. "I'm looking for Garrett Hunt. Have you seen him?"

"The new trooper? That is one delicious-looking man." She closed her eyes and hummed. "Yes, almighty, I wouldn't mind getting a piece of him this summer."

Sonya didn't like the image that picture painted. Davida had a reputation for not only knowing the men, but really *knowing* them.

"He was in here a few hours ago. Bought a bag of trail mix, some jerky, a water bottle. Oh, and some wax."

"Wax?" What would he need wax for?

"Believe you me, I was hard pressed to find it. Wax isn't something that's called for every day." She leaned her impressive bosom on the counter. "Word is that he brought along a surfboard. You ever heard of anything so crazy?"

Now the wax made sense. "Saw it with my own two eyes."

"Get out!" Davida shook her head again. Her hair didn't budge from its sprayed-stiff state. "I really thought he was pulling my leg when he said he was going to 'catch a wave' down at the old Diamond O."

Seeing Davida always paid off. "Why don't you ring me up a bag of chips and a candy bar?" She needed to borrow some wheels. "Any chance you'd let me use your ATV?"

"You headed to the Diamond O?" Davida tilted her head as though to hear Sonya's response better.

The going price for a rented ATV looked like first-hand information. "Yes."

"Now why do you want to meet up with a fish cop with that blustery wind out there?"

Here came the risky part. If Sonya didn't give enough information, Davida would fill in the lines. Too much, and gossip would spread like fireweed that she was shagging a fish cop. "I have some words to say to him regarding his conduct today."

"Going to put him in his place, are you?" A twinkling entered her eyes. "You taking on everyone this summer, Sonya?"

"Gotta throw my weight around to be taken seriously around here."

"Ain't that the truth. Just be careful you don't throw out a hip." Davida handed the ATV's key to her. When Sonya reached for it, she pulled it back. "You *will* fill me on how it went between you two."

Sonya hesitated. Maybe she could walk the distance. It was only six miles round trip to the abandoned cannery. The wind slapped against the metal side of the building with a hard gust. At least one direction would have a headwind. "You have a deal."

Davida smiled and handed over the key along with Sonya's chips and candy bar. "Happy hunting."

CHAPTER SEVEN

He was certifiably insane.

Sonya found Garrett right where Davida had said he'd be. Surfing the waves at the abandoned Diamond O Cannery. She parked the 4-wheeler next to a rusted out old Jeep, alongside the remains of the old cannery's dock. Waves crashed at a height of six to seven feet. Glacial, callous water brutally ate at the rocky beach. Gloomy, heavy laden skies, carrying the promise of rain, gathered overhead.

And the man was out there surfing.

She did have to admire his form. The combination of power and grace she'd witnessed earlier was in high demand now as he rode—no, seemed to command—the wave. His short board sliced back and forth as he carved the water. The temperature had dipped to around forty-eight with the storm, and Sonya knew the water was colder. She'd dressed in jeans, t-shirt layered by a sweatshirt, and a rain jacket and yet she shivered watching him.

Didn't he know how deadly that ocean could be?

Garrett wore what must be a dry suit, as he was a dark shadow against the gunmetal waves. His board, with its flaming yellows and blues, was a beacon of color on the otherwise colorless evening. At least the Coast Guard would know where he'd gone down. No way would they be able to miss that board.

He rode a wave to shore while white water splashed around him with greedy fingers in an attempt to suck him back into its deadly embrace. Upon reaching the rocky sand, he flipped his board under his arm, and jogged up the beach toward her.

"You're crazy, you know that?" Sonya hollered at him. She'd heard rumors that a group of surfers had formed an Alaskan surfing club, but she really hadn't believed that anyone would be insane enough to actually surf that freezing water. Until now.

He smiled a grin that had his eyes alight with amusement, the corners crinkling with deep laugh lines. It was a good look on him and had her repressing the desire to reach out and run her hands over him.

He anchored his board in the dark gray sand next to the Jeep, and tore the skin-tight cap off his head. He grabbed a towel from the seat and rubbed his hair, causing it to spike. Again she had to resist the urge to touch.

"I assume you tracked me down for a reason." His voice was fast and breezy, and if that wasn't sexy enough, he started to strip out of his dry suit. Smooth, tanned, ripped muscle was revealed as he peeled the tight fabric from his upper body.

Sonya swallowed as she took in every inch of power he uncovered. The need to touch him became a hunger. She'd been skipping this kind of treat for a while.

He must have caught the look she couldn't hide, for he slowed his striptease. The cold, blustery wind seemed to heat around them.

"Sonya," he said her name on a groan. Her eyes flicked to his. The amusement was gone, and in its place was fire. "Don't look at me like that."

"Like what?"

"Like you want to eat me up."

If he didn't look so damn delicious, it would be an easier feat to accomplish. He stared at her like he hadn't treated himself in a while, either. The air sizzled and snapped with suppressed appetite.

She needed to be careful here, remind herself of what he was. It was a lot harder with him out of uniform.

"I'd like nothing better than to do exactly that," she heard herself say. "But I'm not an animal driven by my baser urges. I can control myself."

He stalked closer, the top of his dry suit lying loose at his waist. "We're all animals, Sonya, when you strip us bare. Repressing your natural desires can interfere with your biology."

"I happen to fancy black raspberry chip ice cream, but I can stop eating it before I make myself sick."

He cocked a brow as though in a dare. "Afraid too much of me will make you sick?"

"No, not afraid. I know what's good for me and what isn't. You definitely aren't."

"I could be real good for you," he said in a rough tone, taking another step toward her.

She swallowed again.

Damn, this was the hottest foreplay she'd ever engaged in, and they were only talking. Conversations like this invariably lead to something else. She ought to end it here and now. Say what she'd come to say and leave.

"Have you ever lived in the moment, Sonya? Experienced what life has to offer, without thinking of tomorrow?" He took another step closer, towering over her. She was above average height for a woman at five eight, but he still loomed over her with his six-foot-plus frame.

"No, I've never had that luxury." She'd been fifteen when she'd lost her parents and her sister, Sasha. Peter had been only two. He'd been a big, though welcome, surprise to her parents in their later years. The load of responsibility Sonya had taken on, at that young age, prevented her from doing just what Garrett tempted.

"Want to give it a try?" he asked. "Forget who you are. Forget who I am. Could you do that?" His voice lowered to a seductive level and stroked dark fantasies to life.

Her fingers itched to trace each line of muscle in front of her that beckoned.

Could she?

What the hell was he doing?

Garrett knew he had no business goading Sonya into taking a bite of what he offered. He was a trooper. She was a fisherman. If they got physical, it would definitely be something he'd have to deal with "tomorrow." Besides, he doubted very much, that he could walk away from this woman after one night. It'd take at least a couple.

The cold water must have dulled his senses. It had definitely soothed his foul mood. The one she'd been largely responsible for putting him in.

Surfing the Bering Sea had been stimulating, cutting loose and riding a wave that at any moment could have ridden him. There was no way to describe it. Then he'd walked out of that water and seen Sonya standing there under the shelter of the abandoned dock, a log piling at her back, and he'd wanted to take her while the wind screamed around them.

He wanted to make her scream for him.

Garrett watched emotions skitter across her face. Her cheeks blushed from the biting wind, eyes dark and direct as they met his. Was she actually going to pick up the gauntlet he'd tossed her way? It was his turn to swallow as she stepped toward him, her hand pressed against his thudding heart.

"I don't ever forget who I am. When I give myself to a man, we both remember." Her hand took a journey down his chest to his abs, which he couldn't help sucking in. "You wouldn't be able to forget me tomorrow, Garrett. Even if you wanted to."

Christ. Her other hand joined in her exploration of his chest. His breathing was suddenly heavier than when he'd pulled himself out of that freezing ocean. He wasn't chilled now. Far from it. If possible he felt even more exhilarated.

She broke eye contact and stared at her hands, petting him, as though she wanted to venture over every inch of his skin. He was more than willing to let that happen.

"I didn't come here to engage in the physical," she said. "I wanted to thank you for giving us a heads-up today on that hydraulic line." She paused as though forgetting her train of thought, her fingers caressing his abs, the light, exploring touch sending signals to his lower half he knew he shouldn't entertain. She took a deep breath, as if needing strength, and stepped back. He felt the loss of her heat like an extinguished flame.

Meeting his eyes, she added, "I also came to warn you. I don't want you as my protector. You need to treat me like every other fisherman out there on that water."

He captured her elbows and brought her into full contact with his body. "You aren't the same as the others, Sonya. I can't help but differentiate."

"You'll have to." She attempted to pull out of his arms, but he only tightened his hold.

"We might be on different sides of the line, but you enjoyed tying me in knots today." He caught the twitch of her lips.

"Who's tying who up?" she asked. "You just don't like me giving as good as I get."

Damn right he didn't.

"Remember when I told you that I don't play games?" She waited for his nod. "Just because I don't like to play them, doesn't mean I'm not good at them." She smiled, obviously enjoying teasing him.

She also confused the hell out of him. He'd never been confused by a woman before and he didn't like it. Back to those knots. There was one thing he wasn't confused about. She wanted him, and he wanted her.

"This is no game." He leaned down and kissed her, sealed their mouths and tried to forget who they were, while passion and fire flooded his system.

She was right. He was never going to forget her. He felt it in every rapid beat of his heart. He should catch and release right now. Instead, he backed her up against a piling, anchored her to it with his thigh pressed between hers and let his hands roam. Any finesse he usually showed was gone. Sonya brought the animal out in him, and he wanted to feast. She didn't help, with her demanding moan and the arching of her body, as she wrapped her arms around his neck.

She smelled good. Fresh, like citrus and something sweet. Honey maybe, but she tasted better. Like the rarest of fruits. He wanted to peel her naked like a mangosteen. Right down to her pearly white flesh.

"Garrett, we can't do this." Sonya belied her words with a kitten-like sound as he pressed his thigh higher between hers and bit the side of her neck. "Seriously…we must…stop."

She pushed against his chest, her hands losing their intent as they journeyed down his sides. It was enough of a resistance that he shook his head, trying to clear the sexual fog, and focus on her.

"I'm not having sex with you on this beach," she said, her voice raspy and seductive as hell. "No matter how it's portrayed in the movies, sand is not romantic. It gets in places."

"There's the Jeep," he was quick to suggest.

"Well, hell. There's my 4-wheeler, too, but I'm not having sex on it, either."

He chuckled. The reality of their situation caught up to his oversexed, oxygen-starved brain. "I lose my head when I'm around you."

"Believe me, I've figured that out. Your actions out on that water today proved it." She pushed at his chest. "I really need you to let me go."

He breathed deep, inhaling that fervent combination of her, mixing with the smell of rain on the wind. "All right, but I'm going to have to take it slow." His body didn't want to let her go. Come to think about it, neither did his head. She'd said stop. He wasn't so far gone that he'd ignore that road sign. He moved his leg pinning her to the log piling. She closed her eyes and groaned as he brushed against that hot private area of hers, which had him rethinking of releasing her. She was having as much trouble resisting him as he was her. The knowledge was powerful and intoxicating, and he wondered briefly if she'd give in if he pushed?

What the hell was he thinking? He wasn't that kind of man. At least, he'd never thought he was. Sonya had brought more emotions out in him in the last forty-eight hours than he'd experienced with a woman in his lifetime.

He stepped back, releasing her. Immediately, he felt the cold. The only covering he had was the remnants of his dry suit clinging to his lower half. The wind blasted him, and he shivered.

"Might want to get some clothes on," she pointed out, her eyes never leaving his exposed skin.

Now it was his turn to tell her to stop. "Keep looking at me that way and I'll carry you inside this abandoned cannery and pick up where we left off."

She raised her gaze above her as though considering doing just that. Then she shook her head. "There's bound to be spiders in there."

It didn't go unnoticed that she hadn't objected to sex, just to the possibility of spiders. "I didn't think you were afraid of anything."

Her lips parted on a grin. "I don't like it to get around, but spiders—" she shuddered "—really creep me out."

Good to see that she had some girly issues. Since he'd met her, she seemed as much of a brute as any guy he knew, and he'd known some brutes. She followed him to the Jeep where he grabbed a t-shirt and yanked it over his head.

"So we good here?" she asked. The breeze caught her hair and whipped a few more strands lose from her ponytail.

"How do you mean?" He figured he'd better ask for clarification, because he wasn't in a good place where she was concerned. Not by a long shot.

"I don't want you intervening in my business like you did today."

"I'll intervene in any situation that I deem necessary. That's my job."

"You took your job personally."

"I always take it personally. If I have to take you off the water in order to protect you, that is exactly what I'll do."

"B-but—" she sputtered.

He could see her temper heating up again. So he distracted her with a question. "Answer me one thing, Sonya. Why the *Double Dippin'*? Couldn't you have come up with a less controversial name?"

"It's what I'm doing. Why not call it what it is? I don't have a set of balls like you men to carry around. Might as well plaster what I do have for all to see."

"Do you intentionally try to piss people off, or is it a personality flaw?"

"The same could be said about you."

"We aren't talking about me."

"I think you have a problem with strong-willed women. So why don't you work on that, and then we'll see where we end up."

He growled deep in his chest. He did *not* have a problem with strong-willed women. He'd just ended a relationship with one of the strongest-willed women he'd ever met until now. Sonya seemed to be wondering if she'd finally pushed him too far. He took a step closer until his chest almost brushed hers. "We already know where we're going to end up, Sonya. It's just a matter of when and where."

"I wouldn't be too sure of that. I don't jump into bed with just anyone. You have a lot working against you. Humility comes to mind."

"You don't know when to stop baiting, do you?"

"Why bother, when you're still biting?"

He crooked a smile, going from hunter to charmer. He couldn't remember the last time he had this much fun bantering with a woman. "Want to catch dinner? See if we have any subjects in common besides chemistry?"

"The last person I can afford to be seen with is you. Those fishermen already have it in for me. They see me cavorting with a fish cop, and I'm sunk."

Chapter Eight

Aidan motored his skiff, with Lana in the bow, toward their set net site in the river. Sonya hadn't returned to camp last night and he hoped he'd get a chance to talk to her today. He slowed his boat as he noticed the *Albatross*, squatting at where his running line should have been.

"Yo, Harte," Chuck Kendrick hollered from the deck of the *Albatross*. "Top of the morning to ya, asshole." Kendrick gave Aidan a satanic smile as he drifted by.

The man had cut his running line.

"Kendrick, you son of a bitch!" Aidan hollered.

"I'll let Ma know you inquired about her." Kendrick cackled. "Have a nice day."

He was screwed. Fishing was to start any minute, and he had no running line to attach his net to. Where were the fucking fish cops when you needed them?

"Aidan?" Lana's anxious voice came from the bow of the skiff where she sat bundled up in chest waders and raingear. She seemed more a little girl than a woman grown.

Earl pulled alongside in his skiff, his uncle Roland smoking the butt of a cigarette as he reclined in the bow. "We fishing or what?"

"Give me your gun," Aidan demanded, reaching his hand out for the firearm he knew Earl never went anywhere without.

"What the hell for?"

"Are we shootin' people?" Roland sat up, the sound of glee in his voice, as he took an interest in more than sucking on his cigarette.

"Kendrick just cut my running line." Aidan reached his hand out. "Now give me the damn gun."

"Aidan—" Lana's voice wobbled with fear, but Aidan ignored her.

All he saw was red.

"Why the hell didn't you say so?" Earl tossed the Glock underhanded between the two skiffs.

Aidan caught it, cocked it, pointed, and fired three quick shots across the *Albatross's* bow.

Earl's mouth curled in disgust. "You missed."

"I could have hit that boat with my eyes closed," Roland said, turning to Earl. "Didn't you teach this kid how to shoot?"

"I didn't want to hit him," Aidan said. "Just wanted to warn him."

"Give me that gun." Earl shook his head. "You shoot at someone, plan on hittin' 'em." He huffed a breath and curled his upper lip. "You're useless."

"Watch it, old man." Aidan's hand tightened over the butt of the gun he still held.

"Watch what? Watch you sit back and draw your little cartoons—"

"They're graphic novels."

"Whatever. You're still drawing what you don't have the guts to do yourself."

"Would you just shut the hell up!" Aidan wanted to silence the old man for good. Holding the gun in his hand was becoming too much of a temptation.

"Somebody's got to tell you how to be a man."

Aidan gritted his teeth, counted to ten and did what he did best, tuned out his father. He'd been doing it all his life. Sometimes he wondered if the money he made fishing every summer was worth the aggravation of having to tolerate the man. He placed the gun in the dry hold of the stern. If he handed the Glock back to Earl, it was bound to go off "accidentally." He engaged the outboard engine and got back to the business of fishing.

"Lana, hook that running line." Aidan maneuvered the skiff to where the line floated free.

"What are you going to do, Aidan?" Lana's voice shook. She grabbed the boat hook and moved into position at the side of the skiff, careful not to step on the net roped into the bottom of the boat.

Her scared and worried expression tugged at Aidan's temper, and he suddenly felt ashamed over his actions. He shouldn't have shot at the *Albatross*. What if he had actually hit someone? If he wanted to pick a fight with Kendrick, he should do it when Lana wasn't around. There had been a major absence of thinking on his part this morning.

"We're going to tie a Bruce Anchor to the end of the line so we can fish today. Later, when the tide goes out, we'll replace the running line." It would shorten the length of line the Fish and Game allowed the set netters to fish, but he'd be able to fish this tide instead of waiting it out and miss catching anything.

They hooked the line, and working together, attached an anchor to the line and then their net. Then it was a matter of waiting to pick what fish swam into it.

A few hundred feet down the beach he heard Sonya laugh. The musical sound carried easily over the water. Aidan glanced over to see Sonya and Peter joking it up as they laughed and picked fish from their net. The *Double Dippin'* lay anchored at the end of their running line like it was sleeping the afternoon away. She and Peter were picking fish from one of their four sites with their skiff. He didn't see Wes or Nikolai, but knew they'd be showing up soon, probably with a big lunch that Margaret had lovingly packed for all of them. All Aidan had grabbed was a package of jerky and some fruit snacks for him and Lana to share later.

The Savonskis had the best sites on the beach, lying right at the mouth of the river. They raked in the biggest catch as the salmon swam along the shoreline into the river to spawn, while the Hartes always seemed to pick seconds of what their nets caught.

Soon that was all going to change.

One way or another, Sonya would be his. He'd make sure Kendrick got what was coming to him too.

ᒍ

"Aidan's not having a good day," Peter said, resting against the side of the skiff, and wiping the sweat from his brow with the sleeve of his sweatshirt. "Shouldn't we offer to help?"

Sonya dropped the salmon she'd just picked out of the net into one of the brailer bags. She glanced over at Aidan and assessed his situation.

"Aidan can take care of himself." He'd more than proved that this morning when he'd shot at Kendrick. No doubt Kendrick deserved it, and Sonya wouldn't mind seeing the last of him, but she didn't approve of Aidan's methods.

Peter frowned. "That's not very neighborly. What happened between the two of you, anyway?"

"Nothing. We just didn't suit."

"So, because you don't 'suit' we can't lend him a hand?"

Sounded good to her. "Fine, when we get this net picked, we'll run over and see what we can do." Sonya had a feeling what Peter really wanted was to talk with Lana. Sonya glanced back at the Harte's sites. Lana was fishing with Aidan instead of Crafty. She couldn't imagine how tough Lana's life had been with Cranky and Crafty as relatives. For that matter, how had Aidan handled it all his life?

They finished up and headed over to see what they could do for Aidan. Neighborly or not, Sonya didn't want to spend time with Aidan. She didn't want to encourage him. There was no chance of a reconciliation between them, but she had a feeling Aidan didn't see it that way.

"Hey, Lana," Peter greeted with a smile as they came alongside her and Aidan in their skiff.

"Peter." Lana nodded, her face pale, her eyes wide as though she was trying her best to keep it together. She didn't return Peter's engaging smile.

Sonya's heart immediately went out to the girl. She glanced around to see where Cranky and Crafty were and saw them down the beach, picking the other Harte net. Good, wrangling with Aidan was enough. She didn't want to pretend to be "neighborly" with the old rednecks.

"Having trouble?" Sonya asked Aidan. His actions, as he picked fish, were jerky and hasty. He didn't take care with the net, ripping through the knotted diamond pattern when freeing the fish. This was the side of him that she hadn't wanted to see again.

Angry. Cruel.

"Nope. No trouble now," he returned, tearing the gills off a salmon as he yanked it from the net. Blood trailed down the silver scales as he threw the salmon into a brailer bag.

Sonya glanced at Peter, hoping they'd been neighborly enough. She wanted away from here. Peter was talking quietly with Lana, coaxing a small smile from her. She'd give him a few more minutes to brighten the girl's day and then they were history.

"Was it necessary to shoot at Kendrick?" As soon as the words came out of her mouth Sonya could have kicked herself. She knew better than to pour gasoline on a raging fire.

Aidan dropped the net, threw his fish pick down, and straightened to his full height of six two. His hard gaze met hers. Sonya braced herself for his biting comeback. His lips tightened, hands fisted, and then he glanced away. The muscles in his jaw flexed and then smoothed. He turned back to her. "I shouldn't have shot at Kendrick. I'm sorry if my actions concerned you."

Whoa, so not what she'd expected.

Aidan took a deep breath and slowly let it out. "Thanks for coming over and checking on us." He indicated Lana with the movement of his head, letting Sonya know that he was more concerned over how Lana was taking today's mishaps than how his actions reflected on him. "Do you think Peter could invite her over later?" Aidan gestured behind him at Cranky and Crafty. "She could use a breather."

Did he know that caring more for his cousin than himself would lessen Sonya's concerns? Sonya didn't know what to think. Maybe Aidan *had* changed.

"Why don't the both of you come over for dinner after we pull the nets?" Sonya surprised herself by offering. "Grams will be cooking salmon."

Aidan's face finally softened, and he smiled. "Isn't she always?"

Sonya shared his smile. "It's what's readily available. In fact, you can supply it tonight. That is, if you catch anything."

"Oh, I'll catch plenty with enough to spare for feeding you and yours." The gleam in his eyes raised a warning, reminding Sonya that flirting with Aidan wasn't a good idea.

"Yo, guys. We've got company." Peter pointed to the RHIB with the two uniformed troopers fast approaching.

Sonya's heart did a quick jump until she realized that neither one of the troopers were Garrett. Good, she told herself. She didn't need another run-in with that particular fish cop. Hell, what was she thinking, she didn't need a run-in with *any* fish cop.

The trooper cut his engine and drifted over, their wake rolling under them, rocking Sonya's and Aidan's skiffs.

"We had reports that shots had been fired in this area. Any of you know anything about that?" asked the big burly trooper not piloting the RHIB.

Sonya glanced at Aidan. Aidan waited for her to give him up to the cops. "Nope. Haven't heard anything. Just fishing here."

"Uh, yeah," Peter interjected, following Sonya's lead, though she wished he'd keep his mouth shut. "Maybe someone shot at a bear. You know how sound is distorted over water."

The burly trooper stared at each of them individually and then seemed to come to a decision. "Well, since we're here, we might as well check your permits and fishing licenses."

Sonya reached for the sealed bag with the requested materials, kept secure and close to hand in the Velcro pocket of her chest waders.

Damn fish cops never missed an opportunity.

〣

Garrett stood on the deck of the *Calypso* and let the night wash over him. It had been another day full of craziness. Fishermen were a breed apart, most of them gifted with more than their share of deviousness. He should be sleeping, gearing up for another day of insanity, but instead he was on deck face turned into the wind.

Did he hear music? The wind was making a racket as it blew its heart out, but…music?

He strained to catch the notes as they waltzed on the wind.

Sonya. She had to be playing her violin.

"What is that?" Judd asked, joining him.

Struggling to hear the music, Garrett hadn't heard Judd's approach. His SEAL sense must be taking the night off. It had been a long time since someone had snuck up behind him. Not since elementary school when he'd had to keep a watch out for Jimmy the lunch-stealing terror of the fourth grade. Back then, he'd been scrawny for his age. He'd compensated by being silent and sneaky. "I believe Sonya Savonski is playing her violin."

"That rip-off-your-balls woman plays the violin?"

"Yeah. Now shut up." Garrett leaned his arms on the rail of the boat and settled in to listen.

"Damn, she's not half bad," Judd said.

Garrett slid a warning glance his direction.

"Right. Shutting up."

They stood in silence until Skip lumbered on deck from the cabin. Garrett didn't have any trouble hearing him. The man had lost his stealth with the extra pounds he carried. The half-eaten candy bar in his hand wasn't helping either. "Isn't that *Un Giorno Per Noi* from Romeo and Juliet?"

Garrett had no clue what Sonya was playing other than he liked it.

"Beautiful," Skip said, looking as though the music had the power to pull him away from his candy bar.

"Better keep it down," Judd said, "or SEAL-man there's gonna tell you to—"

"Hush," Skip said.

"Well, yeah," Judd whispered, "but you said it a lot nicer."

Skip copied Garrett's pose with his arms leaning on the rail.

Suddenly, the music stopped and the wind went silent. Seconds ticked by, then minutes, and then nothing.

"You don't think she's done do you?" Skip asked, his tone sounding despondent over the prospect. "If we radio her, do you think she'd take requests?"

"Get her to play something happy this time," Judd said. They both looked at Garrett.

"Why the hell you asking me?" Garrett scowled at the men. "How would I know?"

Skip and Judd shared a look. Then Skip asked, "What does her skin smell like?"

"Honeysuckle," he answered without thinking. The scent had been haunting him for days, keeping him up nights.

They smiled.

"You know what she smells like but nothing else about her?" Skip asked. "Women are more than sexual objects."

"Since when?" Judd asked.

Skip elbowed him in the gut. "We don't all think with our little brain." Skip looked at Garrett. "Well, at least I don't. And since I'm the smart one, I'm headed to catch a few winks before we have to baby-sit tomorrow."

"I'm coming too." Judd paused. "What about you?" He glanced at Garrett.

"Yeah, in a bit." He turned back to the many boats anchored up for the night and wondered which one was the *Double Dippin'*.

Then he wondered why he was wondering.

CHAPTER NINE

"Red Fox, this is the *Double Dippin'*. Got your ears on?" Sonya radioed camp on the VHF. She and Wes had finished tendering last night's drift catch to the *Time Bandit* after sending Gramps and Peter back to camp to get some rest.

They'd fished solid most of the week. Each tide was either a drift opening or set netting. Sonya didn't even know what day of the week it was anymore. Their fish poundage was adding up fast. Now, if the price per pound exceeded last year's she'd have no problem with Peter's tuition and paying her mounting debts getting into drifting had set her back.

Wes was currently below catching a few winks. The plan was to get a hot meal, let the drift boat go dry in front of camp, and then sleep until the tide came back in. According to the Fish and Game's latest announcement, they were set netting the next tide, which only gave them maybe five hours of rest.

"Red Fox, come in," Sonya radioed again.

"Morning, Sonya," Grams greeted. "Breakfast is about to be served."

"I was hoping that was the case. Wes and I are floating right out front of the cabin." Sonya looked at the running line to where two skiffs were supposed to be tied up. She pressed the button on the side of the mic. "Do we have a crewman absent for breakfast?"

"No. Everyone's accounted for." Grams's concerned voice registered clearly over the radio.

Shit. "We're down a skiff. Please tell me someone took it for a joy ride and left it somewhere safe." Sonya waited for a reply. She got one. Gramps and Peter scrambled down the trail to the beach, donning their raingear as they hurried.

"Negative on the joy ride," Grams replied. "The boys are on their way."

"Thanks, Red Fox. By the way," she shouldn't ask, "what was for breakfast?" The only food she had on the boat was a jar of peanut butter and a box of stale pilot bread.

"French toast, eggs, bacon, and my homemade cranberry muffins. I'll try and keep it warm."

She'd told herself not to ask. "Roger that, Red Fox. *Double Dippin'* out." Sonya hung up the mic on the clip above her head and hollered for Wes.

He stuck his head up through the hold and yawned. "We at camp already?"

Sonya navigated the drift boat closer to shore. "We've got a runaway skiff to hunt down."

"Huh?" He shook his head as though trying to empty the sleep from it and climbed up the ladder. "Did you say we've got a skiff missing?" He looked at the running line. "Bummer."

"Yep." The surf was calm this morning and she could risk getting right into the shallows. She swung the boat around so Gramps and Peter could wade out into the ocean and climb up the ladder welded to the stern. Gramps was first aboard, leaving Peter to give the boat a push out into the ocean before he climbed aboard.

"I didn't need all three of you," Sonya said as they entered the pilot house, the room getting considerably smaller with their muscled bodies taking up the space. "Wes, Peter, and I can handle this."

"Every pair of eyes helps." Gramps grabbed the binoculars and began scanning the area.

Sonya powered up the jet engine and headed west. She'd just come from the river and would have noticed their skiff adrift with no one aboard. "With the tide going out, we don't have a lot of time. Wes, you concentrate along the shore; Gramps, look out to the bay." Her gaze shot to Peter. "Who tied up the skiff when you returned last night?"

Her brother's mouth tightened. "Why ask when you already know it was me?"

He had a point. "Are you sure you tied it up tight?" She couldn't bring herself to let it rest. She was tired and hungry. The last thing she wanted to do was chase down a skiff that should have been secured.

"I know how to tie up a skiff, Sonya."

"You weren't in a hurry? Distracted?" Had Lana been around and caught his attention? The boy only had half a brain when a girl was around.

"No." He scowled and folded his arms across his chest.

"Let's focus on finding the skiff," Gramps interjected.

Placing blame wasn't helping the situation. There'd be time for that later. Sonya concentrated on piloting the boat while looking for the gray aluminum skiff among an ocean of gray waves. The tide was headed out fast to a minus two. If they didn't locate the skiff soon, it would probably be on its way to Japan. They'd be down to one skiff for the season. That wouldn't do. Not to mention the cost to replace it would eat up all their profits and then some.

"I'm heading on deck." Wes covered another yawn as he left the pilot house and positioned himself at the bow.

"So am I." Peter followed Wes, and Sonya knew he would be dissing her to him.

"You were a bit hard on the boy," Gramps said, still searching through the binoculars.

"Fishing's a hard business. He's got to learn to pay attention to every detail."

"Sonya, we all understand the seriousness of losing the skiff. Don't let the pressure of this season cloud your reasoning. People make mistakes." He lowered the binoculars and met her eyes. "The measure of a good captain is how she deals with those mistakes."

He was right. She shouldn't have automatically assumed Peter was being lax in his job. There were many reasons the skiff could have come loose. The painter's line might have broken or worked its way free in the tossing surf. Things like that happened. Not often, but they did happen.

"Thanks, Gramps."

He raised the binoculars. "Just trying to help."

Wes pointed southwest and Sonya quickly made the corrections. There it was, bobbing in the waves without a care in the world. She felt, rather than heard, her crew sigh with relief.

She brought the boat alongside the skiff, sliding the engine into neutral, while Wes hooked the skiff with the long boat hook and Peter jumped into it. Wes threw him a rope to tie the skiff to the *Double Dippin'*. Peter's movements were fast and sure as he secured the bow first and then the stern.

Sonya cut the engine and joined Gramps and Wes on deck.

The sun broke through the clouds and she lowered her ball cap over her eyes as the aluminum boats reflected the bright light. "How's she look?" From this distance, Sonya couldn't see any damage.

Peter went to the bow and fished the painter's line, where it hung off the side into the water, and held it up for everyone to see.

The line had been cut.

CHAPTER TEN

"That's two acts of criminal mischief," Peter said, sliding his empty plate forward and planting his elbows on the table. "First the hydraulic lines and now the skiff."

They'd just finished the warmed-up breakfast Grams had kept for them and were sitting around the table trying to come up with a game plan.

"'Criminal mischief?'" Sonya parroted. "You've been watching too many cop shows."

"What would you call it, Sonya?" Peter nailed her with his idealistic stare. Peter never saw gray. Everything fell neatly into black and white slots for him. "Be in denial all you want, but we have a problem."

She frowned. "I'm not in denial."

"Yeah, you'd just like to lay the blame on me."

"That's not fair. I apologized for thinking you'd been lax."

"All right, enough," Gramps said, bringing the bickering to a stop. Peter sat back and folded his arms. "Arguing isn't getting us anywhere. It's obvious that we've made some enemies—"

"I wonder how *we* did that." Peter looked at Sonya. It was clear he laid blame for this situation right at Sonya's door. She considered it her due as she'd been so quick to accuse Peter for the runaway skiff. "Corking off Kendrick might not have been the best of moves, in hindsight. Ya think?"

"Not helping, Peter." Grams settled her hand on his shoulder. Peter instantly seemed to calm. Sonya wished she had that ability. She'd raised Peter from the age of two and yet Grams was the mothering force.

"The way I see it, we're going to have to be extra vigilant," Wes added, his level tone soothing the ruffled feathers in the room. "If this continues, and I don't see why it won't, we should take turns keeping watch."

Sonya added, "Someone will need to stay on the *Double Dippin'* at all times. Since I'm her captain, that will fall to me."

"We'll take turns when you get stir-crazy." Gramps nodded. "I agree that we need to keep watch, but we don't need to be paranoid." He narrowed his look on Peter. "No need to be armed or camping out at the sites."

Peter held up his hand. "I want it on record that I voted for arms."

"We got it." Sonya rubbed at the headache brewing in her temples. She needed some sleep and a half dozen Tylenols.

"There's one other thing I suggest we do." Everyone turned to Wes and he continued, "We should contact Garrett and inform him of what's going on."

"I don't think we need to go that far," Sonya was quick to interject. The last confrontation she'd had with Garrett had almost landed the two of them horizontal. She didn't trust herself enough to guarantee their next meeting wouldn't actually end up that way.

"We'll need a paper trail if this continues," Wes said. "It's the smart thing and the right thing."

"I agree with him, Sonya." Gramps leveled his concerned eyes on her.

"Me too," Grams added. "Informing Garrett will add another person to help keep watch."

Sonya stared at Peter. "You have an opinion?"

Peter unfolded his arms and leaned on the table. "If we can't be armed, we might as well have someone watching our backs who is."

$$\text{◊}$$

The last thing Sonya wanted to do was call Garrett.

She sat on a rock having walked down to the beach after their late breakfast. The *Double Dippin'*, and both skiffs, sat dry with the tide out. Cliffs towered above her, and there was just enough of a breeze to keep the mosquitoes and noseeums from feasting on her. Wisps of hair worked free from her ponytail and she tried to secure them under her ball cap. Not that it did any good. The sun played a losing game of keep away with the ever present storm clouds. It was quiet. Most of the fishermen were probably taking advantage of the minus tide and catching up on sleep, which was exactly what she should be doing.

An eagle screeched overhead. She raised her face to the sky and watched, mesmerized, as the majestic bird soared high above her.

Had the eagle seen who'd cut the painter's line to the skiff? What else had it seen?

She picked at the tear in the knee of her jeans. Why had someone decided to mess with her? So what if she was drifting and set netting. In the scheme of things, who really cared? Okay, someone did. Who?

Chuck Kendrick? He loved to cause trouble. She didn't doubt that he got off on it. Other than corking him off the other day, she usually stayed clear of him. The man scared her, though she blustered her way through it every time she was within a few feet of him. If he knew she quaked around him there'd be no telling how far he'd take that tidbit of information.

Kendrick was her bogeyman. Corking him off the other day had been an accident. She sure as hell hadn't planned it.

Could Aidan be pulling these pranks? That thought upset her more than thinking Kendrick had her in his sights. She'd loved Aidan, probably still did in some locked corner of her heart.

Don't go there.

She'd dealt with all that. Aidan didn't deserve her love. Would he mess with her? She didn't like the idea of a man she'd shared herself with, wanting to cause her grief. She couldn't have misjudged his character that much, could she?

Idiot. Black eye, remember. You hadn't seen that coming.

No, she couldn't discount Aidan, which meant she might have an enemy living right next door. She surveyed the Hartes' camp across the creek. They'd shared this section of beach for a long time. Her dad and Earl had actually been friends until her mother had come into the picture. Both men had been enamored with Kyra the summer she'd hired on as a cannery worker, but Mikhail Savonski had won her heart.

A sharp pang of loss intruded—how she missed her parents and her sister. Two halves of one egg, she and Sasha had been inseparable. Sometimes she missed Sasha so much she couldn't breathe. Losing her had been like losing a limb. She'd never be completely whole again.

As far as Sonya knew, she could have pissed off anyone out here. Most kept to themselves, others liked to mess it up. She'd definitely caught someone's attention. Which brought her right back to contacting Garrett.

How did one go about contacting a fish cop anyway? They were always around when you didn't want them, but when you needed them, poof, nowhere in sight. She'd be damned if she'd radio the *Calypso*. It wasn't like you could have a private conversation on the VHF. If she got on the radio, every fishermen out in the bay would know she was contacting the trooper.

She'd have more trouble than she already had if she did that.

So that left her to hunt down Garrett. It wasn't like she could sneak up on the *Calypso* without anyone noticing. Except someone had boarded the *Double Dippin'* without anyone being aware.

Nope. She wasn't about to seek Garrett out. Not going to happen. She'd have to take her chances. Be on her guard, and if Garrett happened across her path then she'd mention the problems they'd been having. Besides, they were on top of things. The chance of more mishaps, now that they were being vigilant, was unlikely.

So much for vigilance.

They'd fished the set net sites during the night tide, returning to camp in the wee hours of the morning. Sonya had anchored the *Double Dippin'* in front of camp, right at the end of the running line. She hadn't gotten any sleep because she'd felt the need to constantly check the boats every half hour. A lot of good that did.

Someone had still gotten by her.

The Fish and Game had closed fishing for the next twenty-four hours to increase salmon escapement up the river, which gave the fishermen a much needed rest before drifting tomorrow.

Not that her crew would get any.

Sonya clenched her fists and wanted to punch some-one, preferably the asshole messing with them. They were down a skiff again, but this one hadn't been cut adrift.

It was left tied to the running line and sinking to the bottom of the damn ocean.

She reached for the mic to radio the cabin, and then set it back on its clip. The first thing her crew was going to ask her was if she'd contacted Garrett. Of course, she hadn't and she'd been fortunate not to have run into him.

Or unfortunate as the case now seemed to be.

There wasn't anything anyone could do for the skiff. It was dead in the water until the tide went back out.

She picked the mic back up and changed to channel sixteen, the trooper's station on the VHF.

"*Calypso* this is…" She stopped and then began again. "Come in *Calypso*."

She waited and then there was a crackle followed by a burst of static. "*Calypso* here." It wasn't Garrett who'd answered the radio. "Please identify yourself."

Damn. "Can we switch to channel fourteen?" she asked, hoping to get off the trooper channel. It would afford them some privacy as long as whoever was listening didn't decide to change channels along with them.

"Roger that."

Sonya changed channels. "*Calypso*?"

"Roger. Whom am I speaking to?"

"I need to talk to Hunt." There was silence except for the occasional blips of static. Sonya waited and hoped, since she'd gone this far, that Garrett was actually on board.

"This is Hunt, over."

The sound of his voice came across the radio as large as life, and her hand shook when she pressed the button to speak into the mic. "I need to meet with you."

Another pause and then. "Sonya?"

Dang it. *He had to go and say her name.* As far as she knew, she was the only Sonya in Bristol Bay. "Can you meet with me?" she repeated.

"Where?"

Now, how to explain where to meet without letting every other ear listening know? "Your surfing haunt."

"Roger. When?"

"An hour?"

"Roger."

Hopefully, she and Garrett were the only ones who knew where he'd surfed after the first day of fishing. She ended the transmission and changed the VHF back to her normal channel. Now how to get to the old Diamond O Cannery? She couldn't very well show up in the *Double Dippin'*. Talk about broadcasting. She glanced down at her wrinkled, slept-in clothes.

What was she going to wear?

CHAPTER ELEVEN

Garrett handed the mic back to Skip. His day just got a hell of a lot more interesting.

"Sonya?" Judd asked. "As in Savonski?" He tore through a piece of jerky with his teeth. Breakfast onboard the *Calypso* was a no frills affair.

"The same." Something must have happened for her to contact him. He doubted she wanted to finish what they'd started the last time they'd been together. Pity. He hadn't had a peaceful night's sleep since. "We need to take a detour."

"We're supposed to be investigating the drift boat fishing in closed waters upstream." Skip's brow creased in a frown as he helped himself to another Oreo.

"I'm sure you and Judd can handle it." Garrett knew Sonya wouldn't be calling if she could help it. The woman wasn't the kind to ask for help. "Something's up." He rubbed the back of his neck. "I can feel it."

"You want us to go with you before we head upstream?" Judd asked, speaking around the jerky in his mouth.

"No." The last thing Sonya would want was a posse of troopers. He knew it had been hard enough on her to call for him, heard it in her voice. "Drop me off at the cannery. I'll make my way with the jeep from there."

"Do you think you could stop in at the General Store and say hello to Davida for me?" Judd looked hopeful.

"I'm sure Skip will wait five minutes for you to say hello."

"It'll take me more than five minutes to say hello to her. Get my drift?"

"We *all* get your drift." Skip shook his head and helped himself to another Oreo. "Man, I miss my wife."

᠕

Garrett found Sonya inside the abandoned Diamond O Cannery, gazing out at the bay through a broken windowpane. Thick wooden planks squeaked under his booted feet as he made his way to her.

She turned, and then grimaced as she looked him over. "Did you have to wear the uniform?"

"It's who I am, Sonya. Who you called." He soaked in the sight of her, from her ball cap, to her worn jeans, and the t-shirt with "Ofishially Wild" written across her full breasts. She'd tied a sweatshirt around her hips, accentuating her waist. One look and he wanted her with a hunger of a starving man. He was getting as bad as Skip. Any minute he'd be whining for his woman. Except he didn't have one to call his own, but he sure wanted to put his name on this one.

Get a grip. He took a step back, keeping plenty of distance between them.

He'd given himself a pep talk in regard to how he'd handle this meeting with Sonya. It was business. He needed to remember his job and the huge conflict of interest that getting involved with her would be.

He *had* to keep his distance.

At least until fishing season was over.

She lived in Soldotna, he lived in Homer. That was a ninety minute drive. After their last meeting, he'd made a call to a buddy and had her investigated. He'd been shocked to find that Sonya Savonski, the headstrong, hell-bent on trouble, sexy woman captain, was a high school music teacher.

The sun slanted through the cracked windows, causing distorted shadows to dance inside the abandoned building. It was quiet, when one expected whistling wind, or the scurry of rodents.

"This place is clean for being abandoned," he commented, taking in his surroundings.

"The villagers use it for drying salmon. Soon it'll be hanging with curtains of fish fillets." Sonya turned back to the window, as though keeping watch. She kept to the shadows instead of standing directly in front of the opening for anyone to see her as they drifted by.

"What's up, Sonya?"

She took off her ball cap, folded it in her hands, and turned to her side so that she could keep an eye on him and the view. "We've had some trouble and my crew voted that we inform you."

Her crew might have voted in the affirmative, but he knew she hadn't. That shouldn't bother him. Keeping a healthy distance from each other was a good thing, but not at the expense of her or her family's safety.

He took a step toward her. Who was he fooling? He wanted to be so close to her that the lines of where she started and he began blurred. "What kind of trouble?"

She reformed the cap she'd been twisting in her hands. "Mischief stuff mostly."

"Mostly?" He advanced another few steps. "Spit it out, Sonya. What's going on?"

"Besides the hydraulics on the *Double Dippin'*, some-one cut one of our skiffs loose yesterday." She took a deep breath, and he realized that she wasn't acting apprehensive over meeting him—at least not much—she was fighting to keep her anger in check. "Now, they've sunk one of the skiffs." She crumpled her hat again and he knew she wished she could tear into the vandal who was causing her trouble.

He reached out and took the cap from her hands. "Keep this up and you're going to need a new hat." The scent of honeysuckle drifted to his nostrils. "Tell me everything that happened."

She filled him in on where they'd found the slices in the hydraulic hoses, the search for the skiff, and the cut rope, and then the reason she'd finally contacted him.

The sunken skiff.

"Have you looked over the skiff yet?"

"No, it's still on the bottom of the ocean. We're waiting for the tide to go out, then we can get to it."

He nodded. "I want to be there with you. I want to see the rope and hydraulic hoses."

She scanned him from top to bottom. "Not dressed like that."

"Sonya—"

"Nope." She shook her head. "Don't even attempt to argue. It's hard enough I'm here with you now. Hanging with a fish cop isn't going to help me. If the other fishermen see that I'll have more trouble then I know what to do with."

He tightened his jaw. It was a new experience to have someone ashamed to be seen with him because of his profession. "If you didn't want my help, why'd you call me?"

"I don't know." She rubbed her hands over her face, and he wondered when she'd last slept?

"Yes, you do." He knew she was frustrated, angry, and worried. Her whole body relayed emotions as though they were signs of an incoming storm. He dropped the ball cap to the floor and put his hands on her shoulders, instinctively rubbing at the tight knots he found. "Sonya. Breathe."

She lifted her head, and their eyes met. Damn, he really should have stayed on the other side of the room. He saw her turbulent emotions change into something else.

Something far more dangerous.

He found it next to impossible to resist a woman who wanted him as much as he wanted her.

One moment, they were motionless, caught up in their physical awareness of each other. The next found them catapulted into each other's arms.

He growled as his mouth met hers, grabbing her flush to him, he slammed their bodies against the wall of the building. His hands fought to free the tied sweatshirt around her waist, and then dove under her t-shirt to find skin.

"No…" Her teeth nipped at his jaw. "Can't…" Her arms tightened around his shoulders. "Do this." Then she climbed up his body and wrapped her legs around his waist.

"Oh, I think we damn well can." His erection rode hard against the heat between her thighs. The seductive sound that escaped her almost had him dropping her to the floor and pounding his body into hers right then and there. Her body shuddered against his and suddenly he wanted time. Not stolen moments in some dusty, drafty, old building. An honest-to-God bed with no chance of interruptions.

He was going to regret this later tonight when he couldn't sleep. "Sonya." He nuzzled the side of her neck, and she arched against him. "Ah, shit, babe." He groaned. "You got to stop moving like that."

She bit his neck and tightened her legs around him. "Then stop moving against me like that." She moaned, and he was helpless to resist taking her mouth again.

One moment Sonya was dead on her feet, so tired she couldn't think straight. The next, she felt like she could supply electricity for the whole state of Alaska. Her skin sizzled, her body vibrated, and she wanted to suck dry every morsel of energy Garrett infused her with.

This was wrong.

She'd promised herself she wasn't going to end up horizontal with him. Though, she hadn't promise anything about being vertical. She'd never had sex against a wall before. Definitely something every woman needed to experience in her lifetime.

What was she thinking? Right, she wasn't. She was very much into feeling at the moment. Boy, did she feel good. No, better than good. She felt down right freaking fantastic.

She moaned, he growled, his teeth biting the cord of her neck. On a sigh of surrender, she angled her head to give him better access. She wanted to give him access to whatever he wanted as long as he continued to make her feel like this.

Garrett's hands sneaked up her rib cage and under her bra. Yes, right there. *Oh goodness gracious halleluiah.* His hands were rough, magical.

Her hips cradled his pelvis and she took full advantage of introducing herself to the generous, unyielding ridge of his erection.

"Sonya, we have to put a stop to this." Garrett thrust against her.

"Uh-huh, right. I know. A few more minutes."

He croaked out a laugh. "Another minute and I'll be inside you."

"And that will be a bad thing, right?"

"So *very* bad."

The way Garrett said "bad" didn't make it sound bad at all. In fact, it sounded way too good, which naturally meant anything that good had to be bad.

She swore.

"Babe, I'm all for that," he muttered, his words strained, "but one of us has to be responsible."

"That's going to have to be you. I'm past that point."

He sucked in his breath and she realized she'd just given him carte blanche to do anything to her he wanted. He groaned and dropped his forehead to hers. She realized that being a cop, Garrett would have responsibility up the yin yang.

"Okay, this is what we are going to do." He met her gaze. "I need you to lower your legs."

"I don't know if I can do that." She really didn't *want* to do that. A few more minutes of riding him like this and she'd feel a hell of a lot better.

"I'd love nothing better than to take you against this wall, but can you honestly say you wouldn't regret it afterward?"

She was too tired to make these decisions. Why did he have to be so honorable? She didn't want to think. She'd been doing too much thinking with all that had been happening. She wanted a moment of oblivion and having Garrett between her legs more than promised a trip.

"You sure know how to spoil a mood, Garrett." She unhooked her legs from around his waist and made sure she rubbed down the length of him as she regained her balance.

Apparently, she'd made her point because it seemed as though Garrett couldn't think clearly now. His eyes were shut tight, lines bracketing his mouth, and sweat beaded his forehead. Having him in such obvious sexual torment shouldn't make her want to smile. But it did.

"Happy now?" She couldn't help goading.

He speared her with a gaze so hot she wished the wall wasn't at her backside so she could step back from the heat.

"Not even close, Sonya."

"Garrett—"

"Give me a damn minute." Garrett's tone was soft and dangerous. He turned and paced the length of the building.

She was quiet and gave him his space. It didn't seem so much fun to torment him when there were still sparks snapping in her own body. In fact, those sparks were better off refueling her anger. What the hell had Garrett been thinking, kissing her like that, pressing his rock-solid body against hers, and then saying they shouldn't be doing this? He'd been the one to torment *her*. With all that she had on her plate, an oversexed fish cop was too damn much.

"You started that," she pointed out.

He glared at her from across the room. "I'm not getting into an argument with you again."

"So you admit it."

"Sonya," he said through clenched teeth. "I understand that you are scared over the criminal mischief you've experienced. Picking a fight with me isn't going to help you."

There was that "criminal mischief" phrase again. It didn't matter if Peter said it or Garrett, it caused a shudder to run through her. Garrett was right. She wanted to fight someone and he was convenient. If she couldn't have sex with him, picking a fight was the second best thing she could think of.

She decided it was best to keep quiet. The only problem was that without the simulation of desire or anger, her exhausted body turned on her. She slid down the wall and sat on the floor. Her hat laid there where Garrett had dropped it when he'd grabbed her. She didn't even have the energy to reach for it. She rested her arms on her raised knees and lowered her head.

She was asleep before she shut her eyes.

Garrett paced the confines of the old cannery, keeping his distance from Sonya. He swore he could smell her all the way over here. He'd never been attracted to a woman to where he couldn't think around her.

How did she do that? Turn him into a walking hormone. He'd had more control in high school than he did around her.

"What time do you figure we'll be able to reach the skiff?" He waited for Sonya's response, and when it didn't come, he turned toward her. Her head was pillowed on her arms as she sat hunched over on the floor, fast asleep. All his pent up passion reduced to a simmer. She was lovely, with her mouth partly open, dark lashes fanning her cheeks. She seemed done in. How long had she been burning the candle at both ends? How long did she think she could get away with it before she collapsed?

The sooner he could get to the bottom of this the better for all of them. Lord knew he couldn't take more moments in her company like the last few.

He walked over and lightly shook her shoulder. On a snort, she jerked awake. He couldn't contain the smile. She was adorable.

"What?" She blinked and straightened like she hadn't just been caught sleeping.

His smile widened. "Let's get down to the beach and see if we can reach your skiff."

She scrambled to her feet. He went to help her and then thought better of it. If he touched her again, he didn't know if he could keep himself off her. Instead, he reached for her forgotten ball cap and handed it to her.

She took it and flipped her pony tail through the opening as she put it on. Then she pointed at him, her finger going up and down. "Uniform." The yawn that surprised her completely ruined her demand.

"Not going to change. Deal with it."

She narrowed her eyes and then seemed to realize that she didn't have much of a choice. Make that any choice.

"Fine."

She made for the exit, but his next words brought her up short. "I'll drive."

"The uniform is bad enough. I'm not going anywhere in the same vehicle as you."

"Sonya, be reasonable. You're too tired to drive."

"I just had a power nap. I'm good to go." She gave him a steady stare that clearly said, don't mess with me.

He let the subject pass since he'd be driving right behind her on the way to the Savonskis' camp in the Jeep. "Let's go then."

"I'll go first. You wait five minutes, then follow."

He folded his arms across his chest. "Not going to happen. I'm leaving *with* you and following *right* behind." He raised a brow when she opened her mouth to argue. "Say another word and I'm carrying you out of here and driving you to camp in my big brown trooper Jeep for all to see."

She snapped her mouth shut and turned on her heel. He tried not to enjoy his short victory or the view of her sweet backside as she swaggered out of the cannery to her 4-wheeler. That was one stubborn woman he was attracted to.

Why couldn't he go for an easy-going homemaker type?

CHAPTER TWELVE

"The skiff *would* have to go dry in the mud," Sonya muttered as she stared at the mudflat the receding tide had revealed. It seemed unassuming, solid even.

The mud was anything but ordinary. It could be deadly.

"Don't worry, Sonya. We won't let the mud take you," Gramps said as he sidled up next to her and Garrett. "Will we, Peter?" Gramps had already greeted Garrett with a hearty handshake. It didn't seem to bother him that a fish cop was on the premises.

Peter, on the other hand, seemed to be in the same mind-frame she was. Until he took in Garrett's sidearm, and perked up.

"Naw, we won't let the mud take you, Sonya." Peter winked. "We need you for fishing."

It was a standing joke that the mud was out to get Sonya. The only problem was everyone thought it was funny except Sonya.

The mud *was* out to get her.

Alaska had many hazardous areas where mudflats thrived. Bristol Bay wasn't immune. The region was blighted with them. They showed themselves at low tide and were made up of fine silt particles, the result of glaciers milling away the surrounding mountains. The mud made a treacherous quicksand—called quicksilt—that sucked at your feet and made it precarious to walk across its deceiving surface. If that wasn't a big enough problem, the mud also contained hidden sink holes. Many an unsuspecting person had been killed when caught in a hole that seemed to have no bottom.

One of those deadly sink holes had almost taken Sonya when she'd been sixteen. The summer after losing Sasha and her parents, she'd fallen prey to one. The mud had grabbed onto her with no intention of letting go. She'd fought for her life, while the incoming tide stealthily crept forward to drown her as Gramps, with the help of the Hartes, had worked frantically to free her from the mud's fatal clutches. Since then, she never ventured into the mud unless she absolutely had to. What really pissed her off was that Wes, Peter, and Gramps never had a problem with the mud.

Unfortunately, the situation with the skiff was one of those absolutes. Another thing to lay at the vandal's feet when they caught him.

Peter had already hooked the trailer up to the 4-wheeler so that they could bring the outboard engine back with them, in a wasted attempt to try and save it. Spending the afternoon drowned in salt water wasn't going to do the aging outboard any good.

The four of them were outfitted in chest waders and ready to face the mud. Well, three of them were ready. Sonya was never equipped to face the mud. Turned out, Garrett was one of those prepared cops who had a pair of waders in his Jeep. Had she really thought he wouldn't be primed for any situation? He'd probably had a handy condom in his pocket when they were at the old Diamond O Cannery, too, just in case.

Wes currently kept watch aboard the *Double Dippin'*. Sonya wasn't taking any chances leaving the drift boat unattended with all that had happened.

"You ready, Sonya?" Gramps asked.

"As I'll ever be," she muttered, wishing she could be doing anything else at the moment. She'd rather have a Brazilian wax than traipse through the mud.

Garrett laid a hand on her shoulder. "You okay?"

The heat from his palm cupping her shoulder made her want to rub against him, much the way a cat would. She stepped forward to break the contact before she did just that. "I'm fine. I just have a healthy respect for the mud."

"You can wait here while we take a look and get the engine," Gramps said, mounting the 4-wheeler behind Peter.

"No." She was running the fishing operation now, and she'd be involved in every aspect of it, whether she liked it—feared it—or not. She turned to the remaining 4-wheeler and climbed aboard, sweat already breaking out over her body.

"Do you want me to drive?" Garrett asked.

"No, I can do it." She could, damn it. If she had to confront the mud, she was definitely driving. She'd be the first to admit she had control issues and wasn't about to put her fate in the hands of anyone else, no matter how capable Garrett's hands seemed to be.

Garrett swung a leg over, and nuzzled up behind her on the seat that hadn't seemed that small a few seconds ago.

"Do you have to sit so close?" She tried to ignore the heat infusing her body with him plastered against her.

"Yes." His breath caressed her ear as his rock-hard chest pressed against her back. "I do."

"You're enjoying this, aren't you?"

"Probably more than I should. Besides, you wanted to drive."

Right, but who was really doing the driving?

She started the 4-wheeler and followed the trail Peter had forged through the mud. She tried to keep her speed steady and stay in Peter's tire tracks, praying that this time she wouldn't get stuck.

Garrett's hands snaked around her waist.

She jerked, which made the handlebars do the same, and the mud grabbed at the tires. "What are you doing?"

"Hanging on."

She gave the ATV a bit more gas and breathed a silent sigh of relief when the heavily treaded tires climbed through the muck. "I'm not going that fast. If you need to hang on to something, there's the rack behind you."

Damn it, she needed to concentrate. This was hazardous stuff she was driving through. Sonya wrinkled her nose as the acrid smell of burning mud, splattering on the muffler, suffused the air.

"The rack's not nearly as nice to hang onto as you," Garrett said, bringing her attention back to him and the incredibly sexy way he nuzzled her neck.

"Garrett," she growled his name and tightened her hold on the handle bars. Her neck tingled where his five o'clock shadow lightly scraped against her skin. It didn't take long for that tingle to ignite others farther south in her body.

"Have I told you that when you get upset, it's sexier than hell?"

"Will you shut up so I can pay attention?" The mud grabbed at her wheels again and this time she had to let up on the gas so the tires didn't dig in. She stood, straddled over the seat, and rocked the ATV, keeping steady on the throttle, until it worked free.

After she regained her seat, Garrett's hands stroked up her sides, flirting with the undersides of her breasts. Her breath caught in her throat. "Garrett," she warned.

"Drive, Sonya. Don't worry about what I'm doing."

She sucked in a much needed breath. "All I can think about is what you are doing."

"You're too wound up. A good massage would do wonders for you."

"Are you volunteering to give me one?" Now why did she go and ask that? Didn't she have enough problems at the moment?

"Anytime."

She slowed the 4-wheeler as they reached the skiff and parked it behind Peter's. She sat there stunned. "We actually made it without getting stuck." It was a first for her.

Garrett leaned in and stole a kiss alongside her neck as he got off the 4-wheeler. "You handled the mud like a pro, Sonya."

Who was the pro, she wondered. "You irritated me on purpose," she accused.

He crooked a smile, his icy-blue eyes full of fun and fire. "Be honest, babe, the last thing you were feeling was irritated." Then he sauntered through the mud as though it was packed sand toward the skiff.

For the first time that day, she felt like laughing. Irritated *was* the last emotion she felt in regard to Garrett.

Hot and bothered came to mind.

Sonya tucked her scattered feelings away and dismounted the 4-wheeler, holding onto her machine, and then Peter's until she made it to the skiff. She wasn't taking any chances of putting her full weight on the mud.

Garrett had jumped into the skiff, having already told Gramps and Peter he needed to be the first to board the boat. Gramps and Peter waited, looking over the side. She joined them, after transferring her hold from the ATVs to the edge of the skiff.

"Got an extra plug?" Garrett asked, investigating the stern. "Looks like whoever did this, helped themselves to yours,"

"Yeah, I brought one." Gramps pulled the plug out of his pocket and handed it to Garrett who screwed it into the bottom of the boat. "Figured if I wanted to sink a skiff, that's how I'd do it."

Sonya mentally kicked herself. She should have been the one who remembered to bring a plug. She probably would have if Garrett weren't occupying so much of her thoughts.

Garrett investigated the rest of the boat. "Whatever evidence the guy left behind, the ocean took care of it." He still scrutinized every inch of the skiff, taking his time to examine the dry holds. Then he removed the top cover of the engine. "Someone's had fun with duct tape here." He fingered one of the many tape-wrapped parts.

"That'd be me," Gramps said. "That engine's lasted us a long time."

"Time to bury it," Sonya muttered.

At least something good might come of the boat sinking. They could finally replace the relic with a new, more dependable model.

Gramps arched his brows in a challenge. "Just you watch, young lady. I'll get that engine up and running again."

Crap. She was afraid of that. Gramps would try to get milk from a bull if he was challenged enough.

The men unbolted the outboard from the stern and strong-armed it into the trailer. Peter double-checked the painter line's knot tied to the running line and they all bailed out the leftover water. Then they returned to the 4-wheelers.

Sonya followed, glad there wasn't any damage to the skiff other than the engine. They did lose two brailer bags and a few fish picks, but the skiff seemed in good shape. It could have been worse.

"Looks like whoever is doing this just wants to cause you problems." Garrett's thoughts must have been running along the same vein as hers. "They could have damaged the skiff to where you couldn't use it for the rest of the season."

"What do you suggest we do?" Peter asked, mounting the 4-wheeler. Gramps climbed on behind him.

"Other than writing up a damage report and being vigilant, there isn't much to go on."

"That's what I figured." Sonya gave Peter and Gramps a pointed look that clearly said they hadn't needed to call in a fish cop.

"It was still smart to contact me." Garrett eyed Sonya with his trooper stare. "If anything else happens, we need a paper trail to prosecute."

"Paper trail," Peter repeated with a smirk at Sonya. "What'd I tell you?"

She decided it was best to ignore everyone and concentrate on getting back to the 4-wheeler without being sucked down into the mud.

Too late.

She knew it. Every damn time.

She worked her foot back and forth, trying to free it from the sucking sludge. She breathed a sigh of relief as she freed one foot and took a step, coming up fast when the mud refused to release her other. She tried not to panic as the mud seized her farther into its grip.

"You really do have a problem with this mud." Garrett walked over to her and took hold of her arm.

"I've said it before, the mud's out to reclaim me." Leaning on Garrett, she pulled her back foot free only to find the front one had settled in the mud enough to anchor it.

"It's all in your head, Sonya," Peter said. "Mind over matter. You think you're going to get stuck, therefore you do."

"Shut up, will you." Frustration ate at her. She hated feeling at the mercy of anything, let alone mud that everyone in her family, even Garrett, seemed to conquer.

"Just saying."

"Well, say it where I don't have to hear it."

"Sonya." Garrett grabbed her attention. "Place your boot into the mud heel first, and then kind of slide, like you're wearing snow shoes."

Pulling on Garrett, she freed another foot and tried what he suggested. She made a few feet of progress, until she heard another 4-wheeler join the party.

Aidan stood astride his ATV heading their way.

This was going to top off her shitty day, Sonya thought, as the mud reached up and gripped her feet tight again.

Aidan cut the engine to his 4-wheeler, and leaned forward to rest his arms on the handle bars. "Having trouble?" He eyed Garrett as though he was the actual trouble. Garrett met Aidan's stare with his glacial blue gaze. It was icy enough to give *her* chills.

Great, Sonya thought.

"Someone removed the plug from the skiff," Garrett said.

Aidan looked at Sonya and then Peter and Gramps. His confusion seemed genuine, but was it?

"You can't mean *intentionally* removed the plug?" He straightened as he glanced back to Peter. "Are you sure someone didn't forget to put it back in after cleaning out the fish slime?"

"Hey!" Peter stood while straddled over the ATV's seat. "I did not forget to screw in the plug. I made sure it was in place when I finished draining the skiff after I tendered. That's a rookie mistake. *I am no rookie.*"

Sonya couldn't blame Aidan for jumping to that conclusion. It was the direction her thoughts had first traveled. "Aidan didn't mean anything by it, Peter. He was just following the same line of questions we all have."

Peter swung his mad gaze her way. "You think I did this?"

"No. I know you didn't. I wish you *had* left the plug out, because it sure as hell beats the alternative." Without a doubt, she knew Peter didn't have a hand in the boat sinking. She wasn't as sure about the man right in front of her. Hadn't Aidan warned her that she'd have trouble this summer?

Peter's stance relaxed somewhat. He looked at everyone in turn, settling on Garrett. "We need to find this guy."

"I plan on it." Garrett's statement invited complete confidence that he'd do exactly that.

"You brought in a fish cop?" Aidan pointed his gaze at Sonya.

"Trooper." Garrett's tone seemed to beg Aidan to say something else derogatory.

"Aidan," Sonya interjected before things got any messier, "this isn't helping."

He seemed to get his ire under control. "What can I do to help?"

"Not much at this point," Sonya said, "other than keeping an eye out for anything out of the ordinary."

"You seem to have a good view of the Savonski's skiffs from your camp," Garrett said. "Did you see anything this morning?"

"No," Aidan said. "I haven't seen anything, but then I spent most of the morning catching up on sleep. I'll keep a watch out now that I know you've had trouble." His gaze landed on her. "You should have come to me first, Sonya."

She turned away, uncomfortable with his wounded expression. No matter their history, she didn't like him hurting.

"Kids," Gramps joined the conversation. "The tide's headed back in. We'd better make for the beach. Peter, let's get this 4-wheeler moving. I have no plans to get wet."

Sonya glanced over her shoulder and gauged the water. It was headed in fast. The tide in Bristol Bay went out in a rush, and returned with a vengeance. One minute you couldn't see the water, and then it chewed hungrily at your feet.

"Got it, Gramps." Peter started the 4-wheeler, but addressed Sonya before he engaged the gear. "Are you going to be okay getting back to camp?"

Meaning, was she going to be able to get out of the mud? It did warm her heart that her usually infuriating baby brother was concerned over her well-being. "Thanks, Peter. We'll be right behind you."

With a wave, Peter turned the ATV and headed back to camp with Gramps and the outboard engine.

Sonya tried to lift her feet. *Stuck.* She glanced behind her to the tide eating up the distance. Don't panic. Deep breaths. Everything would be fine, she mentally chanted.

"You really are mud-impaired, aren't you?" Garrett trudged back to where she wasn't gaining any ground.

"Everyone's got to have one weakness," she muttered. *She should be able to do this, damn it.*

"You have more than one weakness, Sonya," Garrett murmured, giving her a smile that brought to mind what she'd wanted to do with him earlier. Then he swung her up into his arms. A surprised sound escaped her, followed immediately by a squeal of alarm as Garrett stumbled, the mud grabbing thick at his feet. "Don't move," he warned, straining to regain his balance, while at the same time pulling free of the mud.

She tightened her arms around his neck and held herself very still. "Don't you dare drop me."

"Babe, you go down, I go down."

He worked free of the mud, and then fought his way toward the 4-wheeler. Just like any red-blooded woman, she was impressed with the muscle Garrett exhibited as he went all He-Man, carrying her to the safety of her 4-wheeler mount. Sonya tried not to worry about the water coming in like a flood. They needed to move faster, but there was no hurrying through the gelatinous goo. Finally, they reached the 4-wheeler and Garrett set her down on the seat, swiping at his sweaty brow with his arm.

"Next time, let's find a more enjoyable strenuous activity to do together." There was no doubt in her mind to what he was referring to.

Sonya felt the prick of Aidan's glare. She glanced over Garrett's shoulder. Aidan sat like granite astride his ATV. She'd forgotten he was still there. Watching. She flushed hot and then cold.

Aidan's dark eyes were fevered with jealousy.

Chapter Thirteen

"You're welcome to stay for dinner, Garrett," Grams said as she finished filleting a salmon on the bank of the creek below the cabin.

Sonya stood behind Garrett, and shook her head no, but Grams continued even though Sonya knew she'd seen her. "We're having teriyaki salmon with rice, and I've made a yummy lemon cake for dessert."

Gramps and Peter had gone in search of a fifty-gallon drum they could submerge the outboard engine in, hoping to clean out the saltwater. Sonya wished Gramps would just let the engine die.

"Lemon cake?" Garrett swallowed as though dessert had been awhile.

"Yes." Grams nodded with a smile. "Homemade."

Garrett groaned. "You don't play fair. I've been living on what amounts to rations since I got here." He seemed to waver, but then he straightened his shoulders. "Thank you, Mrs. Savonski, but I really need to head back."

Sonya breathed a sigh of relief. Another few hours in Garrett's company and who knew what she'd do. Probably have her way with him. Forget homemade lemon cake, she'd serve herself a slice of Garrett Hunt instead. Then where would she be? Screwed. Not necessarily in a satisfactory way.

Garrett turned to her, and she jerked her thoughts out of the bedroom. His eyes narrowed as he took in the heat flushing her face. She hoped his cop eyes didn't read anything into it.

"I want you to promise to contact me if anything else happens." His ice-blue stare imprisoned hers.

She tried to look away. She did not want to make that promise.

"Sonya." He sighed as he must have read her intent. "I can't help, unless you do."

Damn, why did he have to look at her like that? Like she meant something to him. He was a fish cop. She was a fisherman. Having casual sex with each other was one thing, but the way she felt, and the way he gazed at her, there wasn't anything casual happening between them.

Garrett grasped her hands. "Promise me, Sonya."

"Oh, all right. I promise."

His lips twitched into a crooked smile. "That wasn't so hard."

She scowled. "The hell it wasn't."

He laughed. The sound did funny things to the rhythm of her heart. Garrett gave her one last look and then said his goodbyes. Sonya watched him climb into his Jeep and drive down the beach.

Grams came up alongside her and draped an arm over Sonya's shoulders. "You're sinking fast, aren't you?"

Sonya scoffed. "Grams, he's a fish cop."

She hummed and gave Sonya a knowing smile. "I always did like a man in uniform."

As it turned out, so did she.

Aidan tried to stay away. He really did. He'd been pacing his side of the bluff watching Sonya and that trooper. No matter how he reasoned with himself—using breathing techniques, and visiting his damn screwy happy place—he couldn't keep away.

He waited until the fish cop left, and then found Sonya alone on the beach, mending nets. He could hear Nikolai and Peter discussing the best way to tear into the carburetor of the outboard engine, but with the curve of the bluff, he and Sonya might as well have been alone.

"Why'd you have to bring in a fish cop?" Anger rimmed the edges of his vision, and he couldn't help his biting tone.

Sonya swung around, eyes wide in surprise. He'd approached downwind, and she hadn't heard him. She straightened and gripped the plastic needle she'd been using to patch holes in the net. He knew he was frightening her, a side of him got off on it, the other begged him to rein it in.

"We take care of our own out here, Sonya. Bringing in a trooper will only invite more trouble. The other set netters find out you're getting cozy with a fish cop, you'll have a bigger mess than you can clean up." He took a breath, hoping to calm his temper. "You should have come to me." That more than anything had his anger at a boiling point. Who was he madder at? Her for not trusting him or himself for ruining that trust?

"What if one of our own is causing me trouble?" Sonya asked, with a look that accused.

All the bluster went out of him like a pricked balloon. Of course, she'd think he was the culprit. He'd warned her that her plans would bring trouble. His chosen method of dealing with problems was to fight it out. That was in the past. He would never forget he'd used his fists on her.

130

Seeing things from Sonya's side, it wasn't a huge step to believe he'd do something like this.

He rubbed the back of his neck. How had things between them become so strained? As kids, they'd played together on this very beach. As teenagers, they'd flirted with each other on this beach. Finally, as adults, they'd made love in the tall grass that overlooked this very beach.

"Sonya, I would never intentionally cause you, or your family, harm." She looked away from him, and the pain in his chest seemed to stop his heart.

"Part of me really wants to believe that, Aidan." She flicked the end of the mending needle, and then faced him again, her gaze full of resolve. "The other part of me remembers what you are capable of when you're angry."

He reached out and took the needle from her fingers and lay it on the net mending frame. Then he held her hand in his, lightly tracing her trim nails. "What will it take to make you forget?"

Her sad, solemn eyes met his. "I don't know."

When Garrett had boarded the *Calypso* the night before, he'd filled Judd and Skip in on the incidents that the Savonskis were dealing with. Other than notifying the rest of the troopers to keep theirs ears and eyes out, there wasn't much they could do. The whole situation stunk. Not having a lead or a suspect to question made him feel like a fish caught in a net. It didn't help matters that his gut was telling him Sonya's problems had only begun.

"Want a Coke?" Judd asked, joining Garrett at the rail.

Skip was captaining the boat, and listening for any interesting chatter on the VHF, while he and Judd were stationed on deck with binoculars, keeping an eye out for anyone violating the drift opening.

"Yeah, thanks." Garrett took the soda Judd offered, flipped the top, and drank deep. He'd prefer a thermos of coffee. He was chilled to the bone and needed to work up some steam.

The day was overcast. The constant rain had dropped the temperature into the thirties. Any lower and it would snow.

He'd forgotten how cold a South Naknek summer could be. Fog played on the river, making their job even harder. The AWT planes and helicopters were grounded due to the weather, which left the remaining troopers on the water and shore to police the area. Garrett knew the fishermen were taking advantage of the situation. It was a perfect day to catch fish, by legal means or not.

"Sonya's got under your skin, hasn't she?" Judd casually sipped his Coke while his question hammered into Garrett's consciousness. "Women have a sneaky way about them. Before we know it we're smitten."

Was he smitten? Of course, he was. Sonya consumed his thoughts, his dreams, hell even his job was being taken over by her. Here he was, scouting for violators and hoping he'd catch sight of the *Double Dippin'*. She wouldn't be happy if he "happened" to stop by.

Probably try and fillet him like a fish with her tongue, which actually wasn't that bad an image. He shook his head clear of the picture as Judd rambled on.

"Take Davida for instance," Judd continued as though not needing confirmation over Garrett's state of smittenness. "That woman likes to torment me."

Garrett felt a bit tormented himself. Sonya was like an itch he couldn't reach. It was refreshing to concentrate on another man's woman issues. "Torments you? Do I want to know how?"

"Nothing like that, unfortunately. I went to see her yesterday when you were off with the Savonskis, and she barely gave me the time of day." Judd drained his Coke and then crushed the can into a flat disk.

"Maybe she was busy."

"Too busy for me?" Judd scoffed. "She couldn't get enough of me the last time we were together."

"Maybe that was enough for her." Garrett laughed at the incredulous look Judd sent his way. "Or maybe not."

"Definitely not." He huffed. "You've always had a way with women. Heard your code name in the Navy was Orca. You didn't earn that name from the way you handle a gun. I've seen you shoot, so I assume it's the killer way you have with the ladies."

Garrett slid him a glance. Where had Judd picked up that tidbit of information? He'd been nicknamed Orca for the silent way he killed with his hands, not for his way with women. And he sure as hell could shoot a gun. It just wasn't his weapon of choice.

"Women are just as much a mystery to me as they are to the next man." Garrett finished his Coke and showed Judd that he could crush the can with his bare hands too.

"Well, crap, Hunt. I had high hopes that you'd lead me down the right road. Skip told me to bring her chocolates."

Garrett nodded. "Sounds good. I don't know of a woman who doesn't like chocolates."

"Davida runs the only store this side of Naknek that sells chocolates. I can't go in there, buy them from her, and then give them *to her*. How pathetic is that?"

"Pretty pathetic." So was this conversation. Whatever happened to men being men? Men did not "talk." Girls talked. "Try flowers."

"Where am I going to get flowers? Do you see a florist anywhere? I'd have to have them flown in from Anchorage, and the State doesn't pay me that well."

Garrett rolled his eyes. "Judd, look around." He gestured to the surrounding shore, not that they could see it with the draping fog everywhere. "Go and pick her wildflowers."

"Hey." Judd's whole demeanor brightened. "Now that is a damn good idea. Thanks, Orca."

Garrett grabbed Judd's arm as he lifted his binoculars. "Only SEALs get to call me that." He met Judd's surprised gaze. "Got it?"

"Man, you guys are a breed apart."

Garrett released his hold on Judd, knowing he'd received the message loud and clear. "Damn right."

"Yo!" Skip hollered through the window of the cabin. "A call just came over the radio. The *Double Dippin'* took gunfire, and her captain's been taken to the Infirmary."

CHAPTER FOURTEEN

What had Judd said about SEALs being a tough breed? Knowing that Sonya was hurt had Garrett quaking like an old woman. His pulse pounded until he felt like his heart would beat him to death. He'd had buddies shot down beside him, held one in his arms as he took his last breath, believing his own death would be next, and yet he hadn't been as afraid as he was right now.

Skip had powered the *Calypso* to the cannery and tied up next to the *Double Dippin'*. The side window of Sonya's drift boat was blown free. Jagged pieces of glass still stuck in the edges of the broken frame. Blood trailed down the steps from the pilot house, over the rail, and up the ladder to the dock of the cannery.

"Skip, don't let anyone besides us board that boat." Garrett clenched his jaw.

"You can count on it."

He reached for the ladder. Blood was spattered on each rung. His own raced with dread as he climbed. Judd followed him. They didn't speak as they gained the dock and jumped into the Jeep. He gunned the engine and made for the village, which began on the back side of the cannery.

The commercial area of South Naknek was about a city block long, with the outlying areas dotted with small houses for the hundred or so residents. It was definitely a place you wouldn't get lost in. Main Street consisted of a restaurant/bar, the Pitt, an old Russian Orthodox Church, fire station, school, library, and Community Center. All were within shouting distance of each other.

Tires skidded on the dirt road as Garrett brought the Jeep to a rocking stop. He jumped out of the vehicle and hauled open the door to the Community Center, which housed the offices for the village officials, their one village public safety officer—or VPSO— and the Infirmary. If Sonya was seriously hurt they'd need to call in a helicopter. Then he remembered the fog. No flying meant the village doctor was their only option. How trained would the guy be? What if Sonya was hurt worse than the doc could handle?

Don't borrow trouble.

He grabbed the door to the Infirmary and yanked it open. In the waiting room sat Wes, Peter, and Nikolai, their faces drawn and pale.

"Where is she?" he asked, their solemn expressions making him that more afraid.

Nikolai pointed to the closed door opposite the bench the three of them occupied.

"Damn it to hell, Wanda, that hurts!" Sonya hollered from the behind the barrier.

Garrett nearly dropped to his knees in relief. If she had the energy to yell, she had to be all right. "How's she doing?" he asked Nikolai.

A bit of a twinkle entered Nikolai's worried eyes. "Swearing up a storm. It's a good thing my Maggie May isn't here listening to that potty mouth."

Garrett took a deep breath and slowly let it out. Judd entered the room, having caught up with him. Garrett made the introductions and then got down to business. "Tell me what happened."

"We were pulling in our net when the window to the pilot house exploded," Nikolai began, worrying the rim of his hat in his hands. "It sounded like a gunshot."

"Was Sonya hit?" There'd be a bullet to recover if she was. And, by God, he'd find the gun that matched it.

"Not by a bullet," Nikolai answered, "but she was cut up bad by flying glass."

"There was blood everywhere," Peter said in a hushed voice. The kid looked shell-shocked.

Nikolai patted Peter's back. "She's going to be okay, Peter." By the sounds coming from the exam room, Sonya was holding her own. "That's one tough sister you got."

"Yeah," Peter said, though he didn't sound convinced. Was Nikolai putting on a strong front for the other men? Was Sonya hurt worse than they thought?

"Judd, finish taking their statements. I've got to see Sonya."

Garrett reached for the doorknob, but stopped when Nikolai stood and grabbed his arm.

"Before you go in there, let me give you a few words of advice." Nikolai leaned in, and lowered his voice, "The more scared Sonya gets, the louder and mouthier she becomes."

"Thanks, I'll keep that in mind." He knocked and entered the exam room before a "come in" was issued. He knew Sonya wouldn't want him as a witness to her hurting. The woman liked to put on a tough front. Being someone who did the same, he understood where she was coming from. He didn't give a damn if she didn't want him there. Right now, it was about what *he* wanted. Making sure she was all right was at the top of his list.

Sonya wore a hospital gown toga-style over blood-spattered jeans. Her right shoulder was bare so the doctor could access the cuts that criss-crossed her shoulder and arm. He sucked in his breath when she turned toward him. The right side of her face was traversed with nicks and cuts. Most were superficial and didn't require stitches, but blood had matted her hair from a deep gash, already stitched closed, near her hairline, and two butterfly stitches taped over a slash on her cheek. Half an inch higher and she would have lost an eye.

"Get the hell out of here." She might be wounded, but her voice held enough fire to make him think of stepping back, which he knew was her intent. All bark but not enough strength to bite.

"I'm not going anywhere." He turned to the woman with striking salt and pepper hair, cut just below her chin. She was dressed in pink scrubs with a small moose pattern printed on them, holding a wicked pair of tweezers in her latex-covered fingers. He tried to steel his features into a mask that wouldn't give away how worried and upset he was over Sonya's appearance. "How is she?"

"Who are you?" The woman took in his uniform, not intimidated or impressed.

"Garrett Hunt, Alaska Wildlife Trooper. I'm investigating the incident that sliced up your patient today. And you are?"

"Dr. Wanda Abalmasoff, but everyone calls me Wanda." She turned to Sonya. "You told me you were cut because of a broken window?"

"The window might have been broken by a bullet," Sonya mumbled under her breath, while her eyes shot payback promises at Garrett.

"Sonya," Wanda scolded. "If your injuries are a result of a crime, there are certain procedures that need to be followed."

Garrett bit the inside of his cheek to keep from grinning. Sonya seemed as repentant as a hungry child caught snitching a cookie before dinner. The relief of knowing she would be okay was enough to make him giddy, even though he still relished catching the son of a bitch who'd done this to her.

"Do I need to call Inga?" Wanda asked. At his questioning brow she added, "Inga is our VPSO."

"As a courtesy, you can share whatever information you want to. But this incident happened in open waters, during a fishing period, which falls under my jurisdiction."

Wanda gave him a nod. "If you have to stay, then make yourself useful." She pointed to the cabinet behind him. "I need more gauze. Top shelf on the right."

"No, no, absolutely not," Sonya sputtered in a rush. "I don't want him staying. What happened to patient/doctor confidentiality?"

Wanda raised her brows. "Are you kidding me?"

"No. I'm half dressed and in no mood to entertain a fish cop."

"No entertainment needed," Garrett said. He'd had enough excitement for one day. "You're not getting me out of here, Sonya. Might as well resign yourself to the fact and deal with it." He grabbed the packaged gauze and handed it to Wanda. She took them and dropped them on the tray within easy reach.

"Do you two know each other?" Wanda asked.

"No." "Yes." They both said at once.

Sonya eyed him with retribution. He relished taking whatever she could give him, just as soon as she was up to it.

"Glad you cleared that up." Wanda went to work with the tweezers. Sonya gasped as Wanda pulled a sliver of glass from the deep cut in her shoulder. "Hunt, since you're obviously sticking around, wash your hands." She indicated a sink with a jerk of her head. "Then get over here. I need a nurse."

Garrett scrubbed up, and then snapped on a pair of latex gloves. He knew a thing or two about getting sewn back together. He'd had to stitch himself up a few times. He tore into the package of gauze, trying to separate himself from the pain that Sonya must be feeling. She looked like hell.

When Wanda exchanged her tweezers for a needle filled with a numbing agent, he reached for Sonya's left hand that had escaped the flying glass. Sonya didn't fight him, instead she clamped down on his fingers as the needle pierced the cut. She also added a few more swear words to the others she'd already spewed.

"All right," Wanda said. "While we give that a chance to numb the area, I'll finish cleaning the rest of the cuts on your arm. They aren't deep enough for stitches. You'll have to take care to keep any fish slime from coming into contact with them. I don't have to tell you what kind of trouble you'd be in if you contracted blood poisoning."

Sonya swore again. "Don't tell me I can't fish."

"I wouldn't dream of it," Wanda said. "Just be careful and make sure these cuts are covered up, and disinfect when you're finished fishing for the day."

Garrett gauged what Wanda needed and handed it to her, soaking gauze pads with antiseptic. They worked well together cleaning Sonya's cuts. To keep Sonya occupied, and her swearing at a minimum, Garrett began asking questions. "Tell me everything that happened, Sonya."

Her shoulders slumped as the events of the day seemed to catch up with her. "I was operating the hydraulics. We were pulling in the net—"

"Where were you fishing?"

"Not far off the line at the mouth of the river."

"Who was drifting around you?"

She lifted her hand to rub at her forehead and then dropped it, obviously remembering the stitches. "Uh, let me think." She closed her eyes and grimaced as Wanda's hooked needle pierced the flesh of her shoulder. Garrett took her hand again and gave her a reassuring squeeze. "The *Miss Julie II*, the *Mary Jane*, the uhmm...*Intrepid*." Her eyes flew open and met his. Fear flash in them just before anger flared. "And the *Albatross*."

Chuck Kendrick.

His name sure came up a lot and it always seemed associated with trouble. Garrett nodded. "Okay, tell me what happened next?"

"There was this loud crack and the window shattered. Glass went flying everywhere."

"Where exactly were you?"

"At the wheel. I threw my hands over my head, but not in time to avoid all the glass."

She was damn lucky she wasn't cut to shreds, or worse. "Then what?"

"Gramps and the guys came running. We wrapped the worse of the cuts as best we could, and then Wes and Peter round-hauled in the net. Gramps and I piloted the boat to the cannery, while the boys picked the net." Her gaze suddenly swung to his. "I need to get those fish tendered. They're still sitting in the holds."

He could care less about the fish, but she cared and she'd worry until it was taken care of.

"I'll be right back." He exited the exam room to find Judd writing in his notebook as he took statements. "Which one of you has the permit to sell the drift fish on?"

"Sonya," Gramps said. "The drift permit is in her name. She's the only one who can sell to the tenders unless *you* let one of us do it."

He couldn't bend the law, not even for Sonya. "How long have the fish been in the holds?" The longer the fish stayed onboard, the more chances they took with the tenders not willing to buy them.

"About an hour, maybe an hour and a half."

"Okay, with the weather cold and overcast, there's still time." With the elements like they were today, the fish were basically refrigerated. He returned to the exam room to see Sonya looking exhausted. The ordeal was catching up to her. Dark circles formed crescent moons under her eyes, made more prominent with the white butterfly stitches placed so close. Wanda still sutured the gash in Sonya's shoulder.

"I have to be the one who sells the fish." Sonya looked as though she was geared up for an argument, probably thinking he would insist she couldn't leave, which was exactly what he wanted to do. She was in a tough spot. Fishing was a large part of her livelihood, and the fish wouldn't stay fresh.

"Sonya," Wanda said. "You are in no condition to pilot a boat. You need rest, and pain killers wouldn't be out of order."

"She doesn't have to pilot the boat." Garrett took Sonya's uninjured hand. "She just has to be on the *Double Dippin'* when they sell the fish."

Sonya met his gaze. Most of the fight had gone out of her. Pain and worry reflected in her deep brown eyes, making them almost black. She was crashing fast off an adrenaline high and it was taking its toll.

"Better hurry and get her sewn up," Garrett said to Wanda. "We have to make the tide and she's about done."

"*She's* still sitting here," Sonya pointed out with what little bluster she had left. "You don't have to talk about me like I'm off visiting another dimension."

"Yes, we do." Wanda tied the last knot in a twelve-stitch suture. "I need a few more minutes to finish wrapping this, and I'll give you some pills that will take you to that other dimension."

"I love you, Wanda," Sonya said.

"Yeah, sure you do. All my patients say that when I give them narcotics."

$$\text{ꝑ}$$

Garrett had plenty of help getting Sonya back onboard the *Double Dippin'*.

Too much help.

Sonya was back to cursing with all the attention. Who knew the woman could swear with so much creativity. He'd found himself educated, and he'd been in the military.

Judd had returned to the *Calypso* for the camera and handed it to him so Garrett could document the damage to the *Double Dippin'*. Wes had located a broom and dustpan from someone at the cannery, which Garrett also took.

"You're not going in there without me," Sonya said, her skin ashen, which made the cuts look angry and sore. Funny, he felt like she looked, and if she kept fighting him on every little thing, he'd blow his cool.

"Peter made you a place on deck where you can sit and rest while I investigate."

"This is my boat, and nothing happens on my boat without me present." She might be hurting but she was still as determined as ever.

Nikolai laid a hand on her uninjured shoulder. "Sonya, let him do his job."

She turned to her grandfather. "If you were in my place what would you do?"

"That's not fair," Nikolai said with a frown. "I'm a—"

143

"*Man?*" Sonya supplied for him with a raised brow. "I'm captain. I know you're worried about me, but I'm fine."

Nikolai pursed his lips and huffed. "I don't like it."

She gave him an understanding smile. "I know. How about directing the boys so that we're ready to tender when Garrett and I are through?" Nikolai nodded, though Garrett knew it grated against the man's character, and went to the bow of the boat where Wes and Peter hung out.

"Sonya," Garrett tried again, "You'll be in my way."

"Deal with it." She threw the same words at him he'd thrown at her, when they were at the Infirmary.

He tightened his jaw and clamped his lips shut before he said something he'd regret. Then he turned and marched his way up the stairs into the pilot house. She, of course, followed.

At the door, he slid on another pair of latex gloves before entering. He ordered her to stay. She surprised him and did. He leaned the broom and dust pan next to the door and took out the camera. He snapped a few pictures of the broken window, close-ups of the remaining shards stuck in the frame, and then the spray pattern of the glass.

"Why aren't these windows made of tempered glass?" If they had been, she wouldn't have been cut like she was.

"It wasn't something I thought to ask the previous owner. After this, though, I'll replace all of them with tempered glass."

"Good." He studied the broken pieces of the windowpane, trying not to focus on the amount of blood mixed in with the mess. Most of the glass centered where she would have sat and scattered over the floor. He checked the bunk, making sure no glass was present. "I want you to sit down." Losing as much blood as she had, he was surprised she was still on her feet. Most men wouldn't be,

144

but then most men weren't as stubborn as this woman. She didn't argue with him, and took a seat, leaning her head against the wall. Wanda had given her a gray South Naknek, "Fish Capital of the World" sweatshirt to wear since her clothes had been too bloody to save. He wished she'd take one of the pain killers Wanda had given her, but he understood why she didn't. As soon as he was finished, she'd be tendering fish. It'd be at least an hour or so until she could lie down and rest.

She quietly watched him as he continued to look for a bullet. Frustration ate at him when he didn't immediately find one. The room wasn't that big. The opposite window wasn't broken so the bullet didn't do a through and through. He clicked on the flashlight he carried on his belt, and shined it into the corners of the floor. Nothing flickered back at him, but then his light caught something peculiar. He snapped a picture, then bent and picked it up.

What was a rock doing aboard a drift boat?

It wasn't like someone could carry a rock the size of a walnut onboard in the tread of their boots. Sand yes, small pieces of gravel maybe, but not a rock.

"Have you seen this before?" He held the rock for Sonya.

She shook her head. "No."

"I can't find a bullet. I think your window was shot out with this."

"How? There wasn't a drift boat close enough to throw that small of a rock with enough force to break a window."

"They could if they used a slingshot."

CHAPTER FIFTEEN

This whole situation was surreal. Sonya rubbed at her temple as her headache built.

"We're probably reading more into this than there is," she said. "If that rock broke my window, it was probably an accident. Someone target practicing while their net soaked." That was easier to swallow than someone intentionally shooting at *her*.

"That's one possibility. After the trouble you've already experienced, I'm inclined to think the worst. So should you." Garrett carefully enclosed the rock in a plastic bag and put it in his pocket. He tore off the latex gloves and then took her hands in his, being careful of her cuts. "Sonya, I don't want anything more to happen to you."

He wasn't the only one. She didn't want anything to happen to her either. His eyes traveled over her face. She'd yet to look in the mirror. Wanda had reassured her that the cuts would heal without leaving scars, except for maybe the one on her cheek. The cut at her hairline was a definite, but her hair would hide it. She wasn't vain, at least no more than the next woman, but she knew when she had a moment to look in the mirror, she'd give into the tears she'd held at bay all afternoon. The longer this day lasted the harder it was to hold them back.

Something must have shown in her eyes for Garrett's expression changed from determined lawman to something softer, kinder, and certainly more of an emotional threat. Especially considering her current condition.

"Seeing you hurt today..." He swallowed and slowly blinked, obviously having trouble getting across what he wanted to. That alone, made her want to lean toward him. If he kept this up, she'd beg to be held and comforted, totally destroying the tough-girl image she'd cultivated. "You aren't just another victim, Sonya. You matter to me."

Ah, hell. Why did he have to go and say that? A sniff was the first thing to betray her. Damn it, the tears would come next if she didn't do something fast. "Garrett—"

"Don't say anything. You've had a rough day." He smoothed a strand of hair behind her ear. "When you're feeling better we can—oh shit, don't cry."

"Then quit being so damn nice to me." She swiped at the tears and winced as she hit the butterfly-stitched cut. Her head pounded and if she didn't get these tears stopped, she'd be in real trouble.

Garrett grabbed a paper towel off the roll she kept near the small sink, and carefully wiped at the tears that wouldn't stop. "Everything will be okay. I'll make sure of it."

She cracked a laugh, though it caused her head to ache further. "You can't promise that."

"I'm good at my job, Sonya. I'll find this asshole." His steady stare told her he believed every word he said.

"When you do, I want a few minutes alone with him." She'd take pleasure in getting her hands on the man who thought he could mess with her and hers.

Garrett chuckled. "Until then, let's get you in bed with some pain pills."

"Sounds like heaven." She shut her eyes, just thinking of the bliss checking out would be.

"Who do you want me to call to pilot the boat to tender your fish?"

Crap, she couldn't totally check out until they'd finished tendering. "Wes, he's had the most time at the wheel." Tendering took a bit of finesse, but in her condition she was smart enough to realize that Wes would be the better man for the job.

"All right. I need to leave, but I'll check in with you later." He seemed reluctant to go, but he needed to.

Already Sonya knew the gossip mill had to be buzzing with the *Calypso* tied to her boat. Hell, right now anyone could see inside the *Double Dippin'*, and Garrett stood too close to her.

Word had gotten out about her connection to Garrett. She didn't know how, but she'd felt ostracized from the small community of fishermen fishing with them today.

She had a feeling her troubles were just beginning.

ʃ

Garrett boarded the *Calypso*, where Judd and Skip waited for him. He quickly filled them in on what he'd found aboard the *Double Dippin'*.

"Sonya could be right," Judd said. "This could be an accident. Some kid having fun with a slingshot."

"The other boats were too far away. No kid would have enough power to shoot that distance and break a window," Garrett said. "Besides, with the other troubles the Savonskis have had, I don't buy that this latest one is a random accident. I don't believe in coincidences."

"Garrett's correct," Skip said. "We need to follow this up. I'll give a holler over the radio to see where the other boats are that fished around her today. It might take a while to find them now that the fishing period is over."

"Damn, I was looking forward to some land time," Judd said, his tone wistful.

"Don't you mean some Davida time," Skip said with a knowing look.

"Got that right. If I don't keep showing up at the cannery every now and then to remind her what a great catch I am, she's going to go fishing for another man."

Garrett didn't bother telling him that he was better off losing a woman who wouldn't wait for him. If he did, Judd would probably follow it up with some advice of his own regarding Sonya. Judd had picked up the vibes sweltering between him and Sonya this afternoon. Since Garrett was already confused over his feelings for the woman, he didn't want to invite more opinions. Pushing thoughts of Sonya aside, he focused on the job.

They located the *Mary Jane* first. She was anchored just south of the cannery. The crew was on deck cooking salmon on a Hibachi grill. The sweet, tangy smell caused his stomach to rumble. He couldn't remember the last time he'd eaten well.

The crew groaned as Judd informed them they were coming aboard. Some days it was tough doing a job when nobody wanted you around.

"We ain't doing nothin'," hollered one of the men, dressed in sweats, short boots, and a stained sweatshirt. The man badly needed a shower. The stench overpowered the salmon sizzling on the grill and had the added benefit of silencing Garrett's stomach.

"Hell, we aren't even fishing," added another crewman, similarly dressed and also hygiene-handicapped.

"We're just here to ask a few questions concerning the *Double Dippin'*," Garrett said, taking a step back. How did these guys stand their own stink?

"Heard Sonya had some trouble," Stained Sweatshirt said. "Was she hurt bad?"

"Bad enough," Garrett replied.

"Pretty girl like that should be home making babies, you know what I mean?" He made an insulting hip thrust that had the two other guys hooting

Garrett clenched his fists. Judd took a step forward, grabbing the guy's attention. "Any information you can give us would be helpful."

"Don't have much to tell ya. We were fishing. Heard the news after it had all gone down."

"Who informed you?"

Stained Sweatshirt turned to the third crewman aboard, who was keeping an eye on the smoking salmon. "Ringo, where'd you hear the news about the *Double_D*?"

"Davida at the General Store."

Judd turned to Garrett, and his raised brow seemed to say they should have started their questioning there. They finished their interrogation, getting names, times, and places. Garrett knew in his gut that these guys didn't know anything. It was a relief to get off their boat and take a deep breath of clean air.

They tracked down the *Intrepid* next with pretty much the same results. Treat, the Captain of the *Miss Julie II*, pointed them in the direction that Garrett had wanted to start with.

Chuck Kendrick.

Treat was the first fisherman to regard them as less than fish slime. He was a fit, observant man, around Garrett's age with a shrewdness about him Garrett immediately connected with.

"Sonya's a fine fisherman," Treat said, hooking his thumbs in the belt loops of his jeans. "I hated hearing that she was hurt today. She going to be okay?"

"Sore for a while," Garrett answered steering the subject back to Kendrick. Recalling images of Sonya hurting and bleeding impaired his ability to do his job. "Tell me why you think Kendrick had a hand in this?"

"It's something sneaky the asshole would get off on. Saw Sonya cork off the *Albatross* the first day of fishing. That woman has balls." He chuckled, the sound full of admiration. "It was only a matter of time before Kendrick got back at her for it."

Kendrick's threat of payback seemed to keep most afraid to mess with him. "Have an idea where we might find the *Albatross?*"

"Try the bay. Kendrick doesn't like anchoring in the river with the rest of us. You know, it'd be like a rat sleeping with a pack of dogs. Most of us have something against the man."

"What do you have against him?"

"He sunk my boat." Treat's eyes hardened, and Garrett recognized the man's intention. Some day, somehow, Treat planned on getting his revenge against Kendrick.

Garrett recalled Skip informing him of the sinking of the first *Miss Julie* when he'd arrived in South Naknek. If his memory served him right, there hadn't been enough evidence to charge Kendrick with the crime, even though everyone knew he'd been the one responsible.

"Get the son of a bitch," Treat said. "Sonya didn't deserve what happened to her today."

CHAPTER SIXTEEN

At the insistence of everyone, Sonya was at the cabin being nursed to death by Grams. A whole day had passed. Twenty-four freaking hours. Wes had the *Double Dippin'* anchored off the set net sites where the men could keep watch while they fished the set net opening. Not only was Grams driving Sonya nuts with the constant attention, knowing that the men were fishing and she was stuck cabin-bound, was sending Sonya over the edge of her sanity.

She should be out there with them. Wanted to be. Damn it, she got a thrill picking fish out of the net. Drifting, she was always so busy piloting the boat, running the hydraulics, and keeping an eye out for the rest of the drifters. When they set netted, she actually got to pick fish.

Grams kneaded bread dough at the kitchen table, while Sonya had been confined to lie on the bed and not tax her stitches.

The smell of yeast drifted in the air. Nothing made a place feel homey like homemade bread. Fish camp was the only time during the year Grams went through the effort. She'd pulled her silver curls to the crown of her head and restrained them with a clip, a few fell softly around her flushed face. The woman was beautiful, still striking in her golden years.

Sonya hoped genetics would be as kind to her. Last night, after Grams had carefully helped her wash the blood from her hair, she'd gotten up the nerve to look in a mirror. Her refection had stared back at her in shock, giving her doubts that she'd ever look the same. She'd held it together though. Not a tear had fallen since those few traitors with Garrett.

"You have to quit thinking about it," Grams said, not looking up as she sprinkled more flour over the dough and kneaded it in. "You'll be turning heads just the same as always."

How had Grams known what she was thinking? "I'm not worried about that."

"Don't give me that gibberish. You are too." She slapped the dough into the waiting bowl and tossed a towel over it to rise. "If it were me, I'd be worrying about it." She dusted off her hands and then pulled another bowl out of the cupboard. Then she grabbed packages of chocolate chips, butterscotch chips, peanut butter chips, and M&M's.

Sonya sat up on the bed. "What are you making?"

Grams smiled, her dancing blue eyes twinkling. "Monster mug-up cookies."

"Seriously?" Her absolute favorite.

Grams got out the oatmeal and brown sugar. "Figured we could use a treat."

"Can I help?"

Grams laughed. "If I let you help, you'll eat all the M&M's."

Well, yeah.

"Besides," Grams continued. "You need to lie down and rest."

"Grams, lying down is driving me crazy. I'm not a layabout type of person."

153

"Neither was your father." Grams smile was bittersweet. "When he was sixteen he broke his leg skiing. He wasn't about to miss the rest of the season. He figured that his ski poles worked just as well as crutches. So, one night when your grandpa and I were out on a date, he duct-taped his cast to his ski and tried skiing down the driveway." She laughed at the memory.

"What happened? Did it work?"

"Oh, heavens no. We got home and had to rush him back to the hospital. Not only did he have to have another cast made for his broken leg, he received a matching one for his new broken arm." She shook her head. "I couldn't keep that boy down for nothing."

"Must be where Peter gets his wild hairs."

"Yep, and your father got them from your grandpa."

Sonya already knew that. There were times she had to fight the urge to do something wild herself. It obviously ran in the blood. Why else would she entertain the idea of getting Garrett alone? While he wasn't the man for her, he had the equipment to take care of a few of her urges.

Grams glanced up from mixing the butter, sugar, and eggs together. "Now you're thinking of a man. Your fish cop, by chance?" She reached for the jar of chunky peanut butter and spooned some into the bowl.

There was no point in lying to her. The woman could see through a solid steel door. "He's occupied a bit of my mind lately." More than a bit, if she were honest.

"He's a fine looking man. Nice butt. I can see why you're interested." She scooped four cups of oatmeal into the mix.

"*Grandma.*" Little old grandmas weren't supposed to check out men's butts.

"What woman wouldn't have noticed those tight buns?" Grams laid down the spoon and picked up a pocketknife. She sliced open the many bags of chips, pouring them each into the bowl.

Sonya swallowed. Okay that was it. She wasn't lying here any longer. She stood up and had to fight a wave of dizziness, results of residue from the pain killers she'd taken last night. Her head throbbed for a moment, but it felt good to move around.

"If you're not going to lie down, at least sit," Grams scolded, adding the package of M&M's to the bowl. She saved a handful and set them on the table for Sonya.

Sonya sat and began eating the chocolate pieces one by one. Did anything taste better than chocolate? She didn't think so.

"Sonya, is Garrett being a trooper all that's keeping you from having a relationship with him?"

"As barriers go, it's up there." Sonya popped a few more M&M's, hoping Grams would drop the subject. She wasn't up to discussing what was between her and Garrett.

"You're only a fisherman two months out of the year. What barrier does a trooper pose for a high school music teacher?"

"Logistics?" She didn't like where Grams was going with this. She really hadn't thought about what could happen with her and Garrett when fishing season was over. She didn't know if she wanted to. Fishing was a nice solid wall erected between them. She didn't like Grams poking holes in it.

"What logistics?" Grams asked. "I heard he lives in Homer. That's only an hour away, maybe an hour and a half depending on weather." Grams gave her a measured look. "What's really keeping you from starting a relationship with him?"

It was time for a subject change. "How do you stand being in this cabin all day?"

For a moment, it looked as if Grams wasn't going to let the subject of Garrett Hunt be pushed aside. She must have thought better of it, much to Sonya's relief.

"How do I stand it?" Grams repeated her question. "I treasure it. Don't get me wrong. I love Nikky, but the man can wear on the soul of a priest." She began dropping spoonfuls of dough onto a cookie sheet. "Since he retired, he's always underfoot. I never have time to myself. So, when everyone is out fishing, I get to read, carve, take long walks. Anything I want to. Sure there are chores, but even doing them is a pleasure when it's quiet."

Sonya had never looked at it from Grams' point of view. She'd always felt a twinge of guilt leaving her at camp all the time. It was good to know that she didn't feel like she was missing out on anything.

"Don't think this talk about Garrett is over," Grams said, sliding the cookie sheet into the propane oven. "He seems to be a good man. I love his take-charge attitude." She closed the oven door, set the timer, and met Sonya's gaze with her pointed one. "Besides, he has a strong enough character to equal your own. He'd be a good match for you, Sonya."

"Don't tell me you're playing matchmaker too?" Did she have old maid stamped across her forehead?

"Just telling you like I see it. Garrett's a keeper. A smart woman would recognize that and snag him."

Aidan slapped a piece of cheese between two slices of bread. He was so furious he could barely keep from punching the wall. Knowing that the punch would probably bring the shack down around him kept him from doing exactly that.

Lana sat quietly in the corner. She hadn't said two words to him since he'd found out what happened to Sonya yesterday. She'd buried her face in a book once they'd returned to camp. Classic avoidance. How had she missed the temper gene? She sure as hell would benefit with a bit of fire. What he wouldn't give to have some of her easy-going temperament. It would sure help pave the way with Sonya.

Sonya.

His heart ached.

Why hadn't someone from the Savonskis' camp told him what had happened to her? Didn't they realize how worried he'd be? Not just worried, he was frustrated as hell, and so angry he didn't know if he could pull it back. He'd had to hear the news from Davida. He'd made a run for groceries—seemed they were always out of stuff— after the fishing period had closed, and had picked up more than food.

Davida had said the troopers thought someone had shot Sonya's window with a slingshot. How she got her information, he didn't know, but he did know of someone who was very skilled with a slingshot.

Earl strolled into the cabin and spied the box of food sitting on the table. "Hey, you picked up more vittles." He seemed to be in good spirits for a change.

Why was that, Aidan wanted to know. Was it because Sonya was across the creek, sporting stitches from cuts his father's slingshot might have caused?

"Good thinking, Junior," Earl continued. "We was getting a might low on essentials." Earl rifled through the box, still packed with cereal, snacks, and canned goods. "Didn't you get any more beer?"

"Nope." There was enough drinking going on around here between his dad and Uncle Roland. He wasn't going to supply it for them. If they wanted to get stinking drunk, they could buy the beer themselves.

"Well, why the hell not? You wasted a whole trip to the cannery and didn't get a case of beer. What were you thinking?"

"I was thinking of Sonya." Aidan nailed him with a stare. Earl seemed to take notice that Aidan wasn't in a pretty mood himself. "You have anything to do with that?"

"With what?"

"Don't play dumb with me, old man. I know you heard what happened to her yesterday. Did you have anything to do with it?"

"Settle down, boy. Of course I didn't. How could I?"

"You're damn good with a slingshot. The only other person I know who can come close to you is Roland."

"I don't know if I should feel flattered or insulted. No matter how good I am, I couldn't make a shot like that from shore. Plus, why would I want to hurt Sonya?"

Why did Earl and Roland do half of the mean-spirited things they did? "Maybe you weren't after Sonya. Maybe you just wanted to cause trouble, like with their skiffs."

Earl laughed and shook his head. "You been smoking weed, boy?"

Not since high school. "Where were you and Roland yesterday afternoon?"

"You're overstepping yourself, Junior. You don't have the gonads to go up against me. So pull it back."

Aidan's fists clenched next to his sides. How he wanted to plant one right in his father's face, just like his dad used to do to his mother. Like he'd done to Aidan.

The man more than had it coming.

"Aidan?" Lana's hesitant voice broke through his need for vengeance. "Don't do it."

He turned and met her wide, fretful eyes. He looked back to his father, who seemed to delight in the confrontation. Realization hit him like a rogue wave.

Earl wanted Aidan to take a swing at him. Relished it.

Aidan fell back. He was staring into the cold, mean eyes of his future self, if he didn't gain control.

Earl shook his head in disgust when Aidan stepped back and relaxed his fists. "Sissy boy," he said, turning on his heel and slamming out of the cabin.

"Thank you, Aidan," Lana said. She earmarked the place in her book and rose to her feet. "I really appreciate you holding back. I know it wasn't easy." She combed golden hair back behind her ears with nervous fingers. "Do you really think Uncle Earl and my dad had something to do with Sonya getting hurt?"

"I don't know what to think." Aidan picked up the cheese sandwich he no longer wanted and offered it to Lana. She shook her head. He took a bite, not willing to waste the food even though he wasn't hungry anymore. The sandwich tasted stale with a hint of mold. Time to throw out the rest of the bread, if not the cheese.

"Why would our fathers do something like that?" Lana continued with her questions.

Aidan wished she'd stop. He didn't have an answer for her and he didn't want to think about what Earl and Roland were up to now. If their sick sense of amusement had targeted Sonya and her family, he needed to do more than think about it.

First, he had to see Sonya. "I'm going across the creek."

"Can I go with you?" Lana asked.

"No. I want to talk to Sonya alone. Why don't you see what you can fix for dinner?" He indicated the box of stuff on the table. "There should be something in there. You know how the parents get if they aren't fed on a regular basis." Roland and Earl weren't much different from the wild animals roaming the area. Trouble when full, deadly when empty.

Aidan left Lana to start dinner and headed across the creek and up the bank to the Savonski's cabin. He knocked and entered on Margaret's hollered, "Come in."

The cabin smelled like Christmas. Warm, inviting, sweet. So different from the cold, musty smell of his.

His gaze narrowed on Sonya as she sat at the table with her mug of tea and a stack of cookies. "Oh, Sonya." He swallowed past the lump in his throat at the sight of her injured face.

Margaret was at the sink, finishing dishes. She wiped her hands on a towel and hung it to dry. "Why don't I give you two a moment?"

"That's not necessary," Sonya was quick to interject.

"I've got to bring the laundry in from the line, anyway. I'll just be a minute." Margaret shared a look with Sonya that silenced her protests. Margaret liked to keep things neighborly, and Aidan knew her look had reminded Sonya of her manners.

"I appreciate that, Margaret," Aidan replied, opening the door for her to exit. He was grateful Sonya hadn't informed the Savonskis of what had transpired between them last summer. As far as they knew, Sonya and Aidan had had a tiff. He knew at least Nikolai still held out hope he and Sonya would kiss and make up.

Sonya frowned. "Gramps and the boys will be back any moment."

He'd seen them at the cannery, talking with Chet about the engine that had been sunk. Aidan had plenty of time before they returned. Any time Nikolai got around the machine shop, it took a while to tear him away. "You don't need to be afraid of me, Sonya. I won't hurt you."

"You did."

"I know." It had cost him the one person who'd meant the world to him. "I'll never make that mistake again."

She picked a cookie off the top of her stack and showed some of those manners Margaret had drilled into her. "Want one?"

It wasn't an olive branch, but he'd take it. "Thanks." Aidan sat across from her and bit into the cookie. The taste exploded in his mouth. "Oh, man." He groaned. "Monster mug-ups?" Sonya nodded. "Damn, these are good. How do you have just one?"

She indicated the stack. "You can't. This is my dinner."

They ate in silence for a moment as Aidan cataloged her appearance. "How are you feeling?"

"Fine." She shrugged and then winced as the motion caused her pain. "As long as I don't move much."

The anger he felt now was different than the explosive, out-of-control rage he usually dealt with. This slipped through his blood like oil, coating and smothering, and seemed a hell of a lot more dangerous. "Tell me what happened."

She did, and it was all he could do to keep the knot tight on his temper.

"You think it was an accident?" he asked. Fishing was dangerous, accidents happened. Just the nature of the beast could bring out the worst in people. Limited time, limited catch, limited potential to make a lot of money. "This doesn't sound like an accident."

"That's what Garrett said."

Hunt again. He stuffed a cookie in his mouth to keep the biting words back. Of course, the fish cop *would* be involved. A crime had been committed. At least someone was looking out for her when he couldn't. "Who was drift-ing by you?" She listed the boats, all the while acting as though the whole incident was no big deal. When she mentioned the *Albatross*, Aidan knew he had a target. The son of a bitch deserved whatever mean Aidan could de-liver his way.

"Kendrick makes the most sense," Sonya said. "I don't know who else had the opportunity. I don't know anyone on board the *Intrepid*. The crew of the *Mary Jane* are usually too stoned to hit anything they aim at. Treat, on the *Miss Julie II*, would be shooting at Kendrick rather than at me. So that leaves Kendrick."

Unless someone was a proficient marksman like Roland or Earl, Aidan couldn't help thinking.

If Kendrick was responsible that meant his father wasn't. He knew Earl and Roland didn't have a lot of boundaries when it came to mischief, but thinking that they could have targeted Sonya with their sick little games was more than uncomfortable.

"What are you going to do now?" he asked.

"What do you mean?"

"There's a drift opening tomorrow."

"Yeah."

"Don't tell me you plan on fishing? Cut up like you are."

She tightened her lips and just stared at him.

"You are, aren't you?" His temper flared and a few flames got away from him. "Damn it, Sonya. Why are you doing this?"

"Doing what, Aidan?" She dropped her cookie and sat back on the bench. "Fishing?"

"Look at you? Have you seen your face?"

"Yes." Her eyes wavered and he knew he'd touched a nerve. She wasn't as cool and collected as she appeared.

"You need to take care of yourself. Scars aren't worth catching some damn fish for."

"The permit is in my name. I have to be on the boat."

Aidan took a breath. He understood that there was no calling in sick during fishing. You either fished or lost out. The idea of Sonya out there working, in her condition, more than bothered him.

She flicked him a glance. He hated that look in her eyes. He'd caused that. Only he could fix it. So he swallowed his temper with another bite of cookie. "Be careful tomorrow. I don't want anything else to happen to you." Her eyes widened and he realized she'd expected his normal dressing down. "You matter to me, Sonya."

♃

That was twice in two days that a man had told her she mattered. What was going on? Sonya stared at Aidan who looked so sincere. She knew he cared about her, but she also didn't wanted to be with a man who "cared about a woman" the way he did.

The cookies were making her sick. She probably shouldn't have gorged herself on them. They'd tasted so good, comforting, like the loving hugs her mother used to give her when she was younger.

"Aidan, I appreciate you coming to check on me, but I'm tired." She let all her worry and exhaustion show through. She'd done her best to hide it all day. She didn't want Grams to report to Gramps that she wasn't up to fishing tomorrow. She had something to prove. Not only to herself, but to the other fishermen who might be under the guise that she wasn't cut out to fish. She especially had something to prove to the asshole who'd decided to pick on her. If what happened to her had happened to a man, there would be no question if he'd be fishing tomorrow. There'd be plenty of time to rest and heal after the season was over.

She needed to get rid of Aidan. She didn't like seeing him this way, gazing at her like a kicked puppy. It messed with her resolutions. They'd always been friends, until they'd decided to take that friendship to the next level. How she wished they hadn't. She could use a friend right now. Someone who wasn't looking at her to be captain and call the shots or family members wanting to smother her with concern. Someone who could be a sounding board, where she could vent, get angry, or cry.

Aidan got to his feet. "Get some sleep. But, Sonya, promise me that if you need anything, you'll let me know."

"Thanks, Aidan," she said, wishing, more than she liked, that she could take him up on his offer.

CHAPTER SEVENTEEN

Frustration ate at Garrett like maggots on a dead fish. They'd yet to find Kendrick. It hadn't helped matters that they'd been called away on a search and rescue that had turned search and recovery because some idiot had gotten drunk and fallen overboard. The Coast Guard had been sent in from Kodiak, but they still hadn't found a body. It had been over twenty-four hours. With the way the Bristol Bay tides tore in and out, they weren't going to find one. Just another statistic added to alcohol related deaths in Bristol Bay.

"Garrett," Skip hollered from the cabin to where he stood at the bow, scanning the unusually calm waters of the incoming tide. "Just got a transmission from Miller." Miller was one of the troopers stationed as a spotter on land. "He caught sight of the *Albatross* headed for the line."

Garrett gave Skip a smile full of satisfaction. He glanced at his watch. Drifting was scheduled to open in just under an hour. Kendrick was out early, obviously to claim a choice fishing spot.

"Do you want to intercept?" Skip took one look at Garrett. "Right. Setting a course. But you get to be the one who wakes Judd."

Judd had headed below to catch a few winks before the opening. He wouldn't get many. They were all operating on no sleep and too much caffeine. Garrett knew he was probably not in the best shape to interrogate Kendrick. Not that it would stop him. The man had proved elusive and Garrett wasn't letting the opportunity pass him by.

He managed to get a grumbling Judd out of bed and an energy drink down him just as Skip pulled alongside the *Albatross*.

"*Albatross*, prepare to be boarded," Garrett yelled over the loud speaker. Never had the words been so satisfying to say.

"You're enjoying this aren't you?" Skip asked not needing an answer. He regarded Garrett and frowned. "Maybe I should question Kendrick in your place."

"Kendrick's mine."

Skip shared a look with Judd that Garrett didn't even pretend not to see.

"You boys have a problem?"

Judd slowly shook his head. "Nope."

"You aren't in your right head," Skip added.

"Let me do my job."

"Good enough for me," Judd said, stretching his arms above his head. "Let's go catch us a bird." His comment had the desired effect of cutting the tension.

"Just keep it by the book," Skip said.

Garrett nodded, itching to get aboard the *Albatross* and make Kendrick squirm like the worm he was.

Kendrick stood on deck, his beefy hands fisted on hips that were overshadowed by a robust belly. A scraggly beard mottled his face in calico colors. What hair remained on his head blew like tufts of goose down in the biting breeze. His sharp gray eyes screamed mean. They told Garrett Kendrick had long since buried his soul somewhere in the dark, deep ocean.

"What the hell do you want with me now?" Kendrick hollered as Garrett swung over the rail onto his deck.

"I want answers." Garret stood in front of Kendrick, not intimidated by his size as Kendrick loomed over him. Garrett had taken down bigger men. Judd followed and stood quietly behind him to the left.

"Answers?" Kendrick asked. "Did you have to board my boat for that? We're getting ready to fish." Kendrick's Brutus-arms swung wide, indicating his crew.

Two other men stood nearby, one thin as a rail looking like a tough piece of jerky, the other average, non-descript, except for the tattoo of a skull on his forehead. The guy obviously had no imagination. The three looked like a trio of schoolyard bullies.

"Day before yesterday," Garrett began, "just after two in the afternoon, the *Double Dippin's* window was shattered and her captain injured. You were in the vicinity."

"Is that a fact? Hurt, was she?" A gleam snaked through Kendrick's eyes, turning them an eerie pearl. "How bad?" He gave a sinister smile, showing a row of front teeth badly needing an introduction to a toothbrush.

Garrett wanted to wipe that black smile right off Kendrick's face with an ache so great it made him shake.

Kendrick relaxed against the large fishing reel wrapped with net, and folded his arms across his bulky chest. "Is this what your visit's about? Sonya Savonski? The woman's a looker...at least, she was." He made a clicking sound with his tongue. "That little girl's gonna end up fish food, if she's not careful."

"Is that a threat?"

"Why don't we call it an observation."

Judd grabbed Garrett as he lunged for Kendrick, and held him tight. "He's not worth it, man."

Garrett struggled to shake off his need to retaliate. He clenched his jaw and planted his feet on the deck. He knew better then to let a suspect provoke him. What the hell had gotten into him?

"Ah, personal is it?" Kendrick taunted, obviously enjoying Garrett's momentary loss of control. "I didn't think Sonya would sink low enough to fuck a fish cop."

Fury gnawed at the thin thread of control Garrett hung onto. He wanted to kill the son of a bitch. How had this asshole lived as long as he had without someone doing exactly that?

Judd stepped in. "Did you take a shot at the *Double Dippin*?"

Kendrick buffed his nails on his dirty shirt. "Did anyone see me do it?"

The man was rubbing their noses in it. Kendrick knew if they'd had a witness, he'd already *be* charged with criminal mischief and assault. For the first time in his law enforcement career, Garrett wanted to go vigilante.

"Do you have a slingshot onboard?" Garrett asked, taking over the questioning. He wouldn't let this bully get the better of him.

"Sure. I've got a slingshot aboard. There's also a gaff hook, a few knives, a handgun. You get the idea. This is Alaska. A man never knows what he's going to come up against."

"We'd like to see the slingshot." Garrett doubted it would tell them anything, but it might make Kendrick squirm.

"You gotta warrant?" Kendrick acted bored with the conversation.

So much for squirming. Garrett had no witnesses. He couldn't search the boat without a warrant, and he couldn't haul Kendrick's ass up on charges without him confessing.

He didn't see Kendrick volunteering to do that. Right now, all he had was speculation. The reality of the situation stank like this boat.

Fishy.

Garrett paused. Why *did* the *Albatross* smell so bad? He looked at the deck. It was wet. There had been no rain in the forecast for a change. Had the man been fishing in closed waters? Was that the reason they hadn't been able to find him?

"Judd, something smell fishy to you?" Garrett signaled to Judd, pointing at the wet deck.

"Something does smell rank." Judd caught on.

"What you got in the holds, Kendrick?" Garrett asked. He smiled when not only Kendrick squirmed, but so did his crew.

Gotcha.

"Like I said," Kendrick repeated, his eyes hardening to steel. "You got a search warrant?"

"Don't need one if there's suspicion of illegal fishing." Garrett looked at Judd. "Do we?"

"Nope." Judd's smile was as wide as Garrett's.

He gestured to the skull-tatted crewman. "Open the holds." The crewman glanced at Kendrick. Garrett swore steam wafted off the man's body. The crewman moved toward the hold, bent, and lifted the cover.

"Well, well. What do we have here?" A brailer full of fresh red salmon lay packed like sardines in a can. *Man, he loved his job.* "Open the other holds. Please," Garrett instructed politely, enjoying himself.

Jerky man swore and kicked a bucket. Kendrick eyed Garrett with malice, and Garrett smiled wider in return.

"Didn't you hear?" Judd asked, shaking his head. "Crime doesn't pay."

"Kendrick," Garrett added. "I hope you don't have any priors. You could be looking at jail time, if that's the case." He couldn't help doing some taunting of his own. This was the most fun he'd had in days.

Kendrick stared at him, his face getting redder as each fish hold revealed more illegally caught salmon.

CHAPTER EIGHTEEN

They returned from escorting the *Albatross* to the tender, confiscating the drift boat's catch, and writing Kendrick up for fishing in closed waters. Skip grinned ear to ear, looking happy as he steered the *Calypso* back to the mouth of the river. Garrett filled his empty stomach with a bag of salt and vinegar chips.

They badly needed to get some real food.

"Can you believe Kendrick had eight thousand pounds of illegally caught fish on his boat?" Judd shook his head again, reaching over and helping himself to Garrett's chips.

Yes, Garrett could. The man thought he was above the law. Kendrick had been taught a lesson this morning, and Garrett had enjoyed being the one to teach it. "The State of Alaska is a little richer today."

"Wait until Kendrick shows up in court, and they fine him ten thousand big ones, and possibly confiscate his boat and gear." Judd chuckled and shook his head. "You should have seen the SEAL man, Skip. One minute he was ready to tear Kendrick apart, the next he was smiling like a kid at a surprise birthday party."

"Did you touch Kendrick?" Skip asked, worry stealing his happy grin.

"Naw," Judd answered as he dug his hand into Garrett's bag of chips again. "I pulled him back in time."

Garrett shoved the bag at him and wished he'd stuff his mouth.

"What do you mean you pulled him back in time?" Skip's shrewd eyes narrowed.

"I didn't touch the scumbag," Garrett pointed out, knowing it was too late to stop the unofficial advice Skip would deal out. It sucked that Skip was right. He'd never lost his cool on the job. He knew Sonya was at the heart of the reason why.

"This time." Skip tightened his jaw. "Face it, man. Your relationship with Sonya Savonski is interfering with your ability to do your job."

"I don't have a relationship with Sonya." Hell, they hadn't even slept together. Even though he battled a serious need to. A relationship implied that they were a couple. She was ashamed to be seen with him.

"Right." Judd scoffed, a few crumbs flew out of his mouth. "What would you call it then? I've got an itch for Davida. You're craving Sonya like a starving man craves a meal. You're seriously smitten, dude."

He was seriously something. Question was, what was he going to do about it?

"You need to keep a clear head so there is no conflict of interest," Skip said. "I don't have to tell you where our case against Kendrick would stand, if you'd laid a hand on him."

In the toilet.

He was right. The situation with Kendrick could have gotten out of control. If Judd hadn't been there to pull him back, Garrett didn't know what he would have done.

He needed to do something about Sonya.

J

Once the fishing period had closed for the day, Garrett located the *Double Dippin'*, boarded, and found her captain in a mood that matched the foul weather that had returned. He was dressed in raingear as rain slashed him. Sheets of water fell so hard that it splashed the ocean with enough force to send water raining upward. His gear wasn't doing much to keep him dry. The evening had darkened with the storm-filled clouds showing themselves. Any leftover light from the sun was buried deep under bruised and boiling thunderheads.

"I'm not up for company, Garrett," Sonya said, standing in the open doorway of the pilot house. She'd tied up to the cannery's dock for the night, which made it easy to locate her. He knew if he'd tried to contact her via the radio, he'd be facing more than her cranky attitude.

"This isn't a social call." Garrett planted a foot on the step to the pilot house. "I'd thought you'd like to know what happened with Kendrick."

She seemed to struggle for a moment, but when she glanced around to see if anyone was watching he knew he had permission to come aboard. The weather was angry enough to keep everyone inside somewhere warm and dry. Where he wanted to be.

"Get in here," she muttered.

As invitations went, he'd had better, but the wind and wet were getting the best of him and he hurried up the stairs. She'd pulled homemade curtains—printed with puffins—over the windows, making the area seem smaller, cozier. He could see where she'd patched the broken glass with a sheet of plastic and duct tape. He pushed back his hood, pulled open the snaps to his rain jacket, and soaked in the sight of her. "How are you feeling?"

She tightened her lips before answering. "Fine."

She wasn't fine. The circles under her eyes were more pronounced, though the fire in her gaze was hot enough to warm him. She was dressed in gray sweats, wool socks, and a hoodie with a picture of a large Alaskan mosquito with the words, "Bite Me," written across the front.

He didn't need anymore ideas where she was concerned and wondered for a moment if she chose clothes to dress her body or her mood. Her silky dark hair lay loose around her face and shoulders. She'd combed a section to fall over the bandage on her forehead. The length of hair failed to hide the butterfly stitches marring her cheek. Her long day of fishing had obviously been too long.

"You staying on the boat tonight?" he asked, knowing the answer. She looked dressed for bed. Besides, he doubted she'd planned on heading to camp with the rain pelting outside.

"Yes."

"Alone?" He hoped to God she wasn't going to be alone tonight. Not only for her safety, in case Kendrick decided to cause more trouble.

"No, Peter went for ice cream and pizza. He'll be back soon."

He breathed a sigh of relief. "Comfort food?"

She cracked a smile. "Yeah. I'd really like a serving of KFC's mash potatoes and gravy. My mom used to get me that when I didn't feel well."

He shared her smile. "It's homemade mac'n'cheese for me. No one makes it like my mom does."

They stared at each other until the silence dragged and sexual tension pressed. The pilot house was too inviting, too intimate, and they were too alone.

Where the hell was Peter?

This was not going the way he'd wanted this visit to go. A few moments in her company, and all he could think about was how did he get her into bed? This was definitely going against the plan.

She nervously licked her lips and then blurted out, "Kendrick? You came to tell me what happened."

The name snapped him back from images of her naked in his arms. He'd come here to put a stop to thoughts like that. She was interfering with his job, his sleep, his life. Right now he was supposed to be…oh hell, what was he supposed to do? Right, Kendrick. He quickly informed her what had transpired earlier that day, enjoying her smile when he got to the part of the *Albatross's* illegal take.

"Nice." She grinned, the emotion reaching her eyes, making them glimmer with warmth in the low lighting from the battery operated lantern.

"It made up for not getting him for hurting you." Garrett stepped back and came into contact with the counter behind him. Sonya was pressed up against the bunk across from him.

Only a few feet separated them.

"You don't know for sure that Kendrick was responsible." Sonya brought him back to their discussion.

"He was smug, all but dying to tell me he'd been the one who'd shot out your window."

"I knew he'd get me back for corking him off, but I didn't think he'd take it that far." She picked at the cuff of her sleeve. "I should have."

He frowned. "Is there more I should know here?"

She sighed, raised her hand to run it through her hair, and bumped her stitches. She winced. "Damn, I keep forgetting." She smoothed a length of long bangs over the bandage. "Do you think Kendrick was the one who cut loose and sunk our skiffs? The hydraulic lines?"

"He wouldn't cop to it, but it seems like something he'd get off on. He's been flagged with the illegal fishing. Every trooper in the bay will be keeping an eye on him from now on."

"He's not going to like that."

"No, he isn't. So, continue to be on guard." He angled toward the door, ready to say his goodbyes, but she stopped him with a hand on his arm. He looked up from her fingers wrapped around his forearm to her dark slumberous eyes.

"Garrett. Thanks. I know I haven't been very... uhm...appreciative of your position, but thanks for what you've done for me and my family."

"Sonya." Her name came out as a growl, and he couldn't stop himself from cradling the back of her neck and taking her mouth, being careful of her stitches. She moaned, opening her lips for him, and he sank into her.

He inhaled sharply and instead of releasing her like he knew he should, he dropped his hands from her neck to her breasts, and roughly slanted his mouth possessively over hers.

She arched into him, her own hands cupping his butt and pulling him to her as she met his kiss with demands of her own. Fire flamed at the base of his spine and he pressed his throbbing erection against her. She whimpered. The sexy sound had him losing the last bit of control he held onto. He grabbed her by the hips, lifted, and sat her on the edge of the bunk. He spread her legs and settled hard between them, rubbing his shaft against her sex. She tore her mouth from his and let her head fall back on a cry. The motion was seductive as hell. He kissed down the arch of her incredibly enticing neck, nipping at her fluttering pulse.

His hands slipped under her "Bite Me" sweatshirt to find her breasts bare. He gave a ragged groan. Her nipples were hard and swollen, and his greedy fingers played and plucked them into harder peaks. Her hands went on a trek of their own, snaking under his shirt, knocking off his rain jacket, kneading his muscles until he groaned with pleasure.

He wanted to drown in her. He could feel her heat through the thin barrier of her sweatpants. It'd take nothing to strip her of them, and then he'd be inside her. The thought was heaven and pure hell. He'd already taken this further than he'd planned.

Hell, he'd planned on speaking his peace and getting away from her so this wouldn't happen.

He took a deep breath, but instead of helping to clear his head, he breathed in more of her seductive scent. "You're making this really difficult, Sonya."

"I'm a difficult woman, Garrett." He heard the smile in her voice as her fingers glided over his nipples. His knees shook. "Anything worth having is worth working hard to get."

Damn, but he was willing to work hard for her. Anything she wanted. Any way she wanted it.

No, no. Getting way off track, man. Pull yourself together, and get your ass out of here.

It took everything he had to step back, his breathing shallow and quick. He had to break away from her, save himself. Or he'd be lost.

Her hair was tousled like they'd already gone at each other for hours. Her lips were red and swollen, and begged him for another taste. Her eyes were large dark pools of sinful promises he wanted to cash in.

"You're messing with my job," Garrett blurted out.

"Excuse me?" Those sinful eyes clouded with confusion as she sat up straighter.

"I can't sleep. You're in my head, my blood. I would have taken on Kendrick if Judd hadn't been there to pull me back. I can't focus. Making love with you is only going to make that worse."

"You don't think working each other out of our systems would do the trick?" She adjusted the clothing he'd just had his hands under.

"As much as I like your reasoning, no, I don't." When he finally slept with her, he'd be an addict for sure. That thought alone scared the shit out of him and had him stepping farther back in the confined space. Sonya wasn't the kind of woman he usually hooked up with. There was nothing casual about her. A relationship with her would have expectations. *She'd* have expectations. She wouldn't be content to let him come and go. She'd demand a commitment. Maybe even one that required a ring.

He broke out in a sweat. He was not marriage material. He wouldn't do that to a woman, especially this one. Not when he already cared about her far too much.

"Let me get this straight." She narrowed her eyes and shook her head as though needing to clear her thoughts also. "A no-strings-attached affair is too much for you?"

"Don't kid yourself on the no-strings part." He already felt the pull where she was concerned. The more run-ins like this, the tighter those strings wove together. Her eyes hardened with resolve.

Was he the only one who felt this way?

"I think it's time for you to go." Her frosty tone spoke volumes.

"Sonya—"

"No." She indicated the door not a few feet away. "I think you can find your way out."

Just then footsteps scuffled as someone boarded the boat.

"That will be Peter." Sonya folded her arms across her chest. "He sure took long enough."

The door flew open. "It's raining like—Oh...hi, Garrett." Peter stood in the doorway holding a pizza box from the Pitt, rain splattered on the hood and shoulders of his raingear. "Sorry, Sonya, no ice cream. Davida laughed when I asked if she had any. So I brought you a few candy bars." He held up a bag full of at least a dozen or more. He glanced at Garrett and then to Sonya, obviously feeling the thick tension in the small room. "Everything okay?"

"Everything's fine. Garrett was just leaving." She turned to Garrett and raised a brow. "Weren't you?"

"Yes, I was." He gazed at Sonya, knowing he should say something to fix the mess he'd made of things, but knew whatever he said would make the situation worse. He reached down, picked up the rain jacket Sonya had stripped him out of, and ignored Peter's interested gaze. At the door, he turned. "I'd feel better if you were anchored in front of your camp. Tied up here at the docks, it's like putting a goldfish in a tank of piranhas."

"Garrett," Sonya said, "I'm no goldfish."

CHAPTER NINETEEN

Man, she was tired. Sore, cold, bone-dead tired. She and Peter had just finished picking and pulling the nets at the set net sites. If she ever got through this eternally long line of bobbing skiffs, loaded down with fish, waiting to tender, then she could sleep.

They moved up the line. The *Time Bandit* sat in the channel of the river, large and towering above them. Floating in her shadow, made Sonya feel small and insignificant. Peter sat quietly in the bow. He was tired too. She saw it in the hunching of his shoulders. Was she asking too much of him, of her crew? They hadn't complained, and every night Peter was figuring out his percentage of the take. Money had a way of keeping people working past their stopping point. Next year, she'd better hire another crewman to help with the workload.

Aidan did have a point, she had to concede. He'd told her she didn't have enough crew. They'd make it through this year, but next she'd have to make some changes.

"Finally," Peter said as it was their turn to tender. "How long have we been waiting?"

"Too long." She motored the skiff alongside the tender. Peter grabbed the painter's line and tied a quick clove hitch, securing the bow to the *Time Bandit*. She did the same in the stern and then killed the engine. It was the only engine currently running. She'd tried to talk to Gramps again about buying a new one to replace the drowned engine, but he wouldn't hear of it. Until he had the water-logged one up and running—if fixing it was even possible—they were down to one skiff fishing four set net sites. No wonder she and Peter were so tired.

The tender lowered the crane with the cabled scale for the first brailer. Sonya steadied the scale while Peter ran the ropes through the corner ears of the brailer bag, and then secured them to the hook on the digital scale. Sonya waited for Peter to step back, and then signaled for the tender to pull up the heavy brailer full of fish.

Slowly the hydraulic crane raised the brailer, then it suddenly swung wide. Straight for Peter standing in the bow.

"Look out!" Sonya screamed, watching in horror as the brailer hit Peter. He tumbled overboard into the cold, angry water. Sonya rushed to the edge of the skiff, screaming his name. There was no sign of him in the dark, murky water. "Peter!"

Vaguely, she heard orders yelled from the *Time Bandit* above her. Noise rushed like a waterfall in her ears, an alarm sounded, and everything around her slowed. Please God, she prayed, she couldn't lose another loved one to this damned ocean

Sonya blinked, seeing flames of the past licking the Mystic *as she burned into the ocean. Sasha's screams pierced the night as she struggled in the water. The silence. Frigid, thick water swept her mother, as she bobbed face down on the surface, away from Sonya's grasping reach.*

Peter suddenly surfaced, sputtering, breaking the death-hold of the past Sonya had sunk into.

"Damn, this water is cold," he said.

Sonya choked as tears ran unchecked down her face. She stretched over the edge and tried to reach Peter with her hands, but he was too far. The river current swept him farther as each second ticked away. "Hold on, Peter."

"Onto what?" he asked, fighting his rain gear to tread water.

"Get your chest waders off," yelled one of the guys on the tender. If Peter didn't get them off now, they'd fill up with water and drag him down to his grave.

"T-trying," Peter said, pulling at the snaps on his rain jacket. Then his head dipped under the water again.

"Peter!" *Oh, God.* She was going to lose him too. As though sound were being filtered through a long tunnel, she heard commotion going on above her as the crew on the *Time Bandit* scrambled to help. An inflatable ring landed on the surface of the water where Peter had gone under. Sonya whimpered and ripped off her rain jacket, struggling to unsnap the hooks of her own chest waders, ready to jump in after him.

He finally resurfaced.

"Damn, that w-wasn't easy," he tried to joke. Sonya sobbed and snatched the boat hook, reaching it out into the water for Peter to grab on to. It wasn't long enough.

"I gotcha, Peter," Aidan hollered, appearing from out of nowhere with Lana. He maneuvered his skiff next to Peter. Sonya shook with relief as Aidan pulled Peter into his boat with Lana's help. "Got him, Sonya."

"Peter?" Sonya hollered, not able to control the shrill tone of her voice. She needed to see him, hold him, know for herself that he was okay.

With Aidan's help, Peter stood, soaking wet and shaking. "I'm f-fine, S-Sonya. J-just c-c-cold."

"Sonya, you finish up there," Aidan called. "I'll get him safely back to camp and warmed up." Aidan was already stripping Peter out of his wet outer clothes and giving him the ones off his back. "Don't worry, Sonya. I'll get him back safe. He'll be fine and have one hell of a great story to tell."

Still, she stood at the rail of her skiff not able to look away from her shivering brother.

"Sonya!" She jerked at Aidan's tone and tore her eyes from Peter to meet Aidan's.

"Take care of business, and then join us at camp." He paused, his eyes boring into hers. "Can you do that?"

She glanced at the three remaining brailers full of fish in the bottom of her skiff and then to the men on deck of the tender, waiting for her to give the signal to lower the crane. She stared back at Peter shivering in Aidan's jacket, with Lana's arms wrapped around him. He needed to get warm, and she was holding everyone up.

"Y-yes. I can do that." Her voice gained strength. "Get him back to camp."

"Yes, ma'am." Aidan gave her a proud smile and a salute. Peter sent her a wobbly grin and a thumbs up signal.

Sonya's heart pounded so hard in her chest, that for a moment it was the only sound she heard. Then she straightened her shoulders and motioned for the boom to be lowered. The sooner she finished unloading her catch, the sooner she could get back to camp. Then she'd make sure every hair on Peter's head was okay.

"I don't know how I can ever thank you, Aidan." Sonya had returned to camp to find Grams mothering Peter with cookies and hot chocolate, and Gramps mummifying him with blankets as her brother regaled them with the telling of his impromptu swim. He had a bruise darkening the side of his face where the brailer had hit him. He was lucky that he didn't have a concussion. The brailer had been seven hundred pounds heavy with salmon. If he'd been knocked unconscious when he'd hit the water—

She couldn't go there. Sonya swallowed the cocktail of panic and tears she'd been fighting all afternoon and tried to put forth a calm front. Aidan brushed the side of her arm, stealing her attention.

"Walk with me?" His eyes beseeched her to agree.

She nodded and let him escort her outside. She could use some air.

They walked for a bit in the tall grass behind the cabins, to where the ground leveled onto the flat lying tundra. Yellow buttercups bloomed over the thick, spongy ground, while bees buzzed in a frenzied attempt to gather nectar before the end of the short summer. The breeze blew enough to keep the mosquitoes and gnats from bothering them.

"Are you all right?" Aidan asked.

"I will be." She tried for a reassuring smile, gave up and hugged her arms around her middle instead, ignoring the slight pull of the stitches in her shoulder. "I can't thank you enough for what you did today, Aidan."

"I didn't do more than what anyone else would have done if they'd been in my position."

Sonya disagreed. If it had been someone like Chuck Kendrick there instead of Aidan...

She was ashamed that she hadn't acted quicker herself. She'd frozen like ice at seeing her brother fight for his life as the nightmare of the past faded over the present.

Aidan brushed the side of her uninjured cheek with his fingers, bringing her back from seeing Peter struggling in the cold, deadly water.

"Hey, it's okay. Peter's fine." When she didn't move away he slowly wrapped his arms around her. He rubbed her back, being careful not to touch around the healing cut on her shoulder, and spoke soothing words until her breaths grew even.

It felt good to be back in his arms. Comfortable. She'd missed him, or at least missed what could have been. She let her head rest against the space where his neck met his shoulder, not caring that the action knocked her ball cap to the ground. She breathed in his scent of dark sea breezes and stormy skies. She used to love curling into him and having his strong arms wrap around her, like she was the most cherished thing he'd ever beheld.

"Sonya," Aidan said her name on a groan, his lips brushing against the side of her neck.

Encouraging Aidan was wrong. No matter how good it felt to be held by him again, she had to stop this. She'd thought she'd shut the lid on her feelings for him. She guessed some had slipped out when she hadn't been looking.

"Aidan—"

"Sweetheart, don't push me away." Aidan tightened his arms around her, his grasp desperate. "Just let me hold you."

"I can't do this, Aidan." Her throat thickened with trepidation. Or was it regret? She wasn't sure. "Please, let me go."

Aidan breathed deep, and for a moment, she feared he wouldn't release her. He stepped back, still grasping her upper arms in his calloused palms, his grip loose, being careful with the still-tender cuts on her arm.

"I've changed, Sonya." His dark eyes bore into hers, as though pleading with her to believe him. "You don't have to be afraid of me anymore."

She saw remorse, longing, and sincerity. Could he have changed? If so, was she willing to risk it?

"Heard you had some more trouble." Garrett's voice—hard and sharp—cut through her musings.

Sonya jerked in Aidan's embrace, seeing Garrett over Aidan's shoulder. She immediately took in the uniform, the shades hiding his ice-blue eyes, and the gun at his side—his hand resting right next to the butt of the handle. Without a doubt he didn't like Aidan's hands on her or the situation he'd come upon.

She stepped away from Aidan, who'd stiffened when Garrett had interrupted them, his hands falling away from her. Personally, she was glad for the interruption. She felt like fog had rolled in over her brain when Aidan had touched her. She needed time to clear it out and see the lay of the land.

"Yes, we had some trouble," Sonya said, keeping her voice calm, feeling like she was caught between two opposing forces. "Peter went for an unscheduled swim." She moved to stand between the two men. The testosterone thickening the air was enough to send a wandering wolf hightailing it to higher ground.

"Is he all right?" Garrett asked, not relaxing his stance.

"He's fine," she answered, unsure how to dispel the situation.

"Do you think it was an accident?" Garrett raised a brow. His questioning brow directed toward Aidan.

"Hey!" Aidan took a threatening step toward Garrett.

Sonya pushed her palm against Aidan's chest. She so did not want to be caught like a bone between these two men. "Garrett, Aidan saved Peter's life."

"Convenient." Garrett had yet to move. He stood there like a damn predator waiting for an excuse to attack.

Aidan pushed against Sonya's restraining hand. "Why you—"

"Enough!" Sonya yelled. "This isn't about Peter. Neither of you have a claim on me. So knock it off." She dropped her hand from Aidan's chest. "You want to go all caveman? Fine, but I'm not sticking around to watch." With that she stomped around Garrett with the intention of leaving both men standing there on the tundra.

"Sonya," Garrett's low, warning voice brought her to a quick stop.

She turned back and faced him. "What?"

"I want to know *exactly* what happened today."

The way Garrett said "exactly" told her there was no way she'd be stomping off. Garrett looked at Aidan. "Keep yourself available. When I'm done speaking to Sonya, I want to talk to you."

"What?" Aidan scoffed. "Like don't leave town?"

"If you want to look at it that way."

"Garrett, this is ridiculous," Sonya said, surprised that she was coming to Aidan's defense again. First the gunshots when he'd shot at the *Albatross* and now this, what was with her? Aidan had saved Peter's life when she hadn't been able to move. She owed Aidan more than she could ever repay. "Aidan is a hero."

"Then why the delay in telling me what happened out there today?" Garrett raised that damn eyebrow again. She wished she could see his eyes, instead of her reflection in his mirrored sunglasses. It was like talking to a machine.

"Fine." She gestured wide with her arms. "Where do you want to do this? Here? Or down at the station?" Was there even a police station located in South Naknek?

"Here's fine. Unless you'd prefer—"

"No." She sighed. "Let's get it over with." She glanced at Aidan. "Give us a minute, will you?"

"Are you sure?"

"Yeah."

Aidan looked as though he was ready to wrestle the big, bad fish cop for her if she asked. Aidan rescued her fallen hat and dusted it off before handing it to her. The thought warmed and made her uncomfortable as Garrett watched their interaction.

"Thanks, Aidan." Sonya didn't glance at Garrett as she slipped on her ball cap.

"I'll be in the cabin." Aidan said. "You need *anything* I'm just a holler away." He sent a warning look toward Garrett that bounced off his State Trooper getup.

CHAPTER TWENTY

Just as he was making headway with Sonya, the damn fish cop had to go and show up.

Aidan plodded his way to the cabin. Leaving Sonya in the company of the trooper itched like dried fish scales on his skin. When he'd first seen Garrett Hunt, he'd known the man was trouble.

Sonya practically smoldered with sexual curiosity whenever she looked at Hunt. That sexual energy was supposed to be directed at *him*.

She was his.

He understood that he had things working against him. He didn't come from a settled, loving family like she did. That didn't mean he couldn't provide for her. He made a decent living. His graphic novels had garnered a lot of attention lately. He knew things were financially tough for Sonya. Raising Peter on her own couldn't have been a picnic. She'd have more help from her grandparents, if she asked for it. His Sonya wasn't the type of woman to ask for anything, which was a large part of her appeal. She didn't appear to need anyone. He wanted to change that. If given the right circumstances, Sonya would need him. Today he'd made progress in helping her realizing it.

That was until Hunt had shown up with his accusations. If that trooper had her doubting him, he'd—

Aidan stopped in his tracks. What was he doing? This wasn't who he was. These thoughts weren't his. Sonya wouldn't respond positively to his manhandling her again.

If he laid a hand on Hunt, Sonya's sympathies would be with Hunt. The trooper was right now, talking trash about him. Trying to place the blame on him for what happened with Peter today.

Good luck with that. He smirked. Sonya had seen Peter get hit with the brailer. It wasn't anyone's fault. It *had* been an accident. Pure and simple. It *wasn't* an accident that he'd been close, though. He'd been staying "close" for days. It was a good thing he had. Close enough to step in when he'd seen what had happened.

Having Lana with him had been a godsend. Peter couldn't keep his eyes off her. His cousin was worth her weight in distraction. She didn't even know the blessing she'd added to Aidan's cause. Hunt could try his best to pin this latest accident of Sonya's on him. Aidan hoped he made a good case, because Sonya would surely side with him.

At present, he was her hero, and he was going to stay there.

The feel of her back in his arms was like a soothing ointment. He wanted her back. Wanted the feel of her sweet body next to his. Wanted to lose himself inside her again, and experience that feeling of utter peace and contentment she'd brought him.

ʃ

The second they were alone, Garrett advanced. Sonya stood her ground, though she could swear it shook under her feet. It wasn't fear that had her quaking in her shoes. Hell, she didn't know what it was, but it made her blood pump faster in her veins. She couldn't call the sensation all that unpleasant. Though feeling anything for the man after he'd basically told her she was too much trouble for him, grated on her nerves. Much the way an out of tune instrument always caused her to flinch.

"Are you sleeping with him?" Garrett asked, his tone low, menacing.

"*What?*" His question knocked her off balance. "What does that have to do with what happened today?"

"Answer the question."

What right did he have to ask? He must have read something in her expression for he growled her name in warning.

"Not anymore," she bit out.

"*When?* When did you stop sleeping with him?"

Now he was getting plain nosey. "Not that it's any of your business, but last summer."

"You're fooling yourself if you think it isn't any of my business."

"Excuse me?" she huffed. "You can't just…just—"

"Tell me what happened today."

She took off her ball cap and slapped it against her thigh as she arranged her answers. He had her so off balance she didn't know where to begin. "It really was an accident. The brailer bag swung wide and Peter was in its path." She smoothed her hand over her ponytail and donned her cap, careful of the bandage at her hairline, and pulled the ponytail through the opening in the back. As though in slow motion, she relived the terrifying scene in her head.

"Don't get caught up in what could have happened, Sonya. Just tell me what *did* happen."

"The tender pulled up the brailer, and it hit Peter, knocking him overboard." Her voice broke, but Garrett continued to regard her silently until she pulled it together. She quickly bypassed the fear of praying for Peter to surface and rejoined the facts as they happened. "Aidan pulled him out of the water and brought him back to camp while I finished tendering the fish."

"Where did Aidan come from?"

"Aidan didn't have any part in this, Garrett. He saved Peter's life."

"I don't believe in coincidences, Sonya. Where did he come from?"

"We're both fisherman, Garrett. He must have been in line to tender his fish too."

"Were there fish in his boat?"

"Well…no. I don't think so." Sonya scratched at a mosquito bite on her arm. "He must have just finished tendering before I started to."

"Did you see him in line?"

Sonya thought about the long wait, bobbing on the waves, as fishermen tendered in front of her. "Uh…I'm not sure."

"Okay, that's enough for now."

Sonya laid her hand on his arm. "Garrett, Aidan didn't have anything to do with Peter falling overboard. It was an accident. They happen."

"I don't like the feel of this." Garrett whipped off his sunglasses and wedged them in the opening of his shirt. "My gut's telling me that you're in serious trouble." He wrapped his hand over hers where it rested on his arm. "You've had too many 'accidents.' Peter could have died today. You need to watch out for Aidan."

"I have no delusions where Aidan is concerned. He helped us today, and I'm grateful, but that doesn't mean all is forgotten."

His eyes bored into hers. "What do you mean by that?"

"Nothing. Now, is there anything else I can do for you, officer?" His hand tightened over hers as she tried to yank it free.

"I'm not the kind of man who falls for the brush off. What's between you and Aidan?"

"Nothing," she repeated. "We've already been over this."

"Fine." His expression hardened. "What *was* between you?"

The man wasn't going to let it go and in order to end this conversation and send him on his way, she would have to give a little. "Aidan's always been sweet on me. Last summer we fell together."

"Fell together?"

"I thought I could love him, okay."

He flexed his jaw. "Thought you could?"

She yanked her hand free and he let her go. She paced away from him, bent to pick a yellow flower, and raised it to her nose. "We fit, at least initially. We enjoy the same things. Value the same things. But…"

"But?"

She turned back to him. "Will you stop that?"

"Stop what?"

"That. Repeating what I say, making it a question." She slapped a mosquito, and then flicked the bug off her arm.

"Sonya, I'm a cop, which means I'm a detail kind of man. You're damn good at giving half-truths. You want me to stop. Better start giving me full answers."

She stared at him and then gritted out, "Aidan and I just didn't fit."

"What happened, Sonya?"

She huffed out a breath. "We fought over me wanting to drift. Among other things."

"Why?"

She tossed the flower aside. "That's just it. I don't know why. I don't understand why a fisherman wouldn't want to catch as much fish as he can. Believe me, I know getting into drifting isn't for everyone. First, it's a hell of an investment. I've been fishing out here all my life and I wanted more. To me, investing in drifting made good sense."

"Aidan didn't see it that way?"

"No, he refused to understand that I believe the risk is worth the return. Or will be. He wouldn't see my side of it. He wasn't willing to compromise."

"Neither were you," he pointed out.

"Why should I be the one to compromise? Because I'm a woman?" She threw her hands in the air. "I've dreamed of doing this all my life. So did my dad. He'd been geared up to drift when…"

"When?" he prompted.

Waves of sorrow swirled in the air around her. *Was the past repeating itself?*

"When he was killed." Sonya shook her head trying to clear it. "My dad's death has nothing to do with Peter going for an unscheduled swim."

"Sonya." His voice changed, became softer and had the effect of her fearing what he had to say next. "Wes was found unconscious and the *Double Dippin'* adrift."

"*What?* Is he—" She couldn't voice the question, didn't know if she could handle the answer.

"He's going to be fine. Wanda checked him over and released him. He'll have a hell of a headache, but he'll be okay."

Sonya released a breath, but her hands shook. "What happened?"

"The details are sketchy. From witness accounts we've been able to put together the following scenario. Someone boarded the *Double Dippin'* when she was tied at the cannery's dock, hit Wes over the head and then cut the boat loose. The boat drifted free until it ran into the *Miss Julie II*. Treat jumped aboard the *Double Dippin'* and found Wes. That's when we were notified."

"Where are Wes and the *Double Dippin'* now?"

"She's beached about a half mile from the cannery. Wes is back onboard waiting for the incoming tide. I've already checked the boat over, but you'll want to have a double look." He took a step closer to her. "Kendrick's slipped from our radar. We're looking for him right now. In the meantime, who else might have it out for you, Sonya?"

Her eyes slid to the side and then back to his. "I don't know who would do something like this."

"Yes, you do. Who were you thinking of just now? Harte?"

"No, absolutely not. Aidan wouldn't be behind anything like this."

"As much as I'd like to question Harte regarding this, he happens to have a damn good alibi." His lips tightened. "All this went down about the time Peter fell overboard. Unless Aidan had help, like his father or uncle."

"While I can't see Aidan as a party to this, I wouldn't put it past Cranky or Crafty."

"What would they have to gain?"

"Cranky wouldn't have to gain anything. He just likes to make life miserable for people. Crafty, on the other hand, would have an agenda. He always has an agenda."

"What would his agenda be?"

"I don't know. You'd have to ask him. No one understands how that man's mind works."

"What history is there between you and Kendrick?"

195

"Kendrick's a son of bitch. He likes it when bad things happen to good people. He likes it even more if he's the cause of it."

"What would he have against you or your family?"

"Listen, the only one who has something against Kendrick *would* be me."

"Why you?"

"Do we have to start in with the questions again?"

"That's the only way I get answers. If it bugs you, start volunteering information."

"I come out here every year to fish. That's all I want to do. I don't get involved in the politics between the set netters and the drifters, or jump through the hoops the cannery makes you jump through every year. I just fish."

"Whether you like it or not, you've caught someone's attention and they want to stop you from fishing. The smallest amount of information might be the lead we need to put an end to this before someone gets killed."

She regarded him for a minute and then came to a decision. "Look into the sinking of the *Mystic*."

CHAPTER TWENTY-ONE

Sonya boarded the *Double Dippin'* after making sure Peter would be fine, and entered the pilot house. "Wes," Sonya greeted on a whisper. "How's the head?"

"Pounding." Wes lay on the bunk with an instant cold pack on the top of his head. He'd draped a sock over his eyes to cut out the light. She hoped it was clean. He lifted the toe of the sock, and looked at her out of one eye. "You look as bad as I feel."

"We're quite the pair." And here she'd thought her wounds seemed better today.

"For Halloween maybe."

"I'm so sorry, Wes."

"Don't. What happened today isn't your fault. For all we know Margaret's pissed someone off."

Sonya chuckled. Grams would be the least likely to offend anyone. Wes couldn't be hurt too bad if he was making jokes. Either that or he was dying and putting up a good front. "Maybe these will make you feel better." She uncapped the lid to the plastic container full of Monster Mug-ups.

"They would if you have milk to go with them, and not the powdered stuff?"

She pulled a carton out of the bag she'd carried on board. "I stopped at the General Store."

"Now, you're talking. It's been way too long since we've had fresh milk."

"I can't vouch for the freshness, only that the milk hasn't passed its expiration date. We'd better hurry and drink it." Sonya fetched two paper cups from the cabinet next to the mini fridge, and poured milk into each of them.

Wes gingerly sat up and she passed a cup to him. She hitched a seat beside him, and placed the container of cookies between them.

"I'd thought Peter had scarfed down the last of these."

"This is my secret stash."

He bit into one and moaned with pleasure. "Almost makes getting beamed in the head worth it." He winced as he moved his head too fast. "Almost."

"Garrett told me what he thinks happened. What do you think?"

He was quiet for a long while. Sonya waited. She knew from experience when something really mattered, Wes took his time. He finished his cookie, washed it down with a gulp of milk and then reached for another. "I think Peter's right, and we need to be armed."

That was the last thing she thought Wes would say. He didn't like guns. Even when a bear ventured too close to camp, his last resort was to shoot at it. Scaring it away with loud noises, throwing rocks—that sort of thing was more his style. Never guns. It told her more than words could how shaken he was over what had happened.

"I'm really sorry, Wes. I never thought my decision to drift would bring about all these problems. I knew it wouldn't be easy, but I didn't think someone would go far enough to hurt one of us."

He squeezed her knee. "I've been thinking and I believe whoever is causing us trouble would have done so with or without you drifting. Plus, we have no idea if that was his trigger or if it's something else. It could very well be something that's been brewing for a long time."

"You're talking about the sinking of the *Mystic*?" That was twice today she'd mentioned the *Mystic*.

"A lot of unresolved issues with that."

"I'm the one who lost the most when she went down." Her father, her mother, her twin. "What more could the person responsible want?"

His somber gaze sunk into hers. "You."

𝕁

"What do you know about the sinking of the *Mystic*?" Garrett asked Skip as soon as he boarded the *Calypso* later that evening after returning from Sonya's. He remembered Skip and Judd touching on it during his debriefing when he'd first arrived.

"I wondered when that would come up." Skip sighed and stretched his legs out in front of him, crossing his ankles. "Any time the Savonskis and Kendrick are mentioned in the same sentence, the mystery of the *Mystic* resurfaces."

"Sad, sad times." Judd shook his head, his eyes trained on the aluminum deck of the cabin. "It was my first summer out here." He raised his head and looked at Skip. "It's been what, fourteen years now?"

"Yeah, coming up on the anniversary in about a week." Skip rubbed the back of his neck. "Sonya's dad, Mik, had purchased the *Mystic* around the end of the season."

"Let me guess," Garrett said. "He bought it from Chuck Kendrick."

"Yep." Judd nodded. "Mik wanted to get into drifting." He gave a humorless chuckle. "Like father, like daughter."

"Except Mik had two daughters then," Skip added.

199

Garrett's gut churned. Sonya had lost a sister along with her parents? No wonder she was so protective of Peter. Other than her grandparents, he was all the family she had left. "What happened?"

"The family was on board, taking the *Mystic* for a spin, so to speak." Judd leaned against the wall, stuffing his hands in his pockets. "The boy, Peter, was just a toddler, so he stayed on shore with the grandparents. So it was Sonya, Mik, her mother—Kyra I believe her name was—and Sonya's sister."

"How old was her sister?"

"Twin," Skip added. "Identical. Her name was Sasha."

Shit. Could the news get any worse? "Give me the rest."

"No one knows for sure what went wrong," Skip said, "but from accounts—mostly Sonya's—there was an explosion below in the engine room, and then fire."

Fire aboard a boat was a fisherman's worst nightmare. Garrett hardened his jaw at the thought of Sonya fighting for her life in a no-win situation. "How did they die?"

"Mik was never found and was presumed killed in the initial blast. Kyra had a head injury, one she probably never would have woken up from even if rescue had gotten to her sooner. Her death was ruled as drowning. Along with Sasha's."

"How did Sonya survive?"

"Apparently, Sasha and Sonya were having a race over who could get in and out of their survival gear the fastest. Sonya still had hers on when the explosion happened."

"Not Sasha."

"No. They figured Sonya was in the water for over an hour before she was rescued."

"The boat was never recovered?" Garrett knew the answer before Skip sadly shook his head.

"You know how these tides are. The ocean swept it out to sea along with any evidence that could have been recovered."

"Kendrick has always been suspected because it would be like him to sell a compromised boat," Judd said.

"Actually, back then, Kendrick wasn't so bad," Skip said. "Guess with all the speculation, he must have given in to his true nature."

How had Sonya survived in that cold ocean alone, knowing her family had perished? Died right in front of her. "How old was Sonya?"

Skip answered. "Fourteen or fifteen, I believe." He looked at Judd. "That sound right to you?"

Judd nodded. "Not old enough to handle losing her sister and parents all in one evening."

When was anyone old enough to handle a tragedy like that?

🎣

"Why didn't you tell me?" Garrett demanded, finally locating Sonya down at the Cannery's General Store the following evening. He needed a tracking device attached to her. The woman was never in one place for long. If Peter—keeping watch on the *Double Dippin'*—hadn't informed him that his sister was off shopping, Garrett wouldn't have found her.

Tonight, she wore a t-shirt that proclaimed, "Life is Simple—Eat, Sleep, Fish." It would be nice if life were that easy.

She gave him a once over, scowled at his uniform and then went back to filling her hand-held basket, doing her best to ignore him. "Tell you what?"

"You know what I'm talking about." She added a few packages of jerky and continued down the aisle like he hadn't spoken. "The *Mystic*," he pressed.

The pause in her step was the only indication that the subject rubbed at a tender spot. "I don't like to talk about it." Sonya turned the corner down the next aisle, trying her best to keep him behind her, and grabbed half a dozen Cup of Noodles off the shelf, adding them to her already hefty basket of easy-to-prepare foods.

He reached for the basket.

"What are you doing?" she asked in an angry whisper, holding tight to the handles. She glanced around at the almost empty store. "Would you leave me alone?"

"No one is paying us any attention."

"Don't kid yourself. Davida sees everything."

"What is she seeing here besides me asking you questions?"

"You carry my basket and she'll have us going steady."

He laughed, and she slapped his arm. "Stop that. You can't look like you're enjoying yourself with me."

"Believe me, I'm not." He rubbed his arm as her frown furrowed deeper. He let her have possession of the basket. "Getting off the subject. If you don't want to answer my questions here, then where?"

"Hades?"

"Now who's being funny? You asked me to look into the sinking of the *Mystic*."

"I'm sure your fish cop buddies filled you in on what happened."

"I want to hear the statement from the only eyewitness."

She sucked in her breath and added three packages of Nutter Butters and an equal number of Chip Ahoy's to her basket. "Fine." She carried it to the counter.

Davida looked Sonya over and then glanced at Garrett. "This all for you today, Sonya?"

"Do you have *any* ice cream? I'll even take vanilla, if you have it."

"Not going to happen, Sonya." Davida shook her head, her spiky calico-colored hair not moving. "No matter how many times you ask. Might as well ask me for steak. That would be easier to come by."

"Ooh, a steak would do me a world of good." At any moment Sonya was going to start salivating. "I'm so tired of eating fish. I don't care what they cost. Add a few steaks to the order."

"I said steak *would* be easier to come by than ice cream, not that I *could* come by them." Davida indicated Garrett with long French-manicured nails. The manicure seemed as out of place in South Naknek as a Starbucks. "If it's red meat you're after…" She let the sentence trail off into innuendo.

Sonya scowled and did her best to pretend Garrett wasn't standing next to her. "Just ring me up. Add a case of Mountain Dew, and I need two spark plugs for a 1985 two-stroke outboard engine."

"1985?" she repeated. "I'll check, but I doubt I'll have spark plugs for an engine that old."

"Is Nikolai making progress on the sunken engine?" Garrett asked, leaning on the counter. She'd be hard pressed to ignore him right in her line of vision.

"Unfortunately. If Davida has the spark plugs, he thinks it will be fully resurrected."

"Your grandfather is one of a kind."

A grin softened her face. "Yes, he is."

"You're in luck," Davida said, returning from the back room with a dusty box of spark plugs. "Two, right?"

"How many do you have in the box?"

"Six."

"Give them all to me. It'll save time if Gramps needs more, and he always seems to."

Davida began ringing up the items. She printed out the supply list and handed Sonya the charge slip to sign. While she boxed up the contents, she eyed Garrett. "I'm off at eight, if you want to pass that along to Judd."

"I'm sure he'll be pleased to hear it," Garrett said. Judd had been sulking around the boat like a puppy who'd lost his favorite chew toy.

"You two have plans tonight?" Davida pried.

"Yeah," Sonya said. "I've laundry to finish before the opening. I'm sure Garrett has more fishermen to harass."

"Is that what he's doing with you?" Davida asked. "Haven't heard it called harassment before."

"There's nothing going on between us." Sonya waved her hand as though dismissing the possibility.

"Riiight." Davida gave them a knowing smile.

"Seriously," Sonya stressed. "Nothing."

Garrett grabbed Sonya's boxed supplies. "Come on, sweetcakes. She's going to believe what she wants to regardless of what you say."

"*Garrett.*"

He winked at Davida. "I love it when she growls my name like that." He turned and walked out of the General Store without a backward glance, enjoying the frustrated sounds coming from Sonya as she caught up to him.

"Was that absolutely necessary? Do you have any idea what Davida is going to do with that remark of yours?"

"Not as much as she would have with you denying there's nothing between us. Hell, anyone who gets within a few feet of us can feel the heat."

"Oh, I'm feeling heat all right." Sonya went for the box he carried, but he moved it to the side, out of her reach.

"Nope, supplies are mine until we've had a chance to talk. Pick the place."

She growled again. "Fine. Fisherman's Laundry."

He followed her to the public laundry room, which was empty as it was the dinner hour and most were either eating or catching sleep for the 2:00 a.m. drift opening. He set the box down on the large table opposite three washing machines and dryers. "Why aren't you getting some sleep before the opening in the morning?"

"Because, I didn't have any clean clothes or food for the drift boat." She opened a dryer and pulled out a load of clothes, bringing an armful over to the table. In turn, she emptied the two remaining dryers.

"All these clothes *can't* be yours." He held up a pair of men's boxers with black bears on them.

She grabbed them out of his hands. "It'd be petty of me to only wash my clothes."

"You captain the *Double Dippin'*, set net, drift, shop for groceries, *and* do the laundry?"

"They say a woman's work is never done." She grabbed a pair of jeans and began folding.

"I take it the men are catching some shuteye while you're doing chores."

She folded a t-shirt, and reached for another. "Your point?"

"Why isn't Wes or Peter giving you a hand?"

"Wes has a headache, concussion remember, and Peter's with Lana, living it up after his swim yesterday."

"You still have stitches that aren't healed." He couldn't keep the anger out of his voice.

She slowed the folding of a sweatshirt. "Garrett, what would you do in my position?" She didn't wait for him to answer. "You'd carry on. Which is what I'm doing." She placed the sweatshirt in a growing pile and grabbed another. "I'd rather be busy then laying on my bunk, worrying."

He tucked away his anger and grabbed a t-shirt. He understood. Staying busy kept you from going crazy. "I need you to tell me about what happened the night the *Mystic* sank."

She jerked a pair of pants inside-out. If she wasn't careful she'd tear through the seams. "Why? There isn't more I can tell you that your buddies didn't."

"Sonya." He reached over and stilled her hands. Her eyes flicked to his and he saw anger, remembered-fear, and anguish before she glanced away. "Tell me."

She tore her hands free of his grasp, dropped the jeans, and stalked to the laundry machines and back. She folded her arms across her chest, and faced him. "Do you know that I can't get into the water? Every day I'm on that ocean and I'm petrified if I get more than ankle deep in it." She slid her eyes away from him and gazed at nothing. "I can't even swim in a heated pool without having an panic attack."

He didn't try to placate her with words that he understood. He didn't. He'd lost friends in battle, men he considered brothers, but he'd been trained to accept it, to expect it. Besides, he loved everything about being in the water.

"I *felt* Sasha die," she whispered. The tone of her voice caused his heart to ache. "Losing my parents was devastating, but Sasha was part of me. For the longest time, I couldn't go on without her. I still feel like part of me is missing."

He wanted to embrace her, shelter her from the questions he needed answers to, but he couldn't. The more information he had, the better he could protect her.

"Tell me what happened before the explosion. Where were your parents, your sister?"

Sonya closed her eyes and swallowed. "Sasha and I were on deck, messing with the survival gear." Her voice broke, but she worked through it. She returned to the pile of laundry, picked up a shirt, and began the monotonous chore of folding. "Dad was down in the engine room. Mom was handing him tools." A slight smile touched her lips. "They were arguing over who should be down in the hold. Mom was better with mechanics than Dad was."

"Why was your dad in the engine room? What happened to make him go down there?" He picked up a pair of sweatpants, recognizing them as the pair she'd had on the other night. The ones he'd almost stripped her of. Neatly he folded and placed them on top of the individual piles she'd made.

She narrowed her brow in thought. "There'd been a problem with the lights flickering. You know how a boat lists to the right as it climbs a swell and then lists left as it falls into the gully of the wave?" She continued when he nodded. "Well, each time the *Mystic* listed left the lights flickered off, then back on when we'd listed right." She smoothed the fabric of the fleece sweatshirt in her hands. "Sasha and I thought it was cool. Part of the *Mystic's* mystique." She set the sweatshirt on the pile of clothes.

"Electrical short?"

She took a renewing breath and grabbed another article of clothing. "That's what I think. Makes sense. The boat was also gasoline powered rather than diesel."

Which would have made it a powder keg if an electrical fire started.

"There wasn't enough evidence that Kendrick had intentionally sold my dad a boat with faulty wiring." She reached for a pair of socks and mated them. "Did you know that I had to continue payments on the *Mystic* after she sunk?" She gave an ironic laugh. "It took me ten years to pay Kendrick off." Her lips tightened into a hard line. "Worse than rubbing salt in a raw wound."

"Didn't your dad carry hazard insurance?"

"There hadn't been enough time to obtain a policy. The kicker was that Dad had put up the set net sites as collateral. He'd only made the deal with Kendrick two days earlier."

"Two days?"

"Yeah." She met his eyes with a raised brow. "Interesting don't you think?"

Chapter Twenty-Two

"Yo, Captain," Peter hollered from the deck. "You awake up there?"

Sonya jerked her head up from the wheel. "Yeah, I'm awake." She shook her head and yawned, her jaw popping, and engaged the hydraulics on the large reel which hauled in the net. She'd been resting between the length of time it took for Gramps and Peter to pick the net clean and her needing to operate the reel.

The sun had risen hours ago. The clock on the control panel confirmed it was just after seven in the morning. The fews hours she'd caught before the fishing period had started, after returning from doing laundry, seemed to have hindered more than helped.

Wes was convalescing at the cabin with Grams nursing *him* to death this time. Lucky bastard. He was probably getting a hot cooked breakfast right about now. Sonya's stomach grumbled, but she couldn't drum up any excitement over another cardboard-tasting protein bar. She grabbed a handful of Nutter Butters instead, hoping that if she ate something it would help her stay awake.

Their catch, so far this morning, had been fair, but then she wasn't fishing aggressively. She knew herself well enough to recognize that she was too tired to fight the line and the cutthroat fishermen today. Instead she'd stayed in view of the docks and the more mannerly-minded group of drifters. Besides, she didn't want Gramps overdoing it as Wes wasn't onboard to help pick up the slack. She'd tried to talk Gramps into taking a turn at the wheel and letting her pick fish, but he'd given her a silent stare that was surprisingly loud.

Peter signaled for her to pull in another length of the net. She engaged the hydraulics and the reel slowly began to spin. Suddenly there was a screeching snap, followed by the reel lurching, and then grinding off its track, careening right for Gramps. Sonya slammed the throttle forward, taking the weight of the net off the runaway reel, but not before she heard Gramps howl in pain.

Shit, shit, shit.

Gramps lay pinned between the reel and the pole positioned across the middle of the deck.

"Peter!" Sonya screamed.

"I got him. Keep the tension off the reel!" Peter pushed his shoulder against the reel and heaved until Gramps crawled out from under it, cradling his left arm with his right. Deep lines of pain bracketed his mouth, and his skin was as white as a ghost fish. Sonya throttled the boat forward as Peter rushed to secure a rope around the base of the reel to keep it from somersaulting out of the bow and into the water.

"Gramps?" Sonya yelled, her heart beating a drum solo in her chest.

"Dag nabbit!" Gramps said.

Sonya almost cried in relief. She'd only heard Gramps swear once in her lifetime. When he'd lost his only child, daughter-in-law, and grand-daughter. While Sonya would have colored the air over this, his version of an expletive reassured her and Peter.

"Peter, throw out the anchor," she hollered, powering down the boat once the reel was secured.

"We still got a net out. A fish cop sees us anchored, we'll get written up."

"Let 'em."

Peter hefted the anchor overboard, and Sonya scrambled from the pilot house to the deck. "Let me see," she said to Gramps, reaching for his injured arm.

"I don't think it's too bad," he said. Peter flanked one side while Sonya had his other.

"Let's sit you down." She pulled up the stool they kept on deck for when fishing was slow.

"Now don't go treating me like an old man," Gramps bristled.

"Wouldn't dream of it." She stared into his eyes, letting him know she meant business. "Let me see your arm."

With Peter's help they carefully stripped him of his rain jacket and fishing gloves. His arm was already turning black and blue, but his hand had taken the worst of the blow. It was red and swollen, possibly broken. He put up a blustery front, but Sonya knew he was hurting. They needed to get him to Wanda.

They couldn't do that until they pulled in the net. "All right, this is what we are going to do. I'm going to wrap your arm, in case there's something broken—"

"I don't have anything broken."

"Doesn't matter, we're going to take precautions anyway." Sonya peeled off her sweatshirt—leaving her in a tank top—and used it as a sling, cradling his arm in the body of the shirt and using the sleeves to tie it around his neck. With that done, and Gramps growing paler by the minute, she and Peter helped him into the pilot house and propped him on the bunk.

"I don't want to lay up here like an invalid while you two do all the work," he complained. The complaint didn't have his normal fire behind it.

"When you're captain, you can order me around. Until that day happens, you'll listen to me. Peter, let's round-haul the net in and then you pick while I get us to the Cannery."

"Right, Captain." Peter rushed to follow her orders, which spoke volumes for his worry concerning Gramps. Sonya leveled a narrow look at her grandfather. "Don't even think of getting off that bunk."

"Got it, Captain." He tried to smile, but the effort fell short.

Sonya hurried and joined Peter. They round-hauled in silence, thinking of only speed. Once the remaining net was aboard, Peter pulled anchor and Sonya engaged the engines, motoring them to the cannery. She radioed ahead for medical assistance, and then with only a moment's hesitation, she switched the VHF to the trooper channel and contacted Garrett.

The steel pin that anchored the reel onto the tracks was in her pocket, sheared in two separate pieces.

"Well, I have to say this for your grandpa, he's a much better patient than you are," Wanda said, joining Peter and Sonya in the waiting room of the Infirmary. "Nothing's broken. He'd have been better off with it broken. The ligaments and tendons took the brunt of the injury, though I don't believe anything is torn, just bruised really bad. I've splinted his hand—make sure he keeps it on." She eyed Sonya. "You're down a crewman for the remainder of the season."

This Sonya already figured. She shouldn't have had him on the boat to begin with. He should be retired, playing golf somewhere warm. Not out here, fighting the waves, the cold, the screw-ups.

Garrett entered the room like a charging bear. "How is he?" Sonya was taken aback over the height of worry reflected in his eyes. They were usually the color of glacial ice. This morning they resembled blue flames of propane.

Wanda quickly informed Garrett of what she'd just told Sonya and Peter. "He'll need to keep his hand elevated with cold packs, fifteen minutes on, fifteen minutes off. I'll send him home with pain pills and anti-inflammatories," Wanda instructed. "Make sure he doesn't over do." She turned to go, and then turned back. "Since you're here, Sonya, I want to check your stitches. After that I don't want to see any more of your crew in my Infirmary." She returned to her patient, the door shutting like a final decree behind her.

"What happened?" Garrett asked.

Peter slumped into a seat, looking spent.

"You okay, Peter?" Sonya ignored Garrett for the moment, and took a seat next to her brother. He seemed younger, as if Gramps's injury had taken years off his already young life.

"He could have been killed," he mumbled, his breathing agitated.

"He wasn't. Your quickness saved him from being hurt worse than he was." She rubbed her hand along his tense shoulders. "He's going to be all right."

Peter raised dark eyes to hers. "How did you deal with losing our parents? Losing Sasha? I don't even remember them."

She tossed his hair, which badly needed a cut, and tried for some levity. "I had you to raise, brat."

213

He smiled, though she knew he pulled it out for her benefit. He jerked his head in Garrett's direction. "Go talk to Garrett. I'll wait for Gramps."

"Sure?"

Peter nodded. "I'll be fine." Sonya stood, but his next words stopped her. "We need to get this son of a bitch, Sonya."

She sucked in a breath. He sounded so much like a man, demanding justice. Part of her wanted to reprimand him for swearing, but then she wanted to get the son of bitch responsible too.

She motioned for Garrett to follow her outside. In the precarious state Peter was in, he didn't need to over-hear the conversation she was about to have.

Once outside, Sonya glanced around. The area was deserted, most of the village's occupants still out on the water. Gramps's accident had put a halt to them fishing out the opening.

She brought Garrett up to speed on how Gramps had gotten hurt. Then she pulled the pieces of the steel pin out of her pocket. "These aren't supposed to break."

His knowing eyes met hers. He reached into the inside pocket of his jacket and drew out a plastic bag. Carefully, he picked up the two pieces without touching them.

Realization dawned. "Sorry, I didn't think of fingerprints."

"Chances are we won't recover any. Salt water de-stroys most evidence, but we'll see what we can do. I'll need your prints to rule them out." He studied the pieces of the pin. "I don't see any tool marks where someone could have compromised the pin."

"They didn't need to damage it, just replace it with an inferior metal."

"When Wes was knocked unconscious?"

"That's what I'm thinking." She indicated the pin. "When we checked the boat over, it never dawned on me to inspect that."

"Even if you did, how would you have known it wasn't the original?"

"I wouldn't have. Not until it failed."

"You understand what this means, don't you?"

She nodded her head. "Someone wants me or one of my crew dead."

CHAPTER TWENTY-THREE

"Now don't fuss, Maggie May," Gramps said, though Sonya knew he loved the attention Grams showered on him as she fluffed his pillow and tucked a lap throw over his lower body.

"You just hush and lay there while I get you something to eat." Grams had taken the news of his accident better than Sonya had hoped, but then not much ruffled her platinum feathers. She was one classy bird.

"I've got an errand to do," Sonya said. "You two going to be okay? I'll be about a half hour."

"We'll be fine, Sonya." Grams steady blue eyes met hers. "I've got Barberella if the need arises. Her nod indicated the sawed-off shotgun hanging on the beam above their heads. Grams always gave her guns female names out of respect for being dependable girlfriends.

"I'd feel better if you would keep Gracie with you," Grams said, referring to the small pocket-size pistol she kept beside the bed.

"I appreciate it, Grams, but I won't need Gracie where I'm going." Sonya left the cabin and made her way across the creek to the Harte camp.

"Earl, Roland," she greeted Cranky and Crafty who sat on the broken-down porch. "Is Aidan around?"

"Haven't seen you around much this summer," Roland said, smoking a cigarette.

"You need to get you a man, Sonya," Earl said. "Help with the load you seem determined to carry."

"You sound like Gramps," she replied with a smile, though it was hard to pull off.

"How is Nikolai? He didn't look so good when you brought him home a while ago." Earl rested an ankle on his knee and reclined farther in his rickety chair. Sonya wondered how it held his weight.

"He's fine. A little bruised."

"Good to hear it," Earl said and then quickly followed up with, "That is, it's good to hear he'll be fine. Aidan headed up the bluff. He shouldn't be more than a few hundred yards."

"Check out his shoulders, while you're up there." Roland stubbed out his cigarette with the heel of his boot. "He could help carry your load."

"Thanks." Sonya gratefully turned and headed up the trail. Conversing with Cranky and Crafty was never something she liked to linger over.

She found Aidan reclining on his elbow in the tall grass, his long legs crossed at the ankles. A sketchbook lay opened near his side, a charcoal pencil between his blackened fingers.

"Hey," she greeted, smiling as she startled him. "Am I interrupting?" She knew how involved he became when writing his graphic novels. "I can come back later."

Aidan's eyes cleared of whatever world he'd been visiting. "No, now's fine." He sat up, dropped the pencil in the tin box next to him, and reached his arms over his head and stretched. "I could benefit from a break." He closed the sketchbook, setting it aside, and then regarded her with his intuitive gaze. "What happened?"

She sat next to him in the sweet-smelling grass with the warm sun soothing her temper and a slight sea breeze wafting like a lover's caress over her skin. She told him what had transpired that morning. At first, she hadn't wanted to include Aidan, but he'd always regarded Gramps as an adoptive grandfather. It was time to set things right between them.

Besides, she needed a friend.

She also needed muscle who wasn't overly concerned about the limitations of the law.

Later that evening, Sonya and Aidan parked their 4-wheelers side-by-side in front of the Pitt. The gray salt-weathered board-and-bat siding was years behind a new coat of paint. A neon sign in the window flashed "Sorry We're Open."

The front door grated on rusty hinges as Aidan yanked it ajar for her to enter. The acrid smell of smoke drifted over her and helped to dispel the unwashed body odor of the patrons squatting at the bar. Years of fried food and spilled beer gave the floor a dark patina underfoot. On the jukebox, Johnny Cash's deep baritone sang, "Walk the Line." Balls clacked over scarred velvet as a few fishermen passed the time shooting pool.

The one redeeming quality the Pitt had was its view of the South Naknek River as it poured into Bristol Bay. Plate glass windows flanked the north side of the building. Sonya picked out the *Double Dippin'* beached below on the muddy sand from the outgoing tide. Peter was keeping watch with Gracie for company.

Aidan wrapped an arm around her, leaned down and whispered in her ear, "There he is." He turned her with his body so that she saw Kendrick sitting at the end of the bar. "You sure you want to do this?"

She took off her sunglasses, getting a better look at Kendrick sitting smug at the bar, and anchored them in the collar of her shirt. "I'm dying to do this." This moment had been building for fourteen years.

"The brutes next to him, his crewmen?"

She nodded.

He gave a big sigh. "We could've used Cranky and Crafty as back up."

"I'm counting on those wicked martial art skills of yours to tip the scales." She shrugged. "Who knows, this might end peacefully."

"Uh-huh, and I've got a deed to a goldmine if your interested." Aidan rolled his shoulders. "Remember what I showed you?"

"Yep, let's do this." With all the bravado she could muster, Sonya strutted over to the end of the bar, Aidan flanking her side. "Kendrick, I'd like a word."

"Well, if it isn't the captain of the *Double D*, and who's this?" Kendrick swiveled on his barstool, and raised coarse brows at Aidan. "Your sidekick?" He threw his head back and laughed at his own joke. While his crewmen belatedly joined in, one stocky with a skull tattooed on his bald head, the other looked like a walking Slim-Jim. Kendrick's laugh boomed and echoed in the large room, silencing the patrons as everyone turned their direction. A pool ball, still en route, cracked like a gunshot as it sunk a ball into the corner pocket.

Sonya's legs trembled and she locked her knees. She replayed the image of the reel ramming into Gramps, followed by the haunting memory of fire, and blood, and deadly water. Anger rushed through her veins like a glacial river in summer. It fortified her, made her relish crushing this pissant bully of a man. The feeling intoxicated, seduced her into believing she could take the monster.

"Kendrick, it's time you answered for your sins against me and mine."

"You've had quite the summer, little girl," he commented. "Don't mistake yourself into thinking you're a match for me."

"Oh, I'm no match for bottom feeders." She enjoyed his halibut mouth opening and closing in an attempt for a quick comeback. Apparently, it had been a while since someone had the nerve to offend him.

Red color infused his face, making him look like a candidate for a heart attack. "You have any idea who you're insulting?"

"Oh, am I insulting? Excuse, me. I thought you were comfortable in your skin. Liked to brag and throw your considerable weight around." She poked him in the belly. "Might want to lay off the fried food. Bragging can only take you so far, and table muscle gets in the way."

"You bitch."

"Now, who's being insulting?" She glanced at Aidan, his lips tilting at the corners. "Are you going to let him talk to me like that?"

"Well, Sonya, as I've used the term on occasion myself, I can't rightly tell him not to."

"I see your point." She turned back to Kendrick.

"What game you two playing at?" he asked, his mean eyes squinting.

"Game?" She narrowed her stare and gave Kendrick a glare that stabbed. "I don't play games and I refuse to be toyed by you any longer." She poked him again. Hard. "Lay off me, my family, and my fishing operation. Or you will be floating belly up."

"I haven't messed with you, yet. And I don't take threats from anyone, least of all a little girl and her puppy of a boyfriend."

"Can I hit him now, Sonya?" Aidan asked.

"No, that's what he wants you to do." She had to get Kendrick to throw the first punch. Insults, pushing, and poking hadn't done it. Maybe this would? "Haven't messed with me, huh? Like you didn't sell my dad a compromised boat?"

"She was sound until he got his hands on her. Your dad always did have a problem with his women."

Aidan grabbed her arm, before she could swing, anchoring her clenched fist to her side. Kendrick baited like a pro. She'd be swinging her fistful of rolled quarters first if she wasn't careful.

"My dad did enjoy a woman with passion rather than the dead fish, which I've heard is more to your liking."

That did it.

She saw him move and did what Aidan had taught her. Just as Kendrick's sledgehammer fist flew at her face, she jerked her head back and to the side, taking the power out of the punch. His meaty knuckles grazed her cheek, but even that little force had stars twinkling behind her eyes.

Kendrick was still moving through his swing, when she sucker-punched him in the soft underbelly of his considerable gut, stealing his wind.

Both crewmen went for Aidan. He was art in motion, a roundhouse kick here, a block there. Though a lucky punch did get him on the chin, and knocked him back into Judd—who'd shown up from somewhere—dropping them both to the floor in a tangled heap of arms and legs.

Sonya jumped back as Kendrick roared. His breath returned. He was like a bear with a wounded paw and intent on assuaging his rage with her demise. He came at her like a brick wall. She ducked and side-stepped, and then jabbed her boot into the side of his knee. He howled and went down like a bag of concrete.

Cool.

The few lessons Aidan had schooled her in that afternoon had paid off. A couple of claps sounded throughout the bar, followed by, "You show him, Sonya."

"Break it up!" Garrett stepped between Sonya and Kendrick.

Somehow, she'd known the fish cop would show as soon as she'd seen Judd.

"Don't even try it," Garrett growled at Kendrick as he came up off the floor with a broken beer bottle raised in his hand.

Kendrick backed down, spitting out, "Motherfucker," under his breath.

Sonya couldn't help but smile though her cheek throbbed like a son of a bitch. Baiting Kendrick had been a hell of a lot of fun. Scary as all get out, but exhilarating at the same time. Like taking on Jason in *Friday the 13th*. She'd faced him, punched him, and taken him down.

Who was the coward now, baby?

"What the hell is going on here?" Garrett demanded, staring right at her, his ice-blue eyes freezing the edges off her fun.

"Just having conversation," she replied.

His jaw tightened.

Guess he wasn't receptive to her sarcasm as the entertained crowd. She glanced at Aidan. He was much more in tune to her mood. He had the tattooed crewman in a head lock, while the skinny one lay unconscious on the floor at his feet.

Judd dusted himself off as Davida helped him regain his footing. Aidan's lips smiled at Sonya, and she couldn't help but curve hers in return. Garrett took the whole thing in, and his icy look frosted over.

"I want to press charges," Kendrick boomed.

"What for?" Sonya asked. "Kicking your butt?" The crowd chuckled with her.

"She came in here and started a fight," Kendrick returned. A few agreements came from the spectators.

"Is that true, Sonya?" Garrett asked.

She smiled, enjoying every minute of this evening. "He threw the first punch." She motioned to the nodding crowd. "I have witnesses."

"Did you throw the first punch?" Garrett asked Kendrick.

Kendrick tightened his lips and, if possible, turned a deeper shade of purple.

"Judd, take statements." He pointed to Aidan. "Start with him. Back up is on their way." Garrett grabbed Sonya by the arm. "*You* are coming with me."

"Hey," she sputtered. "I want to press charges." She pointed to her swelling cheek. "He did hit me first."

Garrett took a step and stumbled. He caught himself, and then reached down and picked up a roll of quarters Sonya dropped during the tussle. His incredulous look met hers. "I suggest you keep your mouth shut and come with me."

Looked as though the fun was over.

She glanced back as Garrett pulled her out of the Pitt, her gaze finding Aidan. She mouthed the words "thank you." He grinned and winked at her. Then she caught the murderous look Kendrick sent her.

Chills erupted on her skin. Had she just made matters worse?

CHAPTER TWENTY-FOUR

"Pick the place," Garrett growled once they were outside the Pitt. He still hadn't let go of her arm.

"What?"

"You and me. We are going to talk. Your choices are the *Calypso*, the cannery, or the *Double Dippin'*. Since you're so concerned over what everyone else thinks, pick the place, or I will." His expression was firm and left no room open for discussion. "If I choose, I guarantee you won't like where I take you."

The *Calypso* wasn't even an option. No way would she willingly board a trooper boat. Nowhere at the cannery was private enough. Whatever he had to talk to her about would be all over the bay by next tide if they went there. He hadn't mentioned Red Fox Camp. She didn't want to have any "talk" around her grandparents. Plus, when they found out what she and Aidan had pulled tonight, they would conduct their own "talk" with her.

That left the *Double Dippin'*.

"Fine, my boat. But you're not taking the Jeep." She pointed to the big brown vehicle with Alaska Wildlife Trooper printed on the doors. "I'm not having that trooper beacon parked next to my boat. We'll take my 4-wheeler."

She stomped to the ATV, not liking that she would be seen with Garrett in his uniform traveling the short

224

distance to the *Double Dippin'*. How many fishermen could be out and about? Most should be sleeping. "Here." She picked up the rain jacket she left on the seat of the ATV and handed it to him. "Put this on."

He held his ground, refusing the jacket. If anything his expression went from firm to stone. "You need to get over your problem with my uniform."

"Not going to happen." She shook the jacket as though to reinforce that he needed to put it on.

"Sonya," Garrett growled.

The little hairs on the back of her neck rose and she put the jacket on herself. Maybe if she hunched over and pulled the hood over her head, no one would know Garrett was with *her*. The news of him dragging her out of the Pitt was probably already traveling the cork line. Especially since Davida had been a witness.

With no choice, she got on the 4-wheeler. He mounted behind her. A thrill shot through her as he climbed on. As angry as she was, sexual heat mixed in. She closed her eyes and tried to filter out his enticing scent of power. Closing her eyes was the wrong thing to do. If anything it brought to focus all that he could make her feel.

She revved the ATV and jerked it into gear. She headed down the dirt road to the cannery, and then down the ramp to the beach. With the tide out, she was able to drive the ATV right up to the back of the *Double Dippin'*. Peter met her outside, having heard them pull up, with Gracie riding snug in the waistband of his pants.

"Hey, you're back." He stated the obvious and then frowned when he saw Garrett. "Why'd you bring the fish cop?"

"Trooper," Garrett corrected through clenched teeth. "How many times do I have to say it?"

Peter looked at Sonya. "We aren't in trouble, are we? Don't tell me something *else* happened?" His face went white. "Gramps?"

"Everything's fine. Garrett just wanted to talk to me about…stuff." She shrugged as if Garrett's presence was no big deal. She wasn't going to inform her little brother she and Aidan had pulled a stunt that now began to seem a bit childish. "Why don't you take the 4-wheeler back to camp?"

"Leave the fish cop, er, trooper here with you? Alone?"

"I can handle him," Sonya stated.

"You sure?" Peter asked, eyeing Garrett.

Sonya took a peek. No wonder Peter acted so protective. Garrett's expression was like the calm in a snow globe. One little shake and he'd be all storm.

"Why don't you check on Lana? I'm sure she could use a break from Cranky and Crafty."

That had Peter disembarking. Once he reached the muddy sand, he handed over the pistol. "Keep Gracie with you. I'll see you later." He nodded to Garrett, jumped on the 4-wheeler and roared off down the beach.

Sonya tucked Gracie into the front of her waistband and climbed aboard the *Double Dippin'* feeling Garrett's presence like a kerosene heater set on high at her back. She entered the pilot house and immediately shut all the curtains. There were too many boats dry around her that could see into the wheel house for her liking.

"Okay, let me have it." She sighed. The sooner he reprimanded her, the sooner he could get off her boat and walk back to the cannery.

"Think you can handle me, do you?"

She recalled the careless words she'd thrown at Peter. They'd been meant to reassure, but obviously Garrett had taken them a whole other way. He took a threatening step toward her in the small space, which didn't leave her with much room to move, let alone breathe. His powerful shoulders blocked her view of the rest of the room. All she saw were those shoulders, big and broad, and his chest, roped with muscle. She remembered all too well what his muscles had felt like. The pilot house suddenly seemed not just small, but much too warm.

"How are you going to handle me, Sonya?" His tone had lowered and had the effect of the bottom dropping out of her stomach. It was threatening and sexy as hell. Bringing him to the *Double Dippin'* wasn't the best place she could have chosen after all.

She was having one night of lousy decisions.

"Say your piece, and then get off my boat."

"Do you know how asinine your actions were tonight?"

She had a pretty good idea, but she wasn't going to admit it. At least not to him. "I showed Kendrick that I'm not going to roll over like all the other fishermen out here. He knows I'm watching him now."

"You jeopardized the surveillance we had him under. He'll be more careful now. Sneakier. And since his ego is now at stake, he'll be meaner."

She bit back a smile, remembering how it felt to have Kendrick gasping for breath at her feet.

"You might have enjoyed yourself tonight, but you set my operation back weeks, if not sunk it all together."

She swallowed her smile, suddenly feeling sick to her stomach.

"Why did you do it? Why didn't you come to me first, instead of Harte? I know that Nikolai's injury shook you up, and I understand the need for action, but Sonya, do you have any idea what could have happened to you tonight?"

"I was prepared, and Aidan was with me."

"Against Kendrick and his hoodlums? What if the patrons of the bar turned and sided with Kendrick? As it was, they didn't do anything to come to your aid."

"I didn't need their help. I had things under control."

"No, you didn't. If Judd and I hadn't intervened when we did, the situation would've gone to hell. Where would your family be if you were too hurt to fish? Or worse? What would happen to Peter? Your grandparents? Wes? You are the glue that holds your family together. Without you, they would be lost."

Why did he have to be so damn intuitive? Why did he have to be right? "I was thinking—"

"It's about damn time you started. The attacks you've had are serious. The person behind them isn't playing games. Your grandfather could have been killed."

She turned away from his accusing eyes, breath catching in the back of her throat. He was right. It had been a long time since she'd been ashamed of her actions. Made to feel like an irresponsible child. She didn't like it.

"Sonya—"

"No." She held up her hand, not turning around. "You're right. What I did was stupid and childish."

She felt more than heard him come up behind her. He laid his hands on her shoulders. "And brave." He turned her to face him. "Stupid, but brave. From what I've been able to gather, Kendrick has bullied everyone in this area for years. Nobody has had the guts to stand up to him. Until now." He smoothed the loose hair that had come out of her ponytail, behind her ears. "You scared the hell out of me tonight. Seeing Kendrick hit you took years off my life." He gently brushed the swelling on her cheek.

At least Kendrick hadn't hit the side of her face that had been cut. The force of his fist would have reopened the healing wound.

"You need to be more careful with this face." His fingers lingered. "How bad does it hurt?"

"I barely feel it." She felt something all together stronger. There was a different heat flaring in his eyes now. It warmed her to the very core and had her backing up out of his reach. "You need to leave, Garrett." She swallowed at the intent in his eyes.

Garrett reached for the pistol she'd tucked into the waistband of her jeans and pulled the gun free. The sharp plinking of the bullets ricocheted in the small room as he unloaded and deposited both the gun and the bullets in the small sink behind her.

"I'm not going anywhere."

Chapter Twenty-Five

"You can't stay," Sonya said.

Garrett steeled himself against the flare of unease in her eyes. "We both knew the moment you sent Peter off with the 4-wheeler, I'd be staying." He reached up and released her ponytail, his gaze captured by the strands as they flowed like expensive silk through his fingers.

"The tide is still out," she said then moaned as he ran his hands through her hair and rubbed the tight muscles at the base of her skull. "You can walk back to the cannery," she whispered, her eyes closing as he moved his hands to her neck and massaged the knots he found.

"I'm not going anywhere," he repeated, loving the way she melted in his arms. One minute she was the hard, bust-your-balls fisherman, the next, a soft, seductive woman. "We've been waltzing around each other long enough not to finally dance."

"This is really a bad idea, Garrett."

His hands cradled her face, and he tipped her head back and firmly took her mouth, silencing her objections. She stiffened and raised her hands as though to push him away, but then her fingers curled into the jacket of his uniform and pulled him closer.

"Garrett." She backed away and gazed into his eyes. She wet her lips and he almost hit his knees, ready to beg.

He didn't know if he could leave her this time and didn't want to put it to the test.

"I haven't danced in a long time," she said, her expression soft and hesitant, "and I've never been much of a dancer."

He breathed a sigh of relief. She wasn't saying no, she was nervous. Hell, so was he. He couldn't remember a time when making love with a woman meant so much. "Just follow my lead."

"Wait." She retreated, and he almost groaned when she shook her head. "I can't make love to a trooper."

Not the damn job again.

A flare of anger intruded and mixed with his desire. "Sonya," he warned, his tone strained. There was only so much he could take.

A wicked glint entered her deep brown eyes. "Lose the uniform."

His world turned upside down. Who was taking the lead now? If it got him inside her, he'd gladly let her take control. For a little while anyway. Without a word, he stripped out of the jacket and tossed it on the bunk. Her eyes followed the flick of each button he released on his shirt. He'd never had a woman watch him strip with such obvious want before. It unnerved and titillated at the same time. He pulled the shirt free from his pants and yanked it off his shoulders, hurling it in the direction of his jacket. He paused with his hands on his belt. She needed to do some catching up. "Lose *your* uniform," he ordered.

She swallowed, bit her lip, and reached out a hand, brushing the muscles on his stomach. He sucked in his breath and captured her hand in his, knowing he wouldn't last long if she touched him.

"I'm not in uniform," she said, her voice caressing his skin like crushed velvet.

"Close enough." Tonight her sweatshirt had "Lean Mean Fishing Machine" written across the front. Again, he wondered if she chose her clothes to suit her mood. Considering that she'd taken Kendrick on, had him believing she did. "Every fisherman out here dresses like you do. Sweatshirts, jeans," he glanced to her boots, "reliable footwear."

"How else are we supposed to dress? Heels and short skirts wouldn't look right on the guys and would be too impractical for picking fish."

"Damn, what I would give to see you in high heels and a short skirt." He closed his eyes briefly and enjoyed the image. He'd only seen her in casual attire. Extreme casual. What would he do to see her gussied up?

She gave a seductive tilt to her lips and he could see her cataloging the information away. He'd better be careful what he revealed. Knowing her, she'd find a way to drive him crazy with the information. "I'll have to remember that," she said.

"Unless you're with me, there's no need to remember it."

"That statement sounds like tonight is more than just about sex." Though she hadn't asked a question, it came out like one.

"You have a problem with that?" His heart thudded hard in his chest as he waited for her reply.

"I might." Alarm flickered in her expression, and she retrieved her hand back.

"Get over it. I've had to." He wouldn't let her insecurities feed his. He wasn't made for long term relationships, but with her, he found himself forgoing his usual "boundaries" speech. He pulled her into his arms.

They'd talked enough.

"Garrett, wait—"

"No more waiting." He was done waiting. He was all about having, taking, giving back. He seized her mouth, ending her objections. Here, she was quiet, pliable, demanding. The kiss was too short when she tore her mouth free.

"Garrett."

"Sonya, I can't think straight. Don't make me form sentences." She smiled and disengaged herself from his embrace. He almost begged.

"All I wanted to say was follow me." She lifted the trap door to the sleeping quarters below, bending over, her sweet ass teasing him to the point of pain. She stepped onto the top step of the ladder, and he watched as she lowered herself, rung by rung, that seductive smile of hers promising untold pleasures to be found if he followed.

Like he was staying put.

He was damn lucky he hadn't broken his neck in his rush to join her below. The quarters were tight. A double bed took up most of the room. Shelves, with locked wired fronts to keep the contents in, flanked the wall on one side of the bed. A trunk, obviously for clothes, took up the opposite corner with more shelves colored with the spines of books, above. A half-opened narrow door led to the head.

Sonya had taken off her sweatshirt and had her hands on the hem of her t-shirt when he stepped off the last rung of the ladder. Mesmerized, he watched as she lifted the soft cotton, inch by slow inch, up her body. A simple white bra, encasing soft rounded breasts, was revealed, and it was the sexiest thing he'd ever seen a woman wear. He tamped down the desire to grab her and plunder his face in her cleavage. Next, she teased him by fingering the snap of her jeans.

He couldn't hold back the groan that traveled up his throat. In the small space, it only took him two strides to reach her. He gripped the waistband of her jeans and yanked her close, her breath escaping with a whoosh. One handed, he unhooked her bra and tore it from her body. Her breasts were glorious, soft, and full, with nugget-hard nipples begging for his touch. Her breath hitched and her eyelids shuddered closed, as his fingers twirled the nubs into harder points.

She wrapped her arms around him and pressed her body to his as though to stop the overwhelming sensations. With her supple breasts pressed against his chest, his knees buckled and they fell onto the bed. Lips locked and pillaging, they both fought for dominance. With a rumble from deep within his chest, he flipped her onto her back and held her arms above her head. She undermined him by arching her lower body into his. Damn, but this woman was going to be the death of him.

"Sonya," he growled her name. With his last coherent thought he muttered, "Do I need a condom?"

She froze. "Tell me you have one." Then she kicked him in the back of his calf with her heel. "I told you that it had been a while. So yes, that meant I'm not taking anything to prevent conception."

Without letting go of her hands, he reached into his back pocket, grinding his erection against her in the process, a pleasure punishment for her kicking him. Her groan and returning grind had him clenching his teeth as he pulled out a few condoms and tossed them on the bed. Her eyes closed in obvious relief. He'd begun carrying them after their last heated encounter. She kicked him again. "Hey," he muttered.

"Did you have to tease me like that?"

"It wasn't intentional." He grinned. "Much. For your information, I tested clean two months ago. If you were on the pill, there wouldn't be a barrier between us when I take you."

"I'll get on the pill as soon as fishing season is over."

He gave her a triumphant smile. Whether she realized it or not, she'd just agreed to further a relationship with him once they returned to civilization. Tenderly he kissed her, brushed his lips against hers until she sighed. Then he deepened the kiss, loving how she eagerly opened her mouth to his conquering tongue.

Yet, he was the one who was conquered. She met him kiss for kiss, touch for touch, grind for grind. She was his match. Not only did she hold her own dressed, naked she downright did him in.

He let go of her and shed the remainder of his clothes. She propped herself up on the bed and inspected him up and down.

"You look much better out of that uniform," she said. Her eyes traveled south, centering on his throbbing erection. "Much, much better."

Laughter erupted from deep within his chest, the sound surprising him. When was the last time he'd enjoyed a woman so much? For the life of him he couldn't remember. Sonya teased him with her lips, tormented him with her questing hands, tempted him with her shapely body, and brought him to a level of arousal he'd never felt before. He peeled her out of her jeans, finding thin, barely there, silk panties trimmed in delicate lace. Never had he wanted to unwrap a present so much. Hooking his fingers under the fragile lace, he slowly slipped her out of them. Then he took his time viewing what he'd uncovered.

She squirmed under his stare.

Rather than playing with his newly unwrapped present, as he knew Sonya wanted him to do, he captured her foot and leisurely rolled off her sock, doing the same with her other foot.

"Garrett." Her tone threatened, and her hips arched off the bed as though begging him to delve into her depths.

Instead, he kneaded the curve of her foot, pressing on points that he'd learned from a very knowledgeable woman in the Middle East. Sonya's hips dropped to the bed, and her head twisted on the pillow while she moaned.

"Sonya," he kissed the underside of her toes, "you have incredibly sexy feet." The deep burgundy polish she'd painted her toenails surprised and, if possible, aroused him even further.

"Garrett, Garrett," she chanted his name. "Who taught you how to do that?"

"A woman I met in Kuwait."

"Remind me to send her a thank you card." A whimper escaped her lips and she wriggled on the sheets. "As much as I'm enjoying this, I really need you to get down to business." Her heavy lids shuttered eyes that were deep, dark pools of pleasure. "Can't we come back to the foreplay?"

"God, yes." He crawled up her body and positioned himself at her opening. The head of his shaft nudged the inner folds of her heat and he about came undone. Wet and writhing, she was ready. So hot, so tight, so right for him. She arched her hips, taking him deeper. His possession was a wicked mix of pleasure and pain as he tried to restrain himself from slamming into her. Each inch he gained brought him clenching his teeth and praying he lasted. In a flash, he realized what he'd forgotten. "Shit." He pulled out of her, the friction almost his undoing.

She cried out his name and tried to draw him back inside her with toned legs wrapped around his waist, her heels digging into his ass. Damn, she was strong.

"Condom," he grated out on a curse, searching the bed where he'd tossed them. "I forgot the damn condom."

"I don't care." Her head thrashed back and forth on the pillow. Her hair flowed like silk, thick lashes lay dark against flushed cheeks. She was stunning. The sight of her had him pausing just to look at her.

He swallowed past the lump of emotion suddenly in his throat. "You'll care nine months from now," he said. For the first time in his life, he envisioned what the woman who'd carry his child looked like.

It scared the hell out of him.

Her eyes slowly opened and met his. He thought he recognized yearning. Her lips parted and he wondered what he'd do if she told him to forget the condom. Then she blinked and the moment was gone.

"Need help?" she asked, with a lift of her brow.

How he loved the way she challenged him—when she wasn't pissing him off. "I think I can handle it." He tore the wrapper open, sheathed himself, and slowly reentered her. Her legs tightened around his waist and she arched her hips hard against him, forcing his penetration.

She stole his breath, his control, his domination. A man consumed with making a woman undeniably his, he took her, slammed into her with a force that rocked the bolted-down bed. He spread her legs, hauled her hips off the sheets with bruising fingers, and plundered.

He claimed her with each thrust, strained to be part of her. One with her. He wanted there to be nothing between them. Not her being a fisherman. Not him being a trooper.

Her head fell back on a cry, the curve of her neck summoning him to bite. He closed his teeth on the cord of her neck, loving how she hissed out her pleasure and urged him to take her harder, faster. His climax built at the base of his testicles and he held tight to the slippery threads of his control. Sonya screamed his name, her nails raking down his back, as her inner muscles contracted around his shaft, milking him of his inability to prolong his own orgasm. Another hard thrust and he was helplessly caught in the storm of a devastating climax.

He collapsed into her comforting arms. His body spent.

His soul shaken.

ʓ

Sonya woke to the boat rocking to and fro with the force of the incoming tide. The motion of the waves stroked her against a hard, hot, fully aroused body. Garrett lay behind her, his front pressed to her backside, their legs entwined. His arms were wrapped around her, his clever hands already on patrol. He stroked her body with long sure strokes of a man who'd paid attention to what had thrilled and excited the woman he'd made love to many times during the night.

She hadn't awakened well-rested; rather, well-used and completely resplendent. Did that even make sense, she wondered. She didn't care. Resplendent was the word that had popped into her head and stuck. She was so far past merely sexually satisfied.

Sonya purred, arching her body into the heat of Garrett's, as he lazily continued to caress her with his hands. She turned her head to peer over her shoulder at him. His slumberous eyes regarded her with pure male satisfaction. His soft lips were swollen, much she suspected like hers were. His hand cradled her jaw, and pulled her in for a sweet, good-morning kiss.

"I've never woken on a boat with a sexy woman locked in my arms before," Garrett's voice was rough and raspy, much like the stubble on his chin that grazed the side of her neck as he kissed and nibbled her. "It's erotic as hell." He rubbed the hard ridge of his erection between the cleft of her bottom with the next wave, and her breath caught. He gave a sexy chuckle. "Glad to see I'm not the only one who's getting a rise out of these waves."

Not that they could do anything about them. They'd used up the three condoms he'd tossed on her bed last night. The last one had required a desperate treasure hunt. They'd found it lodged between the mattress and the wall. The memory of how he'd taken her then brought a heated flush to her skin. "Garrett," she moaned as he rubbed his rigid length back and forth against her soft, slick folds, "no more condoms remember?"

He dropped his head to her shoulder and barely smothered an oath. The next wave crested and caused a delicious friction to develop between them as their bodies rolled with the water.

She moaned and arched her back. To know what he could make her feel and then knowing they couldn't consummate their desires was a luscious torture all its own.

Garrett groaned—a rough, aggressive sound that thickened her blood. He grabbed her hips—she thought to hold her still—but instead ground against her as though he couldn't help himself. "Trust me, Sonya." His hands bit into her hips.

Muscles deep within her bore down on emptiness, throbbing to have him inside her. The ache painful.

"Say you trust me," he ground out, his tone desperate, daring. The thick head of his penis penetrated her. She stiffened in his arms, but he was relentless in his mission to fill her. The sensation of the buffeting waves knocked

239

her into him and he took advantage of the motion to completely impale her.

"*Garrett*." His name was a thin whisper of warning on her lips. This wasn't good. He was deep inside her with no protection. Regardless of the amazing sensations spilling throughout her body, the fact still remained, his puppy wasn't covered and she didn't want to get pregnant.

"When was your last cycle?" he demanded, keeping her body locked with his. "Could you get pregnant?"

"Like I'm supposed to remember that while you're—" Another wave hit the boat. She moaned and arched into him, taking him farther inside her.

"*Remember*, Sonya," he growled, the sound taut with lust.

"A few weeks ago. Maybe…I think." She ground her hips back into his fierce thrust. "I'm sure. Pretty much." Hell, she no longer cared if she got pregnant as long as she got off.

Damn him.

She curved her back as he bit her neck in that glorious spot he'd discovered last night. His hands cupped her breasts while he rhythmically thrust into her with the timing of the waves as they pitched the boat back and forth.

"Sonya, I'll pull out," he said in a strained voice. His hand found the button between her legs that had her agreeing to anything he wanted. He'd taken full advantage of the little traitor all night long.

"*Yes*," she hissed. Did she really have a choice?

He rewarded her by flicking and rubbing her sensitive switch while deepening and quickening his thrusts. It didn't take long for her rockets to fire on all cylinders. She didn't worry about being quiet. She was in the bottom of a boat with water all around her. For all intents and purposes they could be the only ones alive, and she responded with abandonment as though they were.

She shuddered in his arms as she returned to earth. "Garrett?" She tried to turn and look at him over her shoulder.

He held her fast. "Don't move." He lay heavy, throbbing and thick inside her, not having climaxed. She felt his muscles tighten and twitch. His arms were bands of live steel and kept her immobile. "Give me a minute."

One push, an arch, a vibrating moan, and she knew he'd be a goner. The power that she held was intoxicating. Rigid ropes of muscles—with corresponding thick veins pumping blood throughout his system—held her fast as though he knew she was tempted. All it would take was one little shove.

A wave broke against the boat's hull.

"*Fuck.*" On a tortured groan, he lost the formidable grip he held over himself and pumped his hips into her like a man possessed, thrusting in long, fast, unrelenting stokes, driving deep.

The way he held her, imprisoned against his body, his leg pressed between hers, one arm across her chest, the other anchoring her hips to his, left her with no alternative but to take what he delivered. It should piss her off to be at his mercy like this, but it had an opposite, thrilling effect. As physically restrained as he had her, she knew she held him within her body just as captive, and it sent Sonya crashing into another orgasm.

Garrett hoarsely hollered her name as his body betrayed him and he climaxed deep within her.

Silence, and the seemingly mocking of the rocking boat, followed the tempest that had raged in the small room. Sensations ebbed and sanity returned. Sonya jerked out of Garrett's arms and scrambled off the bed. "What the hell just happened?"

Garrett opened his eyes and regarded her with intense satisfaction. "You know what happened."

"You said I could trust you!"

He laid his forearm across his eyes as though the action would make the harsh reality of what had happened go away. "I know."

How dare he look so pleased with himself?

He lifted his arm and raised himself on his elbow. She tried to ignore the way his perfectly carved body lay draped, in naked splendor, on her bed. "I'm sorry, Sonya. I thought I could resist. I should have known better."

"I should have too." She should never have let this situation get so far out of hand. "There could be serious repercussions here."

He rubbed his hand over his face, the sound raspy as he scratched over the stubble on his chin. "I know."

"Quit saying, 'I know.' You don't know! This is my body we're taking about. My life. I'm not ready to be a mother. I'm not even a wife!" Gramps wouldn't care for his coveted great-grandchild being conceived before a ring was clamped on her finger. If that happened she saw a lifetime of lectures. Not to mention, the inexcusable example she would provide for Peter.

"Calm down. Chances are good that you won't get pregnant. Couples try for months, sometimes years, and don't conceive."

She raised a brow in disbelief. "Do you really believe that would happen to us?"

"Nope."

"Me, either." Grabbing a change of clothes, she stormed into the head, slamming the door behind her.

She wished, not for the first time, that the boat had a shower. Instead she had to settle for a thorough sponge bath. Knowing Garrett, his little soldiers would be as tenacious as he was. What if one of those soldiers was breaching her unsuspecting girl at this very moment? Sonya laid her hand on her flat stomach, trying to visualize a tiny life just beginning.

No. She straightened. Garrett had to be right. Chances of them having made a baby must be one in...who the hell knew how many? Who figured odds like that anyway? Chances *had* to be just as good that they hadn't. Right?

There was definitely nothing she could do about it now. If she found out she was expecting, *then* she could panic. Until that happened, she had more pressing matters to deal with.

Like a drift opening to fish in a few hours and crewmen to retrieve.

And how the hell to get a fish cop off her boat in the condemning light of morning.

CHAPTER TWENTY-SIX

"Have a good night?" Judd asked, with a knowing smirk, as Garrett entered the cabin aboard the *Calypso* to find him and Skip eating smoked salmon for breakfast.

Garrett glared at Judd until he squirmed in his seat. "Where do we stand on Kendrick?"

"Took his statement, along with his crewmens'." He angled his head. "As you'll expect, they differed from everyone else's in the bar, including Harte's and mine. Remember, I was having dinner with Davida when Sonya and Harte entered the bar and confronted Kendrick."

"Where's Kendrick now?"

Judd rubbed the back of his head. Skip reclined in the captain's chair, hands linked behind his head. The position made him look far from jolly as the shrewd man eyed Garrett with stiff reservations. "First, let's get back to where you've been all night. Were you with Sonya Savonski?"

Garrett clenched his jaw. "Yes."

Skip huffed out a breath and glanced out the window to the river. "Are you aware of the situation you've put yourself in?"

"More than most."

Skip met Garrett's stare. "Again, I have to ask you, is this relationship with Sonya going to interfere with your ability to do your job?"

Since he might have impregnated her this morning, Garrett had to conclude that this time they indeed had a relationship. Whether Sonya would admit it or not, was still in question. As for her interfering with his job, most definitely. "No, it will not."

Skip narrowed his gaze and then straightened, lowering his arms to rest on his knees. "I hope you're right. Kendrick boarded the *Albatross* last night at twenty-three hundred hours. At twenty-three fifty-two, troopers lost her in a fog bank. We have yet to catch sight of her."

"How much time until the drift opening?"

"Just over an hour. I want to cast off in twenty."

"Fine." Garrett turned and headed below to his bunk. Sonya had dropped him off at the cannery where he'd grabbed a shower before finding the *Calypso* tied to the east dock. This time he hadn't argued with her and had worn one of her rain jackets to try and hide his identity. He'd also donned some of Wes's clothes that were on the *Double Dippin'* to try and protect Sonya's reputation. Even though he hated that she was ashamed of his job, he didn't want to cause her grief with anyone over her sleeping with a trooper. Besides, after having one night with her, he knew he'd have to have another, if not a full calendar's. Keeping their sexual escapades covert benefited them both.

At least until fishing season was over. Then everything changed.

He grabbed a fresh uniform, trying to compartmentalize what had happened between them last night, and this morning. Panic ate at him over the reality of the situation he'd put them in. He tugged on his shirt and buttoned it up. He could be a father. The thought had his fingers pausing on the buttons. He'd had every intention of pulling out of her hot, silken body before he'd lost the ability to do so.

He yanked on his pants. So much for good intentions. What had he been thinking? Whenever he was around her, his objective got screwy. What made him think he could hold onto his control when everything showed him control was something he didn't possess around Sonya Savonski?

Sonya finished eating a Snickers bar, and washed it down with a Mountain Dew for breakfast. As breakfasts went, it wasn't one for champions but seemed to do the trick for morning-afters. She propped her feet on the console, crossing her legs at the ankles and leaned back in the captain's chair. Looking out of the windows of the *Double Dippin'*, she scanned the area for Wes and Peter. The sooner they got here the sooner she could cast off and sail away from the *Calypso* docked a few boats east of hers.

She grabbed a couple Chips Ahoys trying to silence the gnawing in her stomach. She could eat until she weighed as much as her boat and that gnawing wouldn't be satisfied.

Damn Garrett for giving her a night of sex that she'd never forget. *Especially, if the result of their hot night ended up producing a child.* Her throat went dry and she almost choked on the bite of cookie she swallowed. She reached for the can of soda.

What would she do if she were pregnant? Would she be able to keep her job at the high school? Could a woman in this day and age be fired for being an unwed mother? How would she care for a child? Daycare might be a necessary choice she'd have to consider, but she could also teach private music lessons at home. She'd been asked by parents before. It would definitely open her options to be a stay-at-home mom, like hers had been. Money was an issue, always had been before. If she were going to have a baby, money became paramount. As well as insurance. She'd need medical insurance, which meant she had to keep her job.

"Ahoy there, *Double Dippin'*!" Peter hollered.

Sonya jumped at the shout, but was grateful for the interruption of her wandering thoughts. Peter and Wes climbed down the ladder to the deck. Finally they could get away from here, away from Garrett, and hopefully distance would quiet her drifting mind. She straightened when Aidan came into view, dropping to the deck behind Wes and Peter.

What was he doing here?

She exited the pilot house and met her crew on deck, her gaze centered on Aidan. He looked...good. His dark hair blew softly around a face sporting a shiner he must have received from their escapade last night. It gave him a rakish appearance that complimented the beard shadowing his jaw from not shaving since fishing had started. While most men would look unkempt, on Aidan it lent him an air of debauchery that was very appealing.

"Hey, Sonya, I invited Aidan along." Peter slapped Aidan on the back. "Time he knew what drifting was all about. Besides," Peter rubbed his hands together, "with all the fish we're going to catch today, we could use the extra crew."

Boy, did she ever need to have a talk with her little brother. Aidan's eyes narrowed as she took her time in answering.

"I decided I needed to see what all the hubbub was about." Aidan gazed at her with those warm brown eyes and his head cocked to the side. "What do you say? Show me the ropes?"

"I don't think this is a good idea."

"Of course, it is," Peter joined in. "Come on, Sonya, you two can brawl together, but not fish together? What kind of example is that?" Peter beamed with a knowing smile.

"He's got you there," Wes piped in with a chuckle, pulling on bibs and exchanging his tennis shoes for boots after boarding the boat.

Asking for Aidan's help yesterday had probably crossed a line that she shouldn't have, looking at it in the brighter light of day, but to kick him off her boat now that he was here would be rude. Besides, she *did* want Aidan to understand the decisions she'd made. If only he had been open to understanding her last summer.

"All right, but you carry your own weight." And no making moves on the captain, she wanted to add. She had all the moves she could take in the last twelve hours. "Cast us off, Peter."

"Aye, aye, Captain."

"Sonya?" Aidan reached out and grabbed her arm. Stepping closer, he studied her face.

"Yes?" Their eyes met and his turned hard.

His jaw tightened, and he let go of her. "Nothing."

Puzzled over his actions, Sonya returned to the pilot house and fired up the engines as her crew, plus one, cast them off from the dock. She turned the boat toward the line, in the mood to fight for her share of the catch today.

The door slid opened and in stepped Aidan, the breadth of his shoulders sucking the air out of the small room. "You slept with that fish cop last night, didn't you?" His eyes were full of anger, accusation, and…hurt?

"Excuse me?" How could he know? Did someone see Garrett leave her boat this morning? Had word swam down the cork line that fast?

"You have that look."

"What look?" What the hell was he talking about?

"The one you always got after we made love. You would develop this glow about you, like heat radiating from the inside out." He swallowed and glanced away for a moment before nailing her with reproachful eyes. "Why, Sonya?"

How dare he make her feel guilty, like she'd somehow cheated on him? They were no longer together. It was none of his business who she slept with and vice versa. "Whatever happened between Garrett and me doesn't have anything to do with us."

He stared at her long and hard, the wounded look in his eyes changing to something dark and dangerous. "Don't kid yourself." Then he slammed out of the pilot house, and stomped his way to the deck where Peter and Wes were readying the net.

A chill chased up her spine.

She reached for the small aluminum pan she kept near the stove. Turning it over, she gazed long at her reflection. Did she give off a "just been satisfied" glow every time she had sex? Why had she never noticed before? Yes, her cheeks were flushed but that could be due to the accusations Aidan had just flung at her. For that matter it could be due to the weather.

Who was she kidding? It was a beautiful morning. Clear, calm, with a caressing breeze.

Suddenly she seethed.

She tossed the pan back to the stove, and it clanged as it hit, rocking until it settled. She wished she had something else she could throw. A glance at the clock told her she had ten minutes until the fishing period opened. The boats in front of her were lined up like an aluminum wall.

Damned if they wouldn't make room for her today.

"Sonya, whatcha doing?" Peter asked as she bumped her way past the *Miss Julie II*.

"You want to show Aidan how to drift, don't you?" she hollered back at him, tired of the men in her life questioning her actions.

"Not if it involves putting ourselves at risk." Peter turned to Aidan, and she heard his words as they traveled into the open window of the pilot house. "What did you say to rile her up? I thought you two were getting along."

Aidan turned and gazed at Sonya, his expression downfallen. "So did I."

The look stabbed her.

Come on already, she had nothing to feel guilty about. She was a grown woman who hadn't had sex in over a year. Hell, she had needs, damn it. She didn't have to explain those needs to anyone. She glanced away from Aidan and focused on finding a place to set out the net in the cramped area crawling with other drifters trying to do the same.

"Five minutes! Peter, get that buoy ready. Wes, keep an eye out." They couldn't put their net out until the clock struck time to fish, but if a fisherman let his buoy fly a little earlier, then all the fisherman dropped their nets. After all, how would the fish cops be able to discern which fisherman dropped their net first?

Time clicked slowly and silence settled over the bay, except for the slow rumble of diesel engines. It was as if the very air waited on baited breath.

"There!" Wes pointed, and Peter let the buoy soar. Sonya gunned the engines and the bay roared as drifters rushed to catch every last fish swimming upriver to the spawning grounds. It was a buzz that never failed to exhilarate Sonya. Forgotten was the risk of being pregnant, the reprimand she'd received from Aidan, the guilt she couldn't seem to squash. Instead, she let the excitement and the fight for fish steal over her.

White fire erupted along the cork line as salmon hit the net. Peter and Wes pointed to areas of the net, hollering a "Hot damn," and "Did you see that?" Even Aidan seemed to forget what had transpired between them as a smile lit his face.

He turned to her, and his smile lost some of its shine, but he nodded to her and Sonya knew he got it. Set netting did bring a portion of this thrill, but not to the heightened level that drifting delivered.

"Hey, hey, Captain. Looky there!" Peter pointed to a ten fathoms section of net where the corks were sunk.

Now that's more like it. A sunk net usually meant they'd caught lots of fish. Wes hollered a, "woo-hoo!" and Peter did a touchdown dance. Even Aidan slapped Wes with a high five. Sonya let the net soak a little longer then hollered that they were going to pull it in. Her crew took up positions, readying themselves for a morning of picking fish and hopefully filling all the holds aboard the boat. She switched on the hydraulics and started pulling in the full net. Now if they could keep that up for the rest of the summer. With the "accidents" they'd been plagued with lately it had been awhile since they'd been able to fish out an opening.

She turned on her iPod that she'd hooked into the stereo speakers placed on deck and Bon Jovi belted out *Wanted Dead or Alive*. She sang along, running the hydraulics as her crew picked fish after fish after fish. Today might be their best day of the season. It was definitely the best stocked net of the season.

She engaged the reel and pulled on the sunken section of net.

"Hold it!" Peter held his hand up like a stop sign. "Something's not right." He leaned over the bow and swiftly turned to her, his face sickly white. "The net's full of…Chuck?"

"What?" She killed the music and leaned out the pilot house window. "What did you say?"

Wes rushed to the side and bent to see what Peter had. He quickly turned back, looking as sick as Peter. "Better call the troopers."

Peter ran for the starboard side and threw up over the edge. Sonya cut the engines while Aidan took a look and Wes tossed out the anchor. Dread lay heavy in her stomach as she made her way to the bow. Dead silence onboard caused her boots to echo like hammer blows on the aluminum deck.

Aidan suddenly stood in front of her, blocking her path. His hands held her shoulders, keeping her in place. "You don't want to look, Sonya."

"Move aside, Aidan. I'm captain of this boat, and I'll handle whatever I have to." He released her, and she leaned over the bow.

There, caught in her net, was Chuck Kendrick.

Floating belly-up.

CHAPTER TWENTY-SEVEN

Sonya radioed the *Calypso*. By the time she'd finished, the anchored *Double Dippin'* had attracted a swarm of drifters. They swooped around her like a flock of squawking seagulls seeking a free lunch. She and Aidan had looped a rope around Kendrick's body so the swift tide didn't work him free of the net. Lord knew Kendrick was in no condition to help himself, as he was seriously dead. They'd also released the tension on the net so that Kendrick sunk under the surface, with the weight of the lead line keeping him under. She couldn't imagine the squawking of the crowd if they caught sight of Kendrick's bloated body.

The main problem—besides the obvious dead body—was that the other drifters were getting downright nasty over the *Double Dippin'* weighing at anchor while her net was still fishing.

"What the hell you playing at, Sonya?" The captain of the *Intrepid* rammed them on the portside. "Set netting in a drift opening? You've got your rigging confused, woman."

A crewman from the *Gale Force* added from starboard, "The *Calypso's* headed this way, and she sure as shootin' better write you up."

Sonya ducked as a can of pop sailed over from the *Intrepid*. The can nearly hit Sonya, exploding on deck in an arc of fizz.

"Hey!" Aidan yelled, ready to take on *Intrepid's* crew.

Sonya grabbed his arm before he could make the leap. "Don't provoke them."

"This is getting dangerous." Wes stepped to her other side so the men flanked her like a pair of bookends. "Somebody's going to get hurt."

"Tell that to Kendrick." Aidan turned to Sonya. "Wes is right, this is dangerous. Too dangerous for a woman like you."

"A woman like me?" she sputtered. The *Intrepid* tossed over another can. This time Sonya caught it and threw it back, taking great satisfaction when it boomed onto the aluminum deck and sprayed one of their crewmen. "What do you mean *a woman like me?*" She turned on Aidan.

"You know, one…who is more…refined. What did you say about *not* provoking them?"

Swearing erupted aboard the *Intrepid* and a few colorful names were directed back at Sonya along with a threat or two. She flipped them the bird. "How's that for refined?" She raised a brow at Aidan.

Did the man even *know* her?

Wes slapped Aidan on his shoulder. "She might be a classical musician, but she has a bit of a rocker in her too."

"I know that, but…Sonya, you can't tell me that you enjoy this?" He indicated the boats, the fishing, the brawling.

She gave a half smile. "Yeah, I do." Though she could have done without the dead body.

The *Miss Julie II* butted her way between the Double Dippin' and the *Intrepid*. Treat's concerned face appeared. "Are you aware of what you're doing, Sonya?"

"Yep." She nodded, shading her eyes from the high sun glinting off the aluminum boat. She'd left her sunglasses somewhere. She made a mental note to check the cabin later. She'd already searched the boat.

Treat studied her and her crew for a moment. Wes stood, arms crossed over his chest, Aidan with his jaw clenched, fists at his side, while Peter sat on an overturned bucket, head resting in his hands. "What's really up? You need help?"

Sonya relaxed a bit and gave him a small smile. "Thanks, Treat, but looks as though help is on the way." She indicated the *Calypso* bearing down on them.

"You're in bad shape if you're looking for help in that quadrant."

"Don't I know it," she muttered under her breath, forgetting how sound traveled over water when Treat chuckled.

"Why don't I stick around, help buffer the worst of them?" He nodded to the *Intrepid* and many of the other drifters of the same ilk.

"It's really appreciated, but I don't expect you to give up fishing to watch out for me."

"Who said anything about not fishing?" He gave her a wily smile. "If you don't mind me rubbing up against you every now and then, my net can drift freely from the stern."

In a sense, Treat would use her as an anchor while he fished. He wouldn't be tied to her but being able to rub up against her helped to keep him stationary.

"Just don't get your net tied up with mine or my boat."

He winked at her. "Don't worry. I'll keep us from getting tangled."

Good, because nobody wanted to be tangled up with her right now.

The *Calypso* cut in along Sonya's starboard side, forcing the *Gale Force* to back out of the way. "*Double Dippin'*, prepare to be boarded."

How she hated those words.

Wes grabbed one of ropes the *Calypso* threw over and Aidan grabbed the other, securing the ropes to the cleats, linking the boats together from bow to stern. Peter continued to sit on the bucket, looking as sallow as tissue paper. He hadn't said a word since losing his stomach contents. She wished she could shield him, send him below deck until it was all over, but she couldn't do that to the man inside of him, or embarrass the boy in front of his shipmates. No matter how much she wanted to shelter him, there came a time when life dictated the course.

Garrett swung over the rail, like a buccaneer ready to pillage. "Sonya?" He whipped off his sunglasses and greedily took her in from head to toe. Her breath caught at the intense flare of heat from his worried eyes. Then his gaze swiveled to Aidan and it turned to ice. "Harte." He took in Peter's sickly appearance and Wes's uneasy one. "What's happened?"

When she'd radioed for the *Calypso* she'd been vague over the reason, just gave them her position and instructed them to hurry.

Judd joined them. "You aware you're sitting at anchor with your net out?"

"Yes."

"What's going on, Sonya?" Garrett moved in closer to her.

She leaned into Garrett to keep her voice from traveling to the other drifters circling around her like vultures. One whiff of Garrett's scent and it was all she could do not to nestle into his strong, protective arms. She had to be tough. A sign of weakness and those vultures would descend. "We caught Kendrick in our net."

"Caught?" His eyes narrowed. "Dead?"

She nodded. "Very."

His lips tightened into a thin line. "Okay." He laid his hand on her arm and slowly rubbed his palm up and down. She took more comfort in the small caress than she should have. "Get your crew and keep out of the way while we do our job."

"I'm not fishing out this period either, am I?"

He shook his head. "Sorry, Sonya."

Garrett turned to Judd and informed him, keeping his tone low, then he picked up his radio and called for backup while Judd returned to the *Calypso.*

"You're calling in *more* troopers?" she whispered harshly. She glanced around at the drifters still watching her like a thick cut of prime rib.

"We can't very well reach the body in a drift boat, now can we?"

"Oh…yeah." She took a deep breath and tried not to think about Kendrick's body bloated like a ghost fish in her net.

"Did you do anything to secure the body or is it floating free in your net?"

"No." She swallowed past the bile in her throat. "We—Aidan and I—looped a rope around his leg—" She slapped a hand over her mouth until the need to be sick passed.

"You okay?" Garrett reached out to touch her.

She held up her hand in a motion to give her a minute, walked over to the cooler they kept on deck, and grabbed a water bottle. She took a long drink, paused and then took another. Screwing the lid back on, she rejoined Garrett.

"Securing the body was good thinking on your part, Sonya."

"Thanks, but it was Aidan who thought of it."

The *Miss Julie II* rubbed against the *Double Dippin'* causing Sonya to stumble into Garrett. He caught her, holding her tight against the hard, warmth of his body, and flashes of what had transpired between the two of them, just hours earlier, sizzled between them.

Garrett set her back on her feet, waited until she was steady, and then let go of her. He turned toward the *Miss Julie II*. "Treat! Quit using Sonya as an anchor and back off."

"I'm only acting as a buffer between Sonya and some of the unsavory fishermen out here."

"I'm all the buffer she needs right now."

"Really?" Treat dragged out. "So that's the way of it? Sonya, seriously? Slumming with a fish cop? You could have set your cap *so* much higher."

"I'm too busy to slum, Treat. Besides, slumming would be going for you," Sonya returned.

"Ouch, Sonya, that hurts."

"Treat," Garrett warned.

"What's really going on here anyway? Someone dead?" Realization dawned across his face. "Shit almighty, that's it, isn't it? Who? Who's dead?"

"Back off, Treat, or I'm confiscating your catch for anchoring."

Treat grumbled but backed his boat off.

Garrett turned as a RHIB arrived with two more troopers aboard. "Stay out of the way, but within earshot in case we need help with your net. Okay?"

She nodded. He reached out and squeezed her arm again and then he was gone, having swung back over to the *Calypso*. She watched as he and Judd dropped from the *Calypso* onto the RHIB. Judd carried a black tool box, and a camera hung around his neck. Garrett carried a body bag.

Sonya lost her morning-after breakfast.

"Yep, that is one dead body," Judd said as he and Garrett floated Kendrick to the surface with the pull of the rope the *Double Dippin'* had secured the body with.

"Yo, *Double D!*" Ringo motored up on the *Mary Jane.* "Are you throwing a party without inviting us?" Ringo caught sight of Kendrick's body as Garrett and Judd pulled it aboard the RHIB. "Holy moly! Damn, Sonya. I heard that you threatened Kendrick last night, but no one believed you'd actually go through with it."

"Listen up!" Garrett yelled in a voice that got the circling drifters's attention. "I'm in the mood to write some tickets. I suggest you all get back to fishing—" he did a three-sixty, staring at all the flocking drifters, "—unless you want a fine for interference."

Mumbling complaints mixed with rumbling diesel engines as the drifters gave them some space. Though not enough to satisfy Garrett. News of Kendrick's death would be brimming over the bay in minutes, if it wasn't already.

Judd started snapping stills as the other trooper— Garrett forgot his name, just that he could eat everyone under the table when it came to King Crab—videoed the scene.

Garrett examined the body but didn't see any obvious signs of injury. "Judd, help me turn him over." They flipped him, and there, in Kendrick's upper back, was a wicked gash.

"Guess this was no accidental drowning." Judd picked up the camera and took some more shots.

Garrett investigated the wound. "A knife didn't do this. Something curved did."

"Like what?"

"Possibly a hook of some sort. A mold will tell us for sure."

"That'll be up to the medical examiner in Anchorage," Judd said. "Skip's probably already radioed for a silver bullet."

"Silver bullet?"

"Yeah, lightweight aluminum coffins for cases such as this. All the evidence and the body get stuffed into the bullet and airlifted to Anchorage. It's not like we have the means or the forensic equipment to completely handle a full investigation. It comes down to old-fashioned legwork out here."

"Gotcha. Hand me the thermometer so I can get a liver temp." Judd handed Garrett the thermometer out of the tool box, and he inserted it into Kendrick's liver.

They finished and zipped the body into the double-lined body bag, leaving it on the RHIB as they boarded the *Calypso*.

"I've called for a silver bullet from King Salmon," Skip said when they joined him in the cabin. "Troopers will meet us at the Naknek City Dock. Hunt, I want Judd staying behind to help you question Sonya and her crew." Skip gave Garrett a long stare. "By the book, Hunt."

He nodded. Here was the test whether or not he could objectively handle Sonya and the job he had to do.

He had his doubts.

"I want statements from everyone onboard and try to get a look around. I'm leaving Corte with you, while I accompany Foster and the body to the dock. We'll reconvene later."

They broke apart. Judd and Garrett boarded the *Double Dippin'* to find her crew much the same as they'd left them.

His gaze immediately gravitated to Sonya. He wanted to hold her. Take her away from all this nastiness. Instead he stamped down his feelings and let the cop inside of him do his job.

"We'll need to question everyone on board," he directed his statement toward Sonya. She was pale yet holding it together better than most in her situation would. Her t-shirt today had a red salmon rocking on an electric guitar with the words, "The Dead Red," written across the top. Life imitating art? "While Judd and I do that, would you mind if Officer Corte takes a look around?"

"You need a warrant for that," Aidan interjected. He'd been shooting daggers at Garrett since he'd arrived.

"Not if Sonya gives us permission." Garrett a raised brow at Sonya. "What do you say?"

"Go ahead." She shrugged. "I have nothing to hide."

Garrett motioned for Corte to take a look around. "All right, this is how it's going to work. Judd and I are going to question you individually. Sonya, can we use your pilot house?"

She nodded. "How long do you think this will take?"

Garrett glanced at her, and her crew, then at Aidan. "Depends on the level of cooperation we receive." He motioned for Sonya to lead the way. "We'll start with you."

"Sonya?" Peter's voice held worry and a touch of anger. It was the first word he'd spoken since losing his breakfast.

She turned to him and took his hand in hers, squeezing it. "Don't worry. Everything will be fine." She turned to Aidan. "Can you and Wes round-haul the rest of the net in?"

"Of course." Aidan reached out and wrapped his arms around Sonya, rubbing her back. "I'll take care of everything."

Garrett wanted to rip them apart. He wasn't sure what he would have done if Sonya hadn't broken out of Harte's embrace.

"Thanks, Aidan." She nodded in Peter's direction. "Keep an eye on him." Without a glance toward Garrett or Judd, she led the way to the pilot house.

Garrett tried to forget what he and Sonya had been doing a mere few hours ago. Sonya dropped into the captain's chair like the weight she carried was getting too heavy to bear. Judd took a seat on the bunk, while Garrett remained standing next to the stove.

Judd flipped open his notebook, and Garrett began asking questions. "Tell me again from the top what happened this morning."

She gave him a run down of her actions since her crew came aboard until they'd pulled Kendrick up in the net.

"That's quite the coincidence," Judd commented. "You're in a fight with Kendrick at the Pitt last night, threatened that he'd be 'floating belly-up', and then he ends up your catch of the day."

Garrett didn't believe in coincidences as a rule. After all, what were the odds? What were the odds that he'd gotten her pregnant this morning? The thought of their child beginning its life inside her right now had all his protective instincts roaring to life.

"Was there a question in there, officer?" she asked, raising a brow at Judd.

"Yeah, I'd like a breakdown of your whereabouts since leaving the Pitt last night."

"Judd, that's not necessary," Garrett said.

"By the book, Garrett."

Garrett ran a hand through his short hair, his jaw clenching. "You don't have to answer him, Sonya."

Her eyes flicked to his and then narrowed toward Judd. "I'm sure he already knows you spent the night with me, so why are we going through this?"

"I need it for the record," Judd said.

"I left the Pitt with Garrett and was with him until around six this morning. Do you want all the salacious details?"

"That won't be necessary." Judd turned to Garrett. "You willing to verify that?"

"You know I am." The steel in his voice was cold and sharp, letting Judd know he'd better watch his step.

Judd turned back to Sonya. "Who else is aware that you two spent the night together?"

She sighed and dropped her gaze, fingering the frayed cuff of her long-sleeved t-shirt. "Uhm…Aidan knows."

"You told Harte?" Garrett asked, his tone unbelieving. Why would she confide in Harte? Unless there was more between them than she'd let on.

Her eyes shifted to the side. "Not exactly."

"What do you mean, 'not exactly'."

Sonya glanced at Judd and then back to Garrett, color staining her cheeks. "It's…personal."

Garrett leaned back and took a deep breath. What had he expected from their one night together? That she'd share everything with him? Care about him? He knew she must have feelings for him on some level, right? If Sonya and Aidan had personal things still between them, where did that put him?

Corte stepped up to the door and knocked. Garrett slid it open. "Excuse me for interrupting, but I found this onboard. Looks like it could be the murder weapon."

Chapter Twenty-Eight

The trooper handed Garrett a gaff hook encased in a large plastic bag. Blood stained the end of the hook. Sonya knew, with the day she was having, that the blood had to be Kendrick's.

"That's not mine," she said, her voice an octave higher than normal. "I don't have a halibut gaff on board. The only hook I have onboard is five feet long, not two. What good would a two foot gaff do on a drift boat? I need one longer than four feet just to reach the water from the sides of this tub." She was rambling but couldn't stop herself. She was smart enough to know how bad this situation was getting. She'd threatened Kendrick last night, in front of a dozen witnesses. Now the murder weapon was found on her boat? Sweat broke out over her body, but she felt cold. Colder than she could remember being in a very long time.

"Sonya," Garrett's voice cut through the fog that was rapidly closing her in. Suddenly he was there, kneeling in front of her, taking her hands in his. "You have an ironclad alibi. We know you didn't do this. You couldn't. Kendrick had been dead between ten and twelve hours. We were together during that time."

She met his eyes. Seeing the reassurance in his should have allayed her fears, but it didn't. "If I use your alibi then everyone will know we were together. If the fishermen find out, I'm going to be blackballed more than I already am."

Garrett let go of her hands and fell back on his haunches. "Let me get this right. You're willing to be arrested and charged with murder rather than let anyone know we were together last night?"

"Dude, that's rough," Judd commented from the bunk.

"No," Sonya said. "It means you have to find the real killer so we don't have to use the alibi."

Garrett got to his feet and walked back to the stove, where he'd positioned himself when he'd entered the pilot house. Sonya tried not to miss his steady warmth. She knew by the tightening of his jaw and the rigid way he held his shoulders that she had hurt him with her refusal to come clean about them. There was a lot at stake here.

"If that's the way you want it." Garrett rubbed the back of his neck. "If the gaff isn't yours—" he picked up the evidence bag "—do you have any idea how it got onboard your boat?"

She racked her brain and came up with nothing. "I've no idea."

"I have one," Garrett said. "Why is Aidan fishing with you today?"

"Aidan? H-he wanted to understand the drift operation."

"He picked today of all days to do that?"

"Another coincidence," Judd interjected, clicking his tongue.

"How?" she asked. "There is no way Aidan could have brought that onboard without one of us seeing him."

Garrett unzipped his trooper jacket, took the gaff hook, stuffed it in his jacket, and then zipped it out of sight.

"No." She swallowed past the bile that had returned. "I don't believe it. I won't. There are other ways to plant something like that. Someone could have dropped it onboard during the night. Or-or planted it when I grabbed a quick shower at the cannery this morning. I was gone about twenty minutes."

"Those are possibilities," Judd seemed to agree until he continued, "but wouldn't you have heard the gaff if someone dropped it onboard during the night? Aluminum boats aren't known for muffling sounds, quite the opposite in fact."

"I wasn't paying attention to noises last night." A bomb could have gone off right on her deck and she wouldn't have heard it, not with all her attention centered on Garrett and what he'd made her feel. She stole a glance his direction and wished she hadn't, as his eyes reflected the same memories she knew hers did.

"Judd, table the gaff for now." Garrett's gaze returned to Sonya as he pulled the hook free of his jacket and held it in his hand. She would never look at another gaff the same again.

"We're back to who wants to hurt you, Sonya." Garrett leaned against the stove and folded his arms across his chest. "It obviously wasn't Kendrick. So we need to go back to the beginning and figure out who wants you off this water. We need names fast, because whoever he is, he proved he's willing to kill to do it."

"Sonya, no matter what the cops might think, I didn't plant that gaff hook on your boat," Aidan said once more as they reached the beach in front of their camps.

Sonya wearily ran a hand over her face. She didn't know what to think. Aidan did have opportunity but did he have motive? The *Double Dippin'* was currently anchored near the running line in front of the cabin with Peter and Wes onboard until she returned.

If she could keep Aidan walking toward their camps, maybe he'd turn in the direction of his when they reached the creek. It had been a hell of day and she didn't see it getting any better. Particularly with the upcoming meeting with her grandparents. It was hard to believe it was only late afternoon. So much had happened in the last twenty-four hours.

It seemed like weeks since she'd been back at camp, when in reality it had only been a day. By the time fishing ended, she'd need a month of sleep to recover from the season. She noticed the outboard engine laying on a tarp under the bluff and almost laughed. She'd bet a steak dinner Gramps had gotten that miserable thing to run. He was probably waiting for Peter or Wes to help him get the outboard bolted onto the skiff.

Aidan grabbed her arm and turned her toward him. She'd almost forgotten he kept step with her. "Sonya, you've got to believe me. I would never do anything to hurt you."

She raised a brow. "Never?"

"Never again." Frustration shown clearly in his expression. "How long are you going to make me pay for that?"

"Name it, Aidan. *Name* what you did to me." Hell, she didn't want to go down this path. She was tired. Tired of crap drifting her way. Tired of men complicating her life. Getting into it with Aidan wasn't something she wanted to face right now. Especially considering the answers she might get.

"Believe it or not, the night I hit you scared me to death." He ran a hand through his hair. "I saw the monster inside me clearly that day. I'd watched Earl beat my mother time and time again. I hated him for it. Still do. But when I couldn't get you to do what I wanted, I turned and did the same to you." He grasped her shoulders. "To the woman I loved. Seeing what I was becoming scared the shit out of me. I got help, and I will continue to get help. There is no way I'll let that ever happen again. I refuse to be my father. Sonya, I love you. Give us another chance. We were good for each other." He dropped his forehead to hers, his arms inching around her waist. "Don't believe the worst of me anymore. Please."

"Aidan." She felt tears tease behind her eyes. She'd believed in them once. Believed that they could be happy together, that they'd marry, have a family. They had so much in common, made sense where she and Garrett didn't, but she couldn't go back. She was either too frightened or too obstinate to try. At some point, her feelings had changed. Whether it was that night he'd shown her a side of him she had no idea existed or later, but something inside her refused to change.

"I don't believe the worst of you, Aidan." She placed her hands on the sides of his face. She'd loved this face. The strong jaw, the warm brown eyes, the sexy tilt of his lips when he smiled at her. She reached up and softly placed her lips against his one last time. Stepping back, she gazed at him with remorse. "I'm sorry. I can't go back."

He pulled her to him and desperately took her mouth. She let him kiss her, tried to even feel what she'd felt with him before. There was nothing. What she felt with Garrett was so much more than she'd ever felt with Aidan. It saddened and scared her at the same time. Aidan's grip loosened, turned gentle as he tried to coax a response from her that she didn't have in her to give. Finally he set her back from him, and let her go. His expression one of resignation.

"It's Hunt, isn't it?"

"No. Yes. Hell, I don't know." She shook her head. "He's not the best choice of man for me to become involved with, but I did…at least, I think we are…involved that is." She bit her lip.

"You barely know the guy."

"How long you know a person doesn't really mean anything. Does it?"

The stain of humiliation colored his face. He slowly shook of his head. "We're never going to get past this, are we?"

"Yes, we will. But we'll never be more than friends, Aidan. You need to understand that and move on."

His heartbroken gaze met hers. "I don't think I can live with that, Sonya."

"You and Sonya looked cozy," Earl commented from the shadows of the porch. The red butt of his cigarette flared to life as he took a long draw. When he exhaled, smoke curled around his head like a crown of death. Aidan had seen this vision many times in his life, even drew one of his seedy characters in his graphic novel after his dad. Not that Earl ever caught on. He'd have to read one of Aidan's novels to see it and that was one thing he knew Earl would never do.

"We were saying good-bye to each other." Or at least good-bye to what they could have been.

"What do you mean good-bye?" Earl's bushy brows hunched over beady eyes. "You going somewhere?"

"She doesn't care about me the way I need her to. We're over. Finished."

"Change her mind. What kind of a sissy-boy are you?" Earl stood and ground the butt of his cigarette under the heel of his boot. "In my day, you wanted something, you went after it until you got it. Show some backbone, boy, and go and get what's yours."

"She isn't mine to get. Besides, she cares for someone else."

"Women are fickle. They change their mind like they change their outfits. Get him out of the picture and chances are she'd be wantin' to wear you."

Aidan gave a humorless laugh. "Right, like what? Bump him off?"

A smile cracked Earl's yellowed, leathered face. "Now you're thinking like a Harte."

The last thing he wanted to do was think like a Harte. It hadn't gotten him anywhere positive in the past. "I'm not going down that road."

Though it would be nice to see the last of the fish cop.

Sonya had spent most of the evening catching up her grandparents on the happenings of the last twenty-four hours. Who knew life could change so much in that length of time? As she had expected, they scolded her for brawling with Kendrick at the Pitt. Peter had given her a heads up over this, but he needn't have bothered. She knew she'd get called on the mat over her actions as soon as they saw her. The news of Kendrick's death went better than she'd hoped, though they were shocked and dismayed over their family having to be a part of something so tragic. The point that they focused on was the development between Garrett and her. Sonya really hadn't wanted to tell them that she'd slept with the fish cop, but figured she needed to prepare them in case the news had to come out. They also took this much, much better than she'd hoped.

"I knew you and Garrett would hit it off the first time I laid eyes on him," Gramps said, nudging Grams. "Didn't I tell you, Maggie May?"

"Yes, dear, you did indeed." Grams gave Sonya a look that said there would be no living with the man now that he considered himself a master matchmaker.

"We need something to celebrate with. Is there any of that German chocolate cake left?"

Grams served them all a slice along with powdered milk to drink. When she joined them at the table, Gramps hit Sonya with the big questions. "So, when you two getting hitched?"

"What? No, no, Gramps. Don't go there. Garrett doesn't seem to be the marrying kind, and I'm not ready for that kind of commitment." Being married would be nice, though, if she turned up pregnant.

"Poppycock. Fear of commitment flies right out the window when you fall in love." He winked at Grams. "Right, Maggie May?"

She reached over and squeezed his good hand. "You're so right." They shared a look that pulled on Sonya's heartstrings. Could she be in love with Garrett? She'd thought she'd been in love with Aidan, but had she really? One thing she did know, she was definitely confused.

They heard an engine pull up outside below the cabin. "I'll see who it is. You two stay there." Sonya opened the door and found Garrett climbing up the path, still dressed in uniform. It didn't look that bad on him, if she were to be honest. What did it mean that the uniform seemed to be growing on her? Somehow she'd known she'd see him again tonight. Was the jumping of her heart due to joy or fear? Or both?

"Sonya." Garrett nodded. "Mind if I come in?"

She opened the door farther for him to enter and indicated that he take a seat at the table. Garrett shook Gramps's good hand first and gave Grams a nod and asked after their health.

Grams offered him a piece of cake that he turned down. "This isn't a social visit," he said, though he gazed at Sonya like he very much wished it were. "We found the *Albatross* earlier this evening."

"Where?" As of this afternoon no one had seen the *Albatross* since the night before. Hopefully there would be some evidence onboard that pointed in another direction besides hers.

He cocked a half smile. "She actually sailed right up to the dock of the cannery. Her crewmen seemed really surprised when they heard what had happened."

"I don't understand. Didn't they question not having their captain onboard?"

"Apparently, they were very inebriated when they returned to the boat. She was still dry when they boarded. They went to bed, and when they finally woke, they found themselves drifting upriver halfway to King Salmon. By then the tide started heading out, and with neither one of them competent enough to pilot Kendrick's boat, they ran aground on a sandbar. They had to wait until the tide came in again to navigate their way back to the cannery. They were expecting to get filleted alive by their captain and seemed relieved that he was in no condition to do that."

"Why wasn't the *Albatross* at anchor?"

"They both swear the anchor had been set before they hit their bunks. I think whoever attacked Kendrick, pulled the anchor. The timeline is a little fuzzy with the temperature of the water being so cold. According to the crew, they left the Pitt, having stayed after Kendrick stormed off not long after you left. They drank, played pool, and drank some more. They left when the Pitt closed, boarding the *Albatross* soon after. "

"So Kendrick's whereabouts from the time he left the Pitt, until he fell into the water are unaccounted for," Sonya said.

Garrett smiled. "You're sounding like a cop."

"Sorry."

"I like it."

Gramps cleared his throat. "Does anyone know where Kendrick went into the water?"

Grams shook her head. "I know he wasn't liked by many, but no one deserves to die the way he did." She shivered.

"Actually we don't know the way he died for sure," Garrett said. "Not until the medical examiner has a chance to exam the body. There was evidence aboard the *Albatross* that Kendrick was set upon there." He reached into the inside pocket of his trooper jacket and pulled out another evidence bag, this one considerably smaller than the one that held the gaff earlier. "We also found these." He handed the bag to Sonya. "How long have you been missing your sunglasses?"

CHAPTER TWENTY-NINE

Sonya slowly reached out for the evidence-wrapped sunglasses from Garrett and looked them over.

Yep, they were hers, but then she'd known they were the moment he pulled them out of his jacket. There was something dark staining the bottom of the lenses. *Blood.* She dropped the glasses as though they'd bitten her.

"How long have they been missing, Sonya?" Garrett asked again.

She couldn't tear her eyes away from the glasses lying there on the table next to her plate of German Chocolate cake crumbs. The eaten cake threatened to make a reappearance. She swallowed, imagining her sunglasses lying on the deck of Kendrick's boat in a pool of his blood. She slid the evidence bag across the tabletop toward Garrett, not wanting to see the sunglasses ever again.

"Sonya."

She ran a shaky hand over her face, closed her eyes for a moment, and then met Garrett's steady stare. "I don't know for sure. I searched the boat this morning when they weren't on the counter where I usually keep them. I'd planned on looking here at the cabin tonight."

He covered her hand with his. "It's really important that you try and remember the last time you wore your sunglasses."

The shock was wearing off, and anger blessedly took its place. "Someone stole my sunglasses and planted them at a murder scene, didn't they?"

Garrett nodded. "That's my theory. So think, when was the last time?"

She leaned back against the wall of the cabin and rubbed her temples. "I had them when we took Gramps to see Wanda. I remember taking them off when Peter and I were in the waiting room."

"What about later that day?"

"You had them when you returned with Nikky," Grams said, lacing her fingers together. "You grabbed them off the table when you headed next door to see Aidan. Remember, you knocked over the card tower I'd been building."

"She's right," Sonya said.

"Were you wearing them when you entered the Pitt to confront Kendrick?" Garrett asked.

"Yes. I remember taking them off when I entered the bar and hooking them into the collar of my t-shirt."

"You didn't have them when we left the Pitt." A knowing gleam entered his eyes.

Sonya felt like the temperature in the room had suddenly increased twenty degrees. Of course, he'd know if she had them on her as he helped to disarm and then undress her later that evening.

"I think it's safe to assume you lost them in the tussle with Kendrick. Now we need to figure out who picked them up and planted them on the *Albatross*. Whoever it is has something against you and against Kendrick. Or was Kendrick just a pawn to frame you?"

"Who would go through all that trouble? I admit I've offended people out here, but no more than anyone else.

We can be enemies out there on water but when fishing's over, we can also share drinks or a meal and laugh it off."

"Someone isn't laughing." Garrett leaned his elbows on the table. "We need a list of everyone who was in the Pitt that night and whoever has threatened, gotten angry with, or insulted you in some way. I don't care how slight, I want names."

"Okay, kids, I need to lie down some," Gramps interrupted, indicating his bandaged hand. "Why don't you two take a walk and let me rest a bit? I'll think on that list, Garrett. Maybe I can come up with something."

"That would be appreciated." Garrett rose to his feet and offered his hand to Sonya.

She felt strange placing her palm in his with her grandparents as witnesses. She thought she caught a twinkle in Gramps' eye before he covered it with a grimace of pain. Was the man still matchmaking? Or was his hand actually paining him enough that he needed to rest? He was getting up there in years, but she'd seen younger men give out before her grandfather would call it quits.

Sonya was silent as she followed Garrett outside. He led the way around the cabin onto the tundra. The dusk of evening painted red and gold streaks across the sky. The breeze was brisk but not cold, blowing from the southeast, which meant they'd probably get rain by morning. Unfortunately wind from that direction would also blow the fish into deeper water. Set netting tomorrow wouldn't fare well. If this kept up, her season would be more bust than bumper.

Garrett came to a stop amongst a meadow of spongy tundra and low-lying wildflowers. Alder bushes dotted areas around them where the plants could get their roots into deeper soil, while the tundra survived on a small amount of loam over ice that never thawed.

"What are you thinking about?" Garrett asked as he turned to face her.

"The cost of Peter's college tuition."

He laughed. "Way to build a man's ego. Here I was hoping you were remembering last night. Why tuition?"

She was glad that he focused on her comment rather than their one night together. She'd been doing her damndest not to think about it, but every few minutes it would sneak into her thoughts. "Well, with everything that has gone down this season, fishing keeps getting interrupted, and to date, I've haven't made much more than expenses. I'd hoped to catch more this summer than what I've caught."

"The season isn't over, yet. It could be worse."

He was right. Here she was concerned over how much money she hadn't made, and Kendrick had lost his life.

"Hey." Garrett cupped her face. "I didn't say that to make you sad. I meant, at least you've made expenses."

"I know. I just couldn't help thinking about Kendrick."

"Why? From all accounts, he made life hell for everyone around him. You included."

"True, but what was he like when he wasn't fishing? We all change a bit out here, become more barbaric, less civilized." A sudden thought struck her. "Do you know if he had a wife, kids? Did he leave a family behind?"

"From what his crewman shared, Kendrick led a solitary life. He preferred it that way."

"Well, that's good." She flushed when Garrett raised a brow. "I mean, it would be tragic if there was a son at home, or a grieving widow. I guess it's even sadder that there isn't, right?"

Garrett smoothed a lock of hair behind her ear that the wind had teased free of her ponytail. "You are something special, you know that. No wonder I can't resist you." He slowly pulled her toward him as though waiting to see if she'd baulk. Instead, she willingly came into his arms, her own snaking tight around his waist. All day she'd had to act competent and convincing while everything fell apart around her. It felt so good to rest her head on Garrett's capable shoulders. Something inside her chest swelled.

"I was proud of you today, Sonya. Not many men could have handled your situation with as much poise or restraint."

She leaned back. "I take it you didn't see me flip off the *Intrepid* or toss my cookies over the side of the boat."

He smiled, and her heartbeat quickened. "It all makes you that much more irresistible to me." He lowered his head, his eyes at half-mast, watching her. Hers fluttered, and she found herself breathless as he brushed his lips softly against hers.

"Wait a minute." Sonya pulled back as a thought struck her and before all reason left her. "According to everything you said earlier, Kendrick's crew had to be on-board when Kendrick was attacked."

"I'm kissing you, and all you can think about is Kendrick?" He gave a crooked grin. "I must not be doing this right."

"I'm serious. You said the boat was dry when Kendrick's crew boarded and went to bed. If Kendrick was attacked on his boat before the crewmen boarded, how did he get in the water?"

"We don't know. His crew didn't notice if he was on-board when they boarded."

"The boat isn't that big, thirty-two-footer just like mine. You've seen my sleeping quarters, not much room. They would have noticed."

"Not if they were too drunk, which also answers your next question. If Kendrick was attacked when the boat was floating, why didn't his crewmen hear anything? Too drunk."

"Kind of convenient, don't you think? What if Kendrick was attacked before they got to the boat? Instead of being pushed into the water, he was pushed over the side of his boat into the mud?"

He looked thoughtful. "We'll have to wait and see what the medical examiner says. You've made an interesting point. With the boat dry, it opens the possibility for someone to board the *Albatross* without anyone seeing or hearing him. He could have snuck onboard and laid in wait. Or boarded when he knew Kendrick was alone. The incoming surf would have washed away any evidence of his approach."

"Meaning the killer could have been a set netter and not a drifter?"

"Exactly."

A gunshot split the air over their heads.

Garrett shoved Sonya to the ground and covered her with his body, but not before she caught sight of Aidan on the opposite side of the bank where the creek sliced through the tundra.

A sawed-off shotgun nestled against his shoulder.

CHAPTER THIRTY

"You okay?" Garrett demanded of Sonya, his weapon already palmed and pointed in the direction of the blast.

"Y-yeah." She was trying to catch her breath, and Garrett knew he'd probably knocked the wind out of her when he'd shoved her to the ground. He shifted to the side to give her more room to breathe. "Was that a gunshot?" she gasped out.

"Yeah, your harmless neighbor is shooting at us."

"That can't be right. There has to be another reason." She sounded almost desperate as though she was trying to convince herself of something different than what her eyes had already seen.

Sonya strained to rise, but Garrett threw his free arm over her and knocked her back to the tundra. "Stay down!"

"This is crazy. Aidan can't be shooting at us. There has to be another—"

Another blast fractured the twilight.

"That's it." Garrett clenched his teeth and tightened his finger on the trigger of his weapon. One shot and this whole mess would be over, and Aidan Harte would be out of the picture. He *knew* Aidan had something to do with the "accidents" that had plagued Sonya all season. "Harte! Drop the gun, and step away from it."

Harte lowered the shotgun from his shoulder but didn't release it.

"Everything's—you're—now." Harte's every other word got carried away on the wind and Garrett couldn't make out what Harte said. All he knew was the man had yet to drop the sawed-off shotgun to the ground.

"Drop the gun!" Garrett rose to a crouched position and held his own weapon on Harte. Harte's face paled, and he dropped the shotgun like it had bit him.

"What in tar nation is going on here?" Nikolai hollered, half-running around the side of the cabin, cradling his injured hand. He was followed by Margaret with her own sawed-off shotgun, at the ready.

"Stay back, and let me handle this," Garrett said, keeping his weapon trained on Harte.

"This—big—understanding," Harte hollered, though the wind continued to pick and choose which words it would allow to be carried. Then he began to point.

"Oh, for heaven's sake," Sonya said from behind Garrett.

"I told you to stay down." Couldn't she follow the simplest of commands? He was trying to keep her alive, damn it.

"Garrett, put your gun down," she said.

"Are you kidding me?"

"I'm sure there's a good explanation." She touched his shoulder. "Let him explain before you go all cop on us."

He *was* a cop, damn it. Harte was lucky he wasn't riddled full of holes right now. Garrett tightened his lips. "Fine, we'll see what he has to say." Then he'd take him down.

ⵡ

"I tried to get your attention," Aidan said again, having joined them from across the creek. They'd all entered the cabin and had taken seats around the table. Garrett and Sonya were on one side, Grams and Gramps sitting cozy across from them, while Aidan sat on Sonya's left at the end of the table. "With the wind, I guess, you couldn't hear me. That bear was within twenty feet of you—"

"If there *was* a bear," Garrett narrowed his brows. "I'd still like to take a look at the area, see if there are any signs."

"Be my guest," Aidan said. "Though I doubt you'd be able to see anything in the dark."

"You couldn't think of another way to get our attention, other than shooting at us?" Garrett continued to fire questions.

"I wasn't shooting *at* you. I was trying to scare off a bear before it stumbled *into* you."

"Isn't it a bit convenient that a bear wandered close while you happened to be in the vicinity with a shotgun handy?"

"I was out for a walk and everyone knows you don't stroll around on the tundra at this time of night without protection." Aidan turned to Sonya. "Which you know better, Sonya."

"I wasn't thinking about bears—"

"That was apparent," he said sarcastically.

Sonya dragged in a deep breath. Aidan must've seen Garrett kissing her. There could be no other reason for the poison in his brown eyes. They'd already gone over this. They were just friends now. He needed to stop playing the jealous boyfriend.

"Okay, kids," Gramps began. "No one was hurt, and the bear was scared off. Aidan, you want a piece of cake?

Maggie May baked up a tasty German Chocolate cake today."

"Yeah." He sighed, though he didn't take his eyes off Sonya sitting next to Garrett. "That'd be great, thanks. By the way, I saw that old outboard of yours on the tarp. Did you get it running?"

"Sure as heck, did." Gramps grinned from ear to ear, and Sonya wished that she'd been the one to bring up the outboard instead of Aidan. She knew Gramps wasn't happy to be no longer fishing, due to his injury. He wanted to be part of the operation, to feel needed, wanted, useful. She should have recognized this and made more of an effort herself. "Want to give me hand tomorrow mounting it on the skiff?" Gramps asked, sounding like a kid who was dying to play with a new toy.

"You can count on me." Aidan took a big bite of cake and groaned with pleasure. "Margaret, if you weren't already married, I'd make a play for you myself."

Grams actually blushed. Sonya didn't like where this was going. Granted, Aidan had always been part of the family, but there needed to be limits, especially since there was no way she was getting back together with Aidan. Her family needed to stop encouraging him too.

"Gramps, I can give you a hand with that engine in the morning," Sonya said.

"Great, Aidan and I can sure use your help. As heavy as that engine is, it'll take all of us with my bum hand."

Well, that went and backfired. If she made a big deal out of Aidan not helping now that she volunteered, she'd come off bitchy. Breaking up was hard to do, she thought. Her family was comfortable with Aidan. She'd have to find a way to be comfortable too. It would be easier if Aidan didn't look at her like a pound puppy in need of a loving home.

"If you'd like help with the engine tonight, I'd be happy to lend a hand," Garrett added.

"Much appreciated, but I'd rather do it when it's a bit lighter outside," Gramps said. "My eyes don't see so well in the dark anymore, and it's a bugger bolting that engine to the skiff."

A silence settled over the group that had tension testing the waters. It was blatantly obvious how comfortable Aidan was with her family and vice versa, while Garrett, though welcomed, didn't have that natural rhythm which had developed with Aidan over the years.

"Well, I'd better be headed back," Garrett said. "The tide will be getting high soon." Garrett rose to his feet, while Aidan extended his, easing back in his seat, like he had all the time in the world and was welcome to stay as long as he wanted.

Sonya wanted to kick his feet from under the table.

"Walk me out, Sonya?" Garrett asked, holding out his hand in what really wasn't an invitation, more of a "this is my woman" message directed toward Aidan.

With both men's eyes on her, Sonya choose to go with Garrett, almost stumbling when Aidan's stare narrowed with temper.

"I need to know what's still 'personal' between you and Harte," Garrett said, as they walked in step across the beach toward his Jeep. A burnished moon glistened over the dark surface of the ocean, painting a coppery trail to the horizon.

"I don't want to get into it." Sonya wished now that she'd decided to stay in the cabin. The day had already been way too long to venture into the past with Garrett.

He grabbed her arm, and swiveled her around to face him. "Too damn bad. Every instinct I have is pointing me in Harte's direction. Now, tell me."

"I can't." She looked past him, down the beach. The area was deserted except for an eagle feasting on a fish that had washed up on shore after falling out of someone's net.

"Can't? Or won't, Sonya?" Garrett pressed.

"What difference does it make?"

"Can't, tells me you don't trust me. Won't, that you are protecting Harte. Do you still care about him?"

She bit her lip. How did she answer that in a way that satisfied them both?

"Sonya." Garrett placed his hands on her shoulders and forced her to look at him, his eyes drilling into hers. "Why are you protecting him?"

"I'm not really. It's just that...I can't even contemplate that Aidan would be behind what happened to Kendrick or the attacks on me and my family." She shook her head and wished she hadn't as a headache had begun to develop. "Aidan has been a part of our family forever. I even thought that someday we would..."

"That you would what? Marry?"

Her eyes shifted to the encroaching tide and then back to his. "To be honest, yes."

"Why didn't you marry?" Garrett swallowed as though the words had been difficult to vocalize. "What happened, Sonya?"

"What always happens when couples aren't meant to be, we had a fight that couldn't be resolved."

"What did you fight about?"

"We've already been over this."

"And we'll go over it again until I get the full picture."

"Fine." She sighed in resignation. "Fishing, remember? We fought over me wanting to drift."

"Why did that break you up? Why weren't you able to work through it? What else happened?"

Here was where it got tricky. If she told him that Aidan had hit her, she knew where Garrett would go with that information. "You need to understand something about Aidan. First, his father, Cranky—I mean Earl—is a real bastard. Aidan grew up in a house where his parents fought. A lot. Earl beat his mother, and even though Aidan hasn't said as much, I think he even beat Aidan."

Garrett's mouth thinned. "Go on."

"That night we fought it got…physical."

"He *beat* you?" His eyes turned to steel.

She took a long time answering but then couldn't find a way around it. "Yes."

"He hit you, and you don't think he could be a part of this?" Garrett threw his hands out to the sides. "A man who would raise his hand to a woman has no limits."

"I knew you wouldn't understand." She folded her arms. The night air suddenly turned chilly.

"Understand what? Don't tell me you think it was your fault? You are not one of those women who feel that they are to blame. Come on, Sonya. Tell me you hit the son of a bitch back?"

This man did know a thing or two about her. "That's beside the point. What I'm trying to get across was that when Aidan hit me, it scared him as much or more than it did me. He hasn't touched me that way since, and I called an end to the relationship. According to Aidan, he's been getting help. He hates what his dad did to his mother and is determined not to turn out like him."

"That's all a nice fish tale, but who's to say part of Aidan isn't just like his father? A part he can't control. I've seen it happen before. Dual personalities: one tows the line, the other is psychotic and believes that if I can't have her, no one else can." He ran a hand through his short hair. "Sonya, Aidan doesn't have an alibi for the night of Kendrick's death. Nor can he verify his whereabouts for when your window was shot out. Not to mention, he had the perfect set up to mess with your skiffs." Garrett indicated the Harte's camp up the beach.

"Yeah, but you're forgetting, I'm his alibi for when Wes was hurt and for the damage that was done to the reel."

"Maybe he had an accomplice. His dad? His uncle? Possibly both of them?"

Sonya vehemently shook her head. "I don't buy it. Aidan wouldn't do that to me. He loves me." He'd told her that very afternoon how much he still loved her, and she believed him.

"Psychotic, remember?" Garrett tapped his temple.

"He might be troubled, but he isn't psychotic."

"Sonya, right now, you can't trust anyone. You can't let whatever you feel for Harte cloud your judgment. You need to be on your guard."

"What about you? Should I be on my guard against you?"

He paused. "Yes." Then his next words threw her into the deep end of the pool minus a lifejacket. "For starters, there's part of me who hopes you're pregnant, because it'll insure that I'm part of your life, regardless if you want me to be or not."

"Whoa." She held her hands in front of her as panic and pleasure warred inside her. "Back up the boat."

"Babe, the boat's sailed." Garrett took a threatening step, scowling down at her. "Do you have any idea what I want to do with you? How hard it's been to concentrate on my job today having you within reaching distance and not being able to touch you?" He hauled her against him now, his body making an impression on hers that caused her knees to weaken. He lowered his face, the breath of his words caressed her lips, prompting them to part with wanting. "If Harte feels about you half the way I do, I feel sorry for the bastard." Then he crushed her lips under the plundering pressure of his.

Her world tipped, or was it Garrett pulling her off her feet? Either way, she knew the ground she walked on was shaky at best.

Rather than do what she should and put an end to this, Sonya scaled his body, wrapping her legs tight around his waist. He groaned and swiveled. Crushing her in his arms, he pressed her against the cold metal side of the Jeep.

"I've wanted to take you into my arms all day." His teeth nipped down her neck. "Kiss you like this." His lips conquered as they persuaded. She felt his frustration, his confusion, his need. "I felt impotent standing by while Judd questioned you like a criminal."

She giggled like a teenager and it felt fabulous, liberating. "You sure don't feel impotent now."

"Far from it." He gave her a devilish grin that promised dark and wondrous things.

They fumbled to free clothing, Garrett cursing the stubborn zipper on her jeans. Salt air had a way of corroding all metals. She didn't care about the cold air hitting her backside as he freed the zipper and tugged off her pants, not when Garrett made her feel like she was in the middle of a raging bonfire.

"You'd better damn well have a condom with you this time, cop."

"I bought a pack at the cannery this morning," he panted. "We're good to go for twelve."

She choked out a laugh. It was heady to not think of consequences, responsibility, or restrictions and, for once in her life, just live in the moment.

CHAPTER THIRTY-ONE

Sonya straightened her clothes, and watched until she could no longer see Garrett's taillights on the Jeep they'd just made desperate love against. A tickled smile seemed to be permanently fixed on her mouth. She'd never done anything so reckless. It felt exhilarating, and naughty, and she didn't even question her reasons for having her way with him. Or did he have his way with her? It didn't really matter, for they'd both had their way and then some. She turned and found herself humming as she sauntered down the beach, taking pleasure in the magical moonlight, the rhythmic waves, and the stirring breeze heavy with the promise of rain.

"Enjoy yourself," Aidan bit out from the dark shadows of the alder bushes that marked the trail leading up the bluff to the cabin.

Sonya squeaked back the scream trapped in her throat. "Aidan? What are you doing?"

"Waiting for you." The tone of his voice caused the hairs on the back of her neck to rise.

Could Garrett be right about Aidan? Was there another side to him? Because she sure as hell didn't recognize the man in front of her right now.

"Why were you waiting for me?" Had he seen her and Garrett together?

Had he watched?

Maybe Garrett's suspicions were correct and Aidan hadn't been scaring off a bear earlier. She scanned him for weapons but didn't see anything except the fisted hands at his sides.

She shivered.

"I *wanted* to talk to you." He stepped from the shadows and the light from the moon shone over the sharp angles of his face, making him look like one of the dark characters in his graphic novels.

"What about?" She swallowed and yearned to take a step back, but held her ground on shaky legs.

He motioned to the empty beach behind her. "Doesn't matter now."

"Listen, Aidan, I don't need to explain my actions to you. I'm free to do what I want."

"Right." He glanced away from her, his nostrils flaring, his jaw flexing, then he turned back to her. "Damn you, Sonya." He grabbed and yanked her into his arms, his mouth crushing hers.

Fear surged inside her like a gale storm. Her arms were pressed to her sides with the force of his hold, his body urgent against hers, bowing it until she felt he'd snap her in two. Aidan was stronger, and desperate. They were utterly alone. Breathing became difficult, and she whimpered as she realized how precarious her situation was.

Suddenly his mouth released hers, and she gulped in air. His bruising hold gentled. His breathing was labored, and his eyes wild. Those eyes searched hers, and she knew he saw the fear and panic swirling in hers.

"I'm sorry, Sonya. Please—" he closed his eyes as though in pain "—don't fear me again." He dropped his forehead to hers and just held her. Gone was the monster and back was the man she'd cared for. "*Damn it,*" Aidan said without any heat and Sonya thought she heard tears in his voice. "He's a *stinking fish cop,* Sonya. How is he preferable to me?"

"I'm sorry." She tried to swallow her own tears climbing up the back of her throat, but a few slipped past her. "I didn't mean for this to happen. It just did." A fat raindrop splattered on her forearm.

"Heaven help me, neither can I." He buried his head in her neck. "I wish to God that I could."

Another raindrop smacked the side of her face and then the heavens shuddered on a sob.

"Where the hell have you been?" Earl asked, followed by a hacking cough that turned Aidan's stomach. "You're wetter than seaweed. Don't you have sense enough to get in out of the rain?"

"Give it a rest, old man." Aidan grabbed a beer and twisted the top off, taking a long swallow. He normally didn't drink, but his heart was breaking and the pain was about to kill him. Seeing Sonya loving Garrett, in a way that she'd never loved him, had Aidan needing to drown out the image seared in his memory.

"Ooh, the boy's getting a backbone," Roland commented from a dark corner of the lantern-lit cabin.

"Yeah, of a jellyfish." Earl chuckled at his own joke. Aidan took a deep drink and tried to wipe his thoughts of Sonya and Garrett clutched together against the side of that Jeep. Why couldn't she have ever let go with him like that?

"So, what had you out in the rain?" Earl asked. "In dire need of a shower?" This time both Earl and Roland cackled.

"I'm sure it has something to do with that pretty drift boat captain on shore leave next door." Roland elbowed Earl. "Don't you think?"

"Gotta be. Only a woman could tempt a man to stay out in the rain, when he should have the good sense God gave him to come in out of it. So, things square with you and Sonya?"

"You could say that," Aidan muttered, taking another swig of the beer and dropping into a chair. The liquid was bitter against his tongue, but the more he drank, the more he found the taste palatable.

"About damn time. You gotta date set?" Earl asked, a smile twisting his normally stoic face, making him resemble the Joker in Batman.

"A date?" Aidan asked, confused. "For what?"

"A wedding, boy."

It was Aidan's turn to laugh, though the sound held no humor. "There's never going to be a wedding between me and Sonya."

"Don't tell me you screwed things up again."

His whole life was nothing but a series of screw-ups. None as big as the screw-up he'd made of his relationship with Sonya. "Yep, I sure did. Fucked it up big time, Pops." He finished the beer, thumping the bottle down on the splintered table, and without a second thought, reached for another.

"Watch your mouth, boy." Roland indicated the loft where Aidan knew Lana was not sleeping, though it was quiet as church up there.

"Why? No one else does around here." He toasted Earl and Roland. "Just following the examples given."

"If you followed my example, you'd make Sonya change her mind," Earl said, his lips twisting into a cruel line.

"What?" Aidan scoffed. "Like you did with her mother?"

Earl's chair scraped against the scarred-plank floor as he leaped his feet. "Shut the hell up. You will not talk about Kyra."

"Why not?" Aidan shrugged. "You have no problem discussing Sonya, but not your own failed attempts with her mother?"

The fist came out of nowhere, slamming into Aidan's cheek with the force of a sledgehammer. Shit, he'd forgotten the lights-out power of Earl's right hook. It knocked him out of his chair and flat onto his back on the floor, his beer spilling into a puddle next to his head.

He should get up and hit the bastard back, but it was just so much more comfortable here on the floor. Besides, the colors swirling in front of his eyes were pretty.

"Get up, you sorry excuse for a Harte," Earl said.

Aidan made out his blurry image looming over him. Now why would he get up for more of what he'd already received? See, he *had* learned a thing or two.

"Earl, leave the boy alone," Roland said, though his voice seemed to come from far off in the distance, instead of across the small room. "Can't you see he's messed up over Sonya? When's the last time you saw the boy help himself to a brewski?"

"What he needs to do is put Sonya in her place." Earl kicked Aidan in the side, seeming satisfied with the grunt of pain that escaped. He walked over to his chair and retook his seat. "Damn kid never learns a thing. Too much like his sorry bitch of a mother."

Aidan continued to lie on the floor with no desire to get up. His only thought before blackness took him was that he wished he'd been able to finish the last of his beer before it was spilled on the floor.

What a waste. Much like himself.

ᘒ

"Dag nabbit!" Gramps threw his rain hat to the ground.

Sonya had met Gramps and Aidan the next morning, as agreed upon, to mount the outboard onto the skiff.

The jinxed outboard lay buried underneath a mountain of mud.

Some time during the night, a section of the bluff collapsed due to the deluge of rain that had fallen and still continued to fall.

Sonya bit back a laugh. Maybe now, they could buy a new engine.

"Don't go thinking what I know you're thinking." Gramps pointed at her.

"What?" She gave him a wide-eyed expression.

"I'll save her. I'll dig her out, clean her up, and she'll be good as new."

"Gramps. It's covered in mud. There comes a time when you have to bury the dead." A chuckle did bubble free after that and she slid a glance toward Aidan. He hadn't said anything since they'd rendezvoused this morning, other than a greeting for Gramps and a nod for her, keeping his distance from her.

Aidan's gaze met hers and his lips curved into a grin.

"Nope," Gramps snapped. "I'll resurrect her. Just you two wait and see if I don't. Wipe those grins off your faces. You look silly. I'm getting out of the rain." He grumbled off down the beach toward the cabin.

A taut silence settled between Aidan and Sonya, while rain spattered around them in big fat drops. They started back the way Gramps had huffed off.

"Listen, Sonya, about last night." Aidan hunched his shoulders into the depths of his rain jacket. "I understand now that we—" he swallowed and gauged the encroaching tide "—can't be together. I don't want the change in our relationship to affect the one I have with your family."

"Of course not, Aidan. I know how much they mean to you, and you mean a lot to them." She slid her hands into the wide sleeves of her rain jacket. "Just so that you know, I never told them what happened between us."

Aidan gave a huge sigh of relief. "I appreciate that."

They fell into step, not completely comfortable with each other but not quite strained either.

"How'd you get the other black eye?" Sonya asked.

Aidan flushed and tightened his lips. "Just one of those things, you know."

She was afraid she did.

"What's your next move?" Aidan asked before Sonya could ask anything else.

It was obvious that he didn't want to talk about how he'd come by the new shiner. Sonya decided now wasn't the time to press. Their relationship was shaky after last night. No sense in rocking the boat. "Set netting this afternoon, just like you."

"No, I meant what's your next move with this Kendrick mess?"

"That will depend on what the medical examiner finds, I guess." She shrugged. "I'd appreciate it if you didn't let anyone know about Garrett and me. The less who know the easier, understand?"

"Yeah, fishermen are already upset with you fishing both gear types. Add you being sweet on a fish cop and your name will be mud."

"Exactly." She lowered her ball cap over her face to help with the rain.

"You sure don't like making it easy on yourself, do you?"

She indicated his new shiner. "I could say the same about you."

Set netting that afternoon turned out to be a bust. Just as Sonya had predicted, the southeast wind had driven the salmon deeper into the bay and away from shore where the nets waited. The rain continued to fall, the wind to blow, and the temperature to drop. All in all, it was chalking up to be one miserable day.

Sonya also felt the piercing looks and the whispered accusations from the other set netters when they passed by. It seemed like the bay hummed with rumors and speculation regarding her involvement in Kendrick's death.

She sat hunched into her raingear at the stern of the skiff, the boat bobbing in the choppy, gray water tied to the running line. Wes was in the bow, sitting much the way she was. Anything to lessen the rain pelting them.

Peter was warm and dry aboard the *Double Dippin'*, anchored off the end of the running line's buoy. Lana kept him company.

There were no fish in the net to pick, as Sonya and Wes had just finished a wasted run-through. Now they sat and hoped that something fishy would swim into it.

Sonya looked left at Aidan huddled down in his skiff. Farther up from him, on the Hartes' other site, were Cranky and Crafty. The weather seemed to appeal to them. They were smoking cigarettes and sucking dry a cooler full of beers. A laugh would cackle over the water every now and then. Mostly they sat and waited for fish like the rest of them.

"This is ridiculous." Sonya stood. "Let's tie up to the *Double Dippin'* and get out of this rain. I'm cold to the bone."

Wes nodded. "I doubt we'll catch any more fish freezing our digits off out here than sitting on the boat where it's warm and dry." He indicated Aidan. "You want to invite him?"

She didn't, but then felt like they'd come to an understanding, and Aidan wouldn't see the overture as an invitation from her this time. "Aidan," she hollered, cupping her hands around her mouth. His head snapped up at his name, like she'd woken him. How could anyone sleep in this weather? "Want to join us aboard the *Double Dippin'*?"

He nodded and started his engine. Sonya did the same. The sooner she was out of this wet, miserable weather the better. Someday she needed to fish on an ocean where she could wear a bikini and actually get a tan.

They met at the drift boat. Sonya left the men to tie the skiffs to the painter's line, so they could drift behind. She stepped up to the pilot house and called Peter's name. She heard some muffled cursing and entered the small room to find Peter and Lana struggling into their clothes. "Whoa."

"It's not what it looks like." Peter pulled his sweatshirt over his head, his face popping up out of the hole.

"It looks as if you two were fooling around." Sonya glanced at Lana. Her shirt was inside out and the blush on her skin rivaled the pink of her shirt. "Better fix your top, Aidan's right behind me."

"Oh, no! He can't find me like this. If he tells my dad, I'm dead."

Letting Crafty know what his daughter had been up to with Peter aboard the *Double Dippin'* went against Sonya's survival instincts too. "Down to the bunks," Sonya said, pointing to the ladder that led below. "He can assume you had to use the head." She heard Aidan and Wes on the steps outside the pilot house. "Hurry."

Lana gave her a grateful look and scrambled down the ladder. Sonya glared at Peter. "How long has this been going on?"

Peter was saved from answering when the door slid open and Wes and Aidan filled the room. Sonya sent Peter a look that clearly said their conversation wasn't over.

"Where's Lana?" Aidan glanced around for his cousin, as he unsnapped his rain jacket.

"Down here," came Lana's muffled reply. "I'll be up in a minute."

"Why don't I make some hot chocolate?" Sonya suggested hoping to cover any questions Aidan might pose over Lana's whereabouts.

"I'll get out the cookies." Peter grabbed a bag of Nutty Butters, obviously thinking along the same lines as Sonya.

"How about I break out the cards?" Wes hung up his raingear on the hooks by the door next to the others, and rubbed his hands together.

"As long as we aren't betting with money this time," Aidan said. "I'm still trying to recover from the last time you cleaned out my pockets."

Lana joined them and Sonya was glad to see her clothing in the right place and her blushing under control. She helped Sonya fix instant hot chocolate for everyone. Cards were dealt around the bunk, Aidan and Wes at opposite ends. Sonya took the captain's chair, which left Lana and Peter to pull out the bench from under the bunk. It was more than cozy in the small room, and it didn't take long for the windows to fog with condensation. Sonya found herself laughing for the first time in a long time. This was another thing she enjoyed about fishing. The camaraderie between friends. Downtime filled with conversation and the occasional game of Rummy.

"I'm out." Wes laid down his hand, much to the good-natured complaints of the others. Points were counted up, and more groans were given as Wes took the lead.

The cards were handed to Aidan for his turn to deal. "So what's everyone planning to buy after the season?" This was another game they hadn't played yet this year. Hearing what everyone dreamed of buying with their percentage of the season's take.

"A new laptop for me." Lana picked up her cards and stacked all the high cards to the left like she always did. She really needed to mix it up, especially playing with Wes who had an eye for such tells.

"I'm hoping I make enough to buy this sweet motorcycle a friend of mine has for sale," Peter said, a dreamy look on his face as he gazed at Lana.

"The one that he wrecked last fall?" Sonya asked. A motorcycle? What about tuition, books?

"He fixed it up and promised me a good deal. Don't worry, Ducky, I know what I'm doing."

The hell he did. He was thinking like a teenager after a thrill, not a responsible adult with college on the horizon. The way he was puppy-worshipping Lana, Sonya knew he had visions of the girl wrapped around him as he drove her to some secluded place where they could be alone.

"What about you, Sonya?" Aidan changed the subject, obviously realizing Sonya was ready to go all parent-like on Peter's behind.

"What about me?" she asked, looking at her cards but not really seeing them.

"What great plans do you have this year? It will be hard to top last year, since you *did* go out and buy a drift boat."

What did she hope to buy with her money? *If* she actually made any. "I haven't really thought about it." Except to wait and see if she were pregnant. Then she'd need every cent she could scrape together.

"Ah, come on. There has to be something you've been wanting?" Aidan pressed, laying down three jacks and ruining the straight she had going.

"Actually, what I would love right now is a pint of Haagen-Dazs black raspberry chip ice cream," she finally said.

"Ice cream? You are my kind of woman." An uncomfortable pause followed Aidan's slip.

"Just so you know, if I had a pint I wouldn't share one bite of it," Sonya added and was glad when a few laughs followed her words. The afternoon had been going along fine and she'd felt like she and Aidan were on better footing. His gaze toward her now was bittersweet, but he smiled as though he was grateful for her dispelling the tension. Sonya realized then that even though they were no longer together, not losing the friends and family connection was just as important to Aidan.

"Well, I plan on buying a cherry red '67 mustang," Wes said, closing his eyes and humming. "Man, that is one sweet ride."

"You and the cars," Peter said. "Don't you already own, like, five?"

"Your point?" Wes asked in all seriousness, which had everyone chuckling.

"How about you, Aidan?" Sonya asked. "What grand plans do you have this year?"

"A house." His smile was wistful. "I've always wanted a real home, and I hope this year, with what I've been saving, I'll have enough for a down payment." His eyes met hers again but then they dropped to the cards he held in his hands.

Sonya knew Aidan's greatest wish was to have a family of his own, and she felt a twinge of sadness she couldn't help provide that for him. He really was a good man and someday, if he continued to work on his issues, he'd be a great one.

"Well, would you look at the grown up?" Peter said. "You live in downtown Seattle, right in the heart of the city. Why would you want to trade that for mowing a yard, fixing a sink?"

"Because it would be mine. A place to raise a family. All the things that make life worth living." He looked at Peter. "Someday you'll realize that."

"Hopefully not any day soon. I'd like to play a bit before I'm saddled with all that responsibility."

"Oh, I don't know," Lana said, picking up a card, shuffling it to the left and then discarding a four from the right of her hand. "A man who's looking to make a life with someone is real attractive."

Peter seemed to sit a little straighter at her words, though Sonya doubted he totally got their meaning. He picked up a card and laid down three sevens, leaving him with only two cards in his hand. "There's plenty of time for that stuff."

Sonya glared at the hand she'd been dealt. She had nothing. "Time flies faster than you think, wolf man."

It was Wes's turn. He laid down three aces and discarded out, winning another hand. How did he do it?

"Sorry folks." His smile clearly said he wasn't.

"Ah, man. Not again." Peter tossed his remaining cards down on the bunk.

"I'm just glad we aren't playing for money." Aidan started counting up the points left in his hand, but then paused, and cocked his ear to the side. "Sonya, I think you're about to have company."

"Double Dippin' *prepare to be boarded.*"

CHAPTER THIRTY-TWO

"Oh, you've got to be kidding me!" Sonya wiped a circle through the fogged up window with the sleeve of her sweatshirt. Sure enough, there was the *Calypso*, bold as brass, right off her portside.

Damn it, she was fishing here. Or at least, she was in a fishing period. Once again, too many nosey set netters would be witnesses to the *Calypso* harassing her. Speculation swam faster than spawning salmon rushing to mate upriver. She opened the window, leaned out, and hollered, "What do you want?"

"It's official business, Sonya," Garrett said, standing strong—and oh so sexy—on deck with his feet braced apart against the choppy waves buffeting the trooper vessel.

What could have happened now? She had everyone she cared about on board.

Except her grandparents.

That thought shook her to the core and had her grabbing her rain jacket, struggling into it while she hurried to the deck. Everyone in the pilot house followed in her wake.

Garrett stood proud and enforcement-like, decked out in his dark blue uniform with matching raingear. A ball cap shielded his face from the drenching sheets of rain that seemed to assault the rest of them who were hunched over in an attempt to lessen the biting downpour. Only Garrett seemed above the elements, as though nothing, least of all, something as weak as water could bend him.

Garrett's face hardened when Aidan stepped up beside her.

"Did something happen to Grams and Gramps?" she asked.

Garrett's face softened and so did his voice, more the lover, than the enforcer. "As far as I know, they're fine, Sonya. This doesn't concern them. We're following up with our investigation into Kendrick's death."

A lot of those words sounded official and caused a shiver of dread to run down her spine. "May we tie up?" he continued.

She was surprised he even asked.

"Uh, sure." Sonya turned to her crew. Wes and Peter grabbed the ropes the *Calypso* threw over, and Garrett, along with Judd, boarded her boat. She caught a glimpse of Skip's face from the cabin of the *Calypso* and it caused another finger of dread to chase after the previous one.

"Sonya," Garrett said, interrupting her eye contact with Skip. "We need to talk with you. Alone." He glanced at her motley crew, his stare dwelling on Aidan.

"Lana and I should be checking our net anyway," Aidan said. "You need anything, Sonya, and I mean anything, we're just a holler away." They quickly dressed in the rest of their gear and went to the stern to pull in their skiff.

"Well, I guess Peter and I should do the same," Wes said, elbowing Peter whose attention had been caught on Lana as she bent over to put on her chest waders.

"Uh, right." Peter turned to Sonya. "That is unless you want us to stay."

"Thanks, but I'll be fine."

"Sure you shouldn't have a lawyer present?" Her brother sized up Garrett, his eyes narrowed. "I know the law, and she doesn't have to talk to you unless she wants to."

"Peter, I'll be fine," Sonya repeated.

"Don't give up your rights, Ducky. You didn't have anything to do with Kendrick and they know it. If things get too hot, demand your right to speak with a lawyer and boot them off the boat." It gladdened her heart to have her baby brother come so strongly to her defense. Wasn't this the same boy, who just weeks ago, hadn't wanted much to do with her? Now he was giving her advice. On legal matters, no less. She hoped he wasn't thinking lawyer as a career choice. The cost of tuition for a law degree had to be outrageous.

"Thanks," Sonya said, "but I can handle this."

Peter turned to Garrett and met his eye, man to man. "I know you're sweet on her, but you hurt her and you'll have me to contend with, comprende?"

To Garrett's credit, he didn't crack a smile, though Judd glanced away to hide his amusement. "You have my word, Peter. I'll do everything in my power to protect your sister." They did some more of that man stare stuff, which must have satisfied Peter, for he nodded, donned his gear, and climbed off the boat into the waiting skiff with Wes.

"We'll be watching. Sonya, you need anything, give us a shout."

"Got it, Peter."

"That's quite the young man you've raised," Garrett said, after Wes and Peter motored off.

A blush of pleasure heated her cheeks over the compliment. "Thank you." She motioned for the men to follow her out of the rain. They entered the pilot house to a mess of empty hot chocolate cups, a half finished bag of peanut butter cookies, and an interrupted game of Rummy. Sonya busied herself cleaning up cups, cookies, and cards.

Garrett pointed to the game. "Who was winning?"

"Wes. He's a card shark. I swear he cheats, but I haven't been able to catch him at it."

Judd and Garrett shared a look.

Sonya eyed both men. "What does that mean?"

"Why don't we all take a seat?" Judd said, standing by the cleared bunk, his body blocking the door. Garrett leaned against the counter, choosing to stand between the two of them, and Sonya settled into the captain's chair feeling anything but in charge.

"How much do you know about Wes Finley?" Judd started.

"Excuse me?" Sonya glanced at Garrett, but he just stared at her as though gauging her reaction. "What about Wes?"

"Are you aware he has a record?" Judd continued.

What the hell was he talking about? Then realization dawned. "You mean his *juvie* record?"

Judd nodded, reaching into his jacket and pulling out his notepad. Flipping through the pages, he came to a stop on the information he was after. "Vandalism, grand theft, assault and battery."

Sonya shrugged her shoulders, hoping they didn't see how much their knowledge of Wes's illicit past upset her. "Who hasn't acted out when they were teenagers? How did you get that information anyway? Those records are supposed to be sealed."

"So, you are aware of Finley's record?" Judd asked. Garrett had yet to say anything. She wondered if it was by choice or orders from his superior.

"Of course." Though the assault and battery was new. "Gramps dropped the grand theft charges after Wes

307

made restitution." She directed her next question toward Garrett. "Did you investigate all of us?"

Garrett met her eyes without flinching. "Yes."

She sucked in a breath. Well, he didn't believe in sugar-coating the truth, now, did he? Neither did she. "Why?"

"It's a murder investigation, Sonya. Part of the job."

"How deep will you dig?"

His eyes were unapologetic as they burrowed into hers. "As deep as I need to."

"Who's next?" she asked, anger making her voice snap. "Peter? Do you think he had anything to do with this? Gramps? Oh, no! It's Grams, isn't it? There's her extensive knowledge of weapons, and everyone knows she has a talent with a knife. A hook would be child's play for her. Let me guess, Aidan's next? Or is Aidan who you're after all along and you're just throwing Wes to the wolves to provide a smoke screen?" She took a breath and raised a brow. "How am I doing?"

Garrett's lips twitched. "Not bad." He turned to Judd. "What'd I tell you?"

"She's quick." Judd nodded, an admiring smile playing along his lips.

"She's also in the room and doesn't have time for this kind of bullshit." Sonya stood to show them the door, but a wave knocked her off balance, and she stumbled back into her chair.

"We're not done," Garrett said in his trooper voice. This time, instead of sending a tingle down her spine, dread returned. She didn't want to hear what he had to say. She knew without a doubt it was going to ruin her already dismal day. "Aidan Harte is an interesting character. How much to do you know about him?"

"A lot. Why don't you just tell me what you came here for? I've got fish to catch."

"You're aware that he writes graphic novels?" At her nod, Garrett continued, "Have you ever read one?"

She met his stare, not liking where this was going. "I know they revolve around spirit totems." She rolled her eyes as she understood where Garrett was going with this. "And there is a smartass heroine who looks a lot like me."

"Are you also aware that he killed her off in his last novel?"

No, she wasn't. She dragged in a breath. "It's fiction, Garrett. The hero is also a shape shifter."

"The hero and heroine were at odds with each other before she was sacrificed."

Sacrificed? She gulped and hoped Garrett hadn't seen her reaction to his words. "What's your point?"

"You don't see any similarities, Sonya?"

"I repeat, Aidan writes fiction. He might take some life experiences and twist them to fit in his novels, but that is all."

"Why was Aidan onboard your boat? Last night he was shooting at us and today you welcomed him aboard?"

"We've been over that. He wasn't shooting at us. He was scaring off a bear." She indicated the once again, fogged up windows. "If you haven't noticed, it's miserable out there. We, including Aidan *and* Lana, were taking a break from the weather. Warming up with a game of cards and having mug-up."

"How much do you know about Earl Harte?"

The swift change in subject knocked Sonya off course. "He's cranky, mean, and not a nice guy. Why?"

"Were you aware that your mother took out a restraining order against him?"

"My...mother?" Where was Garrett headed? She felt like he was leading her through a fogbank. "No." Her brow furrowed. Why hadn't anyone told her about this before? "When?"

"Before your parents married. From what we could tell, your mother dated both Earl and your father the summer she was employed as a cannery worker for Trident. Your dad won out, but Earl wasn't willing to let her go."

"Yeah, but that was...Thirty some odd years ago." Who holds onto a grudge that long?

"The Harte brothers have also spent many a night in jail for criminal mischief, drunk and disorderly, domestic assault, and the list goes on," Judd added, reading from his notes.

"Is this all you have?" Another big wave hit the boat, and she grabbed the edges of her chair. A sloshing sound echoed and distracted her until Garrett's next words interrupted her speculation.

"There's more. We received the preliminary report back from the medical examiner in Anchorage. Kendrick's cause of death is being ruled as a homicide. You were right. He'd been in the mud for a time. They found traces of it in his lungs. His blood alcohol level was over the legal limit. He probably never knew what hit him."

"Also," Judd added, "with his blood alcohol level so high, he probably didn't have a lot of fight in him."

"Meaning, anyone, including me, could have easily gaffed and helped him overboard," Sonya said.

"The gaff stab wouldn't have killed him," Garrett revealed. "The incoming tide, mixed with the alcohol, did. Drunk as he was, the man was beyond helping himself. I'm thinking now the person who attacked Kendrick hadn't planned on killing him. Chances are Kendrick never knew who stabbed him. The attacker probably figured that when Kendrick pulled himself back onboard his boat, and found your sunglasses, he would have retaliated. Not many fishermen have jeweled dragonflies on the frames of their sunglasses. We know you didn't do it, Sonya."

"Yeah, but until you find the real person, I'm all you've got."

"Not with me as your alibi," Garrett said, iron in his voice.

"There is more than one way to be prosecuted, Garrett." Sonya cocked an ear as that same strange sloshing repeated when the boat rocked again with the waves. It sounded like it was coming from below deck. That couldn't be right unless—

She was taking on water.

CHAPTER THIRTY-THREE

Garrett paused in what he'd been about to say as Sonya suddenly went whiter than the condensation clouding the inside of her windows, and jumped to her feet.

"Out of my way." She pushed passed him, out into the rain, and slid down the steps to the deck. Garrett and Judd followed in time to see her lug off the metal manhole cover to the engine compartment.

Sonya swore, but it sounded more like a desperate prayer. She stood, turned, and tried to push through him and Judd again, but Garrett caught her in his arms, the rain making his hold slippery. "What's going on, Sonya?"

"We're sinking." The shock of her words lessened his hold, and she slipped through, running for the pilot house.

Garrett turned to look down into the hold. Sure enough, water was filling the compartment. After a few cranks of the engine, Sonya got it started. She leaned through the window and hollered, "Garrett, grab that hose. Yes, there, wrapped around the hook. Submerge that end into the water while I turn on the pump." She engaged the pump, and water began spraying out of the other end of the hose into the ocean.

"What's going on over there?" Skip shouted from the *Calypso*.

"The *Double Dippin's* taking on water."

"How bad is it? Do I need to untie?"

"Don't know yet," Garrett returned. "Hang tight. We'll keep you posted."

Sonya leaned back out the window. "Judd, get up here."

Judd looked to Garrett. "Who's in charge here?"

"She's the captain. Now get your butt up there and see what she needs."

Judd grumbled about the messed up chain of command, but made his way back up to the pilot house while Garrett concentrated on keeping the end of the industrial-size hose sucking water out of the hold. Sonya dashed back carrying a Mag flashlight. Before he could suggest that he head down into the engine room, she was already lowering herself into the compartment.

"Sonya, let me crawl down there."

"My boat." She glared up at him, donned ear muffs to protect her ears from the noise of the engine. Then she ducked her head and was gone. Garrett kneeled on the wet deck, still holding the hose, and lowered his head into the compartment so he could keep her in his sights.

The situation smelled fishy.

"Hand me that toolbox," Sonya hollered, giving him directions before he could ask, "to your left against the rail."

"Don't touch anything until I take a look."

She scowled. "I have water coming in and you want to take time to look around." She motioned to the rising water she stood knee-deep in. "There *is* no time."

"Sonya, calm down." He knew this situation had to be bringing up horrific nightmares of her family drowning. She was handling it pretty well though, considering. "The pump will take care of most the excess water. Hold the hose and let me come down there." He kept his voice even, mellow, hoping it would help recede the panic he could hear in hers.

"Fine." She steadied the hose as he lowered himself into the tight area.

The sound of the engine, along with the running pump, was deafening in the enclosed space. The pungent tang of oil and diesel mixed with saltwater assaulted his nose.

"There." Sonya pointed, indicating where water seeped in like a garden hose left in the on position.

Garrett bent farther to investigate. He knew about boats, mostly driving and diving out of them due to his SEAL training, but this complicated engine room was above his expertise. He was a cop not a fisherman. "Explain what I'm looking at," he said.

Sonya pointed to a pipe that came up out of the floor with a metal plate bolted over it, where the water was spewing in. "This is the impeller plate, it seals the drain." She indicated the pipe. "When we winterize the boat after the season, and store it at the cannery over the winter, the bolts are loosened to drain any water left in the pump. If left unsealed, ocean water leaks in when the boat is launched."

"I take it no one's fiddled with this since the beginning of the season."

She shook her head. "There wouldn't be a need to."

Garrett bent to get a closer look at the bolts on the metal plate. "Let me see your flashlight." Sonya handed him the Mag. He shined it on the bolts, and fingered the edges of the hex-cut heads. "These are fresh tool marks." Seemed as though someone had been in a hurry to loosen them. Maybe while others onboard were playing a hand of cards? "How long would it take for this much water to spill in?"

"Sitting at anchor, maybe a few hours, could be less." Sonya turned his attention to some cut wires, fingering them. "Look at this. These go to the alarm that's supposed to sound when the water level in here rises. Someone disabled it."

Their gazes met, each serious, though hers still held traces of fear and panic. "Someone tried to sink my boat."

"No," he said, his tone deadly. "Someone attempted to kill you."

ↄ

Wet and freezing, Sonya stood on deck, having just climbed out of the cramped, cold engine compartment, and wiped water out of her face. The unrelenting rain just wetted it again, sinking through her already drenched clothes and into her clammy skin. Now that the crisis was over, the bolts retightened on the impeller plate, and the sinking of her boat diverted, she physically shook from the aftermath. What if they hadn't been able to stop it? What if she hadn't figured out what the sloshing sound had been in time? What would she have done if forced into the open water?

Garrett joined her after settling the heavy engine plate in place. "You okay?" His eyes narrowed.

"Fine," she replied robotically. She was far from fine. She pointed to Wes and Peter busy picking fish, hoping to distract him and herself. "Looks as though the fish arrived." At least that was some good news.

"What happened to your rain jacket?" Garrett snagged her attention again.

For some reason she was having a hard time focusing, as though she didn't want to deal with the reality of what had happened, or what could have happened.

315

"Sonya," Garrett said, his voice sharper this time.

"Hmm?" She'd really like a nap. Wanted to lie down and forget this even happened. Yep, now that sounded like a plan.

Garrett caught her arm. "Hell, you're wet clear through." He steered her toward the pilot house, the action making her dizzy. "We've got to get you dry and warm."

He half-carried her up the stairs. She kept looking at her feet, wondering why they didn't want to move. Guess they were already taking that nap she wanted so badly.

"Judd, fire up the stove and heat some water. Damn fool was out there without her raingear and now she's near frozen. I think she's hypothermic or suffering from shock."

"Am not," Sonya muttered, though no one seemed to pay attention.

Garrett picked her up and set her on the bunk, stripped out of his jacket, and wrapped it snug around her. It was warm and dry from the heat of his body, and she wanted to snuggle into it and sleep for a week. "Stay here. I'll get you some dry clothes." He turned to Judd. "Watch her."

Sonya rested her heavy head back against the wall, her eyelids closing of their own volition. Words came at her like bouncing rubber balls, and she realized that another person had boarded her boat. Sounded like Skip. Great, just what she needed, another trooper. At this rate, they were swarming around her like mosquitoes. She hated mosquitoes. Dang blood suckers. Someone lifted her, and took Garrett's warm jacket away.

"No," she murmured, trying to pull the jacket back over her. Why couldn't everyone leave her the hell alone?

"Hang in there, Sonya," Garrett said.

"Cold." She tried to curl up into a ball but Garrett's hands grabbed and yanked at her clothing.

"I know, honey. I'm going to fix that right now. Guys, go away while I get her out of these wet clothes."

Frigid air slapped against tender skin as Garrett stripped her bare. She couldn't help the whimper that escaped. Then he was stuffing her into a t-shirt, with a sweatshirt over that like she was a child. Next were soft, dry sweatpants, followed by two layers of socks. Garrett then wrapped her tight in a blanket.

"Better?"

"Hmm," was all she could answer. Now, if she could get some shuteye.

"I'm going to dry your hair now," he warned as he pulled the hair tie out that held her ponytail in place. Next, he vigorously towel-dried her hair until it hung loose around her face in damp lengths. "Feeling any warmer?"

"Fine. Sleep now."

"No sleep. Not until I know you're warm and out of danger." He sat her up and forced a hot cup of tea into her hands. "Drink this," he ordered. Seemed like he was doing a lot of that. Wasn't this her boat and wasn't she the one in charge?

He helped her hold the rim of the cup to her lips, and she sipped, grimacing at the taste. "Too sweet."

"Drink it anyway."

She took another sip and then pushed it away. "Enough. Tired."

"I know you're tired. Your body's shutting down. Fight it, babe," he said, his tone quiet but hard.

She looked into his worried eyes and found the strength to drink more of the syrupy tea.

"That's my girl." He set the cup down and then began rubbing her limbs. "Why didn't you tell me you were so cold? Why the hell didn't you put on your raingear?"

"Forgot. Worried about the boat."

"You need to take care of yourself or you're no good to anyone. The boat isn't worth your life, Sonya."

"If the boat sank, I'd be in the water." She shuddered. "Can't let that happen."

He moved to rub her legs and pricks of pain followed. She wanted to push him away, but knew that blood was returning to her limbs, and she'd have to bear through his ministrations. She hadn't realized how much trouble she was in until her body started to seriously shiver in an attempt to warm itself. If she'd been alone—

Judd and Skip entered the pilot house.

"Give you enough time?" Judd asked, looking over Sonya with Garrett's hands all over her. "Or do you need more?"

"She's getting her color back." Garrett continued to rub her limbs, helping the blood circulate.

Skip commandeered her captain's chair. "You seem to be plagued, Sonya Savonski."

"Targeted," Garrett corrected. "I take it you two saw for yourself the damage below?" At their nods, he continued, "This has gone on long enough. We've already got one dead body. I'm not going to let there be another."

"I take it you have a plan?" Skip asked.

"I'm moving in," Garrett said.

"Moving where?" Sonya asked, her voice squeaking, afraid she already knew the answer.

"Here. With you." Garrett tightened his lips.

"How is that keeping your relationship with her from interfering with your job?" Skip asked.

"I'll still be doing my job, just from the *Double Dippin'*."

"Your feelings for her have nothing to do with it?"

"What I feel for her is none of your business. My job is to keep her alive, and that's what I'm going to do."

"I don't think you need to be onboard her boat to achieve that." Skip leaned forward, elbows on knees.

"We've been keeping an eye on Sonya, she's made sure that none of her crew are alone, yet someone was still able to board the *Double Dippin'* sometime in the last few hours and sabotage it. If Sonya hadn't been so tuned to the running of her boat and acted as fast as she did, she'd have sunk. If this had happened when Sonya was sleeping, with the disabled alarm, she would have died. The only realistic course of action is to plant a trooper onboard."

"Wait just a d-damn minute," Sonya interrupted, her teeth chattering as her body shivered. "No f-fish cop is s-staying on my b-boat."

Garrett nailed her with a look that had her biting back the rest of her objections. At least for the moment. "The decision is out of your hands, Sonya."

"We need your help in policing the fishermen, Hunt," Skip said.

"Part of our duties also includes ensuring the safety of the fishermen. We can achieve that better by having me on the inside, posing as one of them."

"P-people already know who you are," Sonya said. "H-how would you pass for a f-fisherman?"

"Not many are going to pay that much attention. They'll be busy fishing. The one who will is the person, or persons, causing you trouble. Hopefully, knowing that I'm on board, he'll think twice before targeting you again."

"Right," she scoffed. "If anything, you'll become a target too. F-fishermen are sneaky. They make a living preying on fast, s-slippery salmon."

319

Skip tapped his fingers together and addressed Sonya, "So you think that by Garrett entrenching himself among your crew, he'll actually lure out the perpetrator?"

"Well, yeah." She rolled her eyes. Weren't cops supposed to be clever?

Garrett gave Skip a shrewd smile. "I have no problem being a mark. Been one before. My main objective is to keep Sonya and her family safe."

"I think he ought to do it." Judd had been quiet during the discussion.

Skip regarded Garrett and Judd, and then looked at Sonya. He pursed his lips and then nodded. "All right, we'll give it a try. But, Hunt, I believe your biggest challenge will be in getting Sonya's cooperation."

Damn straight. It was bad enough that she'd slept with a fish cop.

She was not shacking up with one.

CHAPTER THIRTY-FOUR

Garrett hauled his duffel aboard the *Double Dippin'* and surveyed Sonya's mutinous expression. Skip had been right. Getting her to willingly cooperate with his plan was going to be his biggest hurdle. He'd changed his clothes for more acceptable fishing attire of jeans and long-sleeved t-shirt. Having him out of uniform didn't seem to soften her attitude toward him though.

"This is a stupid idea," Sonya said, her hands fisted on her hips, her legs braced apart on the deck to help buffet the waves battering the sides of the hull. A ball cap rode low over her eyes and covered her hair that still hung loose around her face.

Garrett was relieved to see that her anger had done the trick of warming her up. She seemed ready to breathe fire. "Stupid or not, I'm moving in." He untied the rope at the stern, which secured the *Calypso* to the *Double Dippin'*, and then moved to the rope at the bow.

"This is my boat, and I have a say—"

"Save your breath, Sonya." He unhitched the knot and threw the rope over to the deck of the *Calypso*, and muscled his way past her, up into the pilot house, where he dropped his duffel on the bunk. Through the *Double Dippin's* windows, he watched the *Calypso* set sail. Damned if he wasn't staying put. "Where do you want me to put my things?" He turned as she entered behind him.

Her mouth opened and closed and then opened again, doing that fish mouth thing that he found so adorable. "I'll tell you where you can put your—"

He interrupted her again, but this time by dragging her against him. Her breath rushed out in a whoosh. "Tell me you aren't savoring the chance to make love with me again? Some place more comfortable than against the side of a Jeep." He lowered his voice to a seductive whisper, "Where I can explore your body all night long with no chance of interruption."

Heat of another sort fought with the anger in her eyes, and he couldn't help the smile that teased free.

"Y-you are not sleeping in my bed."

He cocked a brow. "Who said anything about sleeping, sweetheart."

"Why you arrogant, overbearing fish cop." She pushed free of his embrace. "I am not having sex with you again. Been there, done that. Time to cut bait."

Cut bait? What was he? A piece of meat? Only good enough for a one night stand and a frantic fuck against a Jeep? He'd battled panic earlier when she'd been dangerously cold, alarm over more proof that someone wanted her dead. Now he was doing his level best to protect her, *and* she wanted nothing to do with him? It was enough to make any man lose his grip on sanity. He yanked her flush against him and silenced her mouth but good. Hungrily, he slanted his lips over hers, licked into her mouth and made a meal of her until her arms knotted around his neck, and a moan flowed from deep within her throat, as she arched into him.

Now that was more like it. Time to cut bait, my ass.

He knocked the ball cap free of her hair and tunneled his fingers into the loose strands, loving how they felt against his skin, and kept her head prisoner to his plundering mouth.

"Tell me, Sonya," he said, breaking the kiss, his voice hoarse with the effort it cost him to reel back his need. "Was that enough of a lure to welcome me back into your bed?"

Sonya swallowed past the unwanted feelings impeding her better judgment. What had she been objecting to? Sex with Garrett. Now why had she been objecting again? That's right, he'd commandeered her vessel. Well, to be honest, he hadn't taken over the running of her boat, but he'd plowed over her protests as though he had no regard for them or her. She knew he was trying to protect her but—with him on her boat—he'd just put her smack dab in harm's way.

Uniform or no uniform, he was still a fish cop, and every fisherman out there on the water would know it. She might as well use his alibi and end all the speculation, for her reputation was surely ruined with him inhabiting her boat.

"You're sleeping up here." She pointed to the bunk in the pilot house. "Alone. If you insist on staying to protect me, then that's what you are going to do. Protect me and mine. No fringe benefits."

"I can protect you better if I'm close to you."

"No. You need to treat me as just another job."

"You aren't just a job." His eyes narrowed in warning. "I care about you." It looked as though it physically hurt him to say that. Not the declaration every woman dreamt of.

"What does that mean, 'you *care* about me'? Are you in love with me? Want to be with me always and forever, until death do us part? Or is this a summer fling? Not a lot of women out here, and you found yourself some easy entertainment?"

"Babe, there is nothing easy about you." If at all possible, his eyes narrowed even farther, until she barely caught the piercing glint promising a storm to come. "Sonya—"

"No." She held up her hand. "No more." Now she'd had it. "I need a break." She reached for her rain jacket hanging on the hook.

"Where are you going?"

She paused with her hand on the door to the pilot house, not liking that he wanted her to explain herself. "I said I needed a break."

"I don't want you outside in the rain after what happened earlier."

It was hard staying mad at someone who seemed to be looking out for her best interests, but she made the effort. "I'm going to check on the guys, change places with one of them." Anything to get away from him for a while. Until she could reestablish some sort of normalcy or, at the very least, regain authority over her own life, damn it.

"Think again. I'm here to keep you safe, which means I don't leave your side."

"You've *got* to be joking."

"Not laughing, sweetheart. Consider me your shadow until this situation is resolved."

"This won't work. There will be times when I'll need to go set netting, to the cabin, pick up supplies at the cannery, or shower."

"I'll be with you."

She swallowed hard at the vision of them showering together. She knew he hadn't meant it the way she took it, but her mind went right to bubbles and steam, and slick, wet skin sliding against each other. "I need alone time, Garrett. Someone will have to protect *you* from *me*, if I don't get a moment to myself."

"Enough." He grabbed her arm, wrestled her rain jacket out of her hands, and tossed it on the bunk, then he plunked her down in the captain's chair. Leaning over her with his hands resting on the arms, he caged her in. They were both breathing heavy by the time he was done.

"Listen up, Sonya Savonski. I know you're scared and trying to put up a strong front. It's okay to be worried. In fact, it's damn smart. It's also okay to accept help when you need it. And yes, you need it." He laid a finger against her lips to silence her objection. "Wait until I'm finished and then I'll let you have your say." He removed his finger from her mouth. "I know this isn't the best situation, and if you could, you'd choose to do something different. But you can't and there isn't. The season's almost over, and this is a temporary condition. One that will hopefully end to everyone's satisfaction.

"Now—" he straightened and made a come-and-get-me gesture with his fingers, "let me have it."

Damn, she hated that he was right. Hated that she was in this position, and *hated* that she needed his help. "Okay, I might need your help, but I don't have to like it." She sounded like an ungrateful child, but couldn't seem to do anything about it.

"Tell me this, Sonya, if Peter was captain and the attacks and evidence were directed toward him, would you have a problem with me stepping in?"

"That's an unfair question."

"No, it isn't. What are you really objecting to? The situation or me? Would you rather Judd take my place?"

"No," she mumbled under her breath.

"What was that?"

She knew he'd heard her. "No. All right?" She glared at him. "Are you happy now? Yes, I hate the situation but having you here…so close…messes with me, okay?"

"Messes with you how?" He lowered his voice, turning it all sexy again.

"I don't want to care for you and…and with you so near…it makes that harder."

He kneeled down so that they were eyelevel, and tucked a strand of hair behind her ear. "It makes it harder for me too. Listen, I think it might be a good idea to know where we stand with each other." His eyes searched hers, reflecting heat now instead of ice, and she had an overwhelming need to reach out and brush her hands over his squared, muscled shoulders, let his arms hold her tight against his chest, feel his—

"Yo, Sonya!" Peter hollered from outside.

She was grateful for the interruption. She wasn't ready to go where Garrett had tried to take their conversation, and she was afraid any more time in close proximity, she'd have her way with him. Before that happened she really needed to get down with the reality of what she actually felt toward him.

Garrett stood, freeing her from her chair. She grabbed her rain jacket, struggling into it as she rushed on deck to where Peter and Wes idled the skiff alongside the *Double Dippin'*. Unfortunately, Garrett was right behind her like that shadow he'd talked about. She felt the heat generating from his body and was surprised the rain hitting him didn't rise off his massive shoulders in the form of steam.

"We tendered a total of thirty-five hundred pounds!" Peter said. "The fish were all on the ebb tide. Just liked you thought they'd be." He frowned at Garrett. "Why's the fish cop still onboard?"

"Pull the nets and running lines and meet me at the cabin, and I'll explain it to you there. Good job fishing today, guys." She waved them off and regarded the rapidly receding tide, knowing she should have kept a keener eye on her surroundings. See, the man was already messing with her. She turned to Garrett. "All right. If you're going to pose as a fisherman, better start acting like one. We need to pull anchor. I want to be at the cabin before the tide goes out much farther."

"You got it, Captain." Without complaint, Garrett headed to the bow of the boat. She watched him walk, enjoying the way he strutted. Not cocky but confident. He looped the anchor line over the front roller, and she hurried to the pilot house to engage the hydraulics to help drag it in. Once the chain rattled over the roller, Garrett finished manually pulling in the anchor, dragging it on deck, out of the way, next to the rail. She'd seen many men lift heavy objects, but none had quite the effect on her that Garrett produced. Made her remember last night on the beach and how he'd picked her up in his arms, held her against the side of the Jeep, and took her body with his in an act so elemental, so feral, it bordered on claiming.

Being cold wasn't her problem now. In fact, she could use a cooling off period before Garrett joined her. He entered the pilot house too soon, and instead of taking a seat on the bunk, which would give her some much needed breathing room, he stood next to her as she drove. Heat tingled over her skin and made her palms sweaty.

Having Garrett onboard was going to be a trial in more ways than one.

⌡

Later that evening, Sonya had a pow-wow with her family, explaining to everyone what happened to the *Double Dippin'* that afternoon and the new trooper development. Garrett currently kept watch aboard the boat, which was dry in front of the cabin. He'd allowed her to leave to talk to her family as long as she promised not to venture anywhere else. She knew he meant toward the Harte's camp. Her grandparents seemed relieved over the news. Not this afternoon's vandalism, but having Garrett literally onboard.

When she left the cabin to return to the *Double Dippin'*, she was loaded down with a bag of aluminum-wrapped food Grams had prepared. Salmon hunks, homemade dill weed bread, cheddar cheese slices, and the last of the German Chocolate cake. The rain had finally stopped, though the air was still wet as if the weather was only taking a moment to catch its breath.

She saw Aidan waiting for her as soon as she hit the beach.

"Who the hell is that onboard your boat?" Aidan demanded, pointing to Garrett standing on deck.

She quickly brought him up to date.

"What do you mean he's staying on the *Double Dippin'*?"

"Please don't make me repeat it," Sonya said.

"You know what this looks like, don't you?" He leaned into her personal space. "Like you're siding with the enemy."

"Technically, the enemy is siding with me." She felt the need to point out.

"Yeah, I'm sure the fishermen are going to swallow that whopper whole. Why, Sonya? Why would you agree to this?"

"I didn't have much choice in the matter," she mumbled.

"Is it the sex? Couldn't you wait to hook up with him until after fishing?"

She sent him a warning look. "Don't go there."

He ran a hand through his hair and sighed. "Sorry. That was uncalled for."

Silence settled heavy between them and Sonya heard Cranky or Crafty—she couldn't tell which—cackle from down the beach. They were stooped over a makeshift table made of driftwood and broken pilings, a strange lineup of household cleaners littering the sand at their feet. "What are they doing?"

"They missed celebrating the Fourth of July because of weather and fishing. Tomorrow's forecasted to be clear. You know how they are about their fireworks."

Yeah, homemade and hazardous.

"Listen, Sonya, if you feel like you need protection…" He let the sentence trail.

"Thanks, Aidan, but I think its best if we leave the situation the way it is. I could use your help keeping an eye on my family and the cabin."

"Right." The look in his gaze changed from power-less to purpose. "You got it." He reached out his hand and gently grasped her upper arm. "Don't worry about a thing and please…be careful." He leaned in and kissed her cheek. He released her, and with just one backward glance, headed to his camp.

Sonya watched him walk up the beach, shoulders hunched, hands in his pockets, and she knew he'd just said good-bye to her.

She turned, ready to return to the *Double Dippin'*, and came up short when she caught sight of Garrett, standing in the bow, with a pair of binoculars aimed at her.

CHAPTER THIRTY-FIVE

Garrett lay on the narrow bunk and tried to sleep as the boat lightly bobbed with the incoming tide. No breeze gusted against the windows as the weather had cleared, revealing a starry night, which winked at him through the glass as though finding his situation funny.

Who else was laughing at him?

Seeing Sonya with Aidan on the beach, their body language comfortable, intimate, as they stood close to one another still burned in his memory. The way Aidan had touched her. The hold had been brief, but the feeling behind it spoke loud and clear from where Garrett had watched them. Was he kidding himself trusting Sonya that her relationship with Aidan was over? It didn't seem over to him. In fact, lately it seemed he didn't find Sonya without Harte close by.

Too close.

Could that be why she'd put a kibosh on him sharing her bed? Was she confused over feelings she had for both of them? She had to feel something for him, to let caution fly the night they'd had each other against the side of the Jeep. Just the thought of their impulsive loving made him hard.

Ah, hell. No way would he get to sleep with thoughts like that filling his mind.

Garrett rolled to his side. He was going nowhere with this line of questions. He could speculate with the pros, after all he was a cop and that was part of his job. Wondering and worrying about Sonya was driving him nuts. He'd never been this tied up in knots over a woman before, and he didn't like it. He should have kept things casual between them. Hell, he couldn't figure out how his feelings had gotten away from him to begin with.

He strangled the pillow, so tied up over Sonya that he was ready to be committed. He was beginning to think long-term, which was terrifying enough, but the thought of not having her in his life not only troubled but downright saddened him. Saddened him to depths he'd never rappelled down before. He kicked off the sleeping bag roasting him like a toasted marshmallow and willed himself to sleep.

He'd been a SEAL, damn it. There'd been times he'd slept in places that weren't fit to urinate in. He could sleep here. He shut his eyes and let his thoughts drift anywhere except the temptation of Sonya just a few feet below him.

He must have dozed, for what felt like mere minutes, when he found himself instantly alert. A shadow loomed like a ghost over him. Reflex had the gun he'd tucked under his pillow palmed and aimed at the heart of the intruder.

Then he caught a whiff of honeysuckle. "Sonya?"

Shit.

He released the hold on the trigger, his heartbeat stuttering to a halt, and let out a deep breath. "What's wrong?"

"Are you sleeping with a gun?"

"Trooper, remember?" He tried to regulate his breathing. Having his own gun trained on Sonya had stopped his heart. "What's wrong?"

"I can't sleep down there. You need to trade me bunks."

He leaned up on his elbow. "You are not sleeping up here. It's too exposed. If I'm down there, I'll be too far away from you in case there's trouble." He narrowed his eyes to try and see her features better, but the room was too full of shadows. "What's really going on, Sonya?"

She sighed. "Every time I close my eyes, I feel like I'm drowning. I know its stupid memories triggered from the boat taking on water today. The hold is too small, too dark, and I can hear water all around me."

He should have figured today's scare would have generated nightmares of her past. "What if I come down and sleep with you?"

"Just sleep, nothing fishy?"

"If that's what you want." He held his breath hoping she'd say she wanted more.

"That's what I want."

He refused to let out the disappointed sigh stuck in his throat. "Okay."

She turned and climbed the ladder back into the hold. He booby-trapped the pilot house door with the garbage can she had tucked under the sink. Anyone sneaking in would trip over that first, and awaken him if he wasn't already awake. He doubted he'd get any sleep anyway laying next to Sonya and not being able to do anything "fishy." He grabbed his pillow and his weapon, and followed her below.

The room was dark except for a weak beam of light coming from a flashlight, in need of a battery change, hanging from the wall at the head of the bed. It did provide enough light that he didn't run into anything as he made his way to Sonya's bed. The room smelled like her, dark honeyed-flowers with a touch of spring rain.

She scooted in next to the wall, and he took the edge, lowering himself to a night of torture. She wiggled to her left, and then to her right, until finally settling. The boat swayed with the incoming tide. The water surging against the aluminum sides of the hull was different down here than up above in the pilot house. More rousing than soothing.

Sonya pulled the covers up to her chin and began tossing again. It was bad enough that he was deluged with memories of the last time he'd been in this bed with her and the boat had been a rockin'. He didn't need her rolling around giving him even more ideas.

"Sonya," he warned.

"Sorry. I can't seem to get comfortable."

He reached to shut off the flashlight.

"No, don't turn it off."

"It's about to die anyway."

"I know, but it's too dark in here without the light. That's why I wanted to sleep above," she grumbled, somehow making this situation his fault.

"Why don't we talk about something? Get your mind on something else."

"Okay." There was a long pause. "What do you want to talk about?"

Their relationship.

The last time he'd brought up the subject, he'd seen the panic flare in her eyes. Wasn't he the one who was commitment phobic? Had he actually fallen for a woman who feared commitment more than he did? "Tell me about your parents, if it isn't too painful."

"It's not really painful, more bittersweet now. Do you understand?"

He did. Time did that with death. It was the only way the ones left behind could cope with the loss. "Yeah, I understand."

"Mom was one of those really beautiful women. Made-up, she knocked the breath out of you. Even on Sunday mornings, with no make-up, in her ratty pajamas, and her hair doing that bed-head thing, my dad couldn't keep his eyes off her."

Garrett saw the picture perfectly, only it was Sonya lounging around on a lazy Sunday morning in thread-bare pajamas and he was the man unable to tear his eyes from her. "Sounds like they had a good relationship."

"Yeah, they really loved each other and us. It breaks my heart that Peter didn't get to know them."

"Peter's been blessed to have you."

"Thanks." She turned on her side, facing him. "That means a lot, Garrett."

He stayed on his back, facing forward, not wanting to gaze into those warm, seductive brown eyes of hers in the romantic glow of the fading flashlight. He'd try something fishy for sure.

"What about you?" she asked. "Are your parents still living?"

Good, concentrating on his parents would keep him from thinking of her naked. "Yeah, they live in Florida."

"Do you have any siblings?" She asked the question as though realizing she didn't know a lot about him.

"I'm an only child. Dad would have liked more, but Mom had her hands full with me. Since Dad was in the Navy, always away on a mission, and raising me was left to her, she made sure there weren't going to be more Garretts running around."

"That's sad. You would probably have benefited from a sister or brother."

"We probably would have conspired and taken over the chain of command." He chuckled. "No, Mom had it right."

"You couldn't have been that bad."

He'd rather not entertain her with stories of his illicit younger years. No reason to scare her off, since there was a chance she was carrying his offspring. "Let's say I'm solely responsible for Mom going gray before her time." Time for a change of subject. "What's your life like in Soldotna?"

"Quiet. Normal. Boring."

"I doubt boring." He turned his head toward her, not able to resist looking at her as the musical resonance of her voice enticed. "I doubt you could be boring even if you tried."

"Is that a good thing?" her voice lowered almost to a whisper.

He was beginning to get a fishy vibe. "Everything about you is good." He couldn't stop from turning on his side toward her. "And lovely." His fingers trailed down the side of her face to her parted lips.

"You know what I said before, about nothing fishy?" He refrained—barely—from moaning his frustration. Then he felt her hand trailing down his chest. "Would you mind if we forget about that?"

"Are you sure?" He tore his eyes from her lips and met her gaze.

She nodded. "I need you, Garrett."

"How do you need me, Sonya? For just tonight? What about tomorrow?" The day after that? Would she need him then?

"I'm trying to get through today. Can we let tonight be enough for now?"

He wanted to press for more. Had to literally bite back the words that might scare her off. "All right, we'll make the most of tonight."

She sighed into his arms and he realized that with everything she was dealing with, a promise to him for tomorrows she didn't even know if she had, was too much to ask. It was up to him to make sure she had those tomorrows.

Then maybe she'd give them to him.

∫

A piercing boom jolted Sonya and Garrett awake.

"What the hell was that?" Sonya asked, pushing hair away from her eyes. Garrett had already vaulted out of bed, one leg in his pants, before Sonya even sat up.

He finished buttoning his pants, and bare-chested, reached for the gun he'd tucked under his pillow. "Stay here."

"Oh, I don't think so." She jumped out of bed and struggled into the Under Armour that Garrett had stripped from her only an hour or so before.

"Sonya, I don't have time to argue with you."

"Then don't, because I'm not staying put." He looked like he wanted to strangle her. Too bad. She wasn't the type of woman who took orders.

She was the type who gave them.

Garrett crept up the ladder, his gun leading the way, with Sonya hot on his tail. Another whistling bang rocked the night. It sounded like she'd anchored her boat on the frontline of a war zone. Then realization dawned and she started to laugh with relief.

"What's so funny?" Garrett asked as he climbed into the pilot house and helped her up the last rung of the ladder.

"Fireworks. Cranky and Crafty are celebrating the Fourth of July."

"They're a week late." Garrett cautiously peered out the window, motioning for her to stay down below the level of the glass.

"Weather's been bad."

"I don't like this." Another explosion rumbled and flared, lighting up the black sky.

"That was close," Sonya said, worrying her bottom lip.

"Each one's sounded closer than the last." He peered out through the window again. "How far away from shore do you think we are?"

"What time is it?"

The face of Garrett's watch shone green as he checked the time. "Just after two."

"High tide isn't until three. I'd say we're at least a couple hundred yards. Why?" She was afraid she already knew why.

"In case we have to make a swim for it."

She choked out a laugh. "Are you crazy? We're on a boat! We pull anchor, I fire up the engines and we're out of here."

"We might not have that kind of time."

Then she heard what he obviously already had. The coughing of a skiff's motor followed by another boom.

This one rattled what was left of her windows.

Garrett took another peek and quickly slunk down next to her. "Some bastard's shooting bombs at us with a slingshot," he grounded out. He grabbed the mic to the VHF and radioed the *Calypso*, filling them in on their situation and location.

All the words ran together in a buzz of static for Sonya.

"Come on." He grabbed her hand and tried to haul her out of the pilot house. She pulled back, her feet planted like spruce trees.

"I'm not leaving my boat." Her voice shook and her body followed suit.

The captain always went down with the boat.

"Sonya, I know you're scared. But we don't have time for this. He gets any closer and we're in trouble."

"W-what about your g-gun? You can shoot him."

"I'm damn well going to try. You need to be ready in case we have to make a swim for it."

She shook her head, until hair flew in her face from the force of it. "I can't s-swim, Garrett. I can't."

"I'll be with you. It'll be okay."

It didn't matter. She couldn't get in that water. If she did, she was dead.

Garrett pulled her from the pilot house and down the stairs, to kneel next to the rail of the boat. The skiff sounded like it was right alongside the *Double Dippin'*.

"Kyra! I know you're there with that bastard."

"*Kyra?*" Garrett asked, a frown marring his forehead.

"My mother." Sonya was just as puzzled as the look on Garrett's face. "I think that's Cranky. He's confused me for my mom before when he's drunk."

"Why didn't you tell me?"

"Didn't think it was important." She ignored the narrowed stare Garrett sent her.

"Last chance, Kyra," Earl Harte yelled from the skiff as it motored around the side of the *Double Dippin'* where they were hunched down out of sight. "I won't let you leave me for another man. Not again."

Garrett motioned for her to stay down as he rose to peek over the side of the boat. He quickly knelt down and whispered in her ear. "I can't get a bead on him. The skiff's in the shadow of the hull. Can you talk to him? Draw him closer?"

She nodded, the movement jerky, and wet her lips. "Earl Harte? What the hell are you doing?"

"Don't antagonize him," Garrett growled.

"That's how my mom always talked to him," she whispered.

"Kyra? You bitch. What'd I tell you would happen if you chose him over me?"

Sonya shrugged her shoulders. He motioned for her to say something else to Earl, but she was at a loss.

"Y-you said I had another chance," Sonya replied. "Tell me what you want me to do."

Garrett squeezed her hand in approval. "Good, keep him talking. Hopefully it'll buy us time until the *Calypso* arrives."

If it kept her out of the water, she'd recite the constitution. Cranky hadn't responded to the last question she'd asked, which had her worrying her bottom lip again. She was going to chew through it at this rate.

"Earl, tell me what you want me to do?"

"Why, Kyra?" His words slurred. "Why did ya have to do it?"

"Do what?"

"Make me hurt you," he whined.

Hell, this was like déjà vu. This could be Aidan talking to her.

"You haven't hurt me, Earl." Not yet. "And you don't have to. Just tell me what you want me to do?"

"I want you to die, Kyra. And this time, I want you stayin' dead."

A chill sank into her bones. Garrett's hold on her tightened. He rose up again to look over the rail and this time aimed and fired off a shot. A cackling laugh followed, and then a homemade pipe bomb, fuse lit and smoking, whistled into the air, landing a few feet from them.

"*Shit!*" Garrett grabbed her. Before she could utter a protest, she went flying overboard into the black water as the bomb exploded aboard her boat.

Chapter Thirty-Six

Icy needles pierced Sonya's skin as the ocean reached up and eagerly swallowed her. Down, down, down into the depths of hell, invisible talons dragged her to a waiting watery grave. She kicked and lashed. Everything inside her screamed. Water blinded her eyes. Filled her mouth and nose. Smothered, strangled, and squeezed the life out of her.

She broke the surface and choked in large breaths of air. Coughing up the bitter taste of saltwater, she blinked as it stung like acid in her eyes. She thrashed. The deep wrapped around her ankles and pulled at her feet. Water splashed, toying with her as she panicked. Then the killing clutches towed her under again.

There was a score to settle, Sonya knew. Finally understood. She'd cheated this unforgiving ocean before, but she knew she wouldn't be able to again. Her number was being called, and damn it, there was no way she'd avoid answering this time.

Pain exploded in her chest, and her lungs flamed with the need for air.

This was it. Everything she'd feared since she was fifteen. She'd known she'd die this was—the way she'd been meant to all those years ago. She hadn't been destined to live through the *Mystic's* sinking.

Suddenly everything went still and through the murky water, Sonya saw her twin. Floating like an angel, peaceful, beautiful, but sporting that ornery look she always got on her face whenever Sonya did something Sasha didn't like. Sonya reached a hand out for her, but Sasha shook her head, and she swore Sasha mouthed the word "fight." Then she was alone in the freezing darkness. The pressure in her chest returned, burning for breath, the pain worse than anything she'd ever experienced. She struggled, kicked her legs, her arms striking up, angling down, as the motion of swimming returned to her like retained muscle memory.

Her head emerged into the night air and she gasped for breath. Her heart thumped like a drum solo, her breathing choppy as she attempted to gulp in as much air as her body could possible hold. She treaded water and took in her surroundings, while panic still shivered through her. Any minute now the water would reach for her again.

The *Double Dippin'* smoked but wasn't aflame...and a crazed man's voice cackled over the serene darkness of the night.

Garrett.

Where was Garrett? Sonya whipped around, her eyes straining the blackness to find him. He wouldn't have left her. He knew how scared of the water she was—

A body floated face down a few feet from her.

A prayer—a tortured sob—escaped as she swam toward him. Grabbing his arm, she turned him in the water, until his face floated up. Then he sank like an anchor taking her down with him.

Damned if she'd let this ocean steal another person she loved.

Hooking her arm around his neck, she kicked and heaved for the surface with everything she had, relieved to find they hadn't been pulled under far. The cold of the water drained her strength, causing her teeth to chatter. She backstroked for the *Double Dippin'*, dragging Garrett with her, just as a shot ran out.

The bastard was shooting at her now?

Throwing a bomb on her boat wasn't enough? What the hell had she ever done to piss off Cranky?

Once she was out of the water she was going to kill the fucking bastard.

She'd make sure he never hurt her or someone she loved again. Anger heated her muscles, and she made it to the stern, near the ladder. She grabbed the lowest rung with one hand, and rested, still holding Garrett's head above water. How was she going to get him aboard if he didn't wake up?

What if he never woke up? Please God, she silently prayed. *Make him wake up.*

Waves lulled against them, no longer threatening, more like cradling the both of them. As though pitying their useless efforts to stay alive. The evening seemed almost tranquil, hushed, as though pausing to watch. Garrett's head rolled, something warm and sticky brushed her face, and he groaned. Sonya almost sobbed with relief.

Then she heard the engine of Earl's sputtering skiff split the eerie stillness. The mocking serenity of the night bore a shocking similarity to that of a horror movie just before the characters were slaughtered.

Her heart pounded in tune to the theme of Jaws as Earl crept steadily closer.

"Kyrrra? Where are you, Kyrrra?" Earl's sing-song voice sent more shivers coursing through Sonya's body.

With no choice that she could see, Sonya let go of the ladder and swam them around the corner of the stern before Earl saw them. She knew she wouldn't be able to keep them both afloat while Earl played a sick Marco Polo, taking pot shots at them around the *Double Dippin'*.

Swimming to shore was no longer an option. She didn't have the strength to get both Garrett and herself there, and as soon as she left the protection of the *Double Dippin'*, she'd be in open water—easy pickings for Earl, damn-his-cranky-hide, Harte.

Where the hell was the Calypso?

Then she heard another outboard engine roaring toward them. She prayed troopers were coming to the rescue loaded for bear and would take this son of a bitch down. Rather that than a member of her family hearing the explosions and coming to investigate. She couldn't handle it if any one of them were hurt.

The new skiff's engine powered down. "Dad!"

Aidan?

Was he there for backup? For who? Her or his father?

Garrett struggled in her grasp, coughing and giving away their location, as he came to full consciousness.

"Sonya?" he croaked, his tone one of panic as he thrashed in the water.

"Shhh," she whispered near his ear, flooded with emotion that he was alive. Tears clogged her throat. She felt his body jerk with suppressed coughs, relieved he settled and didn't need an explanation regarding their precarious situation. She relaxed her hold on Garrett as he began treading water on his own. She didn't know how much longer she'd have been able to keep them both from sinking.

"You okay?" he whispered back. The concern in his tone brought a lump to her throat.

She nodded, knowing that Garrett wasn't okay, afraid he bled from a head wound.

"Dad, what are you doing?" Aidan asked. "Why are you wasting all the fireworks?"

344

"What fireworks?" Sonya heard the confusion in Earl's voice.

The man was nuts. First he was calling her Kyra and now he didn't remember throwing homemade fireworks at them?

"I'm throwing pipe bombs." He cackled. "They do a fine job blowing up boats. At least they did." She could imagine Cranky scratching his head. "Must've messed up on the mixture. That one didn't do much more than boom and smoke."

"Why don't we head back to camp and try to get the formula right?" Aidan said.

"Sure. Just as soon as I'm done here." Sonya heard the skiff inch closer. The cold was making her fingers numb and her limbs sluggish. Ten minutes was all this water allowed before hypothermia set in. Those minutes were ticking by fast, if not altogether gone.

A flashlight clicked on, shining in Sonya's eyes, blinding her. Garrett moved her behind him, using his body as a shield.

"There you are, Kyrrra," Earl said, sadistic pleasure coming through in his tone. "Thought you could get away from me again, did ya?"

"W-what do you mean, a-again?" Sonya chattered. Was the man off his meds? She twisted to see Earl while Garrett did his best to keep her behind him. His motions were lethargic, and Sonya knew he wouldn't last long. Then his head fell against her shoulder, and his body started to sink. Sonya grabbed him around his trunk.

Enough of this bullshit.

They needed to get out of the water now. They were no better than sitting ducks.

Earl let out another cackle. "Think the *Mystic* caught fire by accident? I rigged the electrical harness."

"You b-bastard." Sonya shook with cold, and anger, and an overwhelming need to wrap her fingers around Earl's neck and squeeze until he flopped like a dead fish in her hands.

"I warned you, Kyra. You never did listen. Guess you'll listen now—" he interrupted himself with a laugh, "—guess you won't, since you'll be dead." His gaze shifted to include Garrett. "Along with your stud." He raised the gun he held in his hand. "That is if the man lives long enough to die."

"Dad! That isn't Kyra. It's *Sonya,*" Aidan said, stressing her name.

"I *know* she's Sonya. What? You think I'm nuts?"

Well, yeah.

"Then why are you calling her Kyra?"

Yeah, why?

"Why would I call her Kyra? Kyra's dead." Then he laughed, the evil sound echoing across the water.

"Dad—"

"When I was your age, Junior, I'd never let a woman get away with making a fool out me like Sonya has you. Fucking a fish cop right under your nose and you just sat back and let her get away with it."

"You're making a mistake. Sonya and I aren't in love—"

"What? You going to tell me you don't love her? That her banging this asswipe doesn't twist your insides? I'm doing you a favor, boy."

"I don't want any favors. Let me handle her on my own."

"Like you've handled her so far? She's made a fool of you, just like her mother did me. I didn't let that bitch get away with it, and I'm not going to let this one either." He turned back to Sonya, his face deformed into a painful, cruel mask. "Why did you have to come back, Kyra?"

"*Sonya*, you psychotic bastard!" she yelled at him. If he was going to kill her, he'd sure as hell better get her name right.

"Whatever." Earl shrugged and raised the gun.

"Earl," Garrett said, raising his head, his voice raspy as though pain had him tight in its grip. "I've already radioed the *Calypso*. Your only choice is to listen to your son."

"Yeah," Earl scoffed. "Like that will ever happen. The boy's an idiot."

"Put the gun down, Dad," Aidan pleaded. "You don't want to do this."

"You're a pain in the ass, you know that?" Earl lowered the gun and swung around to face Aidan, who'd snuck steadily closer in his skiff. Earl smirked when he saw the gun Aidan carried.

"Come on, Dad. Lana made those brownies you like. The ones with the toffee bits crumbled on top. Let's head back to camp where we can have some and figure this all out."

"Why? I've got it figured out." Then, quick as a snake, Earl coiled back to Sonya and Garrett and aimed.

A gun fired…and Earl fell to his knees.

He dropped his pistol, his hand covering his chest where blood bubbled out like black crude oil. His wide-eyed expression sought out Aidan's. "Well, I'll be damned. Who knew you had the balls, son?" A proud smile tilted the side of his mouth, and then he pitched forward into the bottom of the skiff.

CHAPTER THIRTY-SEVEN

"Dad!" Aidan yelled, his skiff smacking into Earl's. "*Oh God, oh God, oh God.*" Aidan grabbed the rail of the skiff, roped the two boats together and jumped into his father's boat.

Aidan's tortured sob clutched at Sonya's heart. From where she treaded water, she couldn't see if Earl was all right, but she didn't think so.

Aidan had always been a crack shot.

Both Sonya and Garrett had jerked when the gunshot rang out, expecting to be shot themselves.

Where the hell were those troopers Garrett had radioed for?

Then she heard another outboard and prayed help was on the way. They needed to get out of this water, which didn't seem as cold as before.

"Sonya!" Peter hollered, his voice anxious. She turned to see Wes and Peter pulling up in the skiff. "Are you okay?"

"Y-yes, but Garrett isn't."

Wes maneuvered as close to them as he could. He and Peter grabbed Garrett under the arms and pulled him out of the frigid water. Sonya swam up to the boat, her actions slow and sluggish, her arms leaden. She reached up a hand, and they pulled her into the skiff.

The night air sliced like shards of ice, stealing her breath. She'd been warmer in the water.

"What the hell's been going on here?" Peter asked, fear causing his voice to crack. "Why are you guys in the water? What's up with Aidan?" They all heard his tormented sobs carrying over the water as the skiffs drifted away from each other with the tide. "What's with all the fireworks? I thought Cranky and Crafty were going to wait 'til tomorrow night." He helped her sit in the bottom of the boat, next to Garrett, since her legs couldn't seem to hold her weight. "Damn, you're cold, Sonya. We've got to get you back to the cabin and warm you up."

She shook her head. "Garrett's h-hurt." She put her hand on his bare chest, relieved to feel air rhythmically breathe in and out. Blood seeped steadily from a gash on his forehead. "We n-need blankets from the *Double Dippin'*. C-cabin's too far away." Wes had already angled the skiff near the ladder at the stern of the drift boat. Peter scampered aboard, while Wes tied them to the boat. "Grab something to h-help stop Garrett's bleeding t-too," Sonya hollered.

Peter was back in moments with two sleeping bags and the first aid kit. Bless him, he'd also grabbed their boots. "Crap, Sonya, the boat's a mess." He draped one of the sleeping bags around her shoulders and handed over a pair of boots. "What the hell went down here tonight?" She grabbed the folds of the down-filled sleeping bag tight around her and struggled to get her wet, frozen feet into her rubber boots.

Garrett moved his head and groaned. "Sonya."

She reached for his hand and held it in hers, bringing their clasped fingers to her chest. "I-I'm right here. H-hang in there, Garrett. W-we'll get you f-fixed up."

349

Wes picked her up and moved her away from Garrett. "You sit here and let Peter and I take care of him." They stripped Garrett's soaked jeans off him and zipped him snug in the sleeping bag. Then Wes covered the cut on his forehead with gauze pads, taping them in place. When they were finished, she crawled back to Garrett's side and brushed a hand over his wet hair.

"There isn't anything more we can do for him until we get to the cabin," Wes said.

She shook her head. "No, you n-need to take him to Wanda. He needs s-stitches, and checked over for a c-concussion," she said through chattering teeth. Aidan's anguished suffering echoed over the water. She had to help him, too, before he did something bad…like turn his gun on himself. "I want you to drop me off with Aidan, and then take Garrett to Wanda."

"No." Garrett struggled to opened his eyes. "Skip and Judd will be here. They can help Aidan."

"They'll a-arrest him and a-ask questions later. That's the last thing he n-needs right now."

"We'll get you two to shore and then come back and help Aidan," Peter suggested. "You need to get dry and warmed up."

"No." She hoped Peter would understand. She knew he was worried about her. "Peter, Aidan just k-killed Earl. I can't leave him a-alone. He n-needs me."

"I *need* you, Sonya." Garrett's hand squeezed hers.

The words warmed her heart and she wished she could go with him, but of the two men, Aidan needed her more right now. She gave Garrett a soft smile and kissed their joined hands. "Garrett, you're the kind of guy who doesn't need anyone."

"Damn it, Sonya." Garrett pushed up to a sitting position, and then his eyes rolled back in his head. He would have fallen back if Sonya hadn't caught him in her arms and helped him lie down. He was quickly losing his ability to fight with her. "Sonya." He swallowed. "Listen—"

"Save your s-strength for Wanda. Y-you'll need it." She ran her fingers alongside his stubbled jaw, and then turned to Wes. "Take me to Aidan."

"You're sure?" Wes asked. "One of us can stay behind with Aidan."

"It'll take b-both of you to get Garrett to Wanda's. I-I don't have the strength."

Wes drew the skiff alongside Aidan's. The two boats drifted recklessly with the incoming tide. Aidan held Earl in his arms, his fractured sobs breaking her heart. She stepped from one boat into the other with Peter's help, the sleeping bag still clutched like a life preserver around her. "Now, get Garrett t-to Wanda. Hurry."

They took off, the skiff on plane as it flew toward the village. Sonya sent a silent prayer that Garrett would be all right and then bent next to Aidan, putting her hand on his shoulder. "Aidan."

"Sonya?" He seemed as though he'd been unaware of her boarding his boat as he'd been caught up in his own hell. "I killed him, Sonya. I killed the son of a bitch." He wiped his nose with his forearm.

"You s-saved my life, Aidan," she pointed out though he didn't seem to hear her.

"Do you have any idea how long I've wanted him dead?" He didn't wait for Sonya to answer as he sobbed. "Most of my life. Even fantasized how I'd do it, if given the opportunity. Never thought I actually do it, though."

He laid Earl's limp body down and curled in on himself. "Goddamn, Sonya." Her name came out on a tortured sob, and she wrapped her arms around him.

"Come on Aidan. L-let's get to shore." The sleeping bag was helping with the cold, but it wasn't enough. She needed to get dry, and Aidan needed to remove himself from Earl's dead body or she was afraid of what he might do.

He angled his head so that he could see her. "How do I face them? Your grandparents? Lana? Oh God, Roland." He shut his eyes on a moan. "He's going to kill me."

"When they h-hear what h-happened, they'll understand."

He shook his head. "Roland won't."

She agreed, but didn't voice it. "Then we'll d-deal with it. But Aidan," she captured his gaze, "I'm going to be in t-trouble if we don't get to s-shore. I'm really c-cold."

He seemed to shake himself free of the horror of the evening's events as he focused on her and what needed to be done.

Sonya breathed a silent sigh of relief. She'd hoped putting herself in Aidan's hands would force him to concentrate on her rather than the realities of what had gone on here tonight. At some point, she would need to deal with those realities herself.

Earl had caused the deaths of her parents and Sasha.

No, not now. She sat in the stern, exhausted, as Aidan untied his skiff and positioned it to be towed behind as he drove his father's boat to shore. Sonya looked over the side at the black tide steadily creeping to shore, trying not to see Earl's dead body as it lay bleeding in the bottom of the boat. She swallowed back the bile that suddenly rose in her throat. Everything she'd believed was wrong, twisted.

They'd lived, fished, next to a killer all these years and had never suspected.

When they reached shore, everyone waited for them. Grams with Barbarella cradled against her chest, Gramps armed with a shovel, Lana clutching a lantern with both hands, and Roland, standing stoic next to her, his hands tucked into the pockets of his dirty cargo pants.

Looked as though Earl's fireworks/pipe bombs had woken up both camps.

"What in dang blazes is going on?" Gramps waded into the surf, his face going pale as he caught sight of Earl's body. "Do we need a medic?"

"N-no," Sonya said, stumbling as the skiff rubbed against the rocky beach.

"Why you wearing a sleeping bag?"

"I w-went for a s-swim."

"What?"

"I'll explain l-later. Right now, I need to get w-warmed up." She looked Gramps in the eye. "Aidan's going to n-need us. P-promise m-me you'll keep an open mind, okay."

Gramps narrowed his eyes but nodded.

"What the fuck!" Roland's voice rang out as he saw their cargo. "Who did this?"

Aidan's face went white, but he squared his shoulders and stood up to his uncle. "I did. I shot him."

"You?" Roland advanced on Aidan, splashing into the surf. "You killed my brother? Your own father?"

"Yes." Aidan swallowed, rolling his lips tight between his teeth as though to hold in his emotions. "He was going to kill Sonya and Garrett."

Grams and Lana gasped. Gramps cursed, and not with one of his colorful adaptations either.

The rest of the their explanations were interrupted as the *Calypso* finally roared up from the south, her bow slicing through the surf, every light onboard blazing like a beacon in the darkness. She cut her engines, and waves rolled like thick black thunderheads from under the hull, their force tossing the skiffs as they crashed to shore. A high powered spotlight pointed at each person on the beach, settling on Grams. Judd's voice came over loud and clear from the *Calypso's* P. A. system. "Lay down your weapons!"

Grams grumbled but laid Barbarella in the sand at her feet. Gramps had already dropped his shovel when he'd waded into the surf.

"Sonya, we were radioed that you and Garrett were under fire," Judd continued, his voice booming over the group. "That better not be Garrett in the bottom of that skiff."

"Head up to the cabin, Sonya," Aidan said, still standing in the stern of the skiff. "I'll explain to them what happened."

"I'll go w-with you. Otherwise they'll arrest you and ask q-questions later."

"I don't care if they arrest me."

"Well, I do. Don't turn m-martyr on me, Aidan."

"They can't come ashore unless one of us goes and gets 'em," Roland sneered.

"We aren't hiding out from the t-troopers," Sonya said. Besides, they had a dinghy. They could get to shore without any problems. "We didn't do anything w-wrong." Maybe Roland had. Earl didn't do anything without Roland. Was Crafty as much to blame for this whole mess as Cranky?

Roland must have read something in her expression. "I'm not waiting around to entertain a bunch of fucking fish cops." He took off toward the Hartes' camp.

"Halt!" Judd's voice rang out.

Roland gave them the bird and kept right on moving. If anything, his gait increased.

"Sonya, it's in your best interest to get one of those skiffs out here and pick us up," Judd hollered. "Now."

"Aidan, take your other skiff," Gramps said. "Leave this one here. Lana, help me beach her on shore. Sonya, you're staying here." Lana handed Grams the lantern and waded into the water, while Aidan did as Gramps instructed.

Sonya was rapidly getting tired, her limbs not wanting to respond, fingers numb. It had been a while since she'd felt her feet.

"Come on, Sonya." Gramps reached his arms up for her. "Let's get you out of this skiff and up to the cabin. Maggie May, run up and heat some water. Lana, you go with her, we'll meet you there."

"Your h-hand. I don't want to h-hurt you, Gramps." Sonya wanted to sink down into the bottom of the skiff, her muscles seeming to atrophy.

"Fiddlesticks," Gramps said, making her smile like the word always did. "The day I can't help my favorite grand-daughter out of a boat, they might as well put me in my grave."

Not a good day for analogies like that one. Sonya put her hands on his shoulders so that most of her weight centered there instead of on his injured hand. Her frozen booted feet landed on the rocky sand and felt as though she'd stood on a bed of sea urchins.

Gramps put a hand around her waist to help her stand. "You're in bad shape, Sonya."

She was afraid he was right. She indicated Earl left in the skiff. "W-what about him?"

"He's not going anywhere."

It was slow going up the beach to the trail with Gramps's help, but once facing the trek to the cabin, Sonya knew she wouldn't make it the rest of the way. Then Aidan was there, accompanied by Judd and Skip. He swooped her up into his arms, and she gratefully rested her head on his shoulder as he carried her up the bluff to the cabin.

Heat blasted her when they entered. Grams had turned up the little propane heater and it was eating up the BTUs.

"Aidan, lay her over there." Grams indicated the curtained-off area where the bed sat. She bustled Aidan out of the room after he'd laid Sonya down. She didn't bother with the questions Sonya knew she was dying to ask, just went to work with Lana's help, getting Sonya out of her wet clothes and into dry ones. Then she piled Sonya high with blankets, stuffing hot water bottles around her. It was heavenly, and Sonya soaked it all up: the undemanding attention, the exquisite heat warming her bones, and the gracious postponement of the troopers' interrogation.

She crashed.

𝖏

Aidan's interrogation started the moment he'd retreated from laying Sonya on her grandparents' bed. She'd seemed so removed from what was happening. As though she'd somehow...left. He couldn't lose her too. She'd been in that water too long, had felt like ice when he'd lifted her in his arms. He prayed they weren't too late getting her care.

They'd returned to the beach, along with Nikolai, after the fish cops had realized Sonya would be no good to them until she was warmed up. The cops had searched his camp for Roland, but there was no sign of him.

Roland wouldn't be found either, not unless he wanted to be.

Now they sat around the fire pit on stumps. The remains of the last fire was nothing but black, cold ashes, much the way Aidan felt inside. More fish cops had shown up to take care of his father's body. Aidan tried to put what they were doing to his father out of his mind. The sound of the zipper, as they sealed Earl into a plastic body bag, caused his stomach to churn.

He'd killed his father. He was a killer.

"Harte." Judd snapped his fingers in front of Aidan's face, breaking into the horrific replaying of what he'd done. "From the top. Again."

Aidan swallowed the bile he'd been fighting since realizing that his *own father* had been the one causing Sonya all the trouble this summer. "I woke around 1:00 a.m. when I heard what sounded like a gunshot or a firecracker. At first, I thought my da—" he stopped himself and had to swallow. If he kept referring to Earl by Dad, he wouldn't be able to hold it together. "I thought Earl and Roland had decided to light their fireworks early—"

"Homemade fireworks, you said?" Judd clarified, looking at his notes. The sun had started to rise, a faint blush in the east, giving enough light for everyone to see too much. "How did your father and uncle know how to make fireworks?"

"Earl was an explosives expert in Vietnam. What he knew he taught Roland and vice versa."

"How did he acquire the necessary ingredients to make fireworks?"

Aidan shrugged. "You can make a bomb using ordinary household materials."

"A bomb?" Judd jumped on the word. "What was it, fireworks or a bomb that your father made?"

"I didn't see him make the pipe bombs, but that's what he was throwing at the *Double Dippin'*. I only saw him make the fireworks." Aidan sighed. Why hadn't he paid more attention to what was happening in his own camp, rather than being so concerned with what was happening with Sonya? Maybe he would have figured this out sooner, before someone had to die.

Nikolai raised his hand. "I can verify the fireworks. I witnessed Roland and Earl both working on them last night. I've seen them do it year after year. They were planning a late Fourth of July celebration for tonight as the weather was supposed to be nice." He paused and then his voice got quiet. "We were going to have a bonfire and roast hotdogs."

"Okay," Judd addressed Aidan again, his pencil scratching on his notepad. "Let's get back to when you realized your father was missing."

"When I woke up, Earl was gone, but Roland was still sleeping. I knew that Earl wouldn't light off the fireworks without Roland. They were a pair when it came to explosives. Turned them into kids." True juvenile delinquents. "Anyway, I got dressed and went to investigate. One of the skiffs was gone and then a bomb went off near where the *Double Dippin'* was anchored."

"It was then that you realized your father was after Sonya?"

Aidan nodded. "I had some suspicions when her window had been knocked out by a rock and it was assumed someone with a slingshot had done it. Earl is—was—real handy with a slingshot."

"Why didn't you come forward then?" Judd asked, his shrewd gaze narrowed.

"I couldn't believe it, or see why Earl would do something like that. It didn't add up." Now he knew different. Acid burped in his stomach again as he replayed the scene in his head of his father confusing Sonya for Kyra.

"So you grabbed the other skiff and made your way to the *Double Dippin'*." Judd pulled him back from the nightmare. "Then what?"

"When I got there Sonya and Garrett were already in the water. I don't know how, but I assumed they jumped overboard to avoid the pipe bomb. Except Sonya would never jump willingly, so Garrett would have had to push her into the ocean."

"She must have been terrified." Nikolai shook his head. "My poor girl."

"What was Earl doing?" Judd steered the subject back to where he wanted it.

"Ranting." Aidan swallowed hard.

"What about?"

Aidan turned to Nikolai. This next part was going to be hard for the man to hear. Hard enough for him to say. "I'm sorry, Nikolai. I didn't know any of this, I swear." He turned back to Judd and Skip. "When my dad drank, he'd sometimes confuse Sonya for Kyra. He was calling her Kyra, telling her that he wasn't going to allow her to make a fool of him again."

"Again?" Nikolai asked, his busy brows furrowing.

"I think the situation between me and Sonya mirrored what happened between him and Kyra years ago, and he refused to let history repeat itself."

"You mean Sonya leaving you for Garrett?" Judd clarified.

It shouldn't have surprised him that these cops knew his and Sonya's history. Whatever Sonya told Garrett about them, he would have shared with his buddies. "Technically Sonya and I have been over for a while. Her decision, not mine. Earl saw it differently."

"Why didn't I see it?" Nikolai said to no one in particular. "Earl had always been jealous of Mikhail. Then when Mikhail decided to get into drifting, with Kyra behind him, Earl went ballistic. He caused all sorts of problems, got the set netters up in arms, the drifters worked up. A Fish and Game meeting was held to see if a set netter drifting was even permissible." He paused as though to gather his emotions. "Chuck Kendrick actually came to Mikhail's defense. We thought later it was because he wanted to unload the *Mystic*. When she sank, it had the effect of sending a clear message to the other set netters of what could happen if any of them followed Mikhail's example."

"So when Sonya announced she was going to do the same thing as her father, it might have snapped something in Earl?" Judd speculated.

Nikolai solemnly regarded Aidan. "Kendrick didn't sell my boy a compromised boat, did he?"

Aidan swallowed once again. Keeping the contents of his stomach down was getting harder and harder as the questions escalated. "No. It was Earl. He admitted to booby-trapping the electrical harness aboard the *Mystic*. I'm so sorry, Nikolai."

"You mean *Earl* sank the *Mystic*?" Skip asked, bending forward. He'd been silent the whole time while he watched, studied, and judged. "*He killed* Mik, Kyra, and Sasha?"

"Yes, and he was just as determined to kill Sonya and Garrett too."

Chapter Thirty-Eight

Garrett sat on an over-turned bucket and leaned against the side of Wes and Peter's skiff as they made their way to the Savonski's camp. His head ached like a son of a bitch, and he was real unsteady. Wanda had sewn him up and complained like the good doctor she was when he insisted on leaving. He knew he had a concussion, but he wasn't seeing double and he was aware of who he was, unlike the time in Iraq when he'd been blown a hundred yards by a bomb planted in the body of a twelve-year-old boy. It had taken him a month to figure out who the hell he was that time. This concussion produced a hell of a headache, and an upset stomach, but it didn't hurt nearly as much as his heart did.

Sonya had actually chosen Harte over him.

He'd promised her he'd keep her safe, and then he'd thrown her overboard into her own version of hell. In his defense, he'd had every intention of helping her in the water, knowing she'd be panicked, but then something had hit him, a piece of shrapnel from the pipe bomb most likely. The last thing he remembered was Sonya saving *his* sorry ass.

He'd bullied his way onto her boat and his own actions had set off a psycho. He'd known this whole mess had been tied to a Harte. He'd just been looking at the wrong Harte.

Why was that?

The answer was a bitter pill. Because he'd wanted Aidan Harte to be guilty, then he wouldn't be competition. He'd be imprisoned. Garrett had done exactly what Skip had feared he would do. Let his feelings for Sonya interfere with his ability to do his job and she'd almost died because of it. Hell, he'd be dead, too, if it wasn't for Aidan.

Wasn't that hard to swallow.

"How you doing, Garrett?" Peter asked from the bow where he stood, holding onto the painter's rope, balancing on the balls of his feet, while Wes drove the skiff full out, flying over the waves.

Other than his breaking heart, pounding head, and nauseous stomach, he was dandy. "Fine," he answered, just as the skiff hit the trough of a wave and banged him hard enough to see stars. Probably the ones laughing at him earlier.

"Sorry about that," Wes said. "Hold on, we're almost there."

Garrett didn't care how many bangs he had to take as long as Wes got them to the camp fast. He'd taken too long at Wanda's. The woman had demanded he be checked over for hypothermia, since he'd shown up in her Infirmary wet, naked, and shivering. She'd rustled up some baby blue scrubs, with little black bears on them for him to wear, and he'd promised to get them back to her. He still held the sleeping bag around him and was forever grateful that the rain had ceased to fall. For once in his life, he had no wish to be wet again any time soon.

"Wow," Peter commented, standing straighter in the bow as they came into shore. "Looks like we're having a party."

Sure enough the place was lit up like a carnival. Troopers canvassed the area, flood lights becoming less effective with the weak sunrise coming up over the bluff. Garrett gingerly stood, holding onto the rail, and took in the scene, fighting the wave of dizziness that threatened to swamp him.

The RHIB was beached next to Aidan's skiff, and Corte and Foster where bagging the body. Farther up the beach, Garrett made out Aidan, Nikolai, Judd, and Skip.

No sign of Sonya.

Bet Sonya was cursing him loud and angry about now, with troopers invading her camp. The alternative didn't bear thinking about. Luckily it was still considered middle of the night and there wasn't a fishing period until later that day, leaving the beach empty of spectators. At least Cranky's dead body didn't have the audience that Kendrick's had.

Wes brought the skiff to shore, and Garrett climbed out into the surf, leaving Peter to help Wes tie up to the running line. He trudged toward the group sitting around the fire pit. He had a job to do. Something he should have been concentrating on instead of letting his emotions for Sonya cloud the reason he'd come to Bristol Bay.

Funny that he'd signed up for this assignment to clear his head of one woman only to have it muddied up over another.

"Nice outfit," Judd smirked as Garrett took a stump between him and Nikolai.

Garrett ignored him and addressed Nikolai, "How's Sonya?"

A look of worry traveled over Nikolai's craggy face. "No news is good news. She's with the women and if I know my Maggie May, Sonya will be just fine. Maggie wouldn't settle for anything less."

Garrett breathed a sigh of relief. If anything had happened to her—

He closed his eyes as the pain in his chest flared. He opened them and regarded Judd and Skip. "Where're we at?"

"Ready for your version of the evening's events," Skip said.

Garrett met his eyes, and tried not to flinch at the condemnation in his. He'd sure fucked up. "Where do you want me to start?"

"The beginning." Cops always started at the beginning.

He began with being jerked awake by the first bomb, leaving out where he'd been sleeping at the time. Nikolai flinched when Garrett recounted tossing Sonya overboard, and he lost himself for a moment in the fear she must have felt being pitched into water black and cold as death. His heart burned with the knowledge of what he'd put her through.

A slight breeze drifted by and an eagle screeched above, while waves lapped carelessly at the shore. The sky flushed pink with promises of a stunning day to come. It all seemed so surreal that the short black hours of the night had been filled with death and confessions.

"I just remember fragments after that." Fighting to stay conscious, struggling to stay afloat, fearing he wouldn't be able to save Sonya, and then the bitter reality that he hadn't saved her. She'd saved herself. Along with Aidan. She hadn't needed him. All Garrett had been was dead weight.

"We need to hear anything you remember," Judd said, settling into the role of good cop while Skip was deep in the role of bad cop. Garrett bet Skip couldn't wait to cut him down, but he was professional enough to wait until they didn't have an audience.

"I remember Earl admitting that he'd caused the sinking of the *Mystic*."

Nikolai glanced away at his words and Garrett knew this night had to be incredibly hard on the man. He'd fished all these years next to the Hartes and hadn't known the part Earl had played in his family's tragedy.

"Did you witness Aidan shooting Earl?" Skip asked.

"Yes. It was self-defense. Sonya and I would be dead if Aidan hadn't reacted as quickly as he had." He met Aidan's eye, knowing he owed the man not only his life but Sonya's. He'd be forever in his debt.

Didn't that suck?

Sonya threw back the mountain of covers and sat up. She'd awakened feeling like she'd been baked too long in an oven. Crispy around the edges and hard as a rock in the middle. The feeling sure as hell beat frozen in a freezer, but she'd had enough. She needed to know if Garrett was okay, and Aidan. The troopers had whisked him away just like she'd feared they would. How was he holding up with their relentless questioning, while he battled the guilt of killing his father? How bad was Garrett's head wound? Had he lost too much blood? She knew the man could take care of himself, but what if tonight had been more than he could handle?

What if—

"What are you doing out of bed?" Thankfully, Grams interrupted her thoughts.

"I'm much better." Sonya reached for a brush to pull her hair back into a ponytail. She really needed a shower. The dried salt from her horrific swim made her feel like a piece of dried meat. Skin tight and gritty. The cabin was quiet. Sonya didn't see any sign of Lana, but Grams had been baking muffins. The tempting smell of cranberries and nuts made Sonya's stomach rumble. She'd exerted so much energy trying to keep her and Garrett afloat she felt like she could eat nonstop for a week.

"Sonya," Grams said, worry wrinkling her brow. "You scared years off my life. I'd feel better if you rested some more."

Sonya wrapped her arms around her grandmother. "I know, and I'm sorry."

Grams hugged her back. "Don't do it again. I don't have that many years left to lose."

"Yes, ma'am." Sonya let her go with a smile. "Where are the men?"

"Still outside pow-wowing around the fire pit."

"Any news on Garrett?" She was afraid of the answer.

"Wes and Peter returned with him about thirty minutes ago."

"He's here?" Wanda had released him? "Have you seen him? Talked to him? How's he doing?"

"One question at a time. From what Wes said, he has a concussion, and Wanda hadn't been too keen on letting him leave. He didn't give her much choice. It took fifteen stitches to close his head wound."

"He should be under observation."

Grams nodded in agreement. "I'm sure you'll tell him that when you see him. You might want to ask yourself why he demanded on returning. His head's got to be paining him something awful."

"You think he came back for me?"

She nodded, her gaze wise. "Don't you?"

Sonya didn't know what to think. Garrett was passionate about his job, but then last night in her bed he'd been pretty passionate regarding her too. A blush heated her cheeks at the memory. Question was, which of the two did he care about more?

The door burst open and Peter rushed in. "Good, you're up," he said when he noticed Sonya. "You feel like going over the *Double Dippin*? If not, the fish cops said they could handle it without you."

"No one's getting on my boat without me."

His knowing grin lit his face. "Thought you'd see it that way." His nose sniffed the air. "Muffins?"

"They still have five more minutes of baking," Grams said, hands on her hips. "Then they need to sit for a few."

"Ah, man." Peter stomped his way back out like a little kid at the end of his patience.

Sonya reached for one of the many hoodies hanging on nails around the cabin. She chose the one which had the words, "Shut up and Fish," blazing across the front.

All she'd wanted to do was fish this season and to date, she hadn't caught enough. This summer had presented more challenges and revelations than she'd bargained for.

She shut the door on those thoughts, not ready to deal with what had been revealed tonight. She didn't know when she would be. Until then, she had a boat to protect from a bunch of nosy fish cops.

She found the men where Grams had said they'd be. Peter and Wes were down the beach, each with a shovel digging out the doomed outboard engine. Gramps must have put them on the chore to keep them busy and out of the way.

Garrett was the first to notice her. "Sonya," he said, rising to unsteady feet, the action causing him to momentarily shut his eyes in pain.

"What are you doing here?" she asked. The man needed to be lying down in a hospital bed.

"My job." Garrett tightened his lips into a thin line. "How are you feeling?"

"Better. How's your head?"

"Fine," he bit out.

"Liar," she returned softly.

"Sonya," Gramps said, his tone chastising her. "It's been a hard night for everyone. Let's not add name calling to it."

"Right." She turned to Aidan. He looked as though he'd aged a decade. She walked over to him and laid her hand on his shoulder. "How are you doing?"

"Been better." He tried for a reassuring smile, which failed miserably and reached up to clasp her hand in his, giving it a squeeze before letting go. He stood and addressed the troopers. "If you don't need me anymore, I'm going to check on Lana."

"You're fine to leave, for now," Skip said. "We'll contact you when the body is ready to be released."

Aidan paled, swallowed, and then nodded.

"Harte, you see or hear anything regarding Roland, you let us know," Skip followed up as Aidan turned toward his camp.

"I will." Then he was gone. Sonya ached for what he was going through. Hopefully Lana would look after him. She was a sweet girl, contrary to her genetics.

"Wait," she asked Skip. "What's the deal with Roland?"

"He's missing," Skip answered. "We'd like to question him."

Sonya looked to the troopers, settling on Garrett. She knew he hadn't taken his eyes off her since she'd showed at the fire pit. She'd felt a weird mix of heat and cold coming from his direction. "You think Roland had a part in this also?"

"He and Earl seemed integrated," Garrett said. "He had to know what Earl was up to, even if he didn't have a hand in it himself."

"You think he did, don't you." She continued not waiting for an answer, "What about the *Mystic*? Do you think he had a part in that too?"

"We don't know. It's one of the many reasons we'd like to talk to him."

Sonya realized how hard this had to be on Gramps. Grams didn't even know yet, unless she'd been filled in when Sonya had slept, but she didn't think so. Otherwise Grams would have mentioned something to her. Gramps would have to be the one to tell her. She reached for his hand.

He took it, holding it in both of his. "You up to looking over the *Double Dippin*?" When she nodded, he asked, "Do you need me there?"

"No, I can handle it. Grams made cranberry nut muffins. I'm sure she's pulling them out of the oven right now. Better beat Peter to them."

Gramps stood and placed his hands on her shoulders, looking deep into Sonya's eyes. "Are you sure you'll be all right?"

Tears clogged her throat as she saw the worry and fear he clearly felt. She nodded and reached out to hug him. His arms enclosed her in a bear hug, and he squeezed the very breath out of her. If he kept this up, she'd be bawling like a newborn. He released her, his own eyes suspiciously wet.

He cleared his throat and turned to Garrett. "Keep her safe."

"With my life," Garrett returned.

"Safe from what?" She frowned. The threat was over now that Earl was dead.

"Until we find Roland and assess his role in all of this, everyone needs to remain on their guard," Garrett said.

Well, fucking fiddlesticks.

CHAPTER THIRTY-NINE

Sonya boarded the *Double Dippin'* with Garrett and Judd. Wes had delivered all of them, including Skip, to the *Calypso*. In turn, the *Calypso* took them to the *Double Dippin'* and then tied up alongside.

"Look at this mess," Judd said, snapping pictures of the destruction with the camera slung around his neck.

Sonya treaded carefully across the deck, taking in the damage. Garrett seemed distant as he stood off to the side. She didn't know if it was from the pain of his head injury or something else. He should be lying down, doing what Wanda had no doubt prescribed.

Her booted feet crunched on glass from the broken windows of the pilot house. The deck and side rails of her boat resembled a pin cushion. She didn't even know what she was looking at. It was like her boat had literally been nailed. A hole had been blown through the aluminum cover in one of the holds, scorch marks flared out in blackened shadows where the bomb had detonated. Most mystifying of all were the nails sticking out of everything.

"The son of a bitch packed the pipe bomb with framing nails," Garrett said, yanking one out of the aluminum side rail. His jaw tightened, a vein in the side of his face pumping in tune to his pulse. It was sexy as hell, and Sonya found herself wanting to concentrate on that rather than the destruction the pipe bomb had caused.

"Bet that's what hit you," Judd said, snapping Garrett's picture. "You're one lucky SOB. A nail to the forehead would have killed a lesser man. It probably ricocheted off that hard head of yours."

Sonya sucked in a breath. She could have lost him. Tears she'd been keeping wrangled sprang free.

Garrett came over to her. "It might look like a lot of damage, but once we get the mess cleaned up, it shouldn't interfere with the running of your boat. Though you'll want a welder to fill in these holes after the season."

She slapped his arm. "That isn't it, you idiot. I don't care about the boat, well I do, but Judd's right." She reached up and gently touched the side of his head where a white bandage covered his stitches. "You could have died."

"As could you." The breath from his words caressed her face.

She'd been strong for her family, but now she wanted his strong arms around her, his broad shoulders carrying the heavy burden of worry, while his body made her forget all that had happened here tonight.

He stepped back from her, putting distance between them.

She turned and pretended to assess the condition of the net while she corralled her scattered feelings. What was wrong with her? She wasn't the weepy kind of woman who needed a man to help shoulder the load. Her emotions must be out of whack.

Was she pregnant? That would account for the weepiness. She'd heard that pregnant women cried all the damn time. She did some calculations, trying to remember when her last period had started. Hell, she wasn't even sure what day it was. With everything that had gone on this summer, how was she to keep track of it all?

One thing at a time.

The net. It would have to be laid out to assess the full damage, but it seemed to have fared pretty well considering. Singed in a few areas that they would have to mend, but it would fish the next opening. The worst of the damage—besides the embedded nails—were the broken windows. Out of the six in the pilot house, she was down to three. The front two windows remained, but one had a perfect spider web crack, which would make seeing out of it difficult if not impossible. The windows over the bunk, and to the side of the captain's chair, were history. Cleaning up the boat would take the rest of the day. Somehow she'd need to find a way to cover up the windows without losing visibility.

Sonya left Garrett and Judd on deck to take a look at the pilot house herself. She entered to find glass shards sprinkled like the devil's confetti over everything. An ocean breeze teased through the broken windows as if finding amusement with her situation. There was lot of work to do before fishing this afternoon. First order of business was to locate a broom.

Did she even own one? A punch of sadness caught and seized her breath.

How did she deal with it all? Everything she'd thought she knew was wrong. Twisted.

All these years, she'd blamed the wrong man. Had her family's actions soured Chuck Kendrick into the ornery man he'd become? Had she been responsible, in part, for his death? The fight she'd started at the Pitt had been unfounded. She'd provoked a man who was innocent. Though innocent did seem the wrong word to describe

Kendrick, but he surely wasn't guilty of what *she'd* charged him with.

Her family had fished next door to a killer all these years. Broke bread with him. Celebrated good seasons and bad, right alongside him.

She'd made love to his son, and would probably have married him if Aidan hadn't shown her a side of himself that she couldn't live with. Earl would have been her father-in-law, grandfather to her children. She shuddered.

"Don't think about it," Garrett said. She hadn't heard him come up behind her. Hadn't realized how long she'd stood there staring at the destruction. "Just focus on the job at hand, and we'll get through this."

"Can I start cleaning up now?"

"Let Judd get some snapshots, and then we'll clean up."

Her gaze flicked to his. "Aren't you leaving with Judd?"

"No. You're stuck with me until Roland's found."

"You're staying?"

His jaw tightened as though he was gearing for an argument. "Yes."

"Good."

His eyes narrowed. "You aren't going to fight me on this?"

"No. I'm too tired and right now, you aren't much of a competitor. Besides, with everything—" she shrugged "—I'd rather not be alone."

ᒍ

Judd showed and shooed them out of the pilot house so he could snap a photo spread. Then he was gone, along with the *Calypso*, leaving Garrett and Sonya alone.

"I need to find a broom," she said.

Garrett assessed her pale skin. She was dead on her feet. "Why don't you have a seat?"

She shook her head. "Need to sweep up this glass." She looked around as though she had no idea where to start. She gazed under the bunk, pulling out the bench. It grated as she dragged it over the broken glass. She peered under the captain's chair, then to cabinet next to the small fridge. A hiccupping sob escaped her. She bit her lip as if to keep it in and yanked open the door to the fridge.

"Sonya." Garrett grabbed her shoulders.

"Where the hell is a broom?" She lost the battle of tears. He pulled her into his arms, and she sobbed into the cartoon scrubs he wore. A hysterical laugh joined her tears. "I don't think I own one. Why don't I have a damn broom?"

"Probably because this is a boat, and you didn't see the need." Garrett held her and rubbed his hands up and down her back in soothing motions. This wasn't about a broom. Until she could deal with all that happened, if she needed to lose it over a broom then she could.

"How am I going to clean up this mess?"

"We'll radio your camp. I'm sure your grandmother has a broom." He was more concerned with pulling the nails out of the aluminum sides and decking of the boat before her family visualized what could have happened to her. The anger that caused his head to pound each time he imagined her flesh pierced with nails made his concussion seem like a paper cut in comparison.

Her sobs subsided, followed by the occasional sniffle and hiccup. He continued to stroke her back, murmuring soothing words into her ear. She snuggled farther into him, and his heart swelled.

Damn, he loved this woman.

He'd known it but had tried to discount his feelings of love for lust. Lust was easier to deal with. Love…

Well, hell, love was so much more.

When he'd thought they were going to die, he'd come face to face with what he felt for her. It was real. It was scary. It was forever.

What did she feel for him? He didn't like this one bit. He liked knowing what he wanted and how to get it. He couldn't make Sonya love him. She either did or didn't. With how she'd chosen Aidan over him, all the evidence pointed to her still in love with Harte. But Garrett knew she cared something for him too.

Where did her heart lie?

Now wasn't the time to hash it out. Not when her world had been blown apart, and the pieces didn't fit neatly back together yet. The best thing he could do was to be there for her. No pressure.

Sonya took a deep breath and blew it out. She straightened in his arms, and he tightened them. "Not yet. Let me hold you a bit longer." She needed some more moments before she faced the clean up ahead, and he needed to feel the comfort of her in his arms. He feared that soon she'd leave them for good, and his arms would be empty.

"Got any ideas how we're going to de-spine my boat?" she asked.

He laughed. She'd had her crying jag, and instead of it sending her to bed, she'd regrouped and was ready to face the practical business at hand. Another thing he loved about her. "Do you have any vice grips in that tool box of yours?"

"Now, *that* I have. In fact, I believe I have two." She choked out a laugh. "No broom, but vice grips, I've got."

"Hey, you know what's important. A broom would only be in the way."

Suddenly she pulled out of his arms, her face flushed, eyes red-rimmed, and vulnerably beautiful. His heart did that swelling thing again.

"I do have a broom." She slapped her forehead. "How could I forget?"

She rushed from the pilot house. He followed to find her lying between the stairs, reaching through the metal slats. He heard a shout of triumph as she pulled out a sad, ratty broom.

"We fly a broom when we catch a hundred thousand pounds of fish. I threw this under here for when we reach our goal."

"You fly a broom?"

"Yeah. It's kind of a symbol of cleaning up. Get it?"

He laughed. "Yeah, I get it." He reached out his hand to her, and she took it. "Come on. Let's get this mess cleaned up so you can catch enough fish this afternoon to put that broom to good use."

The *Double Dippin'* didn't sparkle, but she was clean of bomb debris.

Sonya's crew had boarded for the drift opening, and they'd laid their first set, staying mid-river rather than fighting the line. In a sense, keeping a low profile. Sonya hadn't wanted to provoke any other fishermen with Garrett as loud as the law onboard, and she didn't want to answer questions over what had happened with Earl last night.

Word had already gotten around the bay. She felt the prying stares, had ignored the probing questions. She'd pretty much done a good job of staying in her own little bubble in her broken down pilot house. She'd only been able to cover one of the windows with plastic. The other had to stay open so she could see and converse with her crew.

Luckily the day had turned warm and sunny. The temp flirted around the sixty-five degree mark. A true heat wave for this part of Alaska. Sonya currently wore a short-sleeve t-shirt sporting the words, "Get Reel—Go Fish." The guys were similarly dressed. They'd even had to pass around the bottle of sunscreen. Nothing like being on the water, in an aluminum boat, to produce killer sunburns if they weren't protected.

Wes and Peter were putting Garrett through the paces. Good thing he'd swallowed a few Tylenol. The man was a greenhorn, having only fished with a rod and reel before. Drifting was a different kind of animal.

Sonya consulted the depth finder. She was in four feet of water, drifting over a sandbar. She glanced at the clock and then reviewed the tide charts. Another half hour until high tide, so she was fine drifting where she was. When the tide turned, she'd have to be careful hanging out over the sandbar so she didn't run aground. There wasn't another drift boat within a thousand yards of her. With their deep hulls, they couldn't drift in shallow water and had to steer clear of areas like this one. With its flat bottom, the *Double Dippin'* would be fine in two feet of water.

She raised the binoculars and scanned the cork lines. Not a lot of splashing going on, but hanging over a sandbar *had* to be where the fish were. Salmon liked shallow water and her lead lines were sitting on the bottom. The net had already been soaking longer than she normally preferred. She'd been hoping the sandbar would produce a net full of fish, but no sign of white fire.

There weren't many fishing days left. While she wouldn't call this season a bust—she had made expenses—it sure hadn't lived up to the bumper year she'd hoped.

All she'd gained this year by drifting *and* set netting was more work, less sleep, and too many enemies. She shook her head. She wasn't defeated yet. There was still time and salmon left to catch. She'd turn this season around. Damned if she wouldn't.

She'd given the net enough time. If it hadn't caught any fish, it was time to find another fishing hole. "All right, guys," she hollered to her crew. "Let's reel her in."

She engaged the hydraulics. Peter grabbed the end of the lead lines as the net came over the front rollers, and secured it to the cork line and reel. The reel groaned, and Sonya added more power.

Silver flashing tails and fins flapped over the rollers in a heap of writhing fishermen's currency.

Wes let out a holler.

"Hot damn," Peter added as the salmon-laden net slid slowly over the rollers.

Excitement shot like a sexual thrill through her middle. Hot damn was right. The fish had been caught on the lead lines, which was why there hadn't been a lot of splashing.

The tide still hadn't turned, which meant if they were quick, they could get another chance at cleaning up the sandbar. "Guys, you'll need to pick and round-haul that net in as fast as you can so we can get it back in the water." With Garrett aboard, they'd be strictly adhering to each and every blasted rule.

She'd stumbled across one sweet fishing hole.

Peter scrambled for he knew what work lay ahead. This haul meant a lot to him too. Garrett was going to wish he'd remained on the *Calypso* after today. Peter motioned for Garrett to take the lead lines, while he chose the corks. Sonya couldn't help but feel proud.

She blasted the Beach Boys' "Surfin' USA" for Garrett over the speakers. Wes went to relieve Garrett for a spell. Garrett leaned back and wiped his forehead. He looked up at her sitting snug and comfortable in the pilot house. A smile spilt his face, and Sonya realized, with surprise, that the fish cop was enjoying himself.

As the afternoon progressed, they proceeded to pull in net after net stocked to the gills with fish. Sonya knew it would be a record catch for them this year, if not their best ever. All the fish they'd caught today was pure, sweet profit. Somehow it was made all the sweeter having Garrett a part of it.

She needed to decide what to do about him. The more he integrated himself into her life, the more she liked him there.

Could she be ready for more? She was beginning to believe so.

But what about him?

CHAPTER FORTY

They'd tendered the fish and were proudly flying the broom.

It was the largest catch to be recorded in the Savonskis' fishing history. Her crew was tired, but riding high on accomplishment. They'd tied up to the cannery's dock, and Sonya decided to treat her hard-working crew to pizza from the Pitt. They deserved it. She'd sent Peter after the pizza, leaving Wes to watch the boat, while she headed for the showers. Garrett insisted on shadowing her. By the smell of him, he could benefit from a good cleansing too.

Garrett grabbed her elbow. "I need to stop at the General Store. I'm out of soap."

She lifted her backpack that held her showering supplies. "I've got soap."

"Unless you share a shower with me, I'll need a bar of my own. Besides, I'm sure your soap smells like flowers." He wrinkled his nose. "While I love your smell, not the manly scent I'm after."

She sniffed him and quickly adverted her nose. "Flowers would immensely improve your stench."

"Stench?" He held open the door to the General Store for her and then followed her over the threshold. "I hate to break it to you, babe, but you don't smell all that fresh right now, either."

She glared at him in mock anger. "What a thing to say."

"Just speakin' the truth, ma'am."

"That truth you can swallow."

"Well, well," Davida commented. "Aren't you two getting along like two bears in the woods. Heard you've switched sides of the line, Garrett. How you like fishing?"

"I like it fine, Davida." Garrett didn't take his eyes from Sonya as he admitted it. She felt herself flush from under the heat of his gaze.

Davida cleared her throat, and Garrett glanced from Sonya to her. "I also heard about your troubles, Sonya. I'm sorry."

"Thank you, Davida."

"In your network of news," Garrett said, "have you heard anything about Roland Harte's whereabouts?"

"Nope, not a peep. If I hear anything, I'll let you know." Davida nodded and then got down to business. "So what can I get you two?"

"Soap, shampoo," he scratched his raspy, stubbled jaw, "razor, and shaving cream, if you've got them, and that item I had you special order if it's here."

Davida smiled. "It's your lucky day. It arrived on the morning flight. Give me a minute to rustle it all up."

"What'd you order?" Sonya asked, her curiosity piqued.

"You'll see." His grin was that of a man who had a secret he couldn't wait to share.

"Here you are, Garrett." Davida packed all the items he'd asked for in a bag and then did a quick glance around to see who was watching. She must have deemed the area clear for she reached into the freezer behind her and quickly pulled out a pint of ice cream.

Sonya gasped. *Haagen-Dazs black raspberry chip ice cream.*

"You have a plastic spoon, Davida?" Garrett asked. "I don't think Sonya's going to be able to wait until we're aboard the *Double Dippin'*."

"Already ahead of you." Davida produced the spoon and a couple of napkins.

Sonya took the spoon and the carton of ice cream Davida handed over as though the items were the most precious of objects. To her, they were. Her eyes felt suspiciously wet as she gazed at Garrett. "You got me ice cream?"

"It's your favorite, right?" His eyes narrowed. "Don't tell me I ordered the wrong flavor."

"No. Black raspberry chip is my favorite." She knew how hard it was to get ice cream flown out here, and how high the expense. It was suddenly difficult to swallow as her throat clogged. "Thank you." The words seemed inadequate for the level of gratitude she felt.

"You're welcome."

Davida rang up his purchases. "You tell Judd he needs to do something sweet for me like that. It's not ice cream I want, though. I go weak in the knees for things that sparkle and fit snug—" she held out her ring finger "—right here."

Garrett chuckled and picked up the bag of toiletries. "I'll let him know."

"You do that. I swear the man is denser than a wood boat," Davida mumbled.

They left the General Store. Sonya hid the carton of ice cream from anyone passing by. The frozen treat was like contraband, and she wasn't about to share it with anyone.

Garrett led her down the wooden boardwalk, ending at a hillside ablaze with blooming stalks of fireweed. She followed him up a rarely used trail until they were out of sight of any onlookers. Here, Garrett stomped out a place for her to sit amongst the flowering fireweed.

They sat, and she broke the seal over the pint. The first spoonful had her closing her eyes in ecstasy. The cool, sweet taste slid down her throat like a lover's bold caress. The next spoonful Sonya offered up to Garrett. He didn't say anything except to raise a brow in question. She brought the scoop up to his lips, wetting her own, as he opened his mouth. She slipped the spoon inside.

He closed his eyes and moaned, stirring the ice cream around his mouth with his tongue, before swallowing.

She badly needed to kiss him.

The plastic spoon lay forgotten in her fingers until Garrett took hold of it, scooping up another bite and offering it to her. She opened her mouth, and he slid the spoon between her lips. Tangy, rich raspberries and sinful, dark chocolate burst over her yearning taste buds. She opened her mouth for another bite, and he fed her, taking turns feeding himself. They didn't speak, just shared, soaked up the heat of the late afternoon, as bees buzzed above their heads.

Most of the carton was consumed by the time Sonya lost the hold on her willpower and reached for Garrett, bringing his mouth down to hers. He tasted like her favorite treat, his lips cold from the ice cream, which quickly heated beneath the friction of hers. He gave a guttural moan and leaned his body over hers, laying her amongst the fragrant fireweed and grasses. She reveled in his embrace and wished she had him to herself. In the distance, voices mixed with the sounds of heavy equipment. Screen doors slammed, tires squealed, and a dog barked.

"Damn, Sonya." Garrett pulled back and stared into her eyes. "I'm going to need a cold shower after that kiss."

He wasn't the only one. She reached up and fingered his bandage. "How's your head?"

"Believe me. I'm feeling no pain right now." He gave her a crooked grin. "At least, no pain in my head."

She almost said to hell with the risk of being discovered and begged him to take her here, right now. The only thing that kept the words from escaping her mouth was the fact that she hadn't showered and badly needed to.

"Mind if we pick this up later?" she asked, her eyelids hooded and heavy with the promise of pleasure. "I feel the need to show my appreciation. I know it had to be extremely difficult getting that ice cream out here."

"It *did* cost me a few favors."

"Well, then, your efforts must be rewarded."

"If you insist." He smiled.

"Oh, I do. I do insist."

CHAPTER FORTY-ONE

It was late evening when Sonya anchored the *Double Dip-pin'* in front of camp. She brought the drift boat as close to the beach as she dared in the shallow surf. Peter and Wes waded to shore, leaving her and Garrett to anchor in deeper waters for the night.

Something would be done about the unresolved situation between her and Garrett tonight. If anything, the last twenty-fours had taught her was that time was fleeting, and life was precious. It had also showed her how deeply she loved Garrett.

Before she could make her move, Aidan motored his skiff out to the *Double Dippin'* and asked for permission to come aboard.

"Sonya," Aidan greeted when he climbed on deck. His tone was low and pensive. "Garrett." He nodded, stuffing his hands in his pockets, rounding his shoulders.

"Any word on Roland?" Garrett asked, his feet braced apart, his arms folded over his muscled chest. He looked like a pirate of old, ready to take no prisoners.

"No. No sign of him either. He packed up and left. Didn't even leave a note for Lana."

"Have any idea where he would have gone?" Garrett asked.

Aidan shrugged. "Home is in the Yukon, but if he doesn't want to be found, he won't be."

"Will you be able to fish out the season?" Sonya asked, concerned. With Earl dead, and Roland missing, fishing might be over for Aidan and Lana.

Aidan glanced at Garrett and then addressed Sonya. "Don't know yet. I called into the Fish and Game this morning. Chances are I'll be able to get an emergency transfer for Earl's permit within the next twenty-four hours. We won't be able to fish Roland's."

"Let me know if there is anything we can do," Sonya said.

"Thanks." Aidan ran a hand through his hair. "Sonya...can I talk to you for a minute?" He glanced at Garrett. "Alone."

Garrett's jaw tightened. "Not a lot of space onboard."

Sonya laid a hand on his arm and beseeched him with her eyes to give them some time. She knew she'd won when Garrett expelled a deep breath, his lips twisting with a silent curse she knew he wanted to articulate.

"Fine." He turned and stomped his way up to the pilot house like a two-year-old forced to share his favorite toy and hating every moment of it.

"Sonya." Aidan brought her attention back to him. "I needed to say how deeply sorry I am for the suffering my family has caused you and your family." He paused and stared at Garrett, who made no pretense of not watching their exchange from the broken windows of the pilot house. Aidan took Sonya's arm and led her to the bow. While it didn't block Garrett's view, it did limit what he'd hear.

"Aidan." Sonya waited until his sad eyes met hers. "I don't blame you for what Cranky and Crafty have done. You aren't them."

"Their blood runs through my veins."

"Yeah, and according to my family tree, Stalin's blood runs in mine. You choose what kind of man you are to become. It isn't foreordained because of your bloodline. Don't let this stop you from becoming the man I know you can be."

He indicated Garrett, who'd continued to watch them. She could feel his piercing eyes boring into her back.

"You love the fish cop, don't you?"

"Yeah." She nodded.

Aidan met her gaze. "I hope he makes you happy." He gently tucked a loose strand of hair behind her ear. "You deserve to be happy, Sonya."

"So do you, Aidan. There's a woman out there for you." She gave a soft laugh. "If we'd stayed together, we would have driven each other crazy, you know."

"Maybe." He cleared his throat. "If the cop ever gets out of line, I'd be happy to straighten him out for you."

"Thanks, I appreciate that."

"Okay, well…I'll be going then."

Sonya reached out a hand to stop him. "Aidan. Listen, you need anything with Roland or the, uh, funeral preparations, you can call on us."

"Thanks, Sonya." His eyes seemed suspiciously wet, and he had to clear his throat again. "That means a lot."

She reached out and hugged him. Aidan crushed her against him and buried his face in the crook of her neck. She rubbed his back until he'd composed himself enough to let her go.

He released her. "I'd better check on Lana. She's taking Roland's leaving pretty hard."

"Let her know we're here for her too."

He choked out a laugh. "Peter's already made that perfectly clear. Who knows, maybe someday we'll be related because of those two. You are aware that they hit it off this summer?"

She smiled. "Yeah, but I wasn't sure you knew."

"I caught them snuggled up together the other day. Guess time will tell if they're meant to be." He turned to the rail of the boat and then looked back. "You take care of yourself, Sonya."

"I will. You do the same, Aidan."

She watched him motor back to camp and sent up a prayer for what he'd be going through in the months to come. With a father like Earl, life had never been easy for Aidan. Hopefully now, he'd find some peace and happiness.

She rolled her eyes when she caught sight of Gramps, Peter and Wes heading down the beach toward the skiff carrying the resurrected outboard engine. She couldn't believe they'd actually gotten the thing dug out and cleaned up. Gramps should have let the blasted thing die.

She was smiling when she turned toward the pilot house. It was time to settle things with Garrett, but when she caught sight of him standing there, his eyes frigid, his jaw set, a feeling of dread came over her.

What now?

Garrett figured he'd gotten his answer with the hug Sonya and Aidan had shared. What had he expected? He hadn't told her he loved her. Hadn't solidified their relationship. He'd pretty much let her think this was a summer fling. He had no one to blame but himself. He also wasn't about to give up without a fight either. Damned if he'd lose her to a man whose family had caused her so much pain. Besides, he had one thing going for him that Harte didn't. Chances were he'd impregnated Sonya.

He damn well hoped he had.

She entered the pilot house, and it was everything he could do not to grab and prove that he was the man for her, not Harte.

"All right." She sighed as though bracing for bad news and unzipped her hoodie. "Let me have it. What's happened now?"

He took in the black t-shirt that had been hidden under her jacket. A skull with two red salmon in place of crossbones and the words "Spawn 'Til You Die" blazed across her breasts.

Ah hell, did she know how to bait. "You're marrying me," he blurted out.

"What?" Her eyes widened.

He hardened his tone. "You heard me."

Her mouth opened and closed, and she actually took a step back. He took one forward. She had nowhere to go. They were anchored, afloat on open water, no getaway skiff tied to the side, no one to interrupt them. She was completely at his mercy.

Or, if he were to be honest, he was completely at hers.

"What are you talking about?" she asked, exasperation lacing her voice. "We don't even know if I'm pregnant."

"Pregnant or not, you and I are getting married." Her eyes narrowed and he got a sneaky suspicion that he might not be handling this right, but he couldn't seem to stop himself. He was man enough to admit he was scared of losing her. He felt her sifting through his fingers like grains of sand.

"You aren't the marrying kind, remember?" she pointed out, saying the words he'd believed about himself.

"I changed my mind. Quit being so damn stubborn and say you'll marry me."

She folded her arms across her chest and raised her head in challenge. "I haven't been asked yet."

He growled deep in his throat and then clipped out each individual word. "Will. You. Marry. Me?"

She pursed her lips and narrowed her eyes. "You don't sound very excited over the prospect."

"Damn it, Sonya." He paused, rubbed a hand over his hair, and then added in a calmer, softer voice, "Marry me. Please."

"Why?"

"*Why?*" What did she want? Blood?

"Yes." He thought he saw the corners of her mouth tilt up before she bit her lip. "Why should I marry you?"

He sputtered. "Because…" He took a breath and met her gaze, realizing he'd have to use what was in his heart as bait in order to hook her. "Because, I'm in love with you."

"Well, that's handy." She smiled. "Since I'm in love with you too."

"Now, you listen to me—" He stopped, suddenly daring to hope. "What did you say?"

Her eyes brightened as she closed the space between them. "I said that I'm in love with a trooper."

She'd actually called him a *trooper*, not a damn fish cop. "You're not in love with Harte?"

"No. But he's part of my family. You'll have to deal with that."

"I can deal with anything as long as you're by my side."

"What about our occupational differences?" She raised a brow.

He grinned. "I don't have a problem with you being a music teacher."

"You know that wasn't what I was talking about. If we marry, what do we do about fishing?"

"*When* we marry, not *if*. I'll take my vacation during fishing season. I had fun out there today. But with me as crew, Sonya, you'll have to toe the line."

"I guess if I must," she grumbled.

"Was that a yes?" Hope swelled in his heart, making him light-headed.

"Yes."

"Sonya," he groaned her name, catching her in his arms.

A shotgun blast pierced the air.

In a flash, he had her on the floor of the pilot house and his gun palmed. "What the hell now?"

"Let me up." Sonya struggled against his hold.

"Stay down," he ordered.

"Gramps, Peter, and Wes are out there," she said, panic in her voice. She twisted free of his grip and rushed out onto the deck before he could grab hold of her again.

"Sonya!" He chased after her.

🪝

Sonya's heart pounded, and blood pulsed in her ears. She came to a stop at the rail as her eyes took in the bewildering scene before her. Garrett grasped her in his arms, ready to pull her down to the deck.

"Is that what I think it is?" she asked.

Garrett's hold lessened, and his arms draped around her, his chin falling to her shoulder in relief. He snorted. "Looks as though your gramps just murdered an engine."

Gramps stood with Barbarella cocked to his shoulder. He'd just shot a bullet through the hood of the outboard engine they'd just bolted to the skiff. Smoke drifted from the silent steel carcass. Peter and Wes stood nearby. Peter with his hat over his heart, and Wes with his fingers inter-locked as though in quiet prayer.

Gramps looked downright ticked off.

"Everything all right, over there?" Sonya hollered over the hundred or so feet of water separating them.

Gramps gave a sharp nod and lowered the shotgun. "Son of a biscuit refused to start after all I did to try and save it! Dagnabbit." He blew hair out of his eyes. "Figured it was time to put it out of its misery."

Thank heavens. Sonya wanted to laugh but didn't dare because it would hurt Gramps's feelings. "I think that was a sound decision."

"*Sound?*" Garrett mumbled behind her. She elbowed him to keep quiet. It was all she could do not to bust up in giggles over the relief of a dead engine instead of another dead body.

"Hope I didn't scare you," Gramps called, seeming to realize how Sonya and Garrett might have taken his actions.

"Nope, just wondering what the hubbub was all about." Sonya waved to her family, disengaged herself from Garrett's arms, and turned back to the pilot house. She needed a rest after that scare. Her heart felt like it was going to pound right out of her chest.

"Hubbub?" Garrett asked, following her. "We need to have a sit down and explain a few facts to everyone. Roland is still out there. You know what I thought when that gun blast went off?"

Sonya continued her trek into the pilot house and then down the ladder to the bunk. "Yeah, the same thing I did. Do you really think Roland is laying in wait? Ready to come after us as soon as our guard's down?" She turned to face him as he shadowed her into the small room.

"No, I think we've seen the last of him. Doesn't mean I'm not going to do everything in my power to protect you in case I'm wrong."

"Anything to protect me, huh?" She inched over to him, trailing her fingers down his chest.

"Absolutely anything." Garrett's breath caught as her fingers curled into the waistband of his jeans.

"How about playing big bad trooper to a hell-bent-on-trouble fisherman?"

"We've been playing that all season." His voice went guttural as he pulled her up against his body. "We ought to be pretty good at it by now."

"I think there are still some holes that need mending." An afternoon of "mending" sure as hell would make her feel better.

She screeched as Garrett picked her up and tossed her onto the bed.

He stood tall and domineering next to the edge of the bunk, not taking his eyes off her as he slowly stripped off his t-shirt, and yanked free the snap on his jeans.

She wetted her lips and loved how the action caused his gaze to darken as he followed the trail of her tongue.

He knelt one knee on the bed, and his next words sent a thrill tingling through her core. "Prepare to be boarded."

Oh, how she loved those words.

THE END

NOTE FROM THE AUTHOR:

For the purpose of writing *Hooked*, I kept set and drift gillnet fishermen from fishing the same tides together. During the peak of the salmon run, the Department of Fish and Game will open the fishing periods for both set netters and drifters. It's a mad fight to catch as much fish as we can while fishing the same tides together. As Sonya didn't have enough crew to do both types of fishing during the same tide, I elected not to show this aspect of fishing. It is insane and would have made great material, but it wouldn't fit within the story I was writing.

Also, the Naknek-Kvichak District has not fished the Naknek River since 2007. The Fish and Game stipulates that the Naknek River will open to gillnet fishing when the escapement (number of salmon upriver) of the Kvichak River falls below the projected escapement goals. Any given fishing season we never know if we will be fishing the Naknek River or not until the Fish and Game announce it. Otherwise fishing happens in the bay, which the Naknek and Kvichak Rivers flow into. It's still combat fishing as every drift boat fights to be the first to lay their net on the line. And the fish cops are always outnumbered.

My family was among the first to start both set netting and drifting. Now other savvy fishermen have followed suit, making it even wilder out there. For more information on commercial fishing in Bristol Bay check out the Alaska Department of Fish and Game. http://www.adfg. alaska.gov/index.cfm?adfg=commercialbyareabristolbay. main

A preview of

SHIVER

Tiffinie Helmer

SHIVER

CHAPTER ONE

Aidan Harte stepped out of his rented SUV and right into Hell.

Chatanika, Alaska to be exact, where it was so cold it burned. He'd been born in this forgotten gold-mining town, lost in the interior of the state, north of Fairbanks by about thirty desolate miles.

"Well, Dad, you finally got me back here." And it hadn't been over *his* dead body but that of his father's. Aidan slammed the door shut on the SUV. He was here to exorcise ghosts, while he closed out his father's life. The faster he saw Chatanika in his rearview mirror the better.

Not much had changed in the—what, eleven, twelve years?—since he'd last been here. It was midafternoon and the sun was already headed to bed, it being November. Snow and ice smothered, sending the landscape into a state of unconsciousness, stunting spruce trees, and stripping birch branches until they resembled fragile bones.

Aidan pulled the collar of his coat up around his neck and wished he'd stopped in Fairbanks and bought a parka. His winter coat, which was perfectly adequate for Seattle, might as well have been a windbreaker in this hostile environment.

The outside thermometer on the Tahoe had said two. Now with the sun setting, the temperature would drop fast. Predicted temp for tonight was negative fifteen.

Aidan picked his way toward the family homestead, his feet crunching through the ice-crusted snow. The cabin's roof hung precariously over the rotted porch. The porch had been rotting when he'd last been here the summer he'd turned eighteen. He'd clearly remembered falling through and cutting up his leg. And the kiss he'd received from Raven Maiski. She'd had the power to drive more than pain away with her kisses.

It was eerily quiet. Spooky. The kind of night where you could hear yourself breathe and shadows took on a life of their own. He approached the makeshift fence made of twisted chain link and sharp, rusted barbwire. A chain and corroded padlock secured the front gate as well as a screaming red 'No Trespassing' sign. He should have figured this. Earl Harte had always been under the delusion everyone was out to get him. Many probably were, or had been. It no longer mattered now that the bastard was dead.

Aidan studied the gate. He could climb it and probably get cut from the barbwire or attempt to knock it down. It probably wasn't any better built than the rotting front porch. Problem was, his dad was notorious for booby-traps.

He checked around the gate, looking for wires or sharp instruments, and then gave it a solid kick. The gate swung open.

Well, that seemed anticlimactic.

Puffs of air steamed in front of his face. His breathing increased as he struggled toward the cabin. He didn't want to go in there. Nobody had been living in the dump for four months. Who knew what could have crawled in and died? For that matter, who knew what kind of condition Earl had left it in? His dad had never been the best about picking up after himself.

Aidan took a moment to rethink staying in the cabin while he went through what remained of his father's life. He could get a room at the Chatanika Lodge instead. But then he was sure to run into people—people he didn't want to see. Or, more precisely, people who didn't want to see him.

Maybe he could risk catching a glimpse of Raven.

Nope, the faster he could clean up and clear out the better. No one wanted anymore to do with him than they had his father. No one would miss Earl Harte.

Not even him.

Aidan stepped cautiously, keeping an eye out for anything that looked suspicious. Earl would have a trap or tripwire set on the front entrance that would release something sharp and nasty for anyone stupid enough to bother him. He rounded the corner of the cabin heading toward the back door, hunching his shoulders against the cold and slapping his thin-gloved hands together in an attempt to warm them. The snow was deeper around the side of the cabin. Nothing looked like it had been disturbed. Not even animal prints cut the icy crust of the snow.

Suddenly, he skidded, his arms flailing wide. He regained his balance and looked at what he'd slipped on. A piece of tin. He glanced up and saw where it had fallen off the roof at some point. The place was falling apart. He shook his head and stepped carefully.

Steel teeth of a bear trap sprung, spearing into the flesh of his lower leg.

"Son of a bitch!" He screamed as pain stabbed through his leg.

He clawed at where the teeth of the rusty trap punctured through his jeans, through his boots, and into the tender flesh of his leg. Dropping in the snow, he cried out again as pain seared like fire through his leg, causing him to shake. He moaned through gritted teeth, struggling with the jaws of the trap. Sweat dripped down his face.

He quickly looked around, for anyone—anything—that would help free him from the snare.

Silence.

The only sound was his own choppy breathing, his pounding heart, and his useless moaning. He was alone. He was freezing.

He was seriously fucked.

What kind of sick son of bitch laid traps next to the back door of his own home?

Aidan clenched his teeth, grabbed the edges of the steel-teeth trap, and tried to pry the jaws apart. He roared and strained with everything he had. The effort wasted. Blood soaked through his jeans and dribbled like syrup, staining the snow.

The sun dipped and shadows grew menacing.

And cold seeped in like death.

Aidan's heart grew heavy in his chest. He sat—spent—in the snow, the heat of his body causing the snow to melt through his jeans and freeze next to his skin.

Think Harte, think.

Damn, but it was hard to think when his body was racked with pain. Maybe, he could crawl to the SUV with the trap and drive for help. He scratched around in the snow until he found the chain attached to the anchor of the trap. He heaved until his muscles drained.

No use. The anchor was encased in ice, frozen into the earth.

Come up with something else quick, or you're a dead man.

He patted his pockets, and pulled out his keys. Nothing on the key ring that could help him. He pocketed them and felt around for more. A Jolly Rancher. He snorted out a laugh. Not much of a last meal. Then he found his cell phone.

"Yes!" He flipped it open and dialed 911. No bars. "What the—"

He shook the phone as if that would miraculously gain him coverage. Nothing. He moved the phone around him, over his head, searching for reception. "Come on," he prayed. "Come on." Again, nothing.

It started to snow.

Big, quiet, heavy flakes that smothered the earth. Despair began to settle in, becoming partners with the throbbing pain. He was going to die here. Born and died in the same place. It was kind of funny. Or ironic.

He wondered when his body would be found and by whom. Would it be spring? Or would an animal find him and have *him* for a last meal? He unwrapped the Jolly Rancher and popped it in his mouth. Grape. He grimaced. It tasted like cough medicine.

Chances were good no one would know what became of him. His therapist had encouraged him to return to Alaska, to make peace with his father, and his past. What a laugh.

His editor might be the one to make some noise but not until his deadline was closer on his next graphic novel. He didn't have any close friends. For family, his Uncle Roland was hiding from the law, and his cousin Lana was back in college. She'd miss him, but she'd get over it soon. The only thing they had in common besides the commercial fishing operation was that both their fathers were assholes.

The only people who'd really wonder would be the IRS. What did that say about his life?

He heard a howl. Then another. And another.

Wolves.

God, he prayed they waited until he was dead to feast on his carcass. He laughed, the sound bitter. He'd been born under the sign of the wolf. Conceived under the Northern Lights and born in a blizzard. His Athabascan mother, before the booze had drowned all the love and warmth from her, had strung him tales about the power of the wolf he was supposed to possess.

Guess that had been a load of shit too.

He heard the wolves grow closer. He knew what they'd do. They'd circle him. Enclose him in a death ring. That is, if they were brave enough to venture onto Earl Harte's property. But with a warm meal staked out for them like a buffet, they'd come. They'd surround him, enclosing the circle closer and closer. Yellow beady eyes shining with greed and hunger, gleaming, sharp teeth dripping with saliva, until one of them—the alpha male—would lunge for his throat. At least when that happened, he'd die quickly. He wouldn't feel them tear into his stomach and feast on his organs, shred the meat off his bones. At least, he hoped.

They were closer now. He could hear them breathe.

"Hey, Mr. Harte, nice wheels. Fishing must've been good. About time you got...home." A young, gangly teenage boy, dressed in a fur-rimmed parka and mukluks, skidded to a stop when he saw Aidan. "You're not Mr. Harte."

Aidan had never been so glad to see anyone in his life. "I need help. And we better hurry. I hear wolves."

"Wolves?" The boy scowled in confusion and then smiled. "Those aren't wolves. They're my sled dogs." He ventured closer and saw the trap. "Don't know much about Mr. Harte, do you?"

"More than I wish I did." Aidan gestured to the trap. "Help me out here?"

"I can try." He knelt down in front of Aidan and looked him in the eyes. "You're stuck pretty good. Must hurt bad."

"You could say that." Aidan clenched his teeth. He was also freezing to death. He struggled to his knee for added leverage and grabbed the jaws of the trap.

The boy put his hands next to Aidan's. "Ready?" he asked.

Aidan nodded, and as cold as he was, he began to sweat. They pulled, heaved with all their might, but the springs wouldn't budge. Aidan felt the teeth move but not enough to release his leg.

"All right, break." He moaned. Any minute now he was going to cry like a baby. "What's your name?" Aidan asked, trying to concentrate on anything that could help distract him from the pain. This kid might be the last to see him alive.

"Fox. My name's Fox." Fox tilted his head to the side. "Are you related to Mr. Harte?"

"Yeah," Aidan scoffed. "You could say that."

"Well...are you?" he asked as though the answer meant something. "Either you are or you aren't. What is it?"

"Earl Harte is...was my father."

Fox fell back on his haunches. "You're Mr. Harte's son? The graphic novelist, Aidan Harte?"

A fan? Clear out here? "Yeah." He nodded and wiped sweat off his forehead.

"Whoa." Fox stared at him. Really stared. As though he were looking for something. "What do you mean Mr. Harte *was* your father?" Fox swallowed.

Could the kid have liked Earl? Nobody had liked Earl.

"He was ki—died this summer. I'm here to take care of his effects."

Fox's eyes fell to the ground, and he gave a heavy sigh. "I was afraid something like that had happened when he didn't come back. Seeing the SUV outside his place...well, I thought he'd finally made it home."

"Were you and him...close?" Earl hated kids.

"Kinda. It was a weird relationship." The kid took a deep breath and seemed to collect himself. "You ready to try again?"

"What the hell." They braced themselves and pulled on the jaws of the trap. They heaved and strained until Aidan couldn't help the holler of pain. "Stop. *Shit*." He couldn't take any more of this. Just kill him and get it over with. It wasn't like he had a lot to live for anyway.

"We need help," Fox said. "I'm strong for my age, but this is bigger than me." Fox leaped to his feet. "I'll be right back." He turned toward the back of the cabin, walking in a zigzagging line to the back door. The kid obviously knew where the booby-traps were placed.

Fox entered the cabin and returned with a fur-lined hat and blankets. "Here." He gave the hat to Aidan, who immediately put it on, the flaps big and floppy over his ears, and then Fox carefully wrapped Aidan's legs with the blanket, adding another one around his shoulders.

Aidan fished out the keys in his pocket. "Take the SUV."

Fox shook his head. "My mom would kill me for driving. Besides, it's snowing too hard. I'd probably put it in the ditch. My dogs will get to help faster in weather like this. You hang in there. I'll be back as soon as I can."

"If I'm..." He didn't want to say dead, but that's where he was headed.

"Don't worry. I'll be back before you know it. Think warm."

Aidan heard excited barks and yips as Fox turned the corner and was out of sight. The kid was gone, and Aidan was once again alone in the arctic night.

He tried to disassociate from the pain throbbing in his leg where the metal teeth were clamped around it. It was becoming easier to do as he was losing feeling, either from blood loss or the cutting off of circulation.

He lay down on the hard, frozen ground. Snow fell so thick he couldn't see more than a few feet above him. Sticking out his tongue, he caught the flakes and swallowed as they melted. He used to love doing that when he was younger. Snow had always been magical. Blanketing everything in white. Softening the edges of the harsh landscape. Glowing blue and green in the dark winters when the Northern Lights would dance like spirits in the sky above.

Would Fox be able to make it back in this?

He no longer felt the cold, either because the kid had wrapped him up or because shock had set in. Snow began to cover him, adding another welcomed layer of insulation. He pulled the hood of the hat over his face and closed his eyes.

He didn't know how long he'd stayed like that. Maybe he slept. But suddenly he heard a truck's brakes squealing as it came to a fast stop, then voices and the sound of footsteps crunching through the snow.

"Harte!"

Aidan tried to lift his arm to pull back the hood, but someone beat him to it, dusting off snow that was attempting to camouflage him. He opened his eyes and stared into Lynx Maiski's hard unforgiving face.

Shit. He was hoping not to run into his former childhood comrade.

"I can't believe it," Lynx said. "I thought the boy was suffering from exposure when he told me you were here."

Air puffed from his angry mouth. "Didn't think I ever see you again."

"Can we get me out of this trap before you lay into me?"

Lynx looked him over. "You're not much competition at the moment." He lifted a brow and indicated Fox behind him. "If the kid wasn't so concerned about you, I'd be tempted to leave you."

And he'd be justified.

"If you're going to leave me, shoot me first."

Lynx laughed. "Don't tempt me. Hand me those clamps, Fox." He looked at Aidan. "This is going to hurt."

"Worse than stepping into the damn thing?"

"Wait until the blood gets flowing again." Lynx smiled as though enjoying the picture he painted.

Aidan rose into a sitting position. Fox kept quiet, glancing worriedly at Aidan every few seconds. The kid actually seemed to care. Aidan studied him. Was he Lynx's son? There seemed to be a resemblance of sorts.

Lynx tightened down a C-clamp to the front spring and then attached another to the back. "Fox, you tighten this clap, and I'll do the other. Harte, get ready to pull your leg out. These traps are ancient. It could spring back at any moment. I'm surprised you even attempted to come here, knowing Earl like you do."

"Didn't Fox tell you? Earl's dead."

Lynx paused then continued twisting the clap. "Couldn't have happened to a nicer guy. I hope it was painful."

A bullet to the chest. "Yeah. He felt pain."

"Glad to hear it."

The clamp on his leg started to lessen. He reached out to help pull it out of the trap, as he'd lost most of the feeling in it. The pressure decreased but he couldn't get his leg out. The teeth were caught in the leather of his boots.

"Come on, Harte. *Pull.*" Lynx tightened his jaw. "Who knows how old this trap is. It could go off again at any moment. I don't want the kid hurt."

"Don't worry about me," Fox said. "I'm quick. Let's just get him out."

The kid was wise. Listen to the kid. Finally, the jaws released enough of their hold and he scraped his leg out of the trap. As soon as he was free, the trap sprung, snapping into the air.

"Shit," Lynx said, jumping back. "Your fucking father should have been shot for laying traps like that around here!"

Aidan grabbed his lower leg as feeling began pumping through his veins like hot oil.

"Do you think it's broken?" Lynx asked.

"Don't know. Hurts too bad to tell."

"Fox, bring that sled over here."

Fox positioned a sled next to Aidan and they both helped him into it.

"Let's get out of here. This place always gave me the creeps." Lynx pointed at Fox. "You and I are going to have a talk later on how you know where the booby-traps are hidden."

Fox gulped and looked away.

"Lead us out of here, Fox." Lynx grabbed the rope tied to the sled and pulled, following Fox's trail. They reached a crew-cab 4x4 pick-up with the National Wildlife Refuge seal painted on the side.

Aidan stood with Fox and Lynx's help, using the door of the truck as a crutch. He climbed in, clamping his mouth shut as he bumped his leg.

"Working for the State?" Aidan asked when they were under way. The snow came at them so hard there was no visibility.

"Yep," Lynx answered, concentrating on keeping the truck on the road. How he could tell where it was, Aidan hadn't a clue.

Aidan turned around to Fox, sitting quietly in the backseat studying Aidan. "Thanks, Fox. I owe you my life."

"You're welcome," he said, giving Aidan a hesitant smile.

They pulled into the heart of Chatanika. An old gold mining dredge sat like a metal monster to the left, the main tourist attraction. The old lodge cabin squatted across the street on the right. A few outlying cabins dotted, circling the center of town, vague shadows in the rapidly falling snow.

"We won't be able to get you to Fairbanks in this weather," Lynx said, parking the truck and switching off the engine. He turned to Fox. "Run and get Eva. I'll get him into the lodge."

Fox jumped out of the truck and took off.

Aidan wanted to insist they drive him to Fairbanks. He didn't want to meet any more people from Chatanika. At least he didn't recognize anyone by the name of Eva. She must be new. But if he went into the lodge, memories where going to swamp him. "Who's Eva?"

"My wife. And, lucky for you, an NP. She's the best thing we got in medical care out here." Lynx stepped out of the truck and walked around the front.

Aidan opened the door and gritted his teeth. Getting into the lodge was going to be the easy part. Seeing the occupants of the lodge was going to hurt.

"Ready for this?" Lynx asked.

Aidan didn't know if he was asking about his physical well-being or the emotional havoc to come. "Not much choice in the matter," he mumbled.

Lynx put his arm around Aidan's back. Aidan swung an arm around his shoulder and they hobbled to the front door of the lodge.

The door opened and Fiona, Lynx's mother, stood there, looking the same as Aidan remembered. Round and happy—well, more concerned at the moment—she'd always seemed to make the best out of what life handed her, and it didn't seem as though that had changed. "Aidan Harte! I thought I'd seen a ghost when you pulled up." She quickly looked him over. "Always coming to my place injured in one form or another, aren't you?" She motioned for them to follow her. "Come on. Let's get you patched up. Can't wait to hear the story on this escapade."

A lump lodged in his throat as he looked around the lodge. The walls of its rough homespun interior were decorated with vintage mining materials and snow shoes, while over-sized furniture sat in intimate corners and soft old leather couches flanked the stone fireplace.

Fiona was the closest thing to a mother he'd had growing up, since his own mother had checked out most of the time. Fiona had fed him cookies, washed his scraped knees, and scolded him within an inch of his life when he stepped out of line. Damn, he did not want to deal with these old feelings.

God, he hoped Raven was no longer living here.

Please, he prayed, let Raven be happily married and living in the Midwest somewhere. Far away from Chatanika.

"Bring him in here." Fiona opened the door to one of the guest rooms. The room was decorated simply, with an old quilt on the bed, a wooden rocking chair in the corner, and an old thrift store dresser. Criss-crossed skis hung above the queen size bed, and diamond willow lamps sat on birch nightstands. Nostalgia hit him like a snowplow. The lump in his throat grew.

Lynx threw him down on the bed, and Aidan landed with a bounce. He held up his leg to keep blood from getting on the spread and gave Lynx a dirty look. He didn't care that Lynx hated him, but he needed to take better care with Fiona's things.

"Lynx," Fiona scolded. "That's no way to treat an injured man." She'd grabbed towels from the bathroom, and tore back the quilt, laying the towels down. "All right, Aidan, you can set your leg down now." She gave him a once over. "Whatever did you do to yourself?"

"He got himself caught in one of his father's bear traps," Lynx said with a sneer.

"No." Fiona gasped. "Oh, you poor thing."

Next she was going to be kissing his forehead and smoothing back his hair like she used to do. He wondered if she still had blueberry shortbread cookies in the cookie jar.

"What is Earl thinking?" Fiona tsked.

"Apparently, he's no longer thinking or doing much of anything." Lynx gave a cat-like grin. "Earl's dead."

Fiona sighed. "Well…"

There was no, "Isn't that a shame." Or, "I'm so sorry for your loss." Nobody in the room would shed a tear for Earl Harte.

"I take it you sent for Eva?" Fiona asked Lynx, who nodded. "Good. I'll go and grab some medicinal beverage. Aidan, I'm sure you could use a drink."

Damn right. "Thanks, Fiona. For everything."

"You're welcome. It's good to see you, son." She walked over to the bed and smoothed the hair back on his forehead. "You always did have the best manners around."

She left the room. The lump that had been forming in his throat clogged it closed.

"Suck up," Lynx said. "I'll never understand why she doesn't hate you like the rest us."

He had to clear his throat to speak. "She doesn't blame me for the sins of my father."

"Acorn doesn't fall far from the tree."

"Have you ever seen an acorn tree growing in Alaska?" He tightened his jaw. "And I'm not my father."

Lynx snorted, but looked away like maybe Aidan had touched a nerve.

A woman entered, who Aidan thankfully didn't know. A little thing except for her very pregnant belly, with blond hair cut short and spiked around her pixie face. She reached up and gave Lynx a kiss. Interesting. She also carried a black bag. Must be the nurse practitioner.

"Harte this is Eva, my wife. Eva, this sorry excuse for a man, is Aidan Harte."

"Nice to meet you." She glanced at Lynx when he snorted again. "Are you going to be helpful?"

Aidan couldn't help the chuckle.

"What?" Lynx demanded.

"Just interesting to see who wears the pants in your relationship. Really nice to meet you, Eva." He gave her a full smile.

She smiled back and set the bag on the side of the bed, next to him. "Let's take a look at you. Fox said you were caught in a trap?"

Aidan nodded.

She opened her bag, yanked on a pair of latex gloves, and pulled out scissors. She started at the hem of his jeans and carefully cut up the sides of one leg and then started on the other. "Your pants aren't going to survive. Let's see if we can save the rest of you." She gave him a twinkling smile. "Lynx bring me over that trash can." She indicated the one in the corner. Lynx begrudgingly brought it over. Eva stopped and straightened, looking Lynx in the eye. "If you're going to be like that send someone else in here to help me." She discarded the ruined jeans in the trash can.

"Fine." Lynx made a face, the same one he used to make when they were kids and Fiona would make him do something he didn't want to.

"Good." Eva turned back to Aidan, and threw a crocheted blanket over his lower half, covering batman boxers.

He was going to like this woman. Lynx had grown into a bear of a man. His Athabascan and Tlingit heritage shone through like muscle. His black hair, dark eyes, tanned skinned contrasted with Eva's short blond, blue-eyed, ivory-skinned, fairy looks.

Eva surveyed Aidan's leg. "Good thing you were wearing boots."

Yeah, one thing he had to be grateful for tonight, while so many other things had gone straight to hell.

Fiona entered the room with a bottle of whiskey and no glass. "Better drink up, my boy, before Eva goes any further. She's cute, but wicked." Fiona handed him a bottle and stuffed pillows behind his back when he sat up to drink. He took a long swallow, and relished the burn as it flowed down into his gut. His eyes watered, and he did everything he could not to cough. Not in front of Lynx, who was waiting to insult him. He took another swallow and then handed the bottle back to Fiona, who sat it within easy reach on the nightstand.

"All right, what can I do to help?" Fiona asked.

"Get him to drink more," Eva said, going for the boot laces on his good foot first. "You're going to need a new pair of boots."

"Beats a new leg."

Eva chuckled. "I like a man who can keep a sense of humor at times like this. Unlike someone else I know."

Lynx folded his arms and rolled his eyes.

"I like a woman who's capable and pretty to look at." Aidan flirted back and smiled when Lynx gave him the evil eye. He grabbed the bottle and took another swig. It barely burned at all this time. He swallowed some more, loving how it warmed his blood as it swam through his body.

Eva started on the chewed up boot, cutting through the laces with her sharp scissors. A hush settled over the room, and Lynx and Fiona leaned in. "Step back and give me room to work." She glanced at Aidan. "Why don't you take another drink."

"Sounds like a dandy idear," he slurred. He wasn't much of a drinker. Since his mother had been a lush, he'd stayed away from it. So the alcohol hit him hard and fast, like a moose during rutting season. He downed another long swallow. It was too much effort to get the bottle back onto the nightstand, so he cradled it in the crook of his arm. He was feeling no pain.

Until Eva—the evil fairy from hell—pulled on his boot.

"Ahhh!" He screamed like a baby. He'd tried to keep it in. Even bit his tongue, but with the booze, the holler had escaped.

"Damn, I hope you didn't break this," Eva scolded him like it was his fault he was hurt. "No way we can get you to Fairbanks with that storm out there." She surveyed the situation. "We need to get that boot off. If he broke it we'd better leave it on until we can get him to a hospital. But then what kind of infection has already taken up residence from the trap?"

Aidan quirked a brow. "Are you expecting an answer from me?"

"She likes to talk out her problems," Lynx said, scowling. "Leave her alone."

Aidan took another swig of the whiskey, really getting into the numbing effects.

"How's he doing?" Fox asked, rushing into the room, his eyes wide as he viewed Aidan's leg. "Ooh, that doesn't look good."

Aidan hadn't looked. In fact, he'd looked at everyone and everything in the room, avoiding the sight of his mangled leg.

"Fox, you shouldn't be in here," Lynx said, walking over to him and laying a hand on his shoulder. "Don't you have dogs to feed?"

"That's what I was doing. They're all bedded down for the night." He looked at Aidan, worry shining in his eyes. "Is he going to be all right?"

"He's going to be just fine." Fiona walked around the bed and reached for Fox. "Come with me. I need your help getting him something to eat." Fiona steered him out of the room, giving Aidan a backward glance with a wink.

"Let's get the boot off," Eva announced, tightening her lips. "I think that's the best course of action." She went right to work. Before Aidan could down any more of the bottle, she had his boot off in one quick excruciating yank.

"*Shit. Fuck. Son of a bitch!*" He gasped—had trouble getting his breath back—and started to shake.

"Sorry about that," the demon nurse from hell said. "Guess I could have warned you, but I prefer the rip-off-the-bandage method. Why prolong the pain? Now let's take a look."

The edge of his vision started to blur. God, he hoped he passed out.

Then she walked in.

Raven.

The woman who had haunted him all his life. From his dreams to his fantasies. The woman who had broken his heart.

"So it's true," she said, glaring at him from the doorway, her hands planted on her hips. Her voice was deeper, huskier. It vibrated through him like a stone thrown into a pool of water. She slowly stalked toward the bed. "I can't believe you had the nerve to come back here."

He gazed up into her dark, bewitching eyes. How he had loved to gaze into her eyes for hours as he stroked her soft, honeyed skin. "Why aren't you in the Midwest?" he asked. And he thought dying was the worst thing that could happen to him tonight.

"Midwest?" She frowned and glanced at Eva and Lynx. "Did he hit his head too?"

"Nope," Lynx answered. "But he's had a *lot* to drink." He indicated the half empty bottle, which helped Aidan remember the whiskey snuggled in the crook of his arm.

He took another swig. *Man, that went down nice.*

"Where's Fox?" Raven asked.

"In the kitchen with Mom," Lynx said. "He found Aidan, saved his sorry ass. He also knew how to navigate Earl's booby-traps. It would be interesting to know *how* he knew that."

"Yes, it would. In the meantime, what are we going to do with *him*?" She pointed at Aidan as though he was something rotten that needed to be disposed of.

He wasn't worried. Hell, he was feeling fine. Aidan took another drink and some of the liquid dribbled down his chin. If they were going to kill him, they would have left him to die in the trap. With the temperature dropping to well below zero, he wouldn't have made it through the night.

Eva wiped the blood, rust, and dirt from his leg, while Aidan lost himself in gazing at Raven.

She'd changed since he'd last seen her. At eighteen she'd been a skinny thing. All limbs and sharp angles. She'd gained weight and it had settled in all the right places. She was curvy. The kind of curvy a man could spend hours navigating, losing himself. He remembered the night they'd given each other their virginity. How they'd fumbled, laughed, and spoke of forever. How would it be to lie with her now?

"Ouch." He jerked as Eva poked him. "That hurts."

"Well, yeah." Eva snorted. "You got your leg caught in a trap."

Weren't nurses supposed to be compassionate?

"Lynx, hand me that syringe." She held her hand out. "Yes, that one." She glanced at Aidan. "You've got a lot of crap in these wounds." She glared at him like it was his fault. "I'm going to flush them out with saline and hope we wash out all the debris."

Aidan dropped his head back on the pillow as Eva went to work on him, snapping orders at Lynx for more towels.

"What are you doing back here, Aidan?" Raven asked, her lips flattened into a line. She had such nice full lips that could stretch into a wide, welcoming smile. Why couldn't she have smiled at him when she saw him instead of the scowl that wrinkled her forehead and made him feel like scum? Didn't she have any memories of him that she revisited fondly?

"Earl's dead," Lynx answered for him.

"Well." Raven folded her arms under her breasts—breasts that were considerably larger than they had been at eighteen. "It couldn't have happened to a nicer guy."

"I need those tweezers." Eva pointed to a sterile package in her bag, snapping her fingers for Lynx to speed it up. For such a little thing, she had a Napoleon attitude. She tore into the packaging and pulled out wickedly sharp, stainless steel tweezers. "I didn't get all the debris with the wash. I'm going to have to dig some of it out with the tweezers. Raven, hold his shoulders down. Lynx, you hold his leg immobile. And I mean don't *even* let it twitch." She flicked a glance at Aidan. "You aren't going to like this."

"Surprise," he said. "I haven't liked any of it so far."

She smiled at him as though she approved and then narrowed a look at Raven. "Hold him down."

Raven took a deep breath, her eyes slanting. She didn't want to touch him. But then he didn't want her touching him either, for different reasons all together.

She sat on the edge of the bed and placed her hands on his shoulders. Her scent drifted to him. In all these years she still smelled the same. Earthy. Berries, ferns, exotic underbrush. He vaguely felt Eva poking at him. The real pain came from having Raven so close and discovering he still had unresolved feelings for her hidden in the depths of his mangled heart.

And she still hated him.

"All right, I hope I got it all," Eva said. "That trap must have been decades old and reverting back to nature for the amount of rust I washed out of the wounds. When was the last time you had a tetanus? Earl Harte should he shot for leaving things like that around his place."

Aidan laughed, though the sound was more sardonic than happy. Earl had been shot all right.

"Aidan?" Eva hollered at him. "Tetanus shot? When did you last have one?"

"Can't remember," he mumbled.

"Are you allergic to any antibiotics?"

"Nope."

"Are you all right?" Raven asked, looking suddenly concerned.

"Do you care?"

She tightened her lips, released him and scooted off the edge of the bed. "No."

"Then don't bother asking." He shut his eyes. Man, he was tired. It had been a hell of a day. It had been a hell of a few months. Who was he kidding? His life had always been hell. He'd be better off dead then he wouldn't have to feel. Darkness closed in on him. Not comforting, but numbing.

Whatever. He'd take it.

ABOUT THE AUTHOR

Photo by: Kelli Ann Morgan

Tiffinie Helmer is an award-winning author who is always up for a gripping adventure. Raised in Alaska, she was dragged "Outside" by her husband, but escapes the lower forty-eight to spend her summers commercial fishing on the Bering Sea.

A wife and mother of four, Tiffinie divides her time between enjoying her family, throwing her acclaimed pottery, and writing of flawed characters in unique and severe situations.

To learn more about Tiffinie and her books, please visit www.TiffinieHelmer.com

FUN FACTS

Tiffinie grew up in Fairbanks, Alaska and married one of those wild Alaskan men she loves to write about.

- She spends most of her summers working as a commercial salmon fisherman (er, woman) in Bristol Bay on the Bering Sea of Alaska.

- Huge Stevie Nicks fan, not only her music but her wardrobe too.

- Favorite foods: seafood (fisherman remember), olives, artichokes, mushrooms, cheese in general, and bread. Favorite dessert: pretty much any kind of cheesecake, preferably with chocolate.

- Loves to kayak—seriously loves to kayak—especially sea kayaking.

- She was a foreign exchange student to Finland in high school, and fell in love with the people, the saunas, and their bounty of delectable cheeses.

- She's a bit of a thrill seeker, and finds the older she gets, the bigger the chances she takes.

ALSO BY TIFFINIE HELMER

NOVELLAS

Impact (prequel to Hooked)
Moosed Up
Dreamweaver
Bearing All (sequel to Edge)

BUNDLE

Wild Men of Alaska

NOVEL

Edge

Made in the USA
San Bernardino, CA
05 June 2013